Praise for John Lutz

"John Lutz is a major talent."

—John Lescroart

"John Lutz just keeps getting better and better."

—Tony Hillerman

"John Lutz is the new Lawrence Sanders."

—*Mystery Scene*

"Lutz knows how to seize and hold the reader's imagination."

—*Cleveland Plain Dealer*

"Lutz's real gift is to evoke detective work better than anyone else."

—*Kirkus Reviews*

"Lutz is among the best."

—*San Diego Union*

"It's easy to see why he's won an Edgar and two Shamuses."

—*Publishers Weekly*

Praise for John Lutz

"For a good scare and a well-paced story, Lutz delivers."
—*San Antonio Express-News*

"Lutz is rapidly bleeding critics dry of superlatives."
—*St. Louis Post-Dispatch*

"A thrilling ride for anyone brave enough to sit down and strap in."
—*AudioFile* on *The Ex*

"A thriller-and-a-half . . . a winner . . . fascinating reading."
—*The Daily Sun* on *The Ex*

"Convincing characterizations."
—*The Record* (Hackensack, NJ) on *The Ex*

"Lutz knows how to tighten the suspense."
—*San Antonio Express-News* on *The Ex*

"Likable protagonists in a complex thriller . . . Lutz always delivers the goods, and this is no exception."
—*Booklist* on *Final Seconds*

"Clever cat-and-mouse game."
—*Kirkus Reviews* on *Final Seconds*

"Well paced and entertaining."
– Carl Brookins in *reviewingtheevidence.com* on *Final Seconds*

Praise for John Lutz

"Compelling . . . a gritty psychological thriller . . . Lutz's details concerning police procedure, fire-fighting techniques and FDNY policy ring true . . . draws the reader deep into the killer's troubled psyche."

—*Publishers Weekly* on *The Night Watcher*

"John Lutz knows how to ratchet up the terror. . . . [He] propels the story with effective twists and a fast pace."

—*Sun-Sentinel* (Ft. Lauderdale, FL) on *The Night Spider*

"John Lutz is the new Lawrence Sanders. *The Night Watcher* is a very smooth and civilized novel about a very uncivilized snuff artist, told with passion, wit, carnality, and relentless vigor. I loved it."

—Ed Gorman in *Mystery Scene*

"A gripping thriller . . . extremely taut scenes, great descriptions, nicely depicted supporting players . . . Lutz is good with characterization."

—*www.reviewingtheevidence.com* on *The Night Watcher*

"Some writers just have a flair for imaginative suspense, and John Lutz is one of them . . . truly superb."

—Jeremiah Healy

"A psychological thriller that few readers will be able to put down."

—*Publishers Weekly* on *SWF Seeks Same*

"*SWF Seeks Same* is a complex, riveting, and chilling portrayal of urban terror, as well as a wonderful novel of New York City. Echoes of *Rosemary's Baby*, but this one's scarier because it could happen."

—Jonathan Kellerman

ALSO BY JOHN LUTZ

In for the Kill

Chill of Night

Fear the Night

The Night Spider

The Night Watcher

The Night Caller

Final Seconds (with David August)

The Ex

From Kensington Publishing and Pinnacle Books

DARKER
THAN
NIGHT

JOHN LUTZ

PINNACLE BOOKS
Kensington Publishing Corp.
http://www.kensingtonbooks.com

PINNACLE BOOKS are published by

Kensington Publishing Corp.
850 Third Avenue
New York, NY 10022

All Kensington titles, imprints, and distributed lines are available at special quantity discounts for bulk purchases for sales promotions, premiums, fund-raising, and educational or institutional use. Special book excerpts or customized printings can also be created to fit specific needs. For details, write or phone the office of the Kensington special sales manager: Kensington Publishing Corp., 850 Third Avenue, New York, NY 10022, attn: Special Sales Department; phone: 1-800-221-2647.

Pinnacle and the P logo Reg. U.S. Pat. & TM Off.

First Pinnacle Books Printing: November 2004

10 9 8 7 6 5

ISBN-13: 978-0-7860-1969-4
ISBN-10: 0-7860-1969-7

Printed in the United States of America

For the Royal Aardvarkians,
first among many

For he being dead, with him is beauty slain,
And, beauty dead, black chaos comes again.
—William Shakespeare, "Venus and Adonis"

See my lips tremble and my eyeballs roll,
Suck my last breath, and catch my flying soul.
—Alexander Pope, "Eloisa to Abelard"

1

Jan Elzner jolted awake in alarm.

Something . . . a sound from the kitchen, had intruded in gentle dreams she could no longer recall. She reached over to prod her husband, Martin, but her hand found only smooth sheet, cool pillow. Maybe he'd been awakened before her and had gone to investigate the sound.

Jan smiled, drifting back into shallow sleep, sure that her husband would return to bed and everything would be all right. Probably the sound was nothing, the icemaker doing its work, or a delicately balanced object falling in one of the cabinets. Martin would handle the situation, as he did most things. He was a man who—

A voice.

Unintelligible, but she was sure it was Martin's.

Who could he be talking to at—she glanced again at the clock radio by the bed—three A.M.?

The talking stopped.

Jan opened her eyes wider and lay in the still darkness. The distant sounds of a half-awake Manhattan filtered in through the bedroom windows. A faint, faraway shout, a siren like a distant wolf on the hunt, a growling whisper of traffic below. Night sounds. She rolled over on her back, listening, listening. . . .

Frightened. Though she shouldn't be.

I'm not afraid! There's nothing to fear!

But she knew she was wrong.

Martin never talked to himself. She couldn't imagine it.

Something *clanked,* bounced lightly, then rolled over the kitchen's tile floor.

She swiveled to a sitting position on the edge of the mattress, her heart drumming a rapid message of alarm. She remembered what her grandmother had told her years ago. *The heart knows before the head. Knows everything first.* Beyond the bedroom doorway she could see a rectangle of light from the kitchen, angled over the hall floor. Then the light altered as a shadow passed across it.

What is Martin doing out there?

She stood up, one bare foot on the woven throw rug beside the bed, the other on cool hardwood floor. That was one of the things she and Martin had liked most about their Upper West Side apartment, the polished oak floors. They knew somehow they could be happy there.

And we were happy. Are *happy!*

What did her heart know that her mind didn't?

Fear was like a drug, yet it propelled her through her dread toward the light near the end of the hall. She had to find out—had to know what it was that terrified her. She walked stiff-legged in her silk nightgown, her pale fingers clenched around her thumbs. The only sound she heard now was the faint *thump, thump* of her bare heels striking the wood floor as she lurched toward light and a horrible knowledge she couldn't avoid.

She turned the corner and stood in the kitchen doorway.

Her breathing stopped as she took it all in—the bright kitchen, Martin curled on the tile floor in what looked like a black shadow, the plastic bag and groceries scattered on the gleaming gray surface of the table. A tuna can lay on the floor near Martin's right arm. *That's what I heard fall. It must have rolled off the table.*

She heard herself utter Martin's name as she took a step toward him.

She wasn't surprised—not really—when a dark figure straightened up from behind the cooking island and moved toward her. It was more like a confirmation of what her terror had already told her. Something in his right hand. A gun? *No. Yes!* A gun with something attached to it. A gun with a silencer.

"Please!" She saw one of her hands float up in front of her face. "Please!" *Not me! Not me! Not yet!*

She barely heard the *sput!* of the gun as the bullet ripped through tissue and bone, between her breasts, into her heart, a leaden missile tumbling and tearing through her world, her life, ending her past, her future, everything.

She was still alive on the floor, beyond pain but not horror, as the man with the gun momentarily bent over Martin, then delicately stepped over her, careful not to get blood on his shoes, and continued toward the door.

For an instant she glimpsed the expression on the face of the monster who had taken all that she had and was. *Him!* He was so calm, smiling contentedly, like a simple workman who'd accomplished a routine and necessary task.

He glanced down at her with faint curiosity, then obviously dismissed her as dead.

He wasn't wrong, only a few seconds early.

2

Flash!

Fedderman blinked as yet another photo was shot and the auto winder on the camera whirred like a miniature blender. The crime scene unit was all over the apartment, photographing, luminoling, vacuuming, plucking with tweezers.

The Elzners didn't seem to mind the intrusion. Or the carnage in the kitchen. Not even what had been done to them.

Sudden death did that to people. In the midst of all the horror he'd seen during his time in the NYPD, Fedderman had often thought that was the single mercy.

"About done with these two?" his partner, Pearl, asked the ME, a self-important, meticulously groomed little man named Nift, who, if his life had taken another direction, might have had a film career playing Napoleon. He'd been fussing over the bodies for the last fifteen minutes, giving Pearl and Fedderman some first impressions.

"Sure. You can diddle with them awhile now. Just be sure and zip up when you're finished."

A nasty Napoleon.

Fedderman watched Pearl step hard on Nift's instep, perhaps deliberately, as she moved toward Martin Elzner's body. Those comfortable-looking black shoes of hers, with the two-inch heels to make her appear taller than her five-foot-one stature, could be dangerous.

Nift winced and jerked backward, almost kicking away the tuna can on the kitchen floor.

"Try not to step in any blood," Pearl said.

Then she ignored Nift entirely as she bent down and gingerly pried a Walther semiautomatic handgun from Elzner's dead fingers, then used a pencil inserted in the barrel to transfer the gun to a plastic evidence bag.

Nift glared at her and made for the door, taking his sick sense of humor with him and not looking back. One thing Fedderman knew about Detective Pearl Kasner was that she didn't take any crap from anybody, not even Napoleon. It was the character trait that had gotten her into trouble and sidelined her career. It was why Fedderman liked her but figured she wasn't going to be his partner much longer. Probably this time next year she'd be driving a cab or demonstrating perfume in Macy's.

She was a looker, Fedderman thought, with the great rack and nice ass, and could be an actress or model if she were taller. Searching dark eyes, wavy black hair, turned-up nose, a way about her. Fedderman sometimes mused that if he were younger, unmarried, didn't have trouble getting it up sometimes, didn't have bad breath, a chronically upset stomach, and wasn't balding and thirty pounds overweight, he might make a play for her.

Pearl handed one of the techs the evidence bag with the gun, glancing at Fedderman as if she knew what he was thinking.

She knows. They were partners. Had been for months, since Pearl's troubles began. Neither of them was getting a bargain, and they both knew it. That was the idea. If they got tired of each other's company, that was tough shit. Like with the couple on the kitchen floor.

Homicide had been called in after the radio car uniforms arrived at the scene, called by a next-door neighbor who noticed what looked like a bullet hole in her kitchen wall. When the super had let them in, they discovered the hole was indeed made by a bullet. It had gone through Jan Elzner, then the wall separating the Elzner apartment from the adjacent unit. The uniforms backed out and secured the scene.

Pearl and Fedderman had questioned the tenants on either side of, and above and below, the Elzners. None of them remembered hearing anything like a gunshot, but then Nift had said the killings occurred sometime between two and four in the morning. Sleep was deepest then. Or was supposed to be. Fedderman knew that when people were awake at that time, for whatever reason, terrible things could happen.

He glanced around at the carnage, feeling his stomach kick even after all the years, all he'd seen. He looked at the kitchen table. "How do you figure the groceries? It looks like one or both the Elzners had just come back from shopping and they were putting away what they bought."

Pearl gave him one of her sloe-eyed dark looks. "At three in the morning? In their pajamas and nightgown?"

"It doesn't make sense now, I know. But maybe they shopped earlier and forgot to put stuff away, then remembered and got up and were finishing the job when they started arguing. Hubby got the gun and did Wifey, then himself. It could happen in the real world."

"That would be our world?"

Fedderman didn't want to get into some kind of metaphysical conversation with Pearl. "So whadda we tell Captain Egan, murder-suicide?"

"I don't like telling the prick anything."

"Pearl . . ."

"Yeah, yeah . . . that sure looks like what it was, murder-suicide. Stemming from the pressures of the big city and what comes of marital bliss."

Fedderman breathed easier. She wasn't going to buck the system and cause problems. He had enough problems.

"But it isn't complete."

"Nothing's ever complete," Fedderman said, "but we gotta go with the evidence. Two dead bodies. And what will no doubt be the weapon still in Hubby's hand, powder burns around the hole in his head. It appears he shot the wife, realized what a shit deed he did, then killed himself. The honorable thing. Murder-suicide. Crime solving being on a kinda assembly-line basis with new crimes always demanding our attention, we chalk this one up and move on to the next problem coming down the line."

"Move on but not up," Pearl said.

Fedderman knew what she meant. Even if somehow she kept her job in the NYPD, she wasn't going any higher. Promotions were not for Pearl.

She knew where she stood and so did everyone else, after what she'd done to Captain Egan.

Pearl and Egan.

Sometimes, when he thought about it, Fedderman caught himself smiling.

3

"Ah, it's Quinn, is it?"

The man who had spoken stood in the doorway of the West Side walk-up. He was middle-aged and balding, with a long, jowly face, fleshy purple bags beneath somber brown eyes, and a neatly trimmed downturned graying mustache. A big man, but sagging at the middle, he seemed to have been assembled with mismatched body parts so that his expensive tailored blue suit looked like something plucked off the discount rack.

As only four years had passed, he'd recognized Quinn, and Quinn knew it.

Quinn didn't move from where he sat on the threadbare sofa, facing the door. "It is Quinn," he confirmed unnecessarily to Harley Renz, NYPD assistant chief of police.

Frank Quinn was a lanky, hard-edged man an inch over six feet, with a twice broken nose, a square jaw, and short-cropped dark hair that wouldn't stay combed. But what people remembered about him were his eyes, green, flat, cop's eyes that seemed to know your darkest secrets at a glance. Today was his birthday. He was forty-five. He needed a shave, a fresh shirt, a haircut, new underwear, a new life.

"You didn't lock your door," Renz said, stepping into the tiny, messy apartment. "Aren't you afraid somebody's gonna walk in and steal you blind?"

"To wanna steal anything from here, you'd have to *be* blind."

Renz smiled, which made him look like a dyspeptic bloodhound. Then his expression changed, but he still looked like a dyspeptic bloodhound. "I never told you, but I'm sorry about you and May, the divorce and all. You still see her much? Or the girl? Laura, isn't it?"

"Lauri. May doesn't want to see me. There's no reason to, except for Lauri. And Lauri isn't sure what she wants. What she believes about me."

"Have you told her your side?"

"Not lately. May has her ear and keeps telling her what to think. They're out in L.A. Went there to get away from me."

Renz shook his head. "About all you can say in favor of marriage is that it's an institution. Like prisons and mental hospitals. I was married twenty-six years before my wife ran away with my brother."

"I heard about that," Quinn said. "It was worth a laugh."

"Even I can laugh about it now. That's how things can change in this amazing world. Even *your* shitty situation could change."

Quinn knew what situation Renz meant. Four years ago, Quinn had lost his reputation, his job, and his family, when he'd been unfairly accused of child molestation—the rape of a thirteen-year-old girl. She was a girl he'd never met, much less molested. He knew why he'd been set up. The problem was, he didn't know how.

He'd been a good cop, even a great one, widely respected for his toughness and clever approach to cases. He didn't give up. He didn't back down. He got results.

And in the end, he'd been too good a detective not to notice little things during the investigation of a drug dealer's murder. Quinn had dug deeper, wider, and discovered a network of kickbacks and corruption that involved many of his fellow cops. He was anguished about what he had to do, but he knew, and they knew, that eventually he'd go to internal affairs with his suspicions. Quinn had spoken with his superior officer, Captain Vince Egan, and told him as much.

But somebody else contacted IA first. About the brutal rape of a young girl in Brooklyn. Quinn had been astounded, but not too afraid at first. He was innocent. The accusation had to be a mistake.

He was shown a button found at the scene of the crime, and it matched one that was missing from the shirt he'd worn the evening of the rape. Then, astounding him further, the girl picked him out of a lineup, identifying him by size and build and the jagged scar on his right forearm, even though the rapist had worn a stocking mask.

Quinn knew the accusation wasn't a mistake. It was a preventative.

They confiscated his computer from his desk in the squad room, and on it were three suggestive e-mails to this girl he'd never seen. And there was the worst kind of child pornography on the computer's hard disk.

It looked bad for Quinn, he was told. And he knew it *was* bad. He understood the game. He knew what was coming next.

They were going to show him a way out of his predicament.

And they did. Retirement with partial pension, or he would be charged with child molestation, the rape of a minor.

Quinn realized it must have been Egan who'd tipped off the corrupt cops, and who was part of the corruption himself.

And probably it was the politically savvy Egan who prevented Quinn from being prosecuted, thus keeping a lid on the rot in the NYPD. Quinn, knowing he wasn't going to be believed anyway, understood the arrangement, the addendum to corruption. He was if nothing else a realist.

So he preserved his meager pension, but lost his job and everything else.

Everything.

He hadn't known the devastation would be so swift and complete. His reputation, credibility, and marriage were suddenly gone.

Not only that, he found himself existing only on his partial pension, a pariah unable to find a job or a decent place to live because he was on an unofficial NYPD sexual predator list. Every time he thought he was making progress, word somehow got to whoever controlled his future.

Whoever had put Quinn down wanted to keep him there.

After May left, he missed her so much at first that it affected his health. He thought his aching stomach would turn to stone.

Now, though he thought often of Lauri, he hardly thought of May at all. Renz was right. Things did change.

Quinn had never cared much for Captain Harley Renz. Ambitious, conniving bastard. He liked to know things about people. To Renz, personal information was like hole cards in a poker game.

"You been drinking?" Renz asked.

"No. It's only ten in the morning. What I am now is fucked up with a headache."

Renz drew a tiny white plastic bottle from a pocket and held it out toward Quinn. "Would some ibuprofen help?"

Quinn glared at him.

Renz replaced the bottle in his pocket. "This isn't such a bad neighborhood," he said, glancing around, "yet this place looks like a roach haven."

"The building's gonna be rehabbed, so the rent's cheap. Anyway, I've hired a decorator."

"Johnnie Walker?"

"Uh-uh. Can't afford him."

"Good fortune might change all that. Might throw you a lifeline of money and regained self-respect."

"How so?"

"I'm here."

"You said it was a roach haven."

"It's good to know you're still a smart-ass," Renz said. "You're not completely broken."

Quinn watched him settle into the worn-out wing chair across from the worn-out sofa. Renz made a steeple with his fingers, almost as if he were about to pray, a characteristic gesture Quinn recalled now. He'd never trusted people who made steeples with their fingers.

"My proposition," Renz said, "involves an unsolved homicide."

Despite his wish that Renz would make his pitch and then leave, Quinn felt his pulse quicken. Once a cop, always one, he thought bitterly. Blood that ran blue stayed true. Wasn't that why he found himself sitting around all day drenched with self-pity?

"You know the Elzner murder case?" Renz asked.

Quinn shook his head no. "I stay away from the news. It cheers me down."

Renz filled him in. Jan and Martin Elzner, husband and wife, had been discovered shot to death ten days ago in their Upper West Side apartment. The deaths occurred in the early-morning hours, at approximately the same time. The gun that fired the bullets was found in the dead husband's hand. It was an old Walther .38 semiautomatic. Its serial number had been burned off by acid.

"Like half the illegal guns in New York," Quinn said.

"Seems that way. He was killed by a single shot to the temple."

"Powder residue on the hand?"

"Some. But it mighta been transferred there if the gun was exchanged."

"Burns near the entry wound?"

"Yeah. He was shot at close range."

"Murder, then suicide," Quinn said.

"That's how it's going down. That's what they want to believe."

"They?"

"The NYPD, other'n me. I think the Elzners were both murdered."

Quinn settled deeper into the sprung sofa and winced. His headache wasn't abating. "What makes you different?" he asked Renz.

"For one thing, I intend to be the next chief of police. Chief Barrow's going to retire for health reasons early next year. The department's considering candidates for replacement. I'm one of those up for the job."

"You've got the asshole part of it down pat."

"You were the best detective in homicide, Quinn. You can be that again, if you take me up on my offer."

"I haven't heard an offer," Quinn said. *Christ! Another offer.* He licked his lips. They were dry. "But let's take things in order. What makes you think the Elzners were both murdered?"

"I've talked to the ME, Jack Nift, an old friend of mine."

Quinn wasn't surprised Nift and Renz were friends. A couple of pricks.

"Nift tells me in confidence that the angle of the bullet's entry isn't quite right for a suicide—too much of a downward trajectory."

"Does Nift say it definitely rules out a self-inflicted wound?"

"No," Renz admitted, "only makes it less likely. Also, there's what might be a silencer nick in some of the spent bullets, where they might have contacted a baffler or some irregularity in a sound suppressor, and the gun in Elzner's hand wasn't equipped with a silencer. There were marks on the barrel, though, where one might have been attached."

"But the marked gun and slugs are no more conclusive than the bullet wound angle."

"True," Renz said, "but then there are the groceries."

"Groceries?"

"Some groceries were out on the table, along with a couple of half-full plastic bags, and a can of tuna was on the kitchen floor. The nearest grocery stores and delis don't remember either of the Elzners shopping there or ordering a delivery that day or evening, and there was no receipt in the grocery bags."

"Odd," Quinn said.

"People don't interrupt unbagging their groceries after midnight so they can commit murder, then suicide," Renz told him.

Quinn thought Renz should know better.

He waited for more, but Renz was finished. "That's it? That's your evidence?"

"So far."

"Not very convincing."

"So far."

Quinn stood up and paced to the window, pressing his palm to his aching forehead. He had to squint as he looked down at the street three stories below. The morning was warm but gloomy. Some of the people scurrying along the sidewalks were wearing light raincoats. A few of them wielded open umbrellas.

"Now, what would be the proposition?"

"I want you to investigate the Elzner murder secretly," Renz said, "with my surreptitious help. I'll sit on the evidence as long as possible, so you and I will be the only ones to know it in its entirety. You'll be paid well, and you don't ask where the money's coming from. And if I—you—solve the case and I become the next chief of police, you're back in the NYPD and part of its inner circle."

"A crooked deal."

"Sure, sure. And you're so fucking ethical. I know your reputation, but you mighta noticed you're about out of options. I'm holding out a chance for you. And it's my chance, too. The way it looks, it comes down to me or Captain Vincent Egan as the new chief, and you know Egan's not gonna play it straight."

Quinn had to smile. Renz had gotten his ducks in a row before coming here. Quinn knew something else: Renz would never have come to him with this if somebody higher in the NYPD or in city politics hadn't approved it. Maybe somebody had his suspicions and wanted to place Egan and Quinn, and possibly Renz himself, under a microscope.

"There's no way I can conduct an investigation without Egan and the rest of the NYPD finding out about it," Quinn said.

"Egan won't find out if you work fast enough. And if he does, we'll think of something else. What I'm asking is that you climb outta this physical and psychological shit hole you been in and do your job the way I know you can."

"That last part'd be easy enough," Quinn said, still gazing out the window.

"Not without the first part. Can you manage it?"

Quinn saw more umbrellas opening below, like dark flowers abruptly blooming. He thought it would be nice if the sun would burst out from behind the clouds, send him a sign.

Screw it. He didn't need a sign.

"I can try," he said, turning away from the gloom. "But even if I get it done, I don't see how you can get me back in the NYPD."

"I can if I'm chief."

"All things considered, I don't see why you'd take a chance on me."

"I noticed coming over here, there's a few schools in this neighborhood."

"One right down the street. And there's a church near here, too. I don't pay much attention to either of them."

"I know," Renz said. "That's why I decided to drop by."

4

Moving day.

Claire Briggs stood in the center of the vacant living room, looking around with satisfaction at the fresh paint. She decided the off-white made the pale blue carpet look older, but that was okay for now. She'd spent her budget on paint and what new furniture she needed, and she was grateful she could exchange her tiny basement apartment in the Village for this one.

It was all thanks to her landing a supporting role in the continuing Broadway comedy *Hail to the Chef.* Claire, with her newly dyed blond hair and faux French accent, played Mimi the restaurant owner, in love with her insane but talented sous chef.

A slender woman of medium height who looked taller due to her long neck and erect posture, Claire tucked her fingertips in the side pockets of her tight jeans and walked over to peer out the window.

Twenty-nine stories below, she saw the movers dolly her flea-market antique china cabinet out of the van and roll it down the truck's steel ramp into the street. The cabinet was tightly wrapped in thick padding to prevent damage. She smiled. Claire was glad to have hired this moving company, Three Hunks and a Truck, on the recommendation of one of the dancers in *Hail*. Despite their gimmicky name, they were careful and hardworking movers. Not to mention hunks, as advertised. The moving company, actually more like twenty men and several trucks, based across the East River in New Jersey, was fast gaining a reputation in Manhattan for reliability.

Claire left the window and wandered around the rest of the two-bedroom West Side apartment. She'd had only the living room and kitchen painted; the bedrooms were good enough for now, and only one of them would be used for sleeping. The other would be for storage, a home office, and would contain a small sofa that could be made into a bed—a sometimes guest room. It was a luxury in New York to have an apartment with a spare room, but Claire had always wanted one. It fit into her plans that, even to her, weren't fully formed.

She heard voices, scuffing sounds, then the hall door being shoved open. She went into the living room and saw one of the movers holding the door while another wheeled in the china cabinet. The one with the cabinet was husky and blond, with long, lean features and clear blue eyes, handsome enough to be an actor. And maybe he was one, Claire thought. Manhattan was like that. Anyone might be an actor. Anyone might be anything.

"That wall," she said, pointing. She wanted them to be careful with the old mahogany cabinet, even though it wasn't particularly valuable. She was fond of it, and it would hold the stemmed crystal left to her two years ago by her grandmother, now buried in Wisconsin.

"Nice piece of furniture," said the blond one, as he and his almost-as-handsome dark-haired partner stripped away straps and padding and wrestled the cabinet against the living-room wall. " 'Bout here okay?"

"A little to the left, if you don't mind," Claire said.

"We don't," the dark one said. "You're the boss."

"And a pleasure to work for," said the blond one with a wink.

Claire couldn't help smiling at him. He was definitely a magnetic guy, like a sort of modern-day Viking. If she weren't involved with Jubal . . .

But she *was* involved. She altered her smile, trying not to make it mean too much.

It took the three movers about an hour and a half to bring up the rest of the furniture in the service elevator and place it more or less where Claire wanted it. All the time they worked, the blond one paid special attention to Claire, which seemed to amuse the other two, the dark-haired man and a handsome, bald African American who had a dancer's build and way of moving.

When they were finished, it was the blond one who presented Claire with something on a clipboard to sign and told her she'd be billed. She preferred to write them a check today, she said; she didn't like leaving things hanging. That brought a wide smile to the blond one's face.

"That's good," he said. "You can sometimes get stiffed in this business."

He was waiting patiently for her reply, but Claire decided not to play the double-entendre game. *Strictly business.* She wrote a check, adding a large tip, and handed it to the Viking. He was sweating, standing closer than he had to, emanating heat and a scent that should have been unpleasant but wasn't. Claire had to admit he made her uncomfortable in a way she liked.

He made a show of examining the check, then smiled and said, "My name's Lars Svenson, Claire."

"Lately of Sweden?" She didn't know what else to say and the inane question had jumped out.

"Not hardly," Svenson said. "Well, a few generations ago.

What about Briggs? What kind of name is that? A married one?"

"Not yet," Claire said. "Soon, though."

"Soon is no. The date been set?"

"No."

"Question been popped?"

"Not in so many words. We have an understanding."

He gave her a wide, sensuous grin. "Understandings aren't exactly contracts."

She shook her head no to his obvious intention. "I'm afraid this one is."

Svenson shrugged. "Well, if he turns out to have murdered his last three wives . . ."

She laughed. "Then I'll need a mover."

He gave her a jaunty little salute, then shot another smile at her as he went out the door.

"Whew!" Claire heard herself exclaim.

She walked again to the window and watched below as Svenson swung himself into the truck's cab with the other two men, and the blocky little van pulled away from the curb.

Claire toured the apartment again, checking on where the furniture had been placed. She moved a table closer to the sofa, then exchanged two lamps.

She was standing with her hands on her hips, planning on where to place wall hangings in the living room, when her cell phone chirped in her purse.

She hurriedly crossed to where the purse sat on the floor in a corner and dug the phone from it.

"Claire? It's Maddy," came a woman's voice on the other end of the connection. Madison Capp, the dancer friend who'd recommended the movers.

"Hi, Maddy," Claire said.

"The movers been there?"

"And left. Thanks for recommending them. They were terrific. They didn't dent or scratch anything."

"And they're very decorative, aren't they?"

"I have to say yes."

"Was the big blond one there? Lars whatever?"

"Yeah. Lars Svenson."

"He come on to you?"

"Somewhat. He an actor or something?"

"Nope, just a hunk with a line of bullshit. A friend of mine went out with him after he helped move her into an apartment a few months ago."

"Oh? She give you any reports?"

"Haven't seen her. She left the city. I heard she got a movie part in Europe in one of those erotic coming-of-age flicks. She's bi."

"Bisexual?"

"No, bilingual. But she must have been more than satisfied with Lars in any language."

"Must have been," Claire said, laughing.

"Anyway, you're serious about someone, right?"

"Right. Jubal Day. He's an actor."

"Ah! Played in *Metabolism* in the Village last year?"

"Same Jubal Day."

"Then I can see why you're serious. What's he doing now?"

"*Metabolism*'s touring. He's in Kansas City."

"Too bad he can't be with you. Well, if you need anything, Claire, give me a call."

"I will. And thanks again, Maddy."

"So be happy and get back to nesting."

Claire replaced the phone in her purse and did just that. She continued her rounds of the apartment, touching, adjusting, rearranging, feeling very domestic.

She was feeling that way more and more—domestic. It was strange. Maddy had used the word *nesting*. Birds did that, made a nest, a home. *Homemaking.* That was what was on Claire's mind these days, and there was a deep pleasure in it.

She wondered what was wrong with her.

She realized suddenly that in the excitement of moving, she'd forgotten to check the box downstairs to see if the postal service had started mail delivery at her new address.

At first, when she stood in the tiled lobby and opened the brass mailbox beneath her apartment number, Claire thought she might as well not have bothered. The box was empty except for yet another offer to open a new charge account, and a coupon for free pizza delivery.

Then she noticed the letter-size white envelope scrunched up against the side of the box.

In the envelope was her second major stroke of luck.

It was a gracefully handwritten letter from Aunt Em, her favorite relative, who lived in Maine. The letter was creased and folded around a check.

After Claire had e-mailed the good news about taking over one of the most important roles on Broadway, Aunt Em e-mailed back that she was sending Claire a congratulatory gift. And here it was. Enough money to do what Claire had often told her was one of her fondest desires—hiring a professional decorator. Aunt Em's generous check was the perfect gift, with the new apartment.

Claire thought about calling Maddy back and sharing her good news, then decided against it. Maddy thought about little beyond dancing. Her idea of a well-decorated apartment was one with more than one place to sit.

Which, Claire had to admit, was maybe the reason why Maddy was one of the most frequently employed dance gypsies in New York.

Claire liked Maddy, but she'd always thought a human being should have more than one interest.

She was pretty sure she'd locked the apartment door behind her, so she left the lobby to go outside and walk to the Duane Reade drugstore two blocks down, where she could buy a nice thank-you card for Aunt Em.

It was a beautiful warm day, sunny, so that even the curbside plastic trash bags glistened with reflected light like jewels set along the avenue. Maybe it was only her mood, but people on the sidewalk seemed less preoccupied, more tuned in to the world and happier.

Sometimes, Claire thought, life could be just about perfect.

Also surprising.

5

Pearl lay in bed in her crummy fourth-floor walk-up, staring at the cracked ceiling that needed paint like the rest of the place.

She'd bought decorating supplies last month after renting the apartment six months ago—colonial white latex flat paint with matching glossy enamel. Also brushes, scrapers, rollers, paint trays, plastic drop cloths, even some kind of sponge contraption for trimming corners and around window and door frames. She had everything she needed other than enthusiasm. And time.

Things kept getting in the way, like murders, rapes, robberies, occupying most of her hours and demanding most of her energy.

So the painting supplies all sat in a narrow, shelfless closet in the hall, waiting to be used. Pearl hadn't looked at them in weeks.

The Job, her job, where was it going? She knew where everyone, including her, thought it was going, since the evening she'd had the run-in with that asshole Egan.

* * *

She'd been off duty and had gone into the Meermont Hotel to use the ladies' room, such facilities being rare and precious in Manhattan. To reach the restrooms she had to walk through the Meermont's softly lit, oak-paneled lounge, and she'd heard her name called.

When she'd stopped and turned, there was Captain Vincent Egan seated on the end stool at the long bar.

She'd smiled, wanting to move on, desperately having to relieve herself. But she couldn't ignore or be brusque to the man who commanded her precinct, and who in many ways controlled her future.

"Captain Egan! Hello!" She feigned surprise and pleasure convincingly, she thought, while managing not to stand with her legs crossed.

Maybe she'd been too convincing. Egan slid his bulky, bullnecked self down off his bar stool and advanced on her. Seeing his unsteadiness, looking into his somewhat glazed blue eyes, she realized with a shock he was drunk.

"You undercover?" he had asked, moving close to her so she could smell that he'd been drinking bourbon and plenty of it. She glanced over at his glass on the bar. An on-the-rocks glass, empty but for half-melted ice. "If you're undercover," Egan slurred at her, "you really shouldn't have addressed me as captain."

And I really have to go to the bathroom. "I know that, sir. I'm not undercover. I'm between shifts, on my way to meet someone for dinner, and just stopped in to use the ladies' room."

She saw his eyes gain focus and travel up and down her body. She was wearing a sweater, skirt, and navy high heels. The sweater might be too tight. Pearl had dressed up for the man she was meeting, an assistant DA she'd struck up a conversation with in court. She didn't see much hope that anything might come of the dinner, but still she had to try. Or so she told herself.

Egan had been swaying this way and that, as if he were on the deck of a ship, while he'd stared at her chest. "I've never sheen you sho dolled up."

Uh-oh. He was loaded, all right. She'd heard right the first time; he was slurring his words.

"I've never sheen you sho attractive."

You've never seen me piddle in public.

"You have great . . .," he said. "I mean, I've alwaysh greatly admired you, Offisher Kashner."

"Captain Egan, listen, I've gotta—"

His beefy hand rested on her shoulder. "Politicsh, Offisher Kashner. You are a fine offisher, and I have noted that. A hard, hard worker. Determined. But are you conshidering politicsh's role in your career?" A spray of spittle went with the question.

"Oh, sure. Politics. I really—"

He'd moved to within inches of her, and his fingertips brushed her cheek. "Lishen, Pug—"

"I really don't like to be called that, Captain." She knew it was short for *pugnacious,* but she also thought some of her fellow officers might be referring to her turned-up nose. One of them had even said it wasn't the kind of nose he expected to find on a girl named Kasner. She didn't bother telling him her mother had been pure Irish. She'd instead elbowed him in the ribs, not smiling.

But Captain Egan *had been* smiling, and it was a smile Pearl had seen on too many men. "I happen to know the hotel manager and can get a room here for the night," he said. "We are, I can shee, compatible. That ish to shay, we like each other. I can tell that. It would be in both our intereshst to think about a room." He swayed nearer. "They all have bathrooms."

"Not a good idea, Captain."

"But I thought you had to . . . uh, go." He winked. She realized he thought he was being charming.

"Not that bad, I don't." She moved back so his fingertips were no longer touching her face. The bastard actually thought he was getting away with something, making progress with her. It was pissing her off. If she didn't have to go so bad . . .

"I'm your shuperior offisher, Pug." His hand, suddenly free, dropped to her left breast and stayed there like Velcro. "If you sheriously object—"

He didn't finish his sentence. Pearl did seriously object. She hit him hard in the jaw with her right fist, feeling a satisfying jolt travel down her arm into her shoulder. It was a good punch. It sent him staggering backward to sit slumped on the floor between two vacant bar stools.

He had fought his way up frantically, like a panicked nonswimmer who didn't know he was in shallow water, flailing his arms and legs and knocking over a bar stool he tried to use for support. His broad face was twisted and ugly with anger.

He'd looked amazingly sober then. "Listen, Kasner!"

But Pearl had spun on her high heels and was striding toward the ladies' room, where she knew he wouldn't follow.

She understood immediately the gravity of what she'd done. Knew she'd screwed up. At least there were witnesses in the bar, a lineup of men and a few women, many of them grinning at her in the back-bar mirror as she passed. Hotel guests, most of them. Witnesses. She could locate them if she had to. Asshole Egan would have to know that.

"Kasner!"

Now she did turn. She balled her right fist and raised her voice. "You really want me to come back, Captain Egan?"

He flinched. He was in plain clothes, but he didn't like his rank and name spoken so loudly. Not in these circumstances.

Maybe he knew what she was doing and suddenly realized his own vulnerability, because he seemed suddenly aware of the other lounge patrons and the two bartenders, all staring at him.

He dug out his wallet, threw some bills on the bar next to his empty glass, then stalked out.

Pearl continued to the ladies' room.

When she emerged ten minutes later, calm but still angry, Egan was nowhere in sight.

As she walked swiftly through the bar toward the lobby, she heard applause.

The dinner date was disastrous. Pearl couldn't stop thinking about Captain Egan and what had happened, what she'd done. She couldn't stop blaming herself as well as Egan.

Anger, depression, stress. Pearl's world.

Days had passed, and that world didn't collapse in on Pearl. Word had gotten around, though, like a subterranean current.

Still, there had been no reprisals. Egan was married. There were witnesses to his altercation with Pearl, and he'd been close to falling-down drunk, while she'd been sober. Internal affairs was never involved. No official charges were ever filed. NYPD politics at work.

She, and everyone else, knew that Egan was patiently waiting for his opportunity. Pearl didn't figure to have a long or distinguished career as a cop.

"Damn!" she said to her bedroom ceiling, and tried to think about something else. Her mind was a merry-go-round she couldn't stop. Maybe she should get out of bed and paint.

Yeah, at eleven-thirty at night.

It was one of the few times in her life when Pearl wished she had something other than her work. But she'd had several disastrous romances and had lost her faith in men. Most men, anyway. No, *all* men. The entire fucking gender. None of them seemed to be for her.

Fedderman, being her partner, was the man she spent the

most time with. A decent enough guy, married, three kids, overweight, overdeodorized, eighteen years older than Pearl, and more interested in pasta than sex.

Not much hope there.

The other men in her life, her fellow officers and men she encountered in other city jobs, sometimes made plays for her. None of them interested her. These guys were far more interested in sex than pasta, or anything else. Invariably, they talked a great game, but it was talk. The few guys she'd given a tumble couldn't keep up with her in or out of the sack, and they tended to run off at the mouth. Pearl didn't like that. Pearl figured the hell with them. When it came to what really mattered, they didn't have it.

Maybe she picked them wrong. Or maybe that was just men.

She laced her fingers behind her head and closed her eyes. If she could only meet some guy who wasn't all front. Who wasn't shooting angles or afraid to care and act like he cared. Who wasn't so dishonest with her.

Who knows how lonely I am.

Who isn't so . . .

She fell asleep thinking about it.

Him.

Like she sometimes did on nights when she didn't drink scotch or take a pill.

Lars Svenson wouldn't let the woman sleep. Whenever he knew she was dozing off, he'd lay into her again with the whip. It was a short, supple whip, and about as big around as a shoelace, so it stung and left narrow but painful welts on the woman's bare back.

She couldn't avoid the lashes, because she was lying on her stomach on her bed, her hands tied to the headboard, her feet to the iron bed frame's legs. She couldn't cry out, because a rectangle of silver duct tape covered her mouth.

He lashed her again and she managed a fairly loud whimper.

Lars stood back and smiled down at her. Through the web of hair over her left eye, she stared up at him. He loved the pain in her dark gaze and the message it sent.

He gave her a few more, striking her just so, barely breaking the skin.

It wasn't the first time for her. He'd known that when he picked her up in the Village bar, where she wouldn't have been if she wasn't cruising for this kind of action. She was plump and dark, maybe Jewish or Italian, with a mop of obviously dyed blond hair and the kind of wide smile people called vivacious. He'd seen in her eyes what she wanted. She saw in his that he'd supply it. After only one drink she'd suggested they go to her apartment.

When they'd undressed, he saw that she was even plumper than she'd appeared in clothes. Not exactly what you'd call fat, though.

Lars knew where to look. He saw bruises around her nipples, faint scars on her thighs and buttocks. Her back looked fresh, though. He'd take care of that.

Tiring of using the whip, he propped it in the crack of her ass and went over to the dresser, where he had a cold beer sitting on a coaster so as not to mar the finish. Lars respected furniture.

The woman was sobbing now. He took a sip of beer and regarded her. It might be time to talk to her, softly tell her what else he was going to do to her. Then he realized he'd forgotten her name. It sounded Russian or something and was hard to recall.

He grinned. She wasn't in any position now to refresh his memory.

She twisted her neck, trying to get him in her range of vision, wondering if he was still in the room. He shouldn't have gone yet, leaving her bound and gagged. That was breaking the rules.

Then he remembered. Or thought he did.

"Flo?"

She reacted immediately, tensing her buttocks and straining to look in the direction of his voice.

"If you're a good girl, Flo, maybe I'll take you out for breakfast tomorrow." Letting her know he was staying the long night through.

She managed only one of her whimpers.

He decided the bottoms of Flo's bare feet shouldn't be ignored.

6

Quinn was up late at the kitchen's tiny gray Formica table, smoking a cheap cigar and studying the Elzner murder file. Rather, the copy of the file, which Renz had provided.

He was drinking beer from a thick, clouded tumbler that looked as if it had been stolen from a diner years ago. The foam head had disappeared except for a light, sudsy film along the glass's sides, and the beer was warm.

Quinn exhaled cigar smoke and leaned back away from the open file. There really wasn't much of value inside it. Sure, there were things that didn't quite add up, that suggested someone other than Martin Elzner had fired the shots that killed Elzner and his wife. But almost always in cases of violent death, there were such loose ends, questions that would never be answered. Lives that were stopped abruptly left them behind as if to haunt and not be forgotten. If you were a cop long enough, you didn't expect to ever understand everything.

He propped the cigar in a cracked saucer he was using as an ashtray, then took a sip of beer. There was one thing, though, that stuck like a bur in his mind. The groceries. The

Elzners must have bought them before the stores closed, then were putting them away when the shooting occurred. But no one in any of the surrounding grocery stores or all-night delis, where they might have bought groceries, recalled them being there. Of course it was possible they'd shopped just down the block from their apartment and not been recognized. Or had been recognized and forgotten. People didn't go around paying attention to everything around them in case they might be quizzed later.

So, maybe the groceries were going to remain another of those unanswered questions.

But there was also the gun, a Walther .38-caliber semi-automatic. It was a large enough caliber to make plenty of noise, yet no one in neighboring apartments had heard shots.

That, too, was possible, especially at the time of the Elzners' deaths. But it made the marks on the gun and the bullet nicks all the more likely to have been made by a silencer.

Which, of course, would mean a murderer other than the late Martin Elzner. One who couldn't risk making noise, and who knew no one would bother using a silencer for a murder-suicide. Missing silencer: a killer still at large.

Quinn glanced at his watch, a long-ago birthday gift from May. Past midnight. He decided to go to bed. Renz had set it up for him to visit the Elzner apartment tomorrow morning, so Quinn wanted to be alert, and to resemble as much as possible the man he'd been.

Still am!

He closed the file, then snuffed out his cigar in the saucer and finished the tepid beer that would help him get to sleep.

Quinn was satisfied with his chances. He never expected or needed a brass ring.

A toehold would do.

In the bathroom he brushed his teeth, then leaned close and examined them in the mirror. Too yellow, and they seemed slightly crooked, and maybe that was a cavity way back there. He'd neglected them too long. A trip to a dentist wouldn't be a bad idea for his appearance. He'd lost a couple of molars in a long-ago fight, and broken the bridgework since. Other than that, he still had his own teeth. He smiled, then shook his head at the rawboned, luckless thug looking back at him. Rough. Downright grizzly. Scary.

The smile disappeared and he turned away, sickened with himself.

He'd sunk. He could see it now that he was looking up again. He'd sunk so goddamned far! An outcast, a sexual predator the neighbors whispered about and avoided. He drank too much and thought too much, and spent too much time alone. His wife and his own daughter were afraid of him.

It isn't fucking fair!

He turned again toward the mirror and drew back his fist, thinking of smashing his ruined image, cracking it into fragments so it resembled his broken life.

There again was his sad smile. And his own sad eyes staring back at him. Movie shit, punching mirrors. Heavy-handed symbolism. In real life it accomplished nothing and meant nothing.

Self-pity was his problem. Self-pity was like a drug that would pull him down as surely as any of the drugs on the street.

He went to the closet and rooted through his clothes. Whatever he had, it would have to do until he got an advance on his salary from Renz.

Bum's clothes. Goddamned bum's wardrobe!

Or maybe it wasn't that bad. He didn't have a decent suit but could put together what might loosely be called an outfit. A wrinkled pair of pants, a white dress shirt that had long sleeves and would be hot as hell this time of year, and a blue sport coat that wasn't too bad if he kept the ripped pocket

flap tucked in. Shoes were okay, a black pair, which he'd
bought years ago, that weren't too badly worn and were actually comfortable.

A shave, a reasonable taming of his unruly hair—starting
to gray—and he could still look enough like a cop.

Which he was, damn it!

He was a cop.

A lot of blood.

That was the first thing that struck Quinn the next morning after he'd unwrapped crime scene tape from the door-
knob and let himself into the Elzner apartment with the key
Renz had taped to the back of the murder file.

The Elzners had died in their kitchen. Though it wasn't so
evident in the crime scene photos, it looked as if the wife,
Jan, had dragged herself a few feet before expiring and left
some bloody scratches on the freshly painted white door.
Quinn didn't think the scratches were an attempt at writing a
dying message, more the result of death throes.

Stepping around the crusted dried blood on the kitchen
floor, Quinn made his way to the table. The groceries were
still there. The can of tuna that had been on the floor near the
body was now next to one of the two small, unmarked plastic bags. There were some oranges, a loaf of wheat bread, a
jar of peanut butter. Nothing perishable other than the oranges, according to the file. Also there were two jars of
gourmet strawberry jam.

Quinn didn't touch anything as he leaned down to peer at
the price tags on the jam jars. Expensive.

He left the table and examined the holes in the walls from
the bullets that had gone through Jan Elzner. Two holes. One
wide and jagged, struck by a misshapen, nearly spent bullet
that had passed through too much tissue or bone. The other

hole was as circular and neat as if it had been made by a drill bit, from the bullet that had made it through to the next apartment and led to the discovery of the bodies.

Standing there in the kitchen, Quinn felt something stir deep in his gut. The crime scene didn't feel like murder-suicide. The roughly outlined positions of the bodies, the half-finished mundane task of putting away groceries. No foresight or even rudimentary planning was evident here.

Hubby was supposedly the shooter. If the wife had been interrupted by sudden, violent death while putting away groceries, her body probably wouldn't have dropped where it had. And Hubby wouldn't have been in such a rush to kill himself that he'd knock a can of tuna off the table.

Of course it was all possible.

But it didn't *feel* that way. It felt like murder. And an unlikely, perhaps senseless one. An unsuspecting couple living out their domestic lives, and some evil bastard decided they'd had enough and ended it for them, maybe for no reason other than so he could watch them die. *Evil.* It wasn't a word Quinn shied away from, because he'd learned long ago it was a palpable thing that never quite left where it visited. And it was here, in the Elzners' kitchen, his old and familiar enemy.

Do something about this. You can do something about who did this if you don't screw up.

Quinn realized he'd turned a corner and was assuming the killer wasn't Martin Elzner.

It was the kind of gut assumption any old cop knew not to ignore.

Quinn went into the Elzners' bedroom. Everything was neat in there except for the unmade bed, obviously slept in by two. There was a set of women's pink slippers on the floor near the bed, the kind without heels that you could slide your feet right into. Mules, he thought they were called. But maybe not.

He made a mental note to check and see if Jan Elzner's corpse had bare feet. If so, it suggested she might have awakened suddenly, maybe heard something in the kitchen that alarmed her, and hurried out there, in too much of a rush even to step into her slippers. Which would mean she'd been in bed alone at the time, or she would have alerted her husband.

Interesting, the slippers.

Mules?

Quinn nosed around in the bedroom some more, then the bathroom, finding nothing of use or interest.

He returned to the kitchen and opened the refrigerator. The usual. A carton of milk, now gone bad. Some half-used condiments, a six-pack of diet Coke, two cans of Budweiser. In the door shelves were a bottle of orange juice, an unopened bottle of Chablis, a jar of pickles, and two plastic Evian bottles, one of which was opened and half-empty. And something else: a jar of the same kind of gourmet strawberry jam that was on the kitchen table.

Quinn used a dry dish towel wadded on the sink counter to open the jar. It was almost full of jam.

After screwing the lid back on and replacing the jar, he shut the refrigerator door and tossed the towel back on the counter, near a glass vase containing a small bouquet of neglected yellow roses that had died not long after the Elzners. Then he opened the freezer compartment at the top of the refrigerator.

Three frozen dinners—free-range chicken. *How free were they, really?* Some frozen meat wrapped in white butcher paper. A rubber-lidded dish containing chocolate-chip cookies. Quinn leaned forward and peered into the icemaker basket—full of cubes.

The apartment was warm and the cool air tumbling from the freezer felt good, but he shut the narrow white door and heard the refrigerator motor immediately start to hum. A couple of decorative magnets were stuck to the door—a Statue of Liberty, an unfurled American flag—but there was nothing pinned beneath them. No messages. *Such as, who might try to kill us.*

Quinn figured he'd seen enough. He left the apartment, locking the door behind him and replacing the yellow crime scene tape. He was glad to get away from the smell. Even dry, so much blood had a sickly sweet coppery scent that brought back the wrong kind of memories. Too many crime scenes where death had been violent and gory. Years of cleaning up the worst kinds of messes that people made of their lives and other lives. The woman in Queens who'd slashed her sleeping husband's throat with a razor blade, then mutilated his nude body. The Lower East Side man who'd shot his wife's lover, then three members of her family, then himself. So many years of that kind of thing. What had it done to him that he hadn't noticed? Didn't suspect?

And why did he miss it so?

What had made May leave him so soon after he'd been discredited and lost his livelihood? Had she doubted his innocence from the beginning? Or had she seen something in him that was beyond his awareness?

While he was waiting for the elevator, he examined his reflection in its polished steel door. He looked okay, he decided, with his fresh shave, white collar, and dark tie. A homicide cop on the job.

Except for the shield. There wasn't one.

The elevator arrived with a muted thumping and strumming of cables.

When the gleaming door slid open, a uniformed cop Quinn knew as Mercer stepped out into the hall. A big, square-shouldered guy with squinty eyes and a ruddy complexion. Quinn had only been in the man's company a few times, years ago, and wasn't sure if he'd be recognized.

Mercer nodded to him and politely stepped aside so Quinn could enter the elevator. Quinn nodded back, studying Mercer's eyes.

They were good cop's eyes, neutral as Switzerland.

7

Marcy Graham absolutely and without a doubt had to try on the soft brown leather jacket, and that was what led to the problem.

She knew her husband, Ron, was arguing against buying the jacket not because he disliked it, but because he disliked paying for it. All this talk of it putting weight on her was absurd. Her image in the mirror of Tambien's exclusive women's shop confirmed it. The tapered cut of the three-quarter-length jacket made her look slender. *Not that I have a weight problem.* And the price was unbelievable. Half off because it was out of season.

But later in the years, when the weather was cooler, she could wear such a coat anywhere. What she liked about it was its simplicity. She could accessorize it, dress it up or down. With her blue eyes, her light brown hair, and her unblemished complexion, the soft color of the leather was just right.

"It makes you look ten pounds lighter," whispered the salesclerk when Ron wandered away to deposit his chewing gum in a receptacle that had once been an ashtray. "Not that you need it, but still. . . ."

Marcy nodded, not daring to answer, because Ron was already striding back to where she and the clerk were standing before the full-length mirrors that were angled so you could see three of yourself.

The salesclerk was a slight, handsome man in a blue chalk-striped suit of European cut. He had brown eyes, with long lashes, and black hair slicked back to a knot at the base of his neck. He also wore rings, gold and silver, on two fingers of each hand, and a dangling diamond earring. Marcy knew the earring and rings were enough for Ron not to like him.

"Look at yourself from all sides," the salesclerk urged, nudging Marcy closer to the triptych mirrors. "The coat lends you a certain curvaciousness, doesn't it?" He winked not at Marcy but at Ron.

"Don't try including me in bullshitting your customers," Ron said. He was smiling, but Marcy, and probably the salesclerk, knew he was serious.

The clerk smiled at Marcy. "It's the truth, of course, about what the jacket does for you."

"It's a subjective thing," Ron said.

"Or it's the lines of the jacket complementing the lines of the woman. Or maybe the other way around."

"You really think so?" Ron asked sarcastically. Marcy could see him getting angrier. On dangerous ground now. Close to losing his temper with this slight, effeminate man.

She shrugged and grinned in the mirror at the salesclerk. "I guess my husband doesn't like it, so—"

"Ah! For some reason I thought he was a friend. Or perhaps your older brother."

Ron glared at the clerk. "I'm not quite sure, but I believe I've been insulted."

The clerk shrugged. "It certainly wasn't intentional."

"I believe it was."

The salesclerk shrugged again, but this time there was a different and definite body language to it. A taunt.

Marcy thought he didn't look so much like a harmless salesclerk now, perhaps gay, but not so effeminate. Not the sort of clerk you might expect to find in a semiswank shop like Tambien's that—let's face it—put on airs to jack up prices. His lean body appeared coiled and strong beneath the chalk-striped suit, and she noticed that his manicured hands were large for such a thin man, the backs of them heavily veined. Faded blue coloring, what might be part of a tattoo, peeked from beneath his right cuff. Marcy didn't want to see those hands, with the rings, made into fists.

"Don't push it, Ron, please," she said, starting to unbutton the coat.

"Push it?" But he was looking at the clerk and not Marcy. Unlike Marcy, he didn't seem to sense that the slender male-model type might be a dangerous man.

The clerk smiled. Though possibly fifty pounds lighter than the six-foot-one, two-hundred-pound Ron, he was obviously unafraid. The long-lashed brown eyes didn't blink.

"Why not push it?" Ron said. "I don't appreciate this guy's attitude."

"I apologize for anything you mistook as improper," the clerk said, his smile turning superior and insincere. His teeth were perfectly even and very white.

Ron's face was darkening. Marcy could see the purple vein near his temple start to throb, the way it did when he was about to lose control. Another customer, browsing nearby, a tall woman in designer slacks, a sleeveless blouse, and too much jewelry, glanced at them from the corner of a wide eye and hurried away on the plush carpet.

"Please, Ron, I'm taking the coat off." Her fingers trembling, Marcy fumbled at the buttons. "I've decided I don't want it."

"Can I be of some help here?" a voice asked. A man who stood in a rooted way, as if he had authority, had drifted over to move between the clerk and Ron. He stood closer to Ron. He was short, bald, had a dark mustache, and was wearing a chalk-striped suit like the clerk's, only his was chocolate brown instead of blue. "I'm the store manager."

"I don't think you *will* help," Ron said, "but this jerk was coming on to my wife."

Marcy shook her head. "For God's sake, Ron!"

The salesclerk stood with his hands at his sides, perfectly calm. Almost amused. It occurred to Marcy that he might be one of those small men who felt compelled to pick on large men as a way of proving themselves. The kind of man who'd learned the hard way how to fight and was eager to back up his bravado. Showing off for the lady, but mostly for himself.

"You were *flirting*, Ira?" the manager asked, glancing at the clerk. His tone suggested he was astounded by the possibility.

"Of course not. If it appeared so, I certainly apologize."

Marcy removed the coat, relieved to be out of it, and handed it to the clerk.

He gave her a little bow as he accepted the garment and extended a card to her with his free hand, smiling. "If you think about it and change your mind, I'm Ira."

"She knows you're Ira, and she won't change her mind," Ron said. "And you won't change it for her." He clutched Marcy's elbow. "C'mon, Marcy. We're outta here."

Marcy let him lead her toward the door. She knew he felt he'd topped the clerk and was ready to leave while he was ahead. She was thankful for that. The situation was already embarrassing enough.

"Marcy's a nice name," she heard Ira remark softly behind them.

Ron seemed not to have heard, but she wondered if he had.

8

He stood in the doorway of a luggage shop across the street and watched Marcy Graham leave Fifth Federal Savings Bank, where she worked as a loan officer. She paused in front of the bank's glass doors, set between phony stone pillars, and glanced up at the sky as if contemplating rain, then seemed to reject decisively the idea of going back inside for an umbrella and began walking.

He followed.

He knew her routes and her timetable by now, her haunts and habits. After work, she boarded the subway at a stop two blocks from Fifth Federal. He enjoyed watching her walk. She would stride down the block in her high heels, the warm breeze pressing her skirt against her thighs, her breasts and brown hair bouncing with each step, and she would unhesitatingly enter the long, shadowed stairwell to the turnstiles.

It was a wonder to watch her descend the concrete steps, moving rapidly if there was no one in her way. Almost like a graceful, controlled near-tumble. His eyes took all of her in, the strength and looseness of her legs, the way her arms swung, her hair swayed, her hips switched, motion, counter-motion, the rhythm of time and the cosmos. In some women there was everything.

She would take the train to within two blocks of her apartment building, then walk the rest of the way home, playing out her daily routine, locked in the worn pathways of her life. He knew routine made her feel secure. There was safety in repetition simply because there were no surprises; life was habit and redundancy all the way to the edges of her perception. What a comfort! How wise she was, yet didn't know herself.

Sometimes he followed closely all the way from the bank, taking the same uptown train, even riding in the same car, watching her, imagining. In the gray world of the subway, they were both sometimes lucky enough to find seats. And more often than not, there were the usual subway creeps staring at a woman like Marcy. That meant she didn't pay much attention to him, worrying about the silent watchers who so obviously wanted every part and morsel of her.

The pink and red of her, the hues of her flesh and hidden white purity of bone.

Not that Marcy had to worry about the creeps. She belonged to someone already, even if she didn't yet know it.

He would follow her up to the multicolored surface from the drab subway stop, then down the street to her apartment in the building with the dirty stone facade. Then he'd cross the street and find a spot where he could stand out of the flow of pedestrian traffic and watch the Grahams' apartment windows.

He would see one or the other of them pass from time to time, fleeting movement behind glass panes. Glimpses into another world in which he was only a ghost and she its brightest inhabitant.

Only a few minutes, perhaps ten, would he stay there. Best not to attract undue attention. But it intrigued him that Marcy and her husband were unknowingly walking where he'd walked, touching what he'd touched, maybe sitting in a chair not long cooled from his own warmth. Living, breathing, touching themselves and each other. Being their private selves in the place he'd just left in order to follow her back to it. He didn't shadow Marcy home from work so he could find out where she was going, but to observe her closely when she thought she was alone.

This evening was cooling down and comfortable. It wouldn't be dark for several hours, so the apartment lights wouldn't come on anytime soon. That was a shame, because he particularly wanted to see what would happen this evening between Marcy and Ron. After night fell was when watching was best, when Marcy and her husband moved behind the glass. When, if they happened to glance out, they could see only in—their own reflections and the reflection of their world.

When, even if by chance had they looked precisely in his direction, they couldn't see him.

Color me invisible.

A uniform wanted to see him and only him. Captain Vince Egan was puzzled. It took a lot for a uniformed cop to skip the chain of command and confide in a captain. It meant trouble for the cop if he guessed wrong, and if what he had to say wasn't deemed worthwhile.

Glancing with satisfaction around his paneled office, Egan understood why it took guts for a mere patrolman to approach him. There were framed photos of Egan with various NYPD elites, posed at banquets and various ceremonies with top New York pols. Among the career photos and commendations were a few shots of Egan with show business types, like the old black-and-white photograph of Egan with his arm slung around Tony Bennett, taken years ago in L.A., though Egan always said it was in San Francisco. And there was one in color with Egan chatting with Jennifer Jason

Leigh and Bridget Fonda after a New York movie premiere a while back. Egan with Wayne Newton. All of these photographs were signed.

An impressive office. An impressive and important person must occupy it. Somebody you didn't approach lightly with a shit piece of information or some whine about how the department was run.

Egan was getting tired of waiting. Who the fuck was this guy, and what did he want? And what would be his future after he said his piece and walked out of here?

This better not be about charity. Some kind of pet cause Egan couldn't refuse to contribute money or time to without looking like an ass.

Like the time the guy swallowed his nervousness and asked Egan to make a public announcement about the abominable way chinchillas were treated on chinchilla ranches before they became coats.

What did Egan care about chinchillas? What the fuck actually *was* a chinchilla?

Egan glanced at his watch and wished again the guy would get here. He was already five minutes late, which was inconveniencing people. Like Doris, Egan's uniformed secretary who called herself his assistant, who ordinarily would have left by now but was waiting in the outer office.

Doris, sitting straight as a soldier behind her desk as she always did, like she had a pole up her ass, maybe catching up on some word processing. Egan leaned back in his leather desk chair and thought about Doris. She wasn't a beauty, and Egan didn't usually mix business with fornication, but since her divorce six months ago, Doris was beginning to look more attractive to him. Sure, she was in her fifties, but she still had a shape, and if she wasn't a blue-ribbon beauty, she wasn't butt ugly. And there was another thing Egan liked about her: now more than ever, she needed to hold on to her job.

Egan smiled. Doris was highly ethical and acted around the office like she didn't even have erogenous zones. But with hubby having left her for some younger cunt, she still might come around, like her predecessor. *What some women will do to stay employed.* . . .

There was a familiar three-knock tattoo on the office door; then it opened halfway and Doris stepped into sight.

Was she wearing tighter uniform slacks since she'd become single? She was definitely getting grayer, Egan noticed, and thicker through the middle. Still . . .

"Patrolman Mercer is here, sir."

Mercer. Damn it! He'd told Charlie Mercer not to come here unless it was important. Even now, four years later.

Egan felt suddenly uneasy. *So, maybe it's important.*

He nodded and sat forward in his leather chair, using his right hand to push away some papers on his desk, as if he'd been busy contemplating them.

"Send Officer Mercer in, Doris."

9

Marcy Graham couldn't figure it out, and she wondered if she should even try.

There was the leather coat she'd tried on at Tambien's, the one that had prompted the argument between Ron and that salesclerk who was trying so hard to work her; just doing his job, and Ron got all pissy. It was lying draped over the arm of the sofa, not carelessly but as if someone had carefully arranged it there so she'd see it when she came in. A nice surprise.

Marcy put down her purse on a lamp table and went to the coat, touched it, stroked it. The leather was so soft. That really was what had attracted her to it in the first place. She lifted a lapel, then an arm, and could find no sales tag.

She held up the coat at arm's length and looked it over. There was no clue as to where it had come from. She slipped it on, thinking it felt as good as it had at the shop, and walked to the full-length mirror near the door.

Smiling at her reflection, she turned this way and that, almost all the way around, gazing back over her shoulder as if at a lover she was leaving.

She removed the coat and placed it back on the sofa arm. A gift from Ron? Most likely. In fact, that was the only possible explanation. He felt guilty about smarting off and almost blowing up in Tambien's, and he wanted to make it up to her. It wouldn't be unlike him. He had a temper, but he could be sweet.

She stood with her hands on her hips, staring at the coat. Now, how should she react? What would Ron expect when he walked in the door? Should she leave the coat on the sofa? Maybe it was better to hang it in the closet, play dumb, toy with him and make a game of it. The kind they used to play. Or she could lay the coat on the bed and let *him* find it. That might be interesting. Then she'd show him her appreciation for his unexpected gift, making a gift of herself. The old games.

There was a slight sound in the hall; then the ratcheting of a key in the dead-bolt lock.

The door opened and her options disappeared as Ron stepped into the apartment.

At first he didn't notice her or the coat as he turned and closed and relocked the door. Then he turned back, saw her, and immediately his gaze shifted to the sofa where the coat lay. He appeared genuinely puzzled, but she knew he could act convincingly if he had to, feigning surprise at seeing the coat.

"Isn't that—"

"You know it is," she interrupted, smiling.

"You went back and *bought it*?" She could see his confusion changing now to anger, and silent alarms went off in her head.

"Of course not. You know I didn't!"

"How would I know that?"

"Because you bought the coat and put it there on the sofa so I'd find it when I came home."

He yanked his tie loose violently so it hung crookedly

around his neck, reminding her of a hangman's noose, then jutted out his chin and unfastened his top shirt button. "Now why the hell would I do that?"

Marcy was stunned, searching for words. "I . . . uh . . . Well, I don't know."

Not because you love me. Your eyes and that throbbing vein in your temple say now isn't the time to remind you of that.

"You thought it was a gift from me?" He pulled the narrow end through the knot and let the tie drape loosely around his neck. Almost as if he were preparing to remove it and strangle her with it if that was what he decided.

"What else would I think? I came home from work and there was the coat you knew I wanted."

"And that we didn't buy."

"You could've changed your mind."

"The point is, I didn't change it. So where'd the coat come from?"

"I told you, I assumed it was from you. Who else would have left it there? I was at work all day, and you and I are the only ones who have keys. Except for Lou the super."

Ron shook his head. He might have been angrier, only he couldn't quite figure out who was his target. "Lou's sixty-five years old and couldn't afford a coat like that. Besides, it's impossible to get him in here to fix a leaky faucet, much less shower us with gifts. After the chat I had with him, Lou wouldn't let anybody in here even for a minute without one or both of us being present."

"Then who?"

He clenched his right hand into a fist, holding it close to his chest. "That asshole salesclerk at Tambien's—Ira."

"But how could he? *Why* would he?"

"He knew you wanted the coat." Ron went to the coat and lifted it, then wadded it and tossed it in a heap back on the sofa. "There was no note or anything?"

"Nothing. I found it just like you saw it."

He picked up the coat again and tucked it, still wadded, beneath his arm. "C'mon!"

"Come on where?"

"To Tambien's."

"You're taking it back?"

"No. I never took it *from*! We're giving it back to Ira the wiseass salesclerk, along with a warning."

"We simply can't give this back, Ron! I can't. Let's put this off, think about it some more."

"There's no place else the coat could have come from. Nobody else who might have given it to you."

"How could Ira get in?"

"I don't know, Marcy," Ron said impatiently. "I don't know how magicians guess the right card, either, but they do."

"But why would he give me a gift? What would he expect to get out of it?"

"Jesus, Marcy, what do you think?"

"We only met once, and you were there."

"So what? Maybe he's one of those fucked-up psychos who only have to see a woman once and some kind of weird connection's made."

"I guess that's possible. . . ."

"Goddamned right it is!"

"If it is, I don't want to go near him again."

Ron drew a deep breath, then sighed and dragged his forearm across his mouth, as if he'd just taken a long, sloppy drink from a stream.

"All right," he said. "You stay here. I'm gonna take this thing and return it to Tambien's. We're gonna find out about this! And do something about it!"

And he was out the door and gone.

* * *

An hour later Ron was back, empty-handed. Marcy watched her husband remove his sport coat and drape it on a hanger in the hall closet. He seemed calmer now. His face wasn't so flushed, and the blue vein in his temple wasn't even visible. "Did they take the coat back at Tambien's?"

"No," Ron said. "They claimed they didn't sell it. Said it was sold in at least a dozen shops in and around New York. I told them maybe Ira just walked out with it so he could give it to you. Ira got pissed and I threatened to twist his head off. He just smiled, the little bastard."

"I think he might be dangerous," Marcy said. "There's something creepy about him."

Ron shrugged. "Whatever he is, I told him if he ever came around here again, I'd cut off his balls."

Before or after you twist off his head? "What did he say?"

"That Tambien's wouldn't take the coat in return unless I had a sales slip. He and that numb-brain manager went into their professional salesclerk mode, polite but underneath it acting like assholes."

"So what'd you do?" Marcy asked.

"I told them I didn't want a refund; then I tossed the coat on the floor and walked out the door. You shoulda seen the look on their faces."

"That's an eight-hundred-dollar coat, Ron."

"Not to us, it isn't. It's worse than worthless." He stalked into the kitchen and a few minutes later returned with a glass of water with ice cubes in it. Marcy watched him take a long sip, his head back, the Adam's apple working in his powerful neck.

"You still think Ira somehow sneaked in here and left the coat?" she asked when finally he lowered the glass.

He'd downed half the water. His head bowed, he stared into the glass and swirled its remaining contents around so the ice cubes rattled. "I don't know," he said. "I honestly don't. But if it was him, he won't do something like that around here again. He's been scared away."

Marcy wasn't so sure.

For some reason she doubted if Ira had ever been scared away from anything in his life.

10

This time Harley Renz knocked politely on Quinn's apartment door.

Quinn peered through the round peephole and viewed the distorted police captain. Renz shifted his weight impatiently and raised his elongated arm to look at his watch. Busy man in a hurry, taking valuable time off to talk to a lowlife like Quinn.

Quinn waited awhile, until Renz knocked again, louder, before opening the door.

"Quinn," Renz said simply, nodding hello. "I would've called up on the intercom, but I saw there was sixty years of enamel over the button." He studied Quinn, who was in his stocking feet but was wearing new gray slacks and a white T-shirt, and didn't look quite so like a thug as he had during Renz's last visit. "You got a haircut."

"Got a lot of them cut," Quinn said. "You wouldn't have noticed just one."

Renz smiled. "Some new threads, too. I'm glad you put the money I sent to good use. May I enter your shit can abode?"

"Sure. You're a fit with the decor." Quinn stepped back and to the side, closing the door behind Renz after he'd entered.

Renz sat down on the sofa and crossed his legs, then looked around. "I don't know or care if that's an insult. You've cleaned up the place. No magazines, newspapers, or orange peels on the floor. And is that new mold in the corner?"

"Mold's the same. Orange peels clashed with the carpet, so they had to go. You clash, too."

"Remember I'm your friend now, Quinn. Your way up and back in." Renz made a big deal of sniffing, wrinkling his nose, and squinting. "It doesn't smell as bad in here. Is that insecticide? Or are you burning incense?"

"Have you come to pay me more money?"

"Do you need more?"

"Not yet," Quinn said honestly.

"Come up with anything in the Elzner apartment or murder file?"

"Not much," Quinn said. "The groceries bother me. The strawberry jelly."

"Jelly?"

"Jam, actually. A fairly expensive gourmet brand. There were two jars in with the groceries in the plastic bags and on the kitchen table. And there was a nearly full jar of the same stuff in the refrigerator."

Renz uncrossed his legs and crossed his arms, thinking about that. "Somebody else bought the groceries. Somebody who didn't know the Elzners had plenty of jelly."

"Jam."

"Still odd, though. Two jars . . ."

"Maybe they were a gift from somebody who knew how much one or both of the Elzners liked that kind of jam."

"A gift." Renz made a steeple of his fingers. He liked the idea of a gift, except for . . . "But why would somebody buy the Elzners a gift and then kill them?"

"Maybe he hadn't planned on killing them."

"Maybe." Renz grinned. "And he just happened to be carrying a gun equipped with a silencer. The important thing is, if you're right, it points to a third party for sure. A killer still on the loose."

"A third party who might've left before the Elzners were killed."

Renz sneered at Quinn. "Don't send me up, then bring me down. You're coming around to my way of thinking about this case; you know you are."

"I've moved in that direction," Quinn admitted. He didn't want Renz to think he'd moved almost all the way. "Also, it might be coincidental that the plastic grocery bags aren't the kind that have the name of the store on them. Or it could be the killer deliberately bought groceries someplace where they couldn't be traced by the bags and someone might remember him."

"Very good, Quinn. I was sure you'd have a different slant on this and come up with something new. You didn't disappoint me."

"I'm flushed with pride. Are you here to tell *me* anything new?"

"Yeah. I'm afraid things have changed. Egan found out you're on the case. I think from a uniform named Charlie Mercer."

"Big, square-shouldered guy, blue and brown?"

"Fits him."

"He was coming out of the elevator in the Elzners' building when I stepped in."

"He get a good look at you?"

"Like I got at him."

"Then there's no mistaking it; the bastard must've told Egan." Renz's brow furrowed. "Mercer's made a mistake. One he'll pay dearly for, and sooner than he thinks. Egan's probably already notified the chief's office. Maybe somebody in the news media. That last won't help him."

"Why not?"

Renz's forehead relaxed, but the furrows didn't fade away. "Because I've gone on the offensive. I've notified all my media contacts I've taken a chance on a good man—that'd be you. The safety of the community comes before NYPD politics and petty revenge, so I've asked Frank Quinn to look into the Elzner case because he's the best. If the story's not already on the news, it will be soon, before Egan's. The department won't move to take you off the case, because it'd be bad PR. There was never a criminal charge and a trial in the rape case. The public'll see you as a hero, Quinn. A victim of unsubstantiated rumor who deserves a second chance. I've also assigned a team of detectives to work under your command."

Quinn was surprised. "Team?"

"Two detectives, but you'll have additional temporary help, if and when you need it." Renz leaned forward on the sofa. "You know how it works, Quinn. The killing of a typical Manhattan couple means media by the shit load. Media means pressure. Can you deal with it?"

"I can deal. This team . . . are these good cops you're giving me?"

"Sure, they are. Your old partner from your radio car years, Larry Fedderman, and his new partner, Pearl Kasner."

Fedderman. Quinn almost smiled. Other than the people who'd set him up, Fedderman was probably the only one in the NYPD who didn't think Quinn was guilty of raping a minor. Fedderman had paid for it, in wisecracks and dirty looks and shitty assignments. The word was, he still believed in Quinn. "Fedderman'll do. What about Kasner?"

Renz shifted on the sofa cushion as if he'd just noticed he was sitting on something sharp. "She's got kind of a reputation in the department, but she's also got great skills."

Uh-oh. "Reputation?"

"She's got what you might call a temper. Not so unlike yourself. She gets in the same kinda trouble you used to."

"She in any of it now?"

"Yes and no."

"What's the yes part?"

"Vince Egan made a play for her in a hotel lobby, and she knocked him on his ass."

Quinn stared incredulously. "A working cop swung on an NYPD captain? She's on her way out, then."

"Let's just say she's on the bubble." Renz explained to Quinn that Egan was drunk at the time and there were witnesses. It was the kind of trouble the NYPD didn't need aired in public. An IA investigation had been spiked before it could get under way. "It's the kinda process you should understand," Renz said.

"Egan'll get her some other way."

"Not if you, Pearl, and Fedderman break the Elzner murder case."

Quinn understood Renz's angle better now. He jammed his hands in his pants pockets and paced in his stocking feet. "I don't like this. Too many last chances. How about Fedderman? He got something big riding on this, too? Will solving this case somehow cure him of a fatal disease?"

"You're the one who might be cured of a fatal disease, Quinn. Loneliness and rot."

That one got through. Quinn stopped pacing and turned to face Renz.

"You oughta know last chances aren't so bad," Renz said. "In fact, they're what life's all about."

Quinn felt the anger drain from him. Renz was right.

"You can meet with Fedderman and Kasner tomorrow morning," Renz said. "You name the time and place. I didn't figure you'd want the meet here, since the apartment's not set up for entertaining, even without the orange peels."

"Tomorrow's supposed to be a nice day," Quinn said. "We can meet just inside the Eighty-sixth Street entrance to Central Park, say around ten o'clock."

"That'll work. They'll be in plain clothes."

"I'll watch for Fedderman. What's Kasner look like?"

"You should know Fedderman's put on some weight, mostly around the middle. Kasner's short, a looker with brown eyes, a lotta dark hair, and a good rack."

"And a good punch, apparently."

"A short right," Renz said, grinning as he stood up from the couch. "I got the story from a bartender I know at the Meermont. She knocked Egan ass over elbows. You and Pearl, you oughta get along fine."

"Like salt and pepper," Quinn said, liking Kasner a little already, even though he knew she might be playing a double game, reporting to Renz as well as to him.

"More like pepper and pepper," Renz said, going out the door.

Quinn listened to Renz's receding footsteps on the creaking wooden stairs, then the faint swishing sound of the street door opening and closing.

He wasn't sure what he was getting himself into, but at least his life was moving forward again.

Or some direction.

Pain!

It would never stop. Or so it seemed.

The woman continued crawling toward the door, and the whip continued to lash her bare buttocks, her meaty thighs, and sometimes, to surprise her, her bare back.

She'd known what she was getting into—so this was her own doing, as her father used to say. She was to blame. She bore the guilt like invisible chains. When she'd received the pain and punishment she deserved, she'd be the better for it. The chains would drop away and she'd be pure again.

She was off the carpet now and crawling faster toward the door, knowing she wasn't going to escape, that she had no chance, as always. *A woman with an M.B.A. and a responsible job . . . what am I doing here?* She clenched her teeth and whimpered. She wouldn't scream. That was one of the rules. She'd been commanded not to scream. And if she did, if her neighbors heard and called the police, how would she explain? Her bare knees thumped on the hardwood floor, and her hands made desperate slapping sounds louder than her moans.

The whip whistled near her ear, sending a line of fire across her upper back and curling around her shoulder. It burned again across her tender inner right thigh. He knew how to use a whip, this one.

Ten feet from the door.

The whip set fire to her right buttock. There was less time between lashes now. She crawled even faster, hurting her knees and the heels of her hands. The whip followed, flicking her like a dragon's fiery and agile tongue.

The man standing over her was the dragon.

Afterward, maybe she'd lie with him, cuddled in his arms, and he'd pretend to love her. It wouldn't be real, like what he was doing to her now wasn't exactly real, but that didn't matter. She had no right to expect real.

As she stretched out an arm and her fingertips brushed the door, he clutched her ankles and dragged her back and away from freedom.

It began again.

What am I doing here?

11

Bent Oak, Missouri, 1987.

Two days before Luther Lunt's fourteenth birthday, state employees in Jefferson City dropped a cyanide pellet in the gas chamber, killing Luther's father.

Luther's mother had already been dead for more than a year. She'd died on the same day and in the same way as his sister, Verna, beneath the thunder and buckshot hail of his dad's Remington twelve-gauge. Luther had hunted with the gun twice and knew what it could do to a rabbit. What it had done to his mom and Verna was lots worse.

Seeing it, hearing it, smelling it, even listening to the slowing trickle of blood from his mom's ruined throat, was the kind of thing that stayed in the mind.

Luther cried almost nonstop for days and nights, wondering why Verna had to go tell their mom what she and Dad had been up to. He shouldn't blame her, Luther knew, as she was only twelve, and it was his father, after all, who'd squeezed off the shots from the old double-barrel.

But the fact was, Luther *did* blame Verna, as well as his

mother. They all knew anyway, and it was Verna and his mom who brought it all into the open, who uttered the words that made it real so something had to be done about it. Everything had been going along fine until then. Going along, at least.

And since his father had taken it on himself to start going into Verna's room, he'd stopped coming into Luther's.

Verna's fault.

Verna and his mom's.

Then his father'd been taken from Luther to rot away in a cell in Jeff City, waiting to die when his appeals ran out.

Leaving Luther alone.

"He's suffered something terrible," Luther's great-aunt Marjean from Saint Louis had said of him after the murders, "but I'm eighty-seven years of age and get by hardscrabble on my Social Security. No way I can help the poor thing."

So Luther had gone into the foster-care system, and was taken in by the Black family, Dara and her husband, Norbert. The Blacks had temporary custody of three children besides Luther, who was the oldest. Dara Black, a stout woman with an apple-round face who almost always wore the same stained apron, watched over the children in the old farmhouse, while Norbert was away painting barns and houses in the surrounding countryside.

Luther used to watch her bustle around the house, smiling too much and even sometimes whistling while she got her work done. Luther was aware that she knew and didn't know that Norbert was molesting the children. Nobody ever talked about the subject. Luther thought that was best.

The state paid the Blacks a stipend for their foster care, and Norbert's painting brought in some more money. And it was true Luther would someday have to learn a trade, which was the excuse Norbert came up with to take Luther in as an unpaid apprentice, meaning Luther would do a lot of the heavy work, lugging five-gallon paint buckets, moving ladders and scaffolding, scraping weathered paint off hardwood with Norbert's good-for-shit tools. What Luther learned mostly was how to work all day in the boiling sun.

The day after his father was executed, he ran away.

And eleven months and three days later he was found sleeping behind a Dumpster in Kansas City and returned to the Black farm.

Life as Luther knew it, with its hardships and terrible, intricate balances, began again.

12

New York, 2004.

Anna Caruso remembered.

She had no choice, because now he was back, and they were reminding her of him in newspapers, on television, in conversations overheard in subways and at bus stops and in diners. Frank Quinn, her rapist.

They were also reminding people of his past, of the terrible thing he'd done to her a little over four years ago, but Anna could already sense the drift of the story. Quinn, who had never even stood trial for what he'd done, would be forgiven. After all, he'd never been charged, much less found guilty. And wasn't a rapist innocent until proven guilty? Even a child molester? It was in the Constitution.

That was what the prosecutors had told Anna and her mother and family, how they couldn't arrest and try Quinn because, in the minds of the prosecutors, there simply wasn't enough evidence for an arrest. A big man, a stocking mask, a scar seen by a terrified child in her dim bedroom, a button like one missing from one of Quinn's shirts and a thousand other shirts. Evidence, but not solid. Then there were the child porn sites visited on his police computer. It would all make for emotional but not really substantial testimony, so said the prosecuting attorney. It was a shame the rapist had been smart enough to use a condom, or they'd have DNA to use against him.

On the other hand, Anna might be pregnant.

What the hell kinds of alternatives were those, when whichever happened to you, you'd be wishing for the other?

Anna at eighteen wasn't much bigger than she'd been on her fourteenth birthday. She had breasts now, and her legs and hips were those of a woman rather than a child. But she was still thin, frail, and afraid. Still, in many ways she was the same narrow-faced, brown-eyed girl Quinn had molested, but now made even more beautiful by the sweep of her jaw and her slightly oversize but perfect nose. She was a raven-haired, Hispanic child-woman with a bold, even hawklike look in profile. But when she turned, you saw in her eyes that she was haunted and, in her way, would always remain young and in pain.

Sometimes she wondered if it would have been otherwise except for Quinn. Had he actually somehow altered her exterior as well as interior growth? Had he cursed her for all time?

She looked away from the cracks in her bedroom ceiling and closed her eyes. This was not fair! Especially this morning. *This* is *not goddamn fair!*

For the past several days she hadn't been able to control her thoughts. The dreams were back, which meant *he* was back, his hunched form as he squeezed through her stuck bedroom window in her mother and father's apartment—her mother's now, since her father had left. Quinn, when she'd first seen him. A big man who appeared huge in night and shadow, wearing a stocking mask that disfigured his face and made him other than human. His bent spine had scraped the metal window frame through his shirt, making the only sound in the quiet room. A sound that remained to this day in Anna's mind, that played over and over and begged for meaning and release. She knew it was in her music sometimes, and she tried to stop it.

Anna, a month shy of her fourteenth birthday, had been too terrified to scream. She was paralyzed; her throat was closed, so she had to struggle for breath. There in her perspiration-soaked bed, her panties and oversize T-shirt seemed so little cover and protection.

And they were.

Some of the details of what followed she still chose not to confront. They were hidden somewhere she never wanted to revisit.

She did recall that her attacker's sleeves were rolled up and she noticed the jagged scar on his right forearm. Something told her to remember the scar. *Remember.*

She knew even through her terror and agony that he was being deliberately rough, *trying* to hurt her.

Why? What had she done? She didn't even know this man.

Or did she?

She rejected the notion as soon as it entered her mind, and she concentrated on being somewhere else, someone else, until this was over. Someone else was being humiliated, soiled forever, ruined forever. The sisters at school had warned her, had warned all the girls.

Whores! A whore in the Bible! What could be worse?
You know you're sinning. You know and don't care!

When finally he rose from her, leaving her destroyed and unable to move on the sweat-soaked bed, she saw something pale in the night and knew he was wearing a condom.

She realized later it wasn't for her—it was for him. He didn't want to catch some dreadful disease from *her.* That made what happened all the more demeaning.

"Anna!"

Her mother's voice.

Anna had dozed off again, lost in the old dreams she thought were gone. No, not gone, but finally confined in a place in her mind where they couldn't escape.

But they had escaped. Like tigers. Quinn was back.

"You've overslept, Anna. Get up. This is your big day. What you've been slaving for the past four years. You don't want to be late."

Anna made herself roll onto her side, then sat up gingerly on the edge of the mattress, as if the old pain would be there with the old shame. She was thirteen again. *Unlucky thirteen.*

That was the problem—Quinn had the power again. When she saw his photograph, his name in print, heard people talking about him, she was thirteen even though she was almost eighteen.

She wished she could kill him. The nuns would tell her she shouldn't think such thoughts, but she'd graduated and she could think whatever she wanted now.

She wished she could kill Quinn. That was her almost constant thought.

"You don't want to be late," her mother warned again.

And Anna didn't. She had to concentrate on the present, not the past. Her first day of summer classes at Juilliard. The first day of her music scholarship.

What she'd been slaving for. Her therapy and escape that, as it turned out, hadn't quite worked.

She stood up unsteadily and made her way toward the bathroom.

Unlucky thirteen. Unlucky Anna.

At least she had her scholarship. That was all that was left for her, all that was left inside her . . . her music. Thirteen. A child.

She knew she wasn't going to kill anyone.

13

Quinn sat in the sun on a bench just inside the Eighty-sixth Street entrance to Central Park and watched them approach.

Fedderman looked the same, only a little heavier, the coat of his rumpled brown suit flapping, his tie askew, the same shambling gait. He had less hair to be mussed by the summer breeze, and he seemed out of breath, as if he was trying to keep up with the quick, rhythmic strides of the small woman next to him.

Pearl Kasner seemed to generate energy even from this distance. She was economical, deliberate and decisive in her movements to the point that there seemed something robotic in her resolute walk. She was a study in contrasts of light and dark, a mass of black hair framing a pale face from which dark eyes glared, lips too red, a gray skirt and a black blazer despite the warm morning. It was as if a small child had been given only black and white crayons and told to draw a woman, and here she was, with a compact completeness about her and a vividness almost unreal.

Quinn stood up from the bench, feeling the sun warm on his shoulders. "Hello, Feds."

Fedderman smiled. "Quinn! Back in harness where you belong!"

The two men shook hands, then hugged. Fedderman slapped Quinn on the back five or six times before they separated.

"Make the most of this chance, buddy!" he said.

"Count on it," Quinn told him.

"I'm here," Pearl said.

Quinn looked at her. "So you are. Sorry if we ignored you. Fedderman and I are old—"

"I know," Pearl said, "you go back a long way. You've watched each other's backs, broken bread together, flirted with the same waitresses, fought the same fights. Fedderman filled me in."

Fedderman grinned at Quinn. "This is Pearl. She's a fighter."

Quinn stepped back and regarded Pearl. Despite her sarcasm, she was smiling with large, perfect white teeth. "I've heard that about you, Pearl. A fighter. Also that you have talent as a detective."

"And I've heard about you, Lieutenant."

"Just Quinn will do. Officially, I'm only doing work-for-hire for the NYPD." Quinn buttoned his sport coat to hide ketchup he'd already dribbled on his new tie. "So, everybody's heard about everybody else, except maybe for some things I might tell you about Fedderman. And we all know why we're meeting here."

"Because your apartment's a shit hole," Pearl said.

Fedderman shook his head. "Pearl, dammit!"

"Mine's a shit hole, too," Pearl said. "Tiny, hot as hell, and thirsty for paint."

"Roaches?"

"They won't tolerate the place."

Quinn grinned at her. She was still smiling, a dare in eyes black enough to have gotten her burned as a witch four hundred years ago. Probably, Egan would like to burn her now.

There was something in her favor. *What kind of pain is driving you?*

"Am I the boss?" he asked her. "Or are we gonna have a contest?"

"It'd only be a waste of time," Pearl said.

Quinn decided not to ask her what she meant. "You two go ahead and sit down," he said. "I've been sitting awhile."

When they were on the bench, Fedderman slouched with his legs apart. Pearl sat stiffly, with her notepad in her lap, looking as if she were about to take dictation.

Quinn told them what he'd learned from the Elzner murder file, and what he speculated.

Pearl made a few notes and listened intently. He got the impression her eyes might leave scars on him.

"The jam bothered me, too," she said when he was finished. "An almost full jar in the refrigerator, and they bought two more identical jars when they went grocery shopping."

"Which means they didn't know how much jam they had," Fedderman said, "or they were gonna hole up in their apartment for a few weeks and live on strawberry jam, or someone else did the shopping for them. Someone who didn't know what kinds of foods they were out of."

"Or someone who thought they just couldn't have enough gourmet jam," Pearl said. "I lean toward your possibility number three, that somebody else bought the groceries."

Fedderman leaned forward and scratched his left ankle beneath his sock. Quinn wondered if he still wore a small-caliber revolver holstered to his other ankle. He looked up at Quinn, still scratching. "So, we working on the assumption somebody killed both Elzners?"

"It's the only assumption we've got, " Pearl said, "if you don't want to finish your career doing crap assignments, I don't want to be out of work, and Quinn doesn't want to go back to being a—"

"Pariah," Quinn finished for her.

She nodded. "Okay, *pariah*. I like that. It's so Christian."

"It isn't biblical," Fedderman said, "it's ancient Greek."

She stared at him. "That true?"

"I have no idea. You're so naive, Pearl."

"That I doubt," Quinn said. He made a show of glancing at his watch. "So as of now, we're on the job."

"We don't have anything new to work with," Fedderman pointed out.

"Then we'll work with what we have. Again. You two go back over the evidence and see if there's anything I missed. Then we'll talk to the Elzners' neighbors again. Anyone in the adjoining buildings who might have seen anything. See if there wasn't a dog that didn't bark in the night, that kinda thing. You do the murder file again, Pearl. Fedderman and I will work on the witnesses."

Pearl looked as if she might say something about being assigned to paperwork, but she held inside whatever words she wanted to speak. She knew Quinn was assessing her, testing her. Something told her it was one of the most important tests she'd ever have to pass.

"We'll meet back here at six this evening. If it's raining, the meet'll be at the Lotus Diner on Amsterdam."

"That place is a ptomaine palace," Pearl said.

"I know," Quinn said. "I chose it because I don't think it's gonna rain. Where's your unmarked?"

"Parked over on Central Park West," Fedderman said.

"Let's go, then. Pearl can drop us off at the Elzners' building, then take the car on to the precinct house and get busy with the murder file."

Pearl and Fedderman stood up. Fedderman stretched, extending his back and flailing his arms, which still looked abnormally long even though he'd put on weight. Then he and Pearl walked in the warming sun toward Quinn. They all knew they were probably wasting their time, but nobody objected.

Quinn was pleased with the way their first meeting had gone. Beneath the bullshit and hopeless humor was the beginning of mutual understanding, maybe even respect.

Maybe the beginning of a team.

14

He lay curled in a corner, a folded white cloth clutched in his left hand. He was smiling.

Slowly he raised the saturated cloth to his nose and inhaled deeply of the benzene fumes. Benzene was a solvent not often used these days, but he'd become accustomed to it a long time ago, adapted to it. His drug of choice for the visions and memories long and short.

He inhaled again, his eyelids fluttering. He was back in the Elzners' kitchen, carefully, silently, removing groceries from plastic bags and placing them on the table before putting them away. As usual, he was wearing flesh-colored latex gloves. He giggled, looking down at them in his dream; they were like real fingers, only without fingernails. He reached for the tuna can.

And there was Martin Elzner, the husband. This time he'd been willed there, but he appeared as he had that night—that early morning. Elzner was stunned, his mouth hanging open, surprise, anger, fear . . . all flashing like signs in his eyes. His sandy hair was mussed from turning in his sleep. Had it actually stood up in points like that? It made him look even more astounded to find this stranger in his kitchen, busy at a domestic task.

The stranger—who wasn't a stranger—set the tuna can on the table. The husband's sudden presence in the dim kitchen was a surprise to him, too. Yet not *exactly* a surprise. He was doomed to disappointment and betrayal and knew this could happen, would happen, and he was prepared for it. *Wanting it?*

He smiled.

He inhaled.

Back to Elzner, too astounded even to speak. More fear in his eyes as he saw the gun with its bulky silencer. A terrible understanding. He grimaced and turned sideways, raising a hand as if to wave some irritating insect away if it buzzed near again. *Death could be such a pest.*

Step close. . . . Don't shoot the hand. . . . They must think he died last . . . a suicide, poor deranged creature.

The betrayer would die second.

Close enough. Up came the gun, steady in seconds, inches from his head. The satisfying *putt!* of the silenced gun, like a tiny engine trying once to turn over. Martin Elzner, down with a loud double thumping sound on the kitchen floor.

Backward, step backward, as it actually occurred. The choreography of dreams.

A sudden clattering. His free hand had brushed the tuna can near the edge of the table. *As it actually occurred.* If the sound of Elzner hitting the floor hadn't awakened his wife, the can striking and rolling across the tiles would.

He inhaled. He wondered if the tiles had been damaged. The floor was actually quite attractive. An unusual beige with flecks of—

Enough. There she was as she'd been, standing in the doorway with the sudden alteration of her life, the cancellation of her past and future, all on her face. They knew. *They always knew.*

His hand not clutching the cloth moved down to his

crotch as she instinctively lurched toward her fallen husband, her true love, her only, her lifemate, her deathmate, drawing her, drawing her, gravitation, the inevitable physics of love, the end of love. . . .

The end of love . . .

After a while it was time for the second show. He played in his mind once more that night in the Elzners' kitchen. It amazed him the force of his intellect, the control he had over his recall. He'd reached the point where he could even fast-forward or rewind the reconstruction, as if he were pressing mental buttons, watching the sped-up images moving back and forth across his spectrum of recollection: stop, pause, replay. Slower now—relishing it, seeing it, and reliving it from a more vivid angle. . . .

Unpacking the groceries, the tuna can. There was Martin Elzner, the husband. *Surprise, surprise.* . . . Pause, play, speed up, aim, fire the silenced handgun. The acrid scent of the shot lingering in the air, in his mind. Fast-forward. He inhaled. Jan Elzner was barefoot, in her knee-length flimsy nightgown . . . *half speed.* . . . She sees her husband on the floor, the blood, *a rich scarlet almost black*, and moves toward him, the blood. . . . Wait until she's very near him, almost over him . . . *slow motion.* . . .

Her eyes . . . *what she knew!*

The hand without the folded, saturated cloth moved back down.

He climaxed as he squeezed the trigger again and again.

The colors! The colors are magnificent!

He inhaled.

Finally evening.

It hadn't even hinted at rain that warm summer day, so

Quinn met with his team of detectives again on the park bench just inside the entrance at Eighty-sixth Street. He sat awkwardly but comfortably on the hard bench, sipping from a plastic water bottle he'd bought from a street vender, and watched New Yorkers enjoying their park while there was still daylight and the muggers hadn't yet come out with the stars. There were more people now that it was cooler, a woman pushing a stroller, a few joggers, and some helmeted and padded rollerbladers zooming about like cyber creatures who'd escaped a video game.

Pearl and Fedderman approached together. They looked hot and tired. Pearl's pace was dragging and Fedderman had the sleeves of his white shirt rolled up and was carrying his suit coat slung over his shoulder. Quinn thought back to a time when the younger Fedderman had entered rooms with his coat slung like that on a crooked forefinger over one shoulder and would say "ring-a-ding-ding," like Sinatra when he was a hot item in Vegas and everywhere else. Quinn couldn't imagine that coming out of the older, heavier Fedderman, who carried the weight of his experience on his shoulders along with the coat.

"Ring-a-ding-ding," Fedderman said wearily.

Quinn grinned and Pearl stared at both men. She still looked beautiful, her irises so black in contrast with the gleaming whites of her eyes. Her mascara had run a little with the heat, making the right eye appear slightly bruised, as if she'd gotten into a scuffle sometime today. Not impossible.

"Old joke," Quinn explained.

"Secret male-bonding bullshit," she said.

"Nothing to do with you, Pearl," Fedderman assured her, thinking he was too tired to put up with her if she decided to be in one of her moods.

Quinn thought the brief ring-a-ding-ding jingle could apply to Pearl. She was somehow even more attractive when worn down from a difficult and probably futile day's work. He pulled from beneath his folded sport coat, where they'd stayed cool out of the sun, the other two water bottles he'd bought and handed them up to Pearl and Fedderman. Both detectives expressed gratitude, then uncapped the bottles and took long sips. Quinn watched Pearl's slender pale throat work as she swallowed.

"So what've we got?" he asked when they were finished drinking.

"Nothing new," Pearl said, using her wrist to wipe away water that had dribbled onto her chin, "but at least we're more sure of what we do have. I mean, we've got everything in the file almost goddamn memorized."

"Cop work," Fedderman said with a shrug. He rested a hand on Pearl's shoulder while looking at Quinn. "One thing she hasn't mentioned yet. We questioned the witnesses again and one of the tenants in the Elzners' building, a lonely old guy down the hall, responded to Pearl's feminine wiles."

Quinn took a sip of water and stared at Pearl.

"I use them sparingly and selectively," she said.

"So how did this old guy respond?"

"By remembering something he hadn't had a chance to tell the police. He's three apartments away and was only questioned briefly and by phone."

"So why did you question him?"

"His apartment's by the elevator."

Quinn smiled.

Pearl smiled back. "He can hear the elevator through the wall. Like a lot of lonely old people who live alone, he doesn't sleep well, and he was awake most of the night of the Elzner murder. He heard the elevator, and recalled it because of the late hour. He said he'd never heard it before at that time."

"Two fifty-five A.M.," Fedderman said to Quinn.

"Exactly?"

"He said he looked at his watch," Pearl said. "He sleeps

wearing it. Said it sounded like the elevator stopped at his floor. His and the Elzners'. About twenty minutes later, it went back down."

"He seem credible?"

"Very. And his watch is the kind made especially for old guys with failing eyesight, about the size of an alarm clock and with luminous hands and numerals you could read a book by." She took another sip of water, then watched a wobbly rollerblader for a moment. "It really isn't much."

"It helps fix the time of death," Quinn said.

"So what have you come up with?" Fedderman asked.

"I visited my sister, Michelle."

They both looked at him. "The stock analyst?" Fedderman asked.

"The same."

Pearl shook her head and grinned. "Their credibility's not the highest."

"Not about stocks, no. But Michelle isn't only interested in stocks. She's a math and computer whiz. She runs comparative analyses on other things, sometimes just for amusement. I asked her a question yesterday, and she spent most of last night and some of this morning finding the answer. Insofar as it can be found."

"Question about killers?" Pearl asked.

"Right. She used her sources via the Internet and came up with statistics gathered from and about serial killers. It seems a surprising number of them don't plan concretely but come prepared for murder, compelled to seek situations where they'll have little choice, and the deaths, in their minds, won't be their fault."

"Sounds like public-defender bullshit," Fedderman said.

"He means they set up the situations," Pearl said. "Like teenagers baiting their parents. Grown-ups aren't supposed to lose their tempers, so if they can be made to, whatever comes of it is their responsibility. Or so think the teenyboppers."

Fedderman uncapped his plastic bottle and took a swig of water. "Some of them think that way up to about age seventy."

"It's not the analogy I'd have chosen," Quinn said, "but it's pretty accurate. I think of it as Michelle's scenario-for-murder theory. If the Elzner murders weren't random, if the killer at least expected he'd have to do them and was prepared for it, or even possibly planned it in detail just in case, that means he killed for his own internal reasons. The kinds of reasons that don't go away."

"And?" Fedderman said.

"He's gone through a door that opens only one way, and leads only to another door."

Fedderman shook his head. "You've gotten cryptic in your old age."

Pearl understood immediately. "You saying we should wait for him to kill again?" she asked. "That maybe we got a serial killer here?"

"In the bud," Quinn said, smiling.

The smile sort of gave Pearl the creeps. It wasn't about amusement. It was more the smile of a hunter who'd picked up the spoor of his prey. Who now wouldn't be shaken off, no matter what.

In fact, it was exactly that kind of smile. She knew where she'd seen it before: while walking past a mirror in the bedroom of the sister of a murdered child, when she'd unexpectedly glimpsed it on her own face. It had scared her a little then. It scared her now.

And Pearl wondered, how did Quinn know so much about doors?

Marcy Graham got home from work before Ron. The subway had been a mob scene, and the first train had been so crowded she had to wait for a second. To add to her ordeal, some oaf in a big rush had stepped on her toe as she'd been climbing the steps to the street.

Tired, overheated, irritated, she sat down on the sofa and worked her shoes off. She examined her ankles, which were as swollen as she thought they'd be after a hard day on three-inch heels. The toes of her left foot, which was slightly larger than her right, felt as if they'd been pressed together in a vise. Dressing for success was dressing for discomfort.

Marcy sat and massaged her sore, stockinged feet for a while, then realized she was thirsty. Probably dehydrated after the struggle with crowds and summer heat on her way home.

It seemed too warm in the apartment. She stood up, leaving her shoes lying on their sides on the floor, and padded over to the thermostat. After edging the dial down a degree, she heard the air-conditioning click on. The apartment could be a cool refuge, and would be soon.

It was freshly painted and comfortably furnished. The advance Ron had gotten on his new position at work had been well spent, even if maybe too hastily. Decorating the apartment, buying new clothes they'd both need if they were to stay in style, then paying off old debts, had left the checking account almost in the red.

Marcy swallowed dryly, reminding herself of her thirst.

Feeling a rush of cold air from an overhead vent, she made her way into the kitchen. She was pretty sure there were some diet Cokes in the refrigerator.

And there they were on the bottom shelf, a six-pack, the cans still joined by their plastic harness.

As Marcy worked one of the cold cans loose, then straightened to close the refrigerator door, she noticed a wedge of Norstrum Gouda cheese, her favorite to spread on crackers for snacks. It was shrink-wrapped and unopened, yet she was sure she'd eaten some since the last time she'd bought groceries at the D'Agostino.

She pulled open the plastic meat-and-cheese drawer and saw a half-consumed wedge alongside a plastic container of leftover meatballs. She shrugged. Apparently, she'd bought two wedges when she last shopped. That should be all right. Did cheese ever really go bad? Might it be the only thing in the world that didn't?

Sipping soda from the can, she went into the bedroom, bending down adroitly to pick up her shoes on the way. It would feel good to ditch the panty hose and get into some cool slacks and a sleeveless blouse. She removed her gray skirt and blazer, then sat on the bed and peeled off her panty hose. After draping skirt and blazer on a hanger, she took off her blouse and dropped it in a white wicker clothes hamper. She extended her elbows out and back, in a practiced gesture made somehow graceful, and unhooked her bra, then slipped it off. Bra and panties followed the blouse into the hamper. Nude now, she went to her dresser to get another pair of panties.

When she opened her lingerie drawer, there was a small, flowered box of chocolates. It was lying on top of her folded panties. No note. No card. No explanation.

She picked up the box and examined it more closely. The plastic encasing it hadn't been disturbed, and it was an expensive brand.

A gift from Ron?

Not likely. She remembered the dustup over the coat.

Yet the chocolates *had* to be from Ron. Who else had access to the apartment, to her dresser drawers? And, in truth, the leather jacket that caused all that trouble had to have come from Ron. Unless she bought into the weird idea that Ira, the salesclerk at Tambien's, had a way into the apartment and harbored a compelling crush on her. But the truth was, there wasn't any way Ira could even know where she lived.

Ron. It must have been Ron. But what was going on? Did he have some kind of mental glitch? He'd been under strain with the new position. Marcy knew people weren't always logical. They *did* do inexplicable things and then sometimes denied them even to themselves—like that girl where she used to work who sent people to various addresses for deals on clothes and jewelry. Only the addresses weren't real, and the shops and people she referred to didn't exist except in her mind. Ron's little eccentricity wasn't as serious as that.

So, if he had a kind of mental hitch in his thinking, leaving her gifts and not remembering, what was the harm? It was probably only temporary. So why should she—

Marcy heard the door from the hall open and close. Ron. He was home!

It took her only a second to decide not to mention the chocolates. It sure hadn't helped to show him the coat.

She shoved the box beneath her folded panties and closed the dresser drawer.

Just in time. His shadow rippled over the carpet as he approached the bedroom doorway.

"There you are," he said, smiling when he saw she was nude, in the middle of changing clothes. "I bought you something."

He tossed her a glittering object and she caught it. *Almost weightless.* A thin gold bracelet with a tiny diamond in a plain setting.

"Don't think it's real. Some guy on the street was selling them, and I couldn't resist."

"It's beautiful." She slipped it on her wrist, then rotated it before her as if she were on the Home Shopping Network. Fully clothed, of course.

He watched her, obviously enjoying her pleasure. "It's a pretty well-made knockoff. Either that or it was a hell of a sale."

Marcy went to him and kissed him on the lips, and after a few seconds felt him return the kiss. His arm slipped around, behind her bare back. He truly did love her. So maybe he did have this strange compulsion to buy her gifts, sometimes anonymously.

She could live with that.

15

Quinn finished the last of his spaghetti and used his half-eaten roll to sop up sauce from his plate. He was in his sister Michelle's dining room. She had a spacious—by New York standards—apartment on the West Side with a river view. Never having seen a floater gaffed like a fish and hauled to shore, she obviously didn't think about what Quinn did when she looked at the river.

About once a month she'd invite Quinn over for dinner and prepare spaghetti using an old family recipe for the sauce. Quinn had become tired of the recipe, which called for too much garlic, but he always made it a point to eat all that was served. His sister had been his lifeline to a world where he could hold his head up, and he didn't want to insult her. Besides, the apartment, furnished in expensive modern, was a welcome change from his usual surroundings, and Michelle always served a good red wine with her meals.

Though she ate out most of the time, Quinn knew she enjoyed cooking. Michelle had lived in a lesbian relationship with a woman named Marti in Vermont until six years ago. She'd told Quinn about it after their parents were both dead, not long after the passing of their father. Both their father and mother would have been horrified if they'd known the truth about her, or so Michelle assumed. Quinn, who'd seen the full range of the human spectrum as a New York cop, didn't give it much thought. As far as he was concerned, Michelle's sex life was none of his business.

When Marti had been struck by a car and killed only months later, Michelle returned to New York and put her formidable mathematical ability and her Harvard M.B.A. to work. She was deeply involved now with her job and her computer. Quinn didn't know anything about her love life and didn't ask. Anyway, he was in more of a position to be stoned than to cast the first one.

Michelle poured them both another glass of the excellent Australian red she'd found, probably on the Internet, and surveyed Quinn over the dirty dishes and what was left of the salad and hard-crusted rolls. Four years older than Quinn, she'd put on weight and was a big woman now, but still more large-boned than fat. Though she looked more like their mother, she shared Quinn's square jaw and green eyes. Also his unruly brown hair, which she wore almost as short as his but in a considerably neater style.

"You going to take me into your confidence?" she asked.

"Are you kidding?"

He filled her in on his thinking about the Elzner case.

She stared at him for a moment, then asked, "What about your partners? What sort of people are they?"

She'd met Fedderman years ago and liked him. Quinn told her about Pearl.

"Sounds like the type who thinks outside the box," she said.

He knew she wasn't talking about Fedderman, the good, stolid cop. "There are some who'd like to put her in a box. I think she's a damned fine detective, but she's got a temper and a political tin ear."

Michelle grinned. "And doesn't that sound familiar?"

"Also," Quinn said, "I'm still not completely sure I can trust her."

"Oh? How so?"

"Only because Renz assigned her to me, and I know I can't trust Renz. It's possible that part of her job is to keep him informed about me."

"Spy on you?" Michelle was never one to equivocate.

"Yeah, you could use that word."

"I suppose it's something to keep in mind."

"On the other hand, Renz might simply have assigned her to me because she's—"

"A fuckup."

"Well, she might seem so to him, but she really isn't that. She has . . . maybe too much character."

"Ah. You like her."

"Sure. You can't help but like her. But lots of people liked Hitler before he became Hitler."

"Hitler, huh?" Michelle leaned back in her chair and sipped wine, regarding him over the crystal rim.

"What are you thinking?" he asked.

"Figuring the odds."

"Like always," Quinn said. He didn't have to ask her about the object of her figuring.

He finished his wine, then stood up to clear the table.

It was past nine when Quinn got back to his apartment and found his phone ringing.

He shut the door behind him, crossed the living room in three long strides, and scooped up the receiver.

"It's Harley," Renz said after Quinn's hello. So now they were on a first-name basis. "I got some info for you, Quinn." Almost first-name basis.

"Will I like it?"

"Doesn't matter. Info's info. And does it matter what you like?"

"I hope that's a rhetorical question."

"Or what you hope? Anyway, I talked to my source in the lab. Marks on the gun that was in Martin Elzner's dead hand were definitely made by a sound suppressor attached to the barrel. They're consistent with a Metzger eight hundred model, a rare sort of one-size-fits-all for semiautomatic handguns."

"Never heard of it."

"Neither did I, but then neither of us is a silencer expert. Turns out it's a cheap unit made in China and marketed mostly mail order. Not a lot of them are sold. They advertise in magazines for gun nuts and guys who see themselves as soldiers of fortune and other kinds of armed romantic figures."

"What with the big market in used guns and gun gear, it could be difficult to trace even though it's not a popular item."

"Yep, it mighta changed hands ten times at gun shows, or was sold from car trunks." Renz seemed almost happy about the odds. *That Harley!* "On the other hand, we can try. I'll keep you informed."

Quinn thanked Renz and hung up, thinking it was hard enough to find a particular gun in this wide world, much less a silencer.

But if searching for it helped to silence Renz even a little bit, the Metzger 800 was still doing its job.

Pearl had a late supper alone in her apartment, a Weight Watchers chicken dinner washed down with scotch and water. *My own worst enemy.*

She rinsed out the empy glass and replaced it in the cabinet, and dumped what was left of the dinner into the trash. Dishes done.

Sometimes she wondered what her life would be like if Vern Shults had lived. They'd been very much in love when they were twenty, or Pearl had thought so. What was left of her family had ostracized her for becoming engaged to a devout Catholic. How devout even Pearl hadn't guessed. Vern had announced to her one night after sex that he was breaking their engagement; he'd decided to study for the priesthood.

A week later, he'd been found dead in his bathtub, drowned after apparently falling and striking his head. Leaving Pearl as alone as a woman could be alone.

God moving in His mysterious circles. Pearl trapped in the celestial geometry.

Where she remained trapped.

She watched TV for a while, then didn't think she'd be able to sleep, so she got the glass back down from the cabinet.

Marcy Graham couldn't sleep, knowing the anonymous gift of a box of Godiva chocolates was only about ten feet away in one of her dresser drawers, not fifteen feet away from her sleeping husband. She remembered how unreasonable he'd been about the leather jacket from Tambien's, the problems it had caused.

Even if the chocolates *were* from Ron, he might not admit it. Or for some reason she couldn't understand, he might not even remember leaving them for her.

Marcy waited until her nerve built, then quietly climbed out of bed and opened her dresser drawer. Moving silently, she removed the box of chocolates and carried it into the kitchen.

She couldn't resist opening the box and sampling one of the chocolates.

Delicious! Light caramel with a cream center.

She ate another before closing the box and sliding it into the trash can beneath the sink. Then she tore off a paper towel and placed it over the box so it wouldn't be visible to Ron if by chance he decided to throw away something.

When she returned to the bedroom, she carefully slipped back into bed and lay awake awhile, listening to Ron's deep, even breathing.

She was sure he was still asleep.

She felt safe now.

16

He didn't anger easily. He was beyond that.

He'd thought.

He paced silently. This was an insult, a rejection. A thoughtless, callous act. Who wouldn't anger at the sting? Sting at the slap?

There was no reason to fear making too much noise as he paced. The steady, reverberating buzzing covered the slight sound of his soft-soled shoes on the tiles.

The buzzing, in fact, seemed to be growing louder and was getting under his skin. *Where's it coming from? What's its source?* He'd checked outside, but there was nothing in sight that might be making such a relentless sound. And inside the building no one seemed to be cleaning their carpets or running an appliance without cessation.

The buzzing continued. It was almost as if he were trapped in the confines of a small space and being observed by some gigantic, predatory winged insect that threatened him, that could almost reach him with its painful and paralyzing venom, that would never give up because it knew that eventually it *would* reach him.

Black . . . black . . .

The sound became even louder and more piercing, a buzzing that tripped the frequencies of his body and caused a terrifying vibration in every cell. A buzzing like death and dying. The buzzing of ending and becoming. Of the swarming insects of decay and the whirring of buzzards' wings, of bees and wasps in the damp and dark of the underground. *Beelzebub . . .*

He knew if he didn't do something it would make him scream. And if he screamed . . .

With trembling fingers, he groped in his pocket for the Ziploc plastic bag that contained a folded cloth.

At first Anna Caruso was pleased to be living her long-sought dream, wandering Juilliard's Lincoln Center campus, the library, and Alice Tully Hall, where she knew someday she would give a concert or at least play in the Juilliard orchestra or symphony. It could happen. The Meredith Willson Residence center towered over the campus, but Anna's partial scholarship didn't include residency. She rode the subway each day to Juilliard, usually lugging her viola in its scuffed black case so she could practice at home, as well as in one of the school's many practice rooms.

She'd taken up the viola seriously about six months after the rape. The instrument suited her. It was slightly larger than a violin, tuned a fifth lower, and produced a more sonorous, melancholy tone. While playing it did nothing to cheer her, it was somehow soothing.

Her bliss at attending Juilliard lasted only a few days. Anna was soon disappointed in the way things were going, her progress with her lessons, her relationship with her instructors, but most of all she was disappointed with herself. Discouraged. She was told that was normal. Suddenly she was among musicians of equal or superior talent. It was natural that she should be overwhelmed at first. And, of course, there was Quinn, in her mind and in her music now. Her hatred for Quinn.

As soon as she entered the apartment and saw her mother, she knew something was very wrong. Linda Caruso was slumped on a chair by the phone and obviously had been crying. Her eyes were red and she clutched a wadded Kleenex in her clawlike right hand with its overlong red nails.

"Mom?" Anna went to her, and her mother immediately began sobbing.

When she gained control of herself, she looked with pain in her eyes at Anna. "Your father died a few hours ago. A heart attack."

Anna felt the news like a physical blow to her stomach, and her body assumed the same hunched attitude as her mother's. At the same time, recalling all the things her mother had said about her father, all the old arguments, she wondered how her mother could be so upset. She staggered backward and sat on the sofa.

"But he didn't have a bad heart!"

"He did," her mother said. "We just didn't know it. According to Melba, he didn't even know it."

Melba was Anna's cousin, a chatty fool Anna couldn't stand. "Was it . . . I mean, did he go to the hospital?"

"No, it was sudden. Melba said he didn't suffer. At least there's that." Her mother ground the wadded tissue into her eyes, as if trying to injure herself and started crying again. Her loud, rolling sobs filled the apartment, transforming it. The very walls seemed to weep.

"Jesus Christ!" Anna said.

"Don't curse, Anna. At a time like this . . ."

"All right," Anna said absently. "Will there be a funeral?"

"Of course. He'll be laid out at a mortuary near where he lived. Melba didn't know exactly when or where the funeral will be."

Anna's father, Raoul, had left her mother only months after the rape, and in a way Anna blamed herself for their divorce. Her father had moved into a home on the edge of Queens, near the auto repair shop where he kept the books. Anna had heard the place was a chop shop, where stolen cars were taken and dismantled to be sold for parts, but she'd never believed it.

She visited her father less and less frequently in his sad and solitary home, and they'd gone out for breakfast or lunch and struggled for words, but Anna had never quite stopped loving him. His loss was an unexpected force taking root in her, entangling and weighing down her heart.

Unconsciously she crossed herself, surprised by the automatic gesture. How odd, she thought. Religion wasn't where she'd found any solace. Her music was her religion. Her music that might not be good enough. She felt, just then, like playing the viola.

Her mother stopped sobbing. "Anna, are you okay?"

"No," Anna said.

Marcy Graham had noticed that morning when she poured the half-and-half for Ron's coffee that it was thinner than usual and barely cool.

She opened the refrigerator and laid a hand on jars and shelves as if checking for fever. Not as cold as they should be. When she checked the cubes in the icemaker, she found they'd melted into a solid mass. She wrestled the white plastic container out, chipped away with a table knife, and dumped the ice into the sink.

"Fridge fucked up?" Ron asked.

"Looks that way. I'll call the repairman."

"Nothing should be wrong with it. It's under warranty. Don't let anybody tell you it isn't."

"I won't. Don't worry."

"Think it's safe to use this cream?"

"I wouldn't," Marcy said. She stood back and looked at the refrigerator, less than a year old. Then she opened the door and memorized the phone number on the sticker affixed to its inside edge and went to the phone.

Which is how she found herself here in her kitchen, home early from work to meet the repairman.

He was Jerry, according to the name tag above his pocket, a grungy guy in a gray uniform. But he was young and rather handsome, and he kept his shirt tucked in. A pattern of dark moles marred his left cheek just below his eye and he needed a shave, but still he would clean up just fine. Not what Marcy had expected.

She hoped he wasn't so young he didn't know what he was doing. He had the refrigerator pulled out from the wall and had spent the last half hour working behind it. A stiff black cover lined with fluffy blue insulation leaned against the sink cabinets, and whenever Marcy went to the kitchen to see how Jerry was doing, she saw only his lower legs, his brown work boots she hoped wouldn't leave scuff marks, and an assortment of tools on the tile floor.

Finally, only about an hour before Ron was due home from work, Jerry scooted backward, out from behind the refrigerator, and reached for the insulated panel. It took him only a few minutes to reattach it.

He stood up, came around to the front of the refrigerator, and opened the door so he could work the thermostat. Immediately the motor hummed. He stuck his hand between a milk carton and orange juice bottle, then turned to Marcy and smiled. "Better'n new."

"You sure?" Marcy asked.

"Why? You wanna make a bet it'll stop cooling?"

Marcy grinned. "No. I wasn't questioning your work."

"This was an easy one," Jerry said. "There's a belt attached to the motor that turns a fan blade, so a blower moves cold air and evens out the temperature in the refrigerator. Those belts usually last at least five years before they break."

"My luck," Marcy said.

"Oh, this one didn't break, I'm sure of that."

"What do you mean?"

"If it'd broke, I'd have found it laying there. It's missing."

"Underneath the refrigerator, maybe?"

"Nope. I looked everywhere for it."

Missing? Marcy frowned. "How could it not be somewhere in the kitchen?"

The repairman smiled and shrugged, then leaned down and began tossing wrenches and screwdrivers and things Marcy didn't recognize back into his metal toolbox. "It ain't up to me to figure 'em out. I just fix 'em. You mind if I use your phone?"

Marcy told him she didn't, and listened as he called his office to report he was finished and leaving for his next job.

After she'd signed at the bottom of a pink sheet of paper on a clipboard, he told her she should take care and left.

Alone in the apartment, she felt suddenly afraid. It was one thing for her anonymous benefactor to leave gifts, but why would he sabotage the refrigerator? *Was* that what really happened?

Would Ron have done such a thing? Had he even had the opportunity?

Unexpected presents were one thing. They were eccentric, weird, even, but flattering and not at all scary. Though they sure as hell made you wonder. She stared at the blank white bulk of the humming refrigerator. This was different. This was eerie.

She went to the left sink cabinet and opened it, then reached in through the hinged lid of the plastic trash can and felt beneath the loosely folded paper towel on top. Then she felt deeper beneath the paper towel.

Nothing. At least, not what she expected to feel despite her icy hunch.

She removed the plastic lid and looked to be sure.

The box of chocolates she'd thrown away last night was gone.

Pearl sat at her kitchen table and sipped from a bottle of water. She'd just finished a late-night snack of leftover pizza, which had been warmed and zapped of all form and structure in the microwave. It had become a kind of edible Dalí painting—surreal, like her world.

She could feel the beginnings of trouble, a gentle, hypnotic draw that could deceive and suck her into a maelstrom if she'd let it. If she fell for it.

As she sometimes did.

She found herself thinking about Quinn too often. He'd seemed at first so much older that an affair with him wasn't an option. She wasn't one of those helpless, hopeless women looking for a substitute father.

But he actually wasn't *that* old. Besides, she had a birthday coming up.

It was the weathered look to his features that made him appear older, as if he'd spent a hard life in the outdoors and the sun had leathered and seamed his features. A difficult life, especially lately, buffeted by storms within and without. With a face that suggested character and toughness even if masculine beauty had passed with the years and hard knocks. She could imagine him slouched in the saddle on a weary horse, overlooking a windswept plain. Big white horse, since he was the hero of her imagination.

Bastard belongs in a cigarette commercial, not in the NYPD.

She finished her water and smiled at her own recklessness. She didn't always have to be her own worst enemy. Sometimes she was like a kid who couldn't help reaching out and touching a flame.

She leaned back and looked at the stained and cracked kitchen walls that had once been some weird yellow color. She knew what she should do now. She should paint. Everything she needed to brighten up the place—brushes, rollers, scraper, drop cloths, masking tape, five gallons of colonial white paint—was waiting in the hall closet. And she had the blessing of the landlord. One thing about a dump like this, she could do what she wanted here, short of setting it on fire. Yes, she should paint.

Pearl knew she could spend the next few hours at least getting started on the job, maybe finish a couple of walls, and still have time to get a good night's sleep before meeting Quinn and Fedderman tomorrow morning.

She also knew she wouldn't paint. She had the Elzner case for an excuse.

She couldn't put out of her mind what Quinn had said about the Elzners not necessarily being the first victims, but maybe simply the latest, of a serial killer who did couples. It seemed to Pearl that Quinn was working on insufficient knowledge to make such a statement. On the other hand, this wasn't an ordinary man or an ordinary cop. He'd been right a lot of times in his long career.

Couples. Why would anyone want to murder couples? Resentment? Because they were happy couples and he was single and unhappy? Not likely. How many single, unhappy people were out there wandering around and *not* killing anyone? In New York alone?

Me. I'm a suspect.

So's Quinn.

Depressing thought.

Okay, enough. Time to give up and go to bed.

She stood up from the table and placed her empty glass in

the sink, then went into the bathroom and brushed her teeth. She secured the apartment all the way, chain lock and dead bolt, and turned out the lights, so there was only the illumination from outside that filtered through the flimsy drapes. On her way to the bedroom she gave the hall closet containing the paint and supplies a wide berth and didn't glance in its direction.

At least I didn't succumb to that temptation.

She made a detour into the bathroom to wash down an Ambien, which the doctor had prescribed so she could escape her thoughts and go to sleep. The pills worked okay, but she didn't want to take too many and become dependent, so she spaced them out, trying not to take them on successive nights.

This was a logical night for one of the pills, what with the microwaved pizza's potential effect on her dreams. Pepperoni and anchovies. She wasn't about to give her subconscious and stomach that kind of chance to team up against her. It was a pill night for sure. Her belly was already growling in pizza protest.

Nude but for her oversize dark blue NYPD T-shirt, the window air conditioner humming and rattling away as it sent a cool breeze over her bare legs, she lay on top of the sheets and thought about the Elzner case.

Which led her to think about Quinn.

There he was again, slouched on his damned horse.

C'mon, pill!

17

Marcy Graham woke again from the dream she'd been having lately. Someone would be in the room with her and Ron, standing at the foot of the bed, watching them sleep. She would drift nearer and nearer to consciousness, then come all the way awake with a start.

And there would be no one there.

Again! So real!

She sat up in bed and looked around in the dimness, then relaxed and lay back, noticing her sheet and pillow were damp with perspiration though the room was cool. Ron stirred beside her, then sighed and rolled over onto his side, facing away from her. She took comfort in his bulk, in his nearness.

Yet she couldn't return to sleep, so real was that dream. More real than at other times, she realized. She could almost recall the man's dark form, the silent, motionless way he stood and stared.

But it didn't make sense, any of it. What kind of maniac would want to simply watch other people while they slept?

Unless he wasn't simply watching. Maybe he was making

sure they were asleep so he could . . . do what? Something else? Something more? Knowing he wouldn't be disturbed.

Marcy flung herself onto her side and fluffed her pillow so violently she woke up Ron. He rolled onto his back and looked over at her.

"Somethin' wrong?" His voice was slurred by sleep.

"I can't sleep."

"Yeah. I gathered s'much. Wha's wrong?"

"Nothing."

"Fine."

"Something!"

"What?"

"I don't know."

He breathed in deeply and sighed. "An' you want me to find out."

"Would you?"

Instead of answering, he sat up and opened the drawer of the nightstand on his side of the bed. She knew he kept a souvenir baseball bat there, but while it was a miniature bat, bearing Sammy Sosa's signature, it made a handy club about the size of a policeman's nightstick.

She watched his muscular, slope-shouldered form, dressed in white undershorts and sleeveless undershirt, cross the room and go into the hall, saw the hall brighten as lights in the living room came on. She could hear him moving around out there, checking things, looking where someone might hide, opening closet doors. Master of his domain, stalking a possible enemy who'd gotten through the defenses.

Suddenly uncomfortable alone in the dim room, Marcy climbed out of bed and went to join him. Besides, if by some remote chance an intruder *was* in the apartment, two against one would be better than just Ron—though Marcy sure didn't want to put that to the test.

Ron was standing in the middle of the living room, the miniature bat held low in his right hand.

He looked over at her, hair tousled, eyes sleepy. "Nothing. The door's still locked, everything looks normal, nobody hiding anywhere in here."

"Did you look in the kitchen?"

"Sure. Normal. Everything's okay, Marcy."

"The bedroom."

"Huh? We just left the bedroom."

"There are places to hide there."

"Sure, I guess there are."

She smiled at him. He'd been brave for her. Now he was humoring her. But that meant he was thinking of her, showing his love.

"You wait here while I go check."

He trod barefoot back into the bedroom, looking forward to going back to sleep. But why not give Marcy her way? He was too tired to argue. And he'd been revved up a few minutes ago, thinking maybe she *had* heard something or knew somehow there was someone in the apartment.

Damn, he'd been revved up!

Calmer now, reassured, he entered the dim bedroom and didn't bother turning on the light. As he moved toward the closet door, he held the bat higher. *Anything's possible.*

"Don't forget to look under the bed," Marcy called from the living room.

Ron paused and lowered the bat.

The man lying flat on his stomach beneath the bed switched the long-bladed knife to his other hand, on the side of the bed where he could see Ron Graham's bare feet. Watching the feet gave him some idea of where Graham's face and vulnerable throat might appear any second if he peered beneath the bed. Using the knife might be awkward. It was all a question of body position. Graham would be surprised and horrified and frozen for a second, allowing the opportunity for a quick body shift and a slash with the knife. But the bare feet were so important, where they were, where the toes were pointed. The man with the knife lay very still, his upper body an inch off the floor, watching the pale bare feet, watching. . . .

Ron walked close to the bed and sat down on it. He sure didn't feel like bending over and checking for monsters. He would humor Marcy only so far.

"Nobody under there!" he called to her. "Just a few dust bunnies."

He rose and went to the closet, quickly opened the door, felt afraid as he inserted an arm and parted the clothes to make sure no one was hiding back there in the darkness.

Then he caught himself. He'd bought into Marcy's delusions. *What the hell am I doing?*

Feeling foolish, he grinned and stepped back, closing the door. Shaking his head, he returned to the living room.

"All clear," he told Marcy, who was standing near the sofa looking worried.

She let out a long breath, then hugged him tightly.

He kissed her cool but damp forehead. "Can we go back to bed now?"

"Yeah. I'm sorry. It's just that I've been worried lately and having the damnedest dreams."

"Dreams can't hurt you." He put his arm around her waist and led her back toward the bedroom.

"They can sure as hell scare you."

When they were back in bed, he moved close to her. "Since we're awake . . . ," he said.

She felt her nightgown being tugged and worked upward, and she dug her heels into the mattress and raised her back until her breasts were no longer constrained by the taut material. His fingertips and then his lips were light on her right nipple. Desire moved at the core of her and she raked her fingers through his damp hair. Still she was outside of herself, of what was happening. She wanted to do this, but it was too soon after being so frightened.

He was toying with her left nipple now, not going to stop. She knew him so well. He wasn't going to be talked out of this. And she didn't really want to talk him out of it.

"Can I use my vibrator?" she asked. "I need to relax, and I'm still pretty shook up."

"You'll be shook up in a different way soon," he reassured her.

"Ron . . ."

He raised his head. "Okay." He kissed her between the breasts, using his tongue on her bare flesh, then shifted his weight and stood up. The vibrator was fine with him, anyway. He'd tell her where and how to use it, then let her decide she was ready, then—

"Hurry, please!" she said behind him as he opened the closet door to get the vibrator down from the top shelf. He smiled and didn't answer.

And gasped when he saw the face and eyes staring out at him, felt the cold blade slice in and up toward his heart. Everything was devoured by the searing pain . . . his world, his loss, his love, his hope. . . . All of it fell away and he dropped swiftly and breathlessly in a dark elevator plunging toward blackness.

He tried to say Marcy's name, as if it were the magic that might somehow stop the fall and save him, but that, too, died in darkness.

Marcy, lying back with her eyes closed and massaging her nipples with her fingertips, sensed something was wrong. Then she heard the funny, gasping sound Ron made and sat up in bed as suddenly as if a puppeteer had yanked her strings.

She saw Ron standing against the black background beyond the open closet door, then watched him sink to the floor.

Marcy tried to call to him but made only a strangled, cawing sound.

And out of the closet stepped her nightmare.

Half an hour later, while walking away from the Grahams' apartment building, their killer decided this had been much better than his last late-night encounter.

It was because of the knife.

He'd left his gun in Martin Elzner's hand. The police could do wonders with their ballistics tests, and they could connect gun to crime, therefore he could no longer have it in his possession. It was simply too risky, and he'd learned not to take unnecessary risks within the larger risks that he must take. So, as planned, the gun made a convincing prop.

But it should have been a knife to begin with. Always a knife.

So he'd left the gun, wiped clean of fingerprints other than those of Elzner's dead hand. The silencer, too, was of no further use, so he'd disposed of it by tossing it in a Dumpster. Surely by now it was lost in a vast landfill.

Two days later, at a flea market on the West Side, he'd bought a produce knife, the sort used by warehousemen and shippers of fruits and vegetables. It was a long folding knife, slender, with a bone handle and a high-quality steel blade that would hold an edge.

When he'd bought the knife, he was sure it would do what he needed, and now it had.

18

Most of the blood was from the wife. Quinn could almost taste its coppery scent along the edges of his tongue in a way that brought saliva and a queasy stomach.

Along with Pearl and Fedderman, he stood in the Grahams' bedroom near the body of the husband, Ronald. The dead man was lying tightly curled on his side on the floor, partly encircling most of the blood that had spilled from him, as if he'd tried to conserve the precious substance and failed. The frozen expression on his face suggested he'd experienced an agonized death. Quinn had seen similar expressions on the faces of too many victims of gunshot or knife wounds that incapacitated immediately but allowed a period of suffering before the end.

"That one's pretty simple," said Nift the ME, who was standing near the bed where the wife lay. "He was stabbed once beneath the sternum with an upward angle that got the heart." He motioned toward Marcella Graham. "This one, on the other hand, is more complicated. Over a dozen stab wounds, and deliberate damage to erogenous zones." He motioned toward two lumps in the puddled, crusted blood on the bed. "Those are her nipples."

"Jesus!" Fedderman said.

Nift grinned at the veteran cop's reaction. "I'd say your killer had his beef with the wife, and Hubby had to be eliminated so he wouldn't interfere."

"You're playing detective," Quinn said.

"That's okay," Nift said. "You can play medical examiner."

Quinn ignored him and stuck to business. "Did she die early or late in the game?"

"The pattern of bleeding suggests she died with the last stab wound, to the heart."

"He wanted her to suffer," Pearl said.

"What about time of death?" Quinn asked.

"Early morning," Nift said. "One or two o'clock. Three, three-thirty at the outside. I'll be able to make a closer estimate later."

Quinn had moved to get a different perspective of the room, which was well furnished and looked freshly painted. Most of the furniture looked new.

"They live here long?" he asked nobody in particular, getting into the mode of command again. An assumption of authority that had become part of him. He sent a look Fedderman's way.

Fedderman understood and left the bedroom to talk to one of the uniforms who'd taken the call and were first on the scene. Nobody said anything until he returned a few minutes later.

"The Grahams moved in three months ago. Neighbors didn't know much about them. Guy next door said they argued a lot. He could hear them through the ducts."

"We oughta find out what else he might have heard through the ducts," Pearl said.

Quinn seemed not to have heard her. He was studying the room, the way the dead man lay, the closet door hanging open and how the clothes were draped on the hangers, the way the wife was sprawled on her back with her nightgown up so her breasts showed. What had happened to her breasts. He felt his stomach turn and he swallowed bile that rose bitterly at the back of his throat. All these years on the job, and he still didn't understand how people could do this kind of thing to each other.

He made himself walk over and look more closely at the wife, and at the area around her body.

"Looks like our killer was hiding in the closet," he said, "and surprised the husband when he opened the door. After stabbing the husband, he went for the wife."

"Killer musta gotten blood on him from the wife," Fedderman said.

Quinn wasn't so sure. Someone expert enough with a knife knew how people bled, and could avoid being marked.

"No sign of him having washed up," Pearl said, "but we can check the drains for traces of blood to be sure."

"Maybe she had a lover on the side, and Hubby came home unexpectedly," Fedderman said. "The lover hid in the closet, but maybe made some noise the husband heard and went to investigate. Bad things ensued."

"Hubby must have had time to get undressed and ready for bed," Pearl said with an edge of sarcasm.

"Could have gone that way. The wife's lover mighta been trapped in the closet for hours, hoping for an opportunity to leave before daylight."

"Like in those French bedroom farces," Pearl said.

Nift laughed.

Quinn and the others looked at him.

"Detectives!" Nift said. "Your theories are all bullshit."

Quinn cocked his head at the little man. "Why so sure?"

"You didn't look close enough at the husband. He's still gripping the knife he used to kill his wife, then to stab himself through the heart."

Quinn returned to the husband and got down on one knee beside him. He could see the end of a knife handle in one of the dead hands drawn close to the husband's midsection. He moved an arm slightly to peer at the knife, which appeared to be a paring or boning knife with a long, thin blade.

"Murder-suicide," Nift said.

Quinn nodded. "Looks that way, Detective Nift." He glanced at Pearl and Fedderman and made a slight sideways motion with his head to signal they were leaving. "We'll give you a while, then get back to you about exact time and cause," he said to Nift.

"It'll all be in the autopsy report," Nift said. He looked down at Marcella Graham and shook his head sadly. "Damned shame, great rack like that."

Quinn didn't look at him as he left the bedroom, Pearl and Fedderman following. They made their way through the techs who were busily luminoling the living room, nodding to a few they knew, then went into the kitchen.

"Some blood on the soap," said one of the techs, a curly-haired guy about Nift's size, leaning over the sink. He was slipping a small bar of white soap into a plastic evidence bag. "Looks like somebody washed up here. There'll be more blood residue in the drain."

"If any of it's the killer's blood, we got this asshole's DNA," Fedderman said.

"Then all we'd need is the asshole himself," Pearl said, "and we'd have a match."

"Knife come from there?" Quinn asked, nodding toward an open drawer above one of the base cabinets.

"Probably," said the tech. "That's the drawer where the knives were kept, and it was open like that."

Quinn walked over and peered into the drawer. It had one

of those plastic dividers. He saw an elaborate wine cork puller, spatulas, a long-tined fork, and lots of knives with wooden handles. Like the knife in hubby's hand.

He turned away from the drawer and looked at the refrigerator. It was large and appeared to be fairly new. There was a big clear bowl on top, probably for salads, and next to the bowl a slender glass vase with a yellow rose in it. "Fridge been dusted?"

The tech nodded. "Not that it matters. The way the prints are smeared and overlaid, I can tell you somebody was in here recently wearing gloves."

"Why would Ron Graham have worn gloves?" Pearl asked Quinn and Fedderman.

But it was the tech who answered. "I've seen this before, when it was somebody in the kitchen doing cleaning while wearing rubber gloves. Some women protect their hands that way."

Everybody's a detective, Quinn thought. But the tech was right. Not too much could be made of the gloves. Still . . .

"Found any rubber gloves in here?" he asked the tech.

"Not so far."

"Uh-huh."

Quinn went to the refrigerator and used two fingers to open it. Pearl and Fedderman crowded close to peer inside with him.

"Nothing unusual," Fedderman said in a disappointed voice, feeling cold air spilling out around his ankles as he looked at milk and juice cartons, condiment jars and bottles, soda and beer cans.

Pearl, who'd been standing very close to Quinn, opened the meat drawer, then the produce drawer.

"Cheese," she said, as if about to be photographed.

Quinn and Fedderman looked where she was pointing, near a head of lettuce. There were four large wedges of white cheese there, identical except that one of them was half gone, with the plastic wrapper tucked around it. The labels said the cheese was NORSTRUM GOURMET and it was imported from the Netherlands.

"Look at the price of this stuff," Fedderman said.

"That's why it's gourmet," Pearl told him. "It's probably delicious."

"Four wedges. Or almost four. Stuff must last a long time, and it's pretty costly to be buying it four wedges at a whack."

"And there's no sign the Grahams were planning a party."

Quinn was listening to them, pleased by their acumen and absorption. They were into the case all the way now, as he was. It was much more than a job.

"Dust the cheese for prints," he said.

The tech grinned. "You kidding? Cheese doesn't—"

"The wrappers," Quinn said. "Dust the plastic wrappers." He nudged the refrigerator door shut and glanced at Pearl and Fedderman. "Let's go downstairs."

He didn't say anything while the three of them were in the elevator, waiting till they were outside on the sidewalk and out of earshot of anyone in the building.

"I think it's our guy," he said.

"Yeah," Pearl said. "Making it look like murder-suicide."

"But he used a knife this time instead of a gun," Fedderman pointed out. "Does that add up?"

"If it doesn't touch on his core compulsion," Quinn said.

"Or if he's read the literature on serial killers," Pearl said, "and knows enough to alter his methods."

There was a break in traffic, so they crossed the street to where the unmarked was parked in bright sunlight.

When they were seated in the car—Fedderman behind the steering wheel with the engine idling and the air conditioner on high—Pearl, in the backseat, said, "Nift's gonna go with murder-suicide, and it might wash. The weapon still in hubby's hand, no sign of a break-in. . . ."

"It won't wash for long," Quinn said. "It can't. There was

a chair pulled out from the kitchen table as if somebody'd been sitting there. And there were skid marks on the floor near the bed. Somebody'd been hiding under there and dragged dust with him when he slid out."

"Maybe the husband, hiding and waiting for the lover to show," Fedderman suggested.

"But he was in his underwear," Pearl said. "I think the killer was hiding under the bed. He thought he saw his chance, got out, and was about to leave, maybe out the window, and he heard the Grahams coming and made for the closet."

"Where would the Grahams be coming *from*?"

"I don't know. The kitchen, maybe. They might've both been awake and gotten up for a snack."

Fedderman was quiet for a moment, trying to work out a scenario that made sense where the husband might have slid under the bed in his underwear. Part of a plan. It was difficult if not impossible.

"And there's the cheese," Pearl said. "How many people buy something that expensive four at a time?"

"It happens," Fedderman said. "The rich are, you know . . . different."

"The Grahams weren't the Rockefellers." Pearl looked out the side window, across the street toward the apartment building they'd just left: red brick above a stone facade, green awnings, ivy growing up one corner out of huge concrete planters. No doorman, but a security system with a keypad, buzzer, and key-activated inner door. It wasn't the best building in the neighborhood, but it was a good one. It would be interesting to find out what the Grahams were paying in rent.

Fedderman put the car in drive but didn't pull away from the curb. "We haven't had breakfast, and looking into that refrigerator made me remember I was hungry."

"Maybe there'll be some prints on the cheese wrappers," Pearl said in a hopeful voice.

"I wouldn't count on it," Quinn said. "Our guy must have known whatever he bought for his potential victims might be examined, so he probably wiped everything he carried into the apartment. He's smart."

"So are we," Pearl said from the backseat.

"A cheese omelette doesn't sound bad," Fedderman said.

Quinn smiled, then said, "Drive."

After lunch, while Pearl and Fedderman were questioning the Grahams' neighbors, Quinn sat on a bench in a pocket park on East Fiftieth and called Renz on the cell phone Renz had furnished. It was supposedly a secure line, or nonline, less likely to be tapped than a regular wire connection. Easier to listen in on with a cheap scanner, perhaps, but no one knew Renz had the phone.

"You've solved the Graham case," Renz said when Quinn had identified himself.

"Taken the first step," Quinn said. He had to speak some-what loudly because of an echo effect and the constant trick-ling sound of a nearby artificial waterfall. "We can be pretty sure both Grahams were murdered."

"What's that noise?" Renz asked. "You calling me from a men's room?"

"Maybe you didn't hear—"

"I heard you," Renz cut him off. "Of course they were murdered. Just like the Elzners. That's why I hired you, re-member? I figured we had a repeater and the case would blossom. Thing is, Egan will still be seeing murder-suicide."

"That's what Nift thinks. I let him think it."

"Good. I know the basic facts of this case, though, and after the autopsy Nift will have to reveal everything to Egan."

"I thought Nift was your man in the ME's office."

"He is, right now. But Nift is for Nift. And all he can do is delay. He'll tell Egan it was murder-suicide; then Egan will figure out what you already know. Which is what?"

Quinn explained to Renz about the positions of the bodies, the dust dragged out from beneath the bed, the chair pulled out from the kitchen table, the four wedges of expensive gourmet cheese.

"Cheese this time, eh?" Renz said when Quinn was finished. Then added, "And a knife instead of a gun. We've got a repeater who changes his method."

"It happens," Quinn said. "Our guy's method isn't tied in with whatever makes him tick."

"Whatever makes him sick," Renz said. "That's for you to find out. Get in this motherfucker's mind, Quinn."

"Before Egan does," Quinn said.

"That's our game. How are Pearl and Fedderman working out?"

"They're both good ones. Fedderman's got bloodhound in him. Pearl's a terrier."

"Just so they remember Egan wants to send them both to the pound."

"It's always in their thoughts," Quinn assured Renz.

"I was gonna call you," Renz said, "seeing as cooperation runs both ways. We got a trace on that silencer used in the Elzner case, the Metzger eight hundred Sound Suppressor. In the past five years, one hundred thirty of that model was sold through two outlets: a biannual newsletter called 'Handgun Nation,' and a magazine, *Mercenary Today*."

"And you traced all hundred thirty?"

"It turned out to be easier than we thought. A militia group in Southwest Missouri bought a hundred of them, and they were all accounted for when the government shut down their operation two years ago and confiscated their weapons. The other thirty, we've tracked. They're all accounted for but one. It was bought mail order four years ago from *Mercenary Today* by a guy named Ed Smyth—that's with a *Y*—in Tacoma,

Washington. He says he sold it at a gun show a year later to a bearded man in a pickup truck. No sales record because it wasn't a gun, just gun paraphernalia."

Quinn didn't bother asking about the bearded man in the pickup. "What else do we know about Smyth with a *Y*?"

"That he bought a Russian revolver on that same date. He says he's a collector, and he lists his age as seventy-nine."

"Not our guy."

"Not unless he's the oldest psychosexual serial killer on record. And Tacoma police think he's telling the truth about the silencer. They know him because he's a gun nut, and they say he's honest."

"So we need to track the bearded guy in a pickup who bought the silencer. That should be easy."

"It should be," Renz said, his tone suggesting he'd been waiting for Quinn's sarcasm. "Smyth is a straight shooter in more ways than one. He etched his Social Security number in the silencer. Now we have it, and it's being sent out to various pawnshops and gun dealers. If the beard sold it, we'll nail him."

But Quinn knew he wouldn't be the killer. Whoever they were tracking was too smart to use anything as a weapon that might be traced to him. And there was something else. "Renz—"

"Harley."

"Harley, you've traced silencers sold within the last five years, but what if the silencer was bought before that? There might be hundreds or thousands of them out there you don't know about."

"It wasn't marketed in this country until five years ago." Renz, ready for him again. Quinn could almost see his smirk. Irritating.

"Why didn't you tell me that earlier?"

"Wanted to see if you'd think of it. If you've retained your old sharpness. I've seen cops get old fast, once they retire. And I gotta tell you, Quinn, it took you a while."

"Just keep me informed on the silencer," Quinn said, and pressed the button to disconnect.

He thought he heard Renz laughing as the phone went dead. Quinn almost hoped the silencer they were after had been smuggled in from another country.

Egan sat in his office feeling that everything was pretty much under control. He'd figured double murder faster than anyone predicted, with Nift's help. Renz thought Nift was his man, but Nift was Nift's man only and was hedging his bet on who'd be the next chief. The arrogant little ME called and told Egan right away that the knife found in the husband's hand wasn't the murder weapon. The blades were close, but they didn't quite match the wounds.

The papers and TV had the story the next morning. Egan had seen to it. The New York media became frenetic and inflamed over few things more than a serial killer. Since both couples had been killed around three A.M., and the female victims had been of obvious erotic interest to the killer, the media dubbed him the Night Prowler.

Egan liked it. Leave it to the New York press. Now New Yorkers had a killer they knew by name—nickname, anyway. A killer they could visualize and hate and fear. A star in a city that fed on stars.

He leaned back in his desk chair and grinned at the way things were going. A nocturnal serial killer! Just what was needed to increase the pressure on Renz, Quinn, and that pocket-size bitch Pearl. Fedderman he saw as no problem.

Egan felt confident. This was the kind of fight he never lost.

* * *

The Night Prowler.

Okay, why not? He rather liked it.

"The Night Prowler" set his quarter-folded *Times* aside on the wrought iron table and smiled. He was having a breakfast of soft-boiled eggs and a croissant at a West Side restaurant that had tables set up on the sidewalk outside. Someone driving past in the line of traffic was for some reason envious or offended by the smile and raised a middle finger at him, but he didn't mind. His thoughts were elsewhere, in a very special place the driver would never visit in his paltry, miserable life.

His gaze fell again on the folded newspaper.

The Night Prowler.

Yes, he approved!

And he knew himself well enough to realize that soon the Night Prowler would have to satisfy his special needs. The buzzing would begin again, softly at first, the cacophony and energy of discordant colors. He knew who the next one should be, but she was unmarried and lived alone. And she was apparently without a lover.

Not his type, as the incredibly inept police profilers would say.

Then why does she call to me so in the night?

He should make sure about her. Definitely he should make sure.

His waiter came by and the Night Prowler pointed to the half-eaten croissant on his plate.

"I believe I'll have another. They're delicious."

Why does she call to me so . . . ?

19

It had rained lightly but persistently the morning of Raoul Caruso's funeral, but by the time many of the mourners and family arrived at Anna's father's modest frame house in Queens, the sun was shining. Food—ravioli, salad, and chocolate-chip cookies—had been prepared there by a neighbor who'd been a good friend of Anna's father.

Anna looked at the woman, a dark-eyed, onetime beautiful widow in her fifties who'd put on weight but was still attractive. She wondered if her father and his neighbor had had an affair. The woman, whose name was Lilitta, had certainly been deeply distressed at the funeral.

Anna's father's employer, a swarthy man named Stick, who looked cheap and disreputable even in his expensive suit, had stood next to her at the funeral but didn't drive to the house afterward. Anna's uncle Dale, her father's brother and Melba's father, whom she'd met only half a dozen times, came to the house. He was seated on the edge of the sofa with a paper plate full of ravioli balanced on his knee and listening to a woman Anna didn't recognize, who was sitting next to him. Melba, who was fifteen and made ill by the funeral, was curled in a chair looking as if she wanted to cry and make her eyes even more red and puffy.

With eyes almost as red from crying as Melba's, Anna's mother approached Dale and whispered in his ear. Dale nodded, set his plate aside on a lamp table, and stood up. Anna watched them climb the stairs to the second floor. Lilitta, standing over by a big steel coffee urn, also saw them, and put down her foam cup and followed.

Anna hesitated, then followed Lilitta. As she took the stairs, she looked over and saw that Melba hadn't noticed them and was seated with her head bowed and her eyes clenched shut, absently picking at a zit on her chin.

At the top of the stairs Anna heard voices and went to an open door at the end of the hall.

Her father's bedroom.

The three of them were standing at the foot of the bed, talking calmly, but Lilitta seemed to be holding in anger as well as grief. Anna looked at the bed, at Lilitta, and wondered.

"It's difficult but we oughta do it," Dale was saying. "We're family, and from what Raoul told me"—a glance at Lilitta—"almost family."

Anna's mother saw her and waved her in.

"We're going to look through some of your father's things," she said, "and see what he might have wanted us to take to help us remember him. You should do this, too, Anna. It's posterity."

Anna wondered if the three of them were being sentimental, or actually looking for items of value. Either way, she couldn't stop them, so she decided to play along.

Acting tentative and guilty, as if her father might still be alive, they began opening drawers. Dale went to the closet and yanked open its door, which was warped and stuck on the wood frame. He was about the same size as his late brother and began selectively removing clothes, a shirt, two pairs of slacks, a sport jacket.

"Isn't it a little soon to be doing this?" Anna asked.

Lilitta smiled at her.

"We need to be realistic," Anna's mother said, looking up from the dresser drawer she was rooting through and shooting a glance at Dale.

Anna understood. Her mother feared that if given the opportunity, Dale would return to the house alone and confiscate anything of value.

Dale seemed oblivious of this as he held up the sport jacket to inspect it for wear or moth damage.

Anna's mother removed a wooden box from one of the dresser drawers and placed it on the bed next to the folded slacks. She opened the box and began spreading jewelry out on the tufted white spread.

Anna could see at a glance that all of it was cheap; she recognized the steel Timex watch her father had always worn and sworn by. Lilitta picked up the watch and held it as lovingly as if it were a $20,000 Rolex.

While the other three were occupied by the jewelry on the bed, Anna went to the closet. On the top shelf were stacks of old *Newsweek* magazines, a dusty rotary-style phone, and a shoe box. Anna slid the shoe box down and opened it to find that it contained what looked like a new pair of jogging shoes. As she was returning the box to where she'd found it, she noticed an old wooden cigar box that had been behind it on the shelf.

When she reached for the cigar box, she found it surprisingly heavy. With a backward glance to make sure no one was paying attention to her, she stepped deeper into the closet and lifted the box's lid. The scent of ancient tobacco wafted up to her.

Inside were about a dozen silver dollars with a thick rubber band around them to keep them in a neat stack, and a small revolver.

Fascinated, Anna looked at the revolver, then lifted it from the box and hefted it in her right hand. It felt good, as if it belonged there. It was blue steel with a checked walnut grip, and she could see the dull brass of the cartridge cases in the cylinder and knew it was loaded.

Her father's gun.

Her gun now. Posterity.

My gun.

Possessing it gave her a sense of secret power she didn't want to lose.

Barely hesitating, she slipped the revolver beneath her blouse and tucked its cool steel bulk into her waistband. Later she could go into the bathroom downstairs and transfer it to her purse.

"Anna?"

Her mother's voice.

Anna turned, still holding the open cigar box.

"Whatcha got, honey?"

"Money," Anna said, and held out the box.

The cheap cuff links, rings, and tie clasps on the bed were forgotten as Anna's mother took the box from her hand.

"Not much," Dale said, obviously disappointed. "Twelve dollars."

"Silver ones, though," said Anna's mother. "They might be worth something to a collector."

"Kinda thing the people who'll auction off the household items will keep for themselves. I don't wanna sound greedy, but the fair thing'd be to divide them coins three ways and forget them."

Anna's mother looked at Lilitta.

"He means family," Lilitta said. "Dale, you, and Anna." She held up the Timex. "I'll keep Raoul's watch, if nobody minds."

"No objections," Dale said, and carried the box over to the bed.

"You take my share," Anna said to her mother.

She watched as Dale and her mother carefully meted out the twelve silver dollars, four for Dale, eight for Anna's mother, taking them from the top of the stack in order, one by one, and making it a point not to look at the dates. Lilitta observed the process closely, her face impassive.

Everyone was involved with the money and uninterested in whatever else might have been in the cigar box.

Like the gun tucked firmly against Anna's hip.

Lars Svenson emerged from the Hades Portal Club in the East Village and drew a deep breath of cool night air. He was dressed in black leather from the toes up—black Doc Marten boots, tight black pants, and a studded black vest over a sleeveless black T-shirt.

He hadn't been completely satisfied inside the club, where he was a regular patron. The woman he'd attempted to pick up belonged to somebody bigger and probably meaner. That was actually okay with Lars, as he'd gotten close enough to see that the bruises on her face were dark makeup. So he hadn't scored sexually tonight, and he hadn't scored for dope. Lars still needed relief from his barely contained guilt and rage, which meant he was still looking for meth or cocaine, and for somebody to hurt.

From the time he was a teenager, Lars's relationships with women always led to violence. At first he tried to deny that was what he wanted, what he truly needed, but always the yearning was there, the compulsion only sometimes held in check. Gradually his willpower and his denial eroded, and during the past few years he accepted his need and learned how to lure his victims with feigned concern and kindness.

He soon found that it was like baiting a trap, a contest of

wits his opponents had little chance of winning. He learned to enjoy it. It was like the hunting he used to do in the Minnesota woods—find the game, flush it, and make it yours. The only real difference he could see was that now he was in New York and it was women he hunted. And between hunts he enjoyed going directly to willing victims who endured pain for pay. It was like hunting birds in cages.

Just last week, even after moving furniture all day, he still felt the energy and the need, so he'd gone to a club and used his blond good looks and his pickup skills to get a young woman named Tina to invite him to her apartment.

Lars smiled, remembering Tina's trusting, round face and zaftig body, even fleshier than he'd imagined when she'd stripped off her bra and panty hose. Tina liked to play rough. Or at least she thought she did. Lars had shown her what rough was, once she was tied and gagged and his for the rest of the night.

His smile had become such a wide grin that a passing couple of guys, *faggots,* stared at him as he strode along the sidewalk. He was recalling Tina's futile struggles and muted cries for help, the terror and pain in her eyes, and then the resignation. After all, she'd gotten herself into this, said her eyes, after Lars had patiently explained it to her over and over. It wasn't difficult to get her to believe it; she came with guilt built in, part of the package.

She'd welcomed his advances in the club and even told him she enjoyed bondage and discipline, rough sex with a little pain. Verbal commands and the whip were okay, if used sparingly. B&D and S&M. She hadn't mentioned which she enjoyed more. Her oversight.

In the morning he untied Tina and asked if she wanted to go out for breakfast, but she awkwardly crept from the bed with sore and stiffened limbs and cowered in a corner, staring at him in mute disbelief.

Lars laughed, and as he got dressed, he told her what a stupid bitch she was. He didn't glance back at her when he left the apartment. He wouldn't be surprised to see her again; she might even come looking for him. They were like that, some of them, once you took them to a higher level. They needed to go higher and higher, and Lars was willing to fly them all the way to heaven so they could escape their hell. They'd beg him to, after a while. They'd plead and pledge their souls. What they wanted, they loathed, but their problem was they loved it even more. It was like a drug addiction.

Speaking of which . . . Lars was going to go out of his gourd if he didn't score some dope pretty soon.

He tried to think of something else as he roamed the gray morning streets, watching for possibilities.

The something else was Claire Briggs.

She was the type Lars liked, slender and helpless, fems all the way, natural submissives once they were shown the path, once they were kicked in the ass and shoved along the path. And she lived alone, some kind of actress, probably with a rich family that might come across once he taught her how to mooch.

Claire Briggs. Definitely worthwhile.

Lars spotted a guy he recognized standing outside the entrance to a diner, a gigantic black dude with dreadlocks, looked like a former NFL linebacker who'd taken up reggae. While bigger than Lars, he wasn't as solid. The soft life was making him vulnerable. He was talking to a woman with straight blond hair that hung almost to her ass. The guy's name was Handy and he dealt.

The woman said something about pancakes, then sashayed her ass inside the diner, making the long hair swish. Handy stayed outside, leaning back against the brick wall and smoking a cigarette like it was an art.

"Handy," Lars said when he was about twenty feet away; he didn't want the dealer to miss seeing him and go inside after the woman. "Remember me, my man?"

Handy flicked away his cigarette and gave Lars a wide, gleaming smile. "I remember your money."

"I wanna reintroduce you," Lars said, forgetting all about Claire Briggs.

For the moment.

20

Hiram, Missouri, 1989.

"He's sixteen," Milford Sand said, "of an age when he can damn well work and pull his own weight around here. Hell, I was—"

"I know," his wife Cara said, "you were working in the mine when you were fourteen. This boy, Luther, is the only survivor of a house fire that killed his foster family in Missouri; then he somehow survived almost a year of life on the streets in Kansas City."

"So he's no innocent," Milford said.

"So he needs time to heal body and soul, Milford. Please show him some compassion."

Milford snorted and jammed his arms into his suit coat almost hard enough to split the seams. "He can heal his soul while he's working with his body."

Milford Sand was fifty-three, almost twenty years older than his wife, but he looked as if he could be in his late sixties. His narrow back was bent from sitting hunched over at his desk at the Hiram Lead Mine, where he kept the company books, and his face was pale and pinched. His cheap drugstore spectacles, which were too small, gave him a slightly cross-eyed appearance. Milford monitored the household money the way he tracked expenses at the mine, and there was no point in spending for prescription glasses when the ones on the revolving rack at Drexel's Pharmacy would do just as well.

He studied his thinning brown hair, strained blue eyes, and puckered mouth as he adjusted his tie knot in the dresser mirror. He'd once overheard somebody at the mine say his natural expression was that of a man about to spit. Milford wasn't insulted; the comment hadn't been far off the mark. "The agency said this boy—Luther—has had some experience as a housepainter. I'll talk to Tom Wilde about taking him on as an apprentice."

"I don't know—"

"That's true," Milford interrupted in a weary, tolerant tone. "You *don't* know, and there's no need for you to worry about that part of it. You just try and make the lad feel at home; I'll take care of his employment this summer so he can earn his keep."

"Maybe he should go to summer school. He's already two grades behind."

"Maybe he's simply unable to do the work and needs to learn a trade."

"Milford—"

"I have to get to the office." He snatched up his heavy brown leather briefcase from the floor alongside the dresser, an adroit and powerful motion for such a frail-looking man, and headed for the door. Then he paused. "What time's the agency bringing the boy?"

"One this afternoon. Try and get home if it's at all possible."

"I'll speak to them at the mine." He forced a lemony smile and hurried from the room.

A few seconds later Cara heard the screen door slam downstairs, the hollow thumping of his footfalls on the wooden porch, then after a minute or so the grinding of his car starting in the garage and the crunch of tires on the gravel driveway. Morning sounds. It was how Cara started each long day, listening to Milford leave for the mine.

The mine. All he thought about was the mine, his job, numbers, and lead. Profit and loss, this column or that. Cara thought the lead in the air was probably poisoning the whole town.

It was certainly poisoning their marriage.

Luther was surprised by the house that Saturday afternoon. He'd expected something smaller. This was a cream-colored frame monster with gray trim, a gallery porch, and a steep, tiled roof with lots of dormers. It looked like the house Luther had seen in Hansel and Gretel drawings—only much, much larger. There were a few other houses something like it on the wide, tree-lined street, but this one was the biggest and in the best condition even though it was old like the rest of them. The yard around it was wide and level, with a low stone wall in front and with lots of trees and shrubs. There was a long gravel drive that ran to a garage in back that looked newer than the house.

It was warm when he and the woman from the state agency got out of the air-conditioned car. There was plenty of shade in the yard, and twenty or thirty industrious sparrows pecking away busily on the green lawn. The sparrows all took flight when Luther slammed the car door. He hefted his lumpy duffel bag and walked around the car toward the wide wooden porch steps.

The porch was shady and had viney potted plants and a glider and rocking chair on it. "Looks like Norman fuckin' Rockwell lives here," Luther heard the agency woman mutter under her breath. She was slender, with lustrous blond hair, and was better-looking than most of the state employees. Luther knew she would have been pissed off if she was aware of how he'd been studying her.

Their footsteps made noise on the plank floor, and the front door opened before the agency woman pushed the doorbell button.

Inside, the woman introduced herself to Mr. and Mrs. Sand as Helen Simpson, which was a good thing because Luther had forgotten her name somewhere on Interstate 40. He watched and listened as she went through the routine that was so familiar to her, complete with smiles and pats on Luther's shoulder at proper intervals; then she left the house and walked down the drive to her dusty white agency car. Business finished.

And there sat sixteen-year-old Luther Lunt with his new foster parents. The three of them listened to gravel crunch as Helen Simpson backed her car out of the drive. Then it was quiet in the big three-story Victorian house that Milford Sand and his wife had restored.

Luther would be the only charge here, which he liked. And he liked the wife, Cara, right away. She was kinda old— maybe even in her thirties—but still pretty, with her curly dark hair and brown eyes. She had an oval face that looked like it belonged in one of those heart-shaped lockets you opened up to see the photograph. And she smiled at Luther as if she meant it.

On the other hand, the husband, Luther's new temporary father, acted like he had a stick up his ass. While working the streets as a male prostitute in Kansas City, Luther had seen his kind of little weasel before. He thought he might need the wife to protect him from Mr. Sand. He was sure, just by looking, that she wasn't like Mrs. Black.

Cara—Mrs. Sand—was smiling at him. "Would you care for a glass of lemonade, Luther?"

Time for the act. "I sure would, Mrs. Sand."

She stood up from the sofa, where she'd been seated next to her husband. For a moment she looked as if she might cry. "I wouldn't expect you to call me mother, Luther, but Cara would do fine."

Milford stood up also. He bent over and brushed imaginary lint or dust from his pants. "I'd like to stay, but I need to get to the mine."

"Mine?" Luther asked.

"The Hiram Lead Mine, where I'm head of accounting."

"Sounds neat," Luther said.

Milford nodded solemnly. "It is neat." He pecked Cara on the cheek. "I'll be back in time for dinner, dear. Bye, Luther."

"Bye," Luther said to his retreating back.

Cara went into the kitchen, then returned with two glasses of lemonade. She handed one to Luther, then sat down again on the sofa across from the wing chair where he sat.

"He works so hard," she said of her husband. "Even sometimes on weekends. When they're behind at the mine."

"Yes, ma'am." Luther sipped lemonade and glanced around. "You sure got a beautiful house, all the room and nice furniture."

"Why, thank you, Luther. Mr. Sand and I spent months restoring it. The first two floors are done, and we'll get around to the third-floor bedrooms someday." She took a sip from her tall, frosted glass and crossed her legs, tugging down her flowered skirt demurely to cover her knees. "We sanded the floors, brought the kitchen up to date. . . . It's such a job, keeping up with an old house. It never stops."

"Maybe I can help," Luther said.

"Why, thank you." She smiled. "Maybe you can."

"I know you and Mr. Sand are putting yourselves out for me."

"Not at all. We volunteered because we like to help children—young men—like yourself. And if it'll make you feel any better, Mr. Sand's going to speak to someone about help-ing you learn a trade. A housepainter. You've done some of that, haven't you, where you came from?"

"I can paint some," Luther said. His voice was tight, re-membering the fire spreading over spilled paint, gaining glowing life, burning in a widening circle and filling the house with fumes. He'd thought the other kids were gone and the house was empty except for the scumbag Norbert, and Dara, who didn't care. They were supposed to be all by themselves, fucking in the upstairs bedroom, not paying at-tention while the fire spread. It was when the screaming started that Luther—

"More lemonade?"

"No thanks," Luther said, grinning shyly at Cara. "I best be getting unpacked, if that's okay."

Cara placed her glass on a coaster and stood up. "Of course it's okay. I'll show you your room. I hope you'll like it."

"I will," Luther said, following her.

The next Monday, after a breakfast of pancakes and eggs prepared by Cara, Milford drove Luther into town to intro-duce him to Tom Wilde.

Wilde's Painting Company was a green-and-yellow flat-roofed building that looked as if it had once been a corner service station. A rusty and dented Ford pickup truck and a newer-looking white van were parked outside. The van was lettered with the company name and phone number and had racks on top and three paint-splattered aluminum extension ladders lashed to them. One of the pair of overhead doors was open to reveal a shadowed interior of shelves lined with paint cans and folded canvas drop cloths. Nearby were sev-eral stepladders, a pair of wooden sawhorses, and stacks of white plastic five-gallon paint buckets.

Milford parked his blue Ford Fairlane sedan at the curb, diligently setting the emergency brake even though they were on level ground. He said nothing as he and Luther got out of the car and walked toward the building.

Luther thought the old pickup truck looked interesting and wondered if he'd be driving it. Driving Norbert Black's pickup was the only thing he'd found enjoyable about working for Norbert. Of course Luther didn't have a driver's license, which never bothered Norbert but might be of concern to Tom Wilde.

As they got closer to the building, Luther detected the familiar scent of paint thinner. Then he saw in the dim interior of the building a stocky figure in white overalls, standing at a workbench with his fists on his hips. Drifting from what had obviously once been a service bay for cars came the thumping and vibrating rhythm of an electric paint mixer violently shaking a gallon can of paint.

The man at the workbench sensed he wasn't alone and turned. He was between thirty and forty, with kindly, handsome features arranged in a permanent, squinting smile. He had bushy brown hair and a somewhat oversize, lumpy nose threaded with red veins. His was the sort of face that made you like him at once, or at least trust him. Luther saw now that his white overalls were splattered with a rainbow array of paints.

The man reached behind him and switched off the frantically thumping mixer; in the silence he looked at Luther and smiled wider. "This the lad?"

"This is him," Milford said, and formally introduced them.

"I'm told you have some experience as a painter," Wilde said. He had a soft, precise way of speaking, like a teacher.

"Some," Luther told him. "Painting barns, some houses."

"That oughta be good enough. Pay's every two weeks, minimum wage. That's about all I can afford."

"That'd be fine."

Nobody spoke for a while; then Milford said, "I'll leave you two to tell paint stories and get acquainted." He looked at Wilde. "I might have to work late at the mine. Can you drop Luther off at the house after you're finished with him?"

"Won't be a problem."

Luther and Wilde watched as Milford returned to the Ford. He glanced back and waved to them as he was lowering himself behind the steering wheel; then he drove away fast, making the car's wide back end dip.

"He sure seems to like his job," Luther said.

Wilde laughed. "A kinda workaholic. And don't let his frail appearance fool you. He spent time in the military as a ranger, then some years at hard labor in the mine while he was getting his accounting degree. You never want to mix it up with him, Luther." As if reminded of his interrupted task, he turned on the paint mixer again, then motioned with his head. He and Luther walked outside, where it wasn't so noisy and they could talk.

"We got a job today?" Luther asked, still trying to imagine Milford Sand as a hard ass tough guy. It was just possible.

"Sure do. You good at cutting in?"

"Cutting in?"

"Trimming with a brush."

"I've done that," Luther said. He had, a few times. Mostly for Norbert he'd lugged materials, scraped and sanded, or rolled paint onto large surfaces, doing the backbreaking work. Maybe painting where there were wasps or hornets nearby on hot days beneath the eaves of barns or farmhouses.

Wilde looked at him in a way that made Luther think he was taking his measure. "What you have to know, Luther, is I'm no ordinary painter. There are tricks to this trade. I can match colors perfectly, tell people what color schemes will work, tint and layer paint so things show their best, make rooms look larger or smaller, create light and shadow where none really exist. You understand what I'm saying?"

Luther nodded. "You're kinda like an artist."

Wilde grinned. "Sometimes, Luther . . . sometimes. What I am all the time is a craftsman. That's why people hire me. That's what I need you to be working toward—craftsmanship. Use your God-given talent and don't abuse it, and it'll take care of you. You believe that?"

"Maybe."

"An honest answer." Wilde walked back inside and switched off the mixer, then came back out into the sunlight. "Craftsmanship. You interested?"

"I think so," Luther said honestly.

"Me too," Wilde said, and patted him on the arm. Not *We'll find out*. He was on Luther's side. "Help me load the van and we'll go spread some paint and cheer up our corner of the world."

Surprisingly, the day went fast for Luther. He found that he *was* interested in painting, if it was done the way Tom Wilde did it.

They worked on an old house on the other side of town, a three-story Victorian, which was something like the Sands' house, that was being totally redecorated. It was ideal for the task of teaching.

During the next few days Wilde showed Luther how to stencil a border around a room, how to tint paint and shade the beveled edges of door panels to make them appear recessed so the doors looked thicker, how to use the mixer and paint scale to match colors precisely from only a tiny paint chip. Luther applied himself carefully and didn't make too many mistakes. The ones he did make didn't seem to upset

Tom Wilde, who helped to correct them. Wilde worked steadily but not fast; he was more interested in results than in making money on the job.

The week went by, almost without Luther realizing it had happened.

His days flew past, and in the evenings he enjoyed watching Cara Sand work around the house, dusting, vacuuming, preparing dinner for Milford, who always seemed to arrive home late from his job at the mine. Cara had those wonderful dark eyes, and Luther couldn't help staring at the roundness of her hips beneath her housedress, the graceful turn of her ankles. There was something about her flesh, its creaminess, that made him yearn to touch it. He was sure she didn't suspect he was thinking of her in that way, and he didn't want her to guess. Sometimes in her presence it was an effort not to get an erection, which she might notice if for some reason he had to stand up suddenly. It wasn't just the way Cara looked, her lush body and perfect eyes and lips; it was her smile and the way she listened to people when they talked—really listened.

Luther loved most of all to watch Cara working in the kitchen, the way she stood at the sink, up against it, with its edge pressed into her stomach, making her round breasts appear even larger, while she peeled potatoes or washed dishes. He studied how her clothes clung to her and her calf muscles gave shape to her legs when she stretched to reach things high in the cabinets.

She caught Luther once staring at her when she stooped low to reach something toward the back of the refrigerator, but she pretended not to have noticed. He knew she'd caught him looking, though, and she knew he knew—a special and unspoken secret between them. It was the things people didn't say that made them close.

Cara was somehow able to sense when Luther was hungry and would prepare snacks for him. Once she even baked him a peach pie after he mentioned it was his favorite. Her voice became like music. "My growing boy," she would call him as she placed food before him, with that smile that flooded his heart.

Luther began to dream about Cara almost nightly. On some mornings he'd discover he'd had an orgasm in his sleep. But his dreams were not only carnal; in his mind Cara was a lady. He never considered actually touching her, or declaring how he felt about her. *You didn't shit in your own nest* was something he learned early on the streets. But Milford, Luther decided, was crazy to spend so much time at his job.

The Saturday after getting his first paycheck, Luther walked down to the drugstore and bought a razor and shaving cream, which he barely needed, and a bar of soap that was better than the cheap stuff provided by Milford that left him itching and scratching.

It was at the drugstore that he first heard people talking about him, and where he first heard the gossip about Tom Wilde.

21

New York, 2004.

Quinn got the phone call from May late at night.

"Frank?"

Even though he was in bed and half-asleep, he recognized her voice immediately. Besides, she was the only one who called him by his first name.

He scooted back to lean into his wadded pillow and pressed the plastic receiver harder to his ear. "Something wrong, May?"

"Something I have to tell you. I'm sorry to call so late, but I couldn't sleep thinking about it."

"Is it about Lauri?"

"No. She's fine."

"We still don't speak," Quinn said.

"I know. I'm sorry about that, Frank."

Are you? It was you who turned her against me. If you'd believed in me . . .

Quinn sighed, wondering what kind of trouble was coming his way. "So what else are you sorry about?" he asked.

"How you might take what I'm going to say."

"I'm lying down." Trying to make a joke of it.

"I'm going to be married."

Quinn felt as if the ceiling had dropped on him, though he knew he shouldn't care. May was no longer his wife and hadn't been for years.

Still, they shared a history; they were part of each other. *Married! Jesus!*

"Who's the lucky man?" he forced himself to ask, loathing how trite and hollow it sounded.

"Elliott Franzine. He's a cost accountant."

Whatever that is. "A successful one?"

"Reasonably. He works hard."

"Sounds like a settled, secure guy who keeps regular hours." *Not like a cop.*

"He is. You know that's what I always needed, security."

"There's really no such thing, May."

"Then call it predictability. That's what was missing in our marriage. It's the uncertainty that eats away, Frank."

She was right about that. He'd seen it with too many cops' marriages. "Yeah, I can understand that, May. I wish you and . . ."

"Elliott."

". . . Elliott the best. I really do."

"Frank—"

"Life moves on."

"What about *your* life? How are things going for you? Some of the news about those New York murders is reaching us here on the other coast."

"I'm back on the force, in a way. But you might call it a probationary situation. It's kind of my last roll of the dice."

"It'll work out for you, Frank. I've got a feeling."

Do you have a feeling I didn't rape Anna Caruso?

But he didn't put the question into words.

They talked for a while longer, about their daughter, the upcoming wedding, where May and Elliott were going on their honeymoon—Cancun. At least it was a place where Quinn and May had never been.

After hanging up, Quinn couldn't come close to going back to sleep.

May Franzine . . .

Around midnight he gave up and climbed out of bed. He went into the kitchen and got down an unopened bottle of scotch from the back of a cabinet shelf.

May and Lauri Franzine . . .

What was he, disappearing?

It was raining the next morning, so Quinn went to meet Pearl and Fedderman at the Lotus Diner on Amsterdam.

It was a long, narrow place, with wooden booths along a wall of windows opposite the counter. A haze of cooking smoke hung just beneath the high, stamped tin ceiling. There were half a dozen customers eating breakfast alone, three at the counter, three in the booths. Two of the ones at the counter were having only coffee and reading the *Post,* probably about the Night Prowler. The scent of overfried bacon made Quinn a little queasy the moment he came through the door. The line of booths went beyond the counter and windows. He sat in one of the back booths and was trying without much success to get down coffee and a glazed doughnut while waiting for his detective team.

He'd used an umbrella and walked here from his apartment in order to clear his mind. It had worked to an extent, but his head still ached and his stomach objected to the half bottle of scotch he'd killed last night. His ankles felt cool every time somebody came or went, and the draft from the open door flowed over his pants cuffs that were still wet from his walk through the rain.

Pearl was the reason for the latest cool draft. She'd driven her unmarked here alone. Fedderman and a detective named

Drucker had worked late yesterday evening questioning the Grahams' neighbors who held jobs and weren't available during weekdays. Fedderman and Drucker were going to reinterview neighbors in adjacent buildings today and would arrive soon in Fedderman's plain Ford Victoria.

Quinn started to stand to make himself noticeable, but Pearl spotted him and walked toward the booth. She had on black slacks today, black boots that looked waterproof, and a black raincoat that was trimmed in green and came to her knees. She wasn't carrying an umbrella.

She unbuttoned the coat, draped it over a brass hook on the opposite wall, and slid into the booth to sit across from him. He saw the alarm on her face. "You look like shit, Quinn."

He knew he should take offense but didn't; she was, after all, right. "Tough night."

She made a face as she got a whiff of his breath. "And you smell like a still."

"I did imbibe."

He explained what had happened, telling her almost everything about May's late-night phone call. Once he'd begun talking, he couldn't stop; the words were inside him like winged things that had to get out, had to be heard and shared.

Her reaction surprised him. "Your sleeve's unbuttoned. Your cuff got dunked in your coffee."

Quinn looked down and saw the brown triangular stain on his dangling white shirt cuff. He tried to button the cuff with his left hand but couldn't. His fingers were trembling in a way they hadn't for months.

Pearl reached across the table and deftly fastened the button. "Is Feds bringing Drucker by here this morning?"

"That's the plan," Quinn said.

"Let's change the plan. You don't want anybody else to see you like this. I'll drive you home."

Quinn must have noticeably recoiled at the thought.

"On the other hand," Pearl said, "there might be some booze left in that bottle. You're going to my place and catch up on the sleep you should have had last night."

"Pearl, I really don't think I'm at that point."

"You look like a goddamn wino, Quinn. C'mon."

She stood up and reached for her coat.

Quinn looked again at his stained cuff and his unsteady hands. His head throbbed and his stomach was sour. He decided not to argue with Pearl. He trailed her meekly out of the diner.

As they were walking toward the car, she said, "I think you need a real breakfast instead of that jolt of caffeine and sugar you were working on."

Pearl taking care of him. Maternal Pearl. Quinn couldn't help wondering where this might lead.

"After you get something to eat, you sack out on my sofa and I'll tell Fedderman and Drucker you're not feeling well today."

"Listen, Pearl . . ."

"Don't thank me, Quinn. And don't question what I say. It'd be best if you skipped working today and were sharp tomorrow, instead of being a booze zombie two consecutive days."

Less than an hour later he sat with his sleeves rolled up at her tiny kitchen table, where she served him a cheese omelette and toast with a glass of orange juice, no coffee.

When he'd finished breakfast and was ensconced on Pearl's sofa with his shoes off, she tinkered around in her bedroom a few minutes, then left. He opened a narrowed eye and caught her smiling at him as she went out the door.

It was a particular kind of smile that Quinn recognized, both affectionate and proprietary.

Lord, Lord, Lord . . . , he thought, and dropped into a sleep blacker than black.

* * *

Claire had just finished washing the bedroom windows when there was a knock on the door. That was odd, she thought. Someone had bypassed the intercom and somehow gained entrance to the lobby and elevators.

On the other hand, not so odd. Probably whoever was knocking had simply entered along with another visitor or one of the tenants. Or maybe for some reason the intercom wasn't working today.

Claire's lover, actor Jubal Day, had lost his role in *Metabolism* when it folded last week in Kansas City; he was back in New York with Claire. He'd decided to stay with her, even if it meant having to accept roles he didn't want in off-off-Broadway theaters with folding chairs and leaky ceilings. Though she feigned disappointment about the Kansas City play, Claire was delighted. Handsome, lanky Jubal, with his tousled dark hair and piercing blue eyes, belonged with her. Belonged *to* her.

As she entered the living room, still holding the folded rag she'd been using on the bedroom windows, he was standing up from where he'd been dozing on the sofa. She grinned and waved him back down, since he looked too sleepy to be coherent anyway, and continued to the door.

When she opened it, she needed a few seconds to recognize the man standing in the hall. He was tall, blond, and muscular, wearing a black suit with a black pullover beneath the coat.

He smiled. "Lars Svenson," he reminded her.

"I know. It took me a while."

"I'm not always a furniture mover. I have another life."

Claire grinned. "Everybody has several."

"I thought in this one," Svenson said with an easy confidence, "I'd come by and see if you wanted to share a little of it."

"Uh, Mr. Svenson . . ."

He shook his head, widening his smile that was too obviously meant to charm. "Claire, it's Lars. And I don't mean any harm. It's just that for some reason you stuck in my mind. I move furniture for a lot of people, and usually it's just a job. But—"

He stopped talking abruptly and his expression changed. The smile was gone as if Claire had Windexed it off with the rag in her hand.

"Somebody looking for a job?" Jubal asked behind her.

Svenson recovered nicely and the smile was back. "Already did the job," he said, his full attention now aimed at Jubal. "I just came by to make sure everything was to the lady's satisfaction. We do that."

"We?"

"Mr. Svenson was one of the movers who schlepped all our furniture up here," Claire said.

"You shittin' me?" Jubal asked Svenson, nudging Claire a few inches to the side. "You mean you actually get dressed up like a Midwesterner's idea of a New Yorker and visit all your customers days later to make sure you put the sofa in the right place?"

"Mostly, we only do that with the pretty ones." Svenson's smile was the same, but something had changed in his pale eyes. "I know you're not Claire's husband; are you her brother?"

"Closer than her brother."

Svenson's unblinking gaze didn't waver, but now he seemed amused rather than angry. "Like maybe her bodyguard?"

"Among other things," Jubal said. Claire caught something in his voice; he was afraid, but he wasn't backing off.

"Hopefully, bodyguarding isn't necessary," Svenson said. "Hopefully."

Svenson smiled again at Claire, then nodded. "If you decide you want anything rearranged, you know how to get in touch with me." He backed away, then turned and sauntered to the elevator, not in any rush. Everything in his body language said he was in control and unconcerned.

Claire made a move to close the door, but Jubal reached out above her and held it open. They both watched until the elevator arrived.

"Thanks again for the business," Svenson said to Claire, and gave a little wave as he stepped inside and the elevator door slid closed behind him.

"Guy's some creep," Jubal said as he shut the apartment door and latched it.

"He does have a nerve," Claire agreed, "coming back like that."

"And he doesn't look at all Swedish. I doubt his name's really Lars Svenson."

"We can't hold that against him," Claire said jokingly. "Your own name's been changed."

"That's common among actors, but not furniture movers."

Jubal slumped down again on the sofa and used the remote to switch on cable news. The screen was split four ways to accommodate two men and two women in severe business garb arguing about the Supreme Court. It reminded Claire of a rerun of *Hollywood Squares* that had gotten out of hand.

She went into the kitchen and got a fresh bottle of Windex from beneath the sink to use on the spare bedroom's windows.

Whether he was Swedish or not, she couldn't get Lars Svenson out of her mind, which aggravated her because she knew that was exactly what he wanted.

Well, not exactly. He was, after all, a man.

Claire realized she wasn't really attracted to Svenson. At least not in the usual way.

She was afraid of him.

22

The woman in the mirror hadn't been rich before, or what she'd describe as poor, and hadn't been married before. This was quite a change. The woman was smiling.

The mirror, bolted to the wall near the door to the hall, was a leftover from the previous tenant. Reflected in it was Mary Navarre, a woman in her twenties, with her mother's ginger hair and her father's Spanish eyes, and what he used to call her noble nose. She was of average height and slender, dressed in a light tan Gucci knockoff she'd bought before the inheritance.

Mary turned away from the mirror and looked around the spacious apartment on West End Avenue. She began mentally placing her furniture, which was still in a rental storage building in New Jersey. She was grateful again for the inheritance, but she would have preferred to wait a few years.

She missed her mother, who'd drowned while swimming off the coast of Florida five years ago. And she missed her father, who'd died of emphysema six months ago, soon after her marriage to Donald Baines. She and Donald hadn't thought they could make it on one salary, even though he'd received a raise along with his transfer to the New York office, so Mary assumed she'd have to find some kind of work in or around Manhattan.

However, they'd been shocked when they learned after her father's death that Mary, his only living child, would receive almost a $1 million inheritance.

Mary's father, Hector, had arrived in the United States in 1980, one of the Marielitos that Castro had allowed to leave in order to empty Cuba's prisons and mental institutions. Hector Navarre had been imprisoned for killing a man in a machete duel over a woman. The man happened to be a deputy commissioner of the state. It had happened when Hector was still a teenager, but he'd been in prison for almost twenty years.

When he suddenly found himself free in Southeast Florida, he'd made the most of his situation. He saved his money and within a year had opened a dry-cleaning establishment with a partner who'd supplied most of the cash. Hector's end of the deal was sweat equity. Within another three years, they'd opened three more dry cleaners in Miami. Hector secured financing, bought out his partner, and further expanded the business, establishing cleaners in Fort Lauderdale and on the other side of the state in Tampa. When he died, he still had much of the money obtained from selling to a franchise operator five years ago, almost immediately after his wife's death.

It truly is a great country, Mary thought, and not for the first time. She didn't plan to waste this opportunity provided by her father's money. The wealth carried with it an obligation. She would delay having a child and attend New York University in the spring. Eventually she'd obtain a degree, the first in her family. Perhaps she'd go into the dry-cleaning business. Donald had no problem with any of her plans. He wanted her to succeed.

He wasn't flawless as a husband, but he did wish her the best.

Luck in love and money, having the right parents, the right husband, being in the right place at the right time. It was what life was about, and whatever happened, you had to make the most of it, because it could also swing the other way.

The intercom rasped, startling her. Mary crossed the room to it and pressed the button.

The decorator was downstairs, precisely on time for their appointment. She buzzed him up.

They would go over preliminaries and make plans for the apartment. Mary would listen carefully to his advice, then deliberate and tell him what she preferred.

For the first time in her life, she knew exactly what she wanted.

The Night Prowler strolled along Broadway at ten that evening and ignored everyone going in the opposite direction. He didn't like making eye contact with passersby; he wanted no connection, no relationship to take even tenuous hold. He managed his life and his time and chose his relationships carefully. All kinds of relationships. He kept his colors bright.

He paused and looked across the street to where a glowing red sign sent its brightness shimmering over diners at an outside café, lending a glow to the hair of the women and a satanic hue to their features. The women, caught laughing with heads thrown back, daintily dipping spoons into soup, leaning back in their chairs and smiling, raising skewered meat or salad to red lips, talking intently over coffee or dessert. Even at this distance their jewelry glinted like bright taunts attached to the softness of their flesh. The men seated across from the women leaned toward them, close to them, drawn by the timeless thing that had drawn reptilian ancestry and still lived.

Fools with their fools!

A waiter emerged from the restaurant, and diners at one of the tables stood up to leave. An oblivious bicyclist pedaled by like a haughty trespasser. The tableau was ruined and became part of past and memory.

Almost nothing in the world was perfect. For God's sake, he, among all, understood that. But once concessions were made, choices settled, plans laid and carried out—there could be perfect moments. Imbalances in the cosmos could be shifted, measurements recalibrated, objects and colors brought into sharp focus. Colors could be felt and heard like music. *Like music!*

So much better than the gray buzzing, a maelstrom of all colors, a breakdown of order and control.

The universe would come to bear and press down and in, until finally pressure triggered action. *Beneath the smooth flesh, bones, bleached white and beautiful, an absence of color.*

Then the kaleidoscope would lurch and there would be new patterns and colors and hopes and order and design. There would be internal silence, almost. There would be a new mystery even if the same old need survived.

The need was immortal because love and hate and betrayal never changed. Not of their own accord.

They had to *be* changed.

In the brightness of an intersection, the Night Prowler glanced down at the name he'd scrawled five times in red ball-point ink on the inside of his wrist, where his blood pulsed and coursed visibly in a blue map of destiny.

Mary Navarre.

* * *

"You okay today?" Fedderman asked the next morning when he approached Quinn and Pearl, who were seated on the park bench off Eighty-sixth Street. He was wearing his usual baggy brown suit and had a folded *Newsday* tucked beneath his right arm.

"Still a little shaky," Quinn said. "You and Drucker learn anything yesterday?"

"Not really. The usual *see no, hear no, tell no.* A next-door building in New York can be like another world." He looked more closely at Quinn. "You sleep in your clothes?"

"Sort of. Those nighttime cold medicines knock you out."

Fedderman looked at Pearl, who'd said nothing since his arrival. Not like Pearl. He sighed, and Quinn watched his eyes and saw his old partner catalog information in his mind.

Quinn knew it wouldn't do any good to tell Fedderman he'd spent the night on Pearl's sofa and nothing happened between them. Feds would believe what he chose, but he'd keep his mouth shut about it.

Fedderman held out the folded newspaper. "You might wanna look at this."

"We take another flogging in the press?"

"You in particular. There's an interview in there with Anna Caruso."

Quinn unfolded the paper and saw the photograph of a beautiful young woman with dark hair and somber brown eyes. Not a child. No one he remembered.

But there was her name beneath the photo, and there was the old accusation in her eyes.

In the interview she recounted her rape by Quinn, then talked about her life now, how she'd put the horrible experience behind her. Or thought she had. Here it was again because Quinn was getting another chance. One he didn't deserve. No one had served a day in prison for what had happened to her, and that injustice still haunted her. She didn't like it, but she could live with it, she told the interviewer.

Her father died recently, and she was concentrating on coping with that and going ahead with her music. With her life.

She played the viola and that was therapeutic. She wouldn't be afraid, or think about Quinn. She would be fine, she said. People shouldn't worry about her. People had better things to do. She had better things to do.

Hate burned between the lines.

23

Donald was out of town and wouldn't be back until tomorrow night. After lunch at the Café Un Deux Trois, Mary reminded herself she was moderately wealthy and took a cab instead of a subway to the apartment on West End Avenue. She needed to take a few measurements and reconsider the window treatment for the master bedroom. Nothing must disturb the magnificent view.

As soon as she opened the apartment door, she saw the bouquet of fresh yellow roses. The flowers were in a clear glass vase, on a metal folding chair that was the only piece of furniture in the room.

Mary went to the bouquet and saw that there was a card attached by a green ribbon. But when she gingerly reached in among the thorns and maneuvered the card to where she could examine it, she found it blank.

She looked for some other marking on the flowers or the rounded vase, but there was nothing to indicate who'd sent the flowers or delivered them.

But Mary knew who'd sent them. Donald. He'd ordered them by phone so she'd find them when she came to the apartment, as he knew she would today and every day until they moved in.

It was so like him; he was thoughtful that way.

Still, it was odd that he hadn't instructed a message be placed on the card. Or maybe he thought the blank card would heighten her interest and surprise.

He knew her so well.

Mary loved to be surprised.

"There doesn't seem to be much of a pattern to the murders," Pearl said. They were driving along in the unmarked. She was behind the wheel, with Fedderman beside her, Quinn in the backseat.

"Other than they took place in the kitchen," Fedderman said, "and there were items around, food and such, that didn't seem to belong."

"Marcy Graham and her husband were killed in the bedroom," Pearl reminded him. She made a quick left turn in front of a delivery truck, pissing off the driver and drawing an angry blast of the horn. "Screw you," she said absently, while smoothly avoiding a pothole. Trash was still piled at the curb, waiting to be picked up, and its cloying smell wafted in through the car's vents. None of the car's occupants remarked on the odor; they were used to mornings in New York.

They were on their way to the Graham apartment to look over the crime scene again and try to find something they'd missed. That was what it had come down to, covering already explored territory, hoping for something like a matchbook with a message written inside it, a forgotten receipt for the murder weapon, a hidden safe-deposit box key, like in TV or the movies. Why *couldn't* it happen in the play called *Real Life*?

"There's a pattern," Quinn said, "just not clear yet, even at the edges. It'll continue to emerge, no matter how hard our Night Prowler tries to disguise it."

"I like it you're so sure of yourself," Fedderman said.

"These scuzzballs are all slaves to compulsion, Feds. It's why they have to kill in the first place."

"He's been a pretty successful slave up to this point," Pearl said.

"The kitchens," Quinn said. "If you think of the apartments as sets in a play, the murders began in the kitchens, even if the Grahams were actually killed in their bedroom. Something drew them from their bed, maybe a sound in the kitchen, where the murder weapon came from, where the extra gourmet cheese was placed in the refrigerator. The killer was probably hiding in their closet, but he'd stopped off first in the kitchen."

"Some weird play," Fedderman said. "Like something by that Mammal guy."

"Mamet," Quinn said. He and May had gone often to live theater. It was their singlemost expensive indulgence. Quinn hadn't been lately.

"Isn't the mamet some kind of little animal?"

"No."

"Did you ever get around to seeing *The Lion King*?"

"No."

"You think something formative happened to our guy in a kitchen and he never let it go?" Pearl asked.

"Sounds right," Fedderman said before Quinn could answer. "Assholes like this, they can go on a killing spree if their eggs are runny. I don't see how that helps us much. The trouble is, our killer's crazy and we haven't got inside his mind yet. Maybe there's no pattern to the killings because he's a certifiable fruitcake without any pattern to his thinking."

"Three things," Quinn said from the back of the car. "The kitchens, the food items that were out of place, and the fact that the victims were reasonably attractive married couples living in apartments in Manhattan. That's the pattern."

"Except that I got a kitchen," Fedderman said. "And my wife and I used to live in an apartment in Manhattan. And if you looked in our refrigerator, you'd find things so out of place you'd be afraid to eat them."

"He's got a point," Pearl said, "even though he left out reasonably attractive."

"He usually does have a point," Quinn told her. "That's how he'll keep us honest."

Quinn looked out the dirt-streaked car window at the Grahams' apartment building.

"We're here."

Wherever here *is.*

24

Hiram, Missouri, 1989.

A breeze blew in low off the river, carrying rain that settled as a warm mist. Painting outside became impossible; the colors diluted and ran as soon as they were applied. So Tom Wilde postponed the exterior job, which was his only work at the time, and sent Luther home for the day. He dropped him off in front of the Sand house about two o'clock in the white van with the ladder racks on top, telling him they needed to get an early start tomorrow and they'd have a long day, so Luther should make sure he got a good night's sleep.

Luther waved to Wilde and watched the van sway around the corner, its wipers sweeping the wide windshield. He clomped up onto the wood porch to get out of the mist and started to ring the doorbell.

Then he remembered—he lived here. This was his home. At least for a while.

He drew back his hand from the doorbell button and tried

the door. It was unlocked. He pushed it open and went inside.

Will I always feel like a trespasser?

At first he thought the house was completely quiet, maybe unoccupied; then he heard a faint sound.

Someone was humming.

He made his way in the direction of the sound, to the kitchen, and there was Cara humming a song he didn't recognize while she rolled dough for a pie. She was perspiring slightly, so her face glowed, and each time she leaned forward and ran the wooden rolling pin over the dough, her large breasts swayed beneath the thin material of her blouse.

She stopped flattening the pale ellipse of dough, wiped the back of her wrist across her moist forehead, then picked up a red sifter that looked like a can with a crank and sprinkled more flour on the dough. As she put down the sifter, she saw Luther and stopped humming.

"You been watching me, Luther?" She was half smiling, not seeming to mind if he'd been quietly observing her. She smelled like sweat and peaches.

"Just for a few seconds, ma'am. I liked watching. You seem to enjoy your work. Cooking, I mean."

Her smile widened. "Baking, you mean."

"Well, yeah, sure." He shifted uncomfortably. It wasn't like him to be ill at ease in the presence of a woman, after his experiences in Kansas City. But he knew what those women wanted, how to act for them and toward them. This was . . . well, a lady. There were miles of distance between a woman and a lady.

"C'mon over," she said. "Sit and talk with me awhile, Luther."

He sidled over to the table, pulled out one of the wooden chairs, and sat, a self-conscious teenage boy not quite sure where to situate his arms and legs.

"This is gonna be another peach pie," she said. "Special for you."

Luther didn't know what to say. He mumbled his thanks.

"How you and Mr. Wilde getting along?" Cara asked, leaning into her rolling again.

"I like him fine," Luther said, trying not to look at her breasts. He found himself wondering about the Sands' sex life. It couldn't be much, the way they were so bitter to each other just beneath almost everything they said. And that was when Milford wasn't flat out ignoring his wife. Luther knew Milford could turn mean with Cara; he'd overheard some of their bedroom spats. Once, he even heard a slapping sound. Maybe Milford had hit her. Then again, maybe that was what she wanted. Luther recalled a woman with a rich husband back in—

"Luther? You still with me, boy?"

He grinned. "Still here, ma'am."

"You call me Cara, you hear?"

"I hear, Cara."

He was trying to find a word describing how he felt with Cara here in the kitchen. *Peaceful* was the best he could do. He felt at peace. There hadn't been much of that in his life. Was this how it was to have a mother?

He doubted it. There was something different here.

Cara placed the rolled-out dough in a pie plate, shaped and patted it down, and cut away the excess. Then, very adroitly, she began using her fingers to puff up the crust in little scallops around the plate's edge.

The motion brought her face close to Luther's. He could feel the heat of her breath and smell her perspiration. She turned her face toward him, smiling, her eyes only a few inches from his, her lips only a few inches. . . .

Then he found himself kissing her.

Thought hadn't been involved; there hadn't been time to think *not* to do it.

But now he thought about what he was doing. About what a total idiot he was. What a risk he was taking. Fear cut through him.

She'll tell Milford. What will Milford do?

Worst of all, he liked Cara. A lot. And now look what he was doing!

Oh, God!

When he was about to pull away, confused and upset with himself, she leaned forward and began kissing him back, hard, using her tongue. Their lips still locked, she came around the corner of the table to bend at the waist so she could reach him better where he was seated in the chair. Luther felt the chair lean sideways, then topple as its legs slid on the tiles, and he and Mrs. Sand—Cara—were suddenly on the kitchen floor, their bodies pressed close together.

All of a sudden, he was the other Luther, from the cruel streets of Kansas City. The Luther without hopes or dreams or illusions. He knew women in ways far beyond his years. He knew what Cara wanted, how to treat her.

She's playing in my backyard.

One of his hands snaked inside her blouse, the other began working her denim slacks down over her hips and buttocks. She moaned and fumbled to unfasten his belt buckle.

Luther kissed her again, then drew his head back, slowing this down. Her breath was hissing in the quiet kitchen and she was staring up at him, her breasts trembling as they rose and fell.

A beat. A pause. They could change their minds here. Change the future. They both knew it. Embarrassed grins, hurried buttoning and zipping, and it could be as if this never happened.

They helped each other undress. Neither wanted to take the time to go into one of the bedrooms. There was a heavy woven throw rug on the floor in front of the sink. Luther folded it in quarters and slid it beneath Cara's raised hips before using his mouth on her, then mounting and entering her.

If she was surprised by Luther's experience and lack of

inhibition, she didn't show it. Yet there was a glint of wonder and confirmation in her eyes. He knew now that her sex with Milford had been lacking, and that she was in new territory, and he, Luther, was her expert guide. But she was the expert on what sex could mean, and where it could carry them. They had so much to teach each other.

He showed her what he knew and how well he knew it.

And he was eager to learn from her.

For Luther, this wasn't simply sex. It was love.

Luther began going home every day for lunch. Hiram wasn't that big a town, so wherever the painting jobs were, usually it wasn't that far to walk. If Tom Wilde suspected anything, he never let on.

Cara would take Luther into the bedroom now, and Luther knew he was enjoying her where Milford lay with her. Being in the master bedroom seemed to make it better for Cara. She'd clamp her legs tight around Luther and bite his bare shoulder, or grab a handful of his sweat-damp hair and urge him on.

Cara never talked about her life with Milford, never complained. It seemed enough to her that she had Luther.

One afternoon after sex, when Luther lay with his head on Milford's pillow and looked across white linen at Cara, he said, "I hear some gossip now and again about Tom Wilde."

She laughed. "Is all of that still floating around? Been a lotta years ago." She turned onto her side, dug an elbow into the pillow, and propped her head sideways on one hand. "What is it you heard, Luther?"

"That Tom used to teach at the high school and got himself in trouble with some of the boys there."

"Yep," Cara said. "Same old rumor. And that's all it is, Luther. You think Milford and I would let you go to work for a child molester?"

"Not you," Luther said.

"*Luther!* Milford's not *that* kinda man!"

"How do you know the rumors about Tom aren't true?"

"No witnesses ever came forth, Luther. It was just stories floated around by people that wanted Tom Wilde to lose his job. The father of some boy was said to have complained to the board of education, but if that's so, whatever he said stayed a secret. And none of the boys came forward to point an accusing finger."

"So what happened?"

"What happened is Tom Wilde lost his job. This is a small town, Luther, and it don't take chances with child molesters teaching school, even if they're just *suspected* child molesters." She leaned over and kissed him lightly on the lips. "Luther, you don't worry any about Tom Wilde in that regard. I know some other stories about him, concerning some of the so-called ladies of the town, and I tend more to believe those rumors."

So did Luther, whatever the rumors. He'd been with child molesters, with Norbert Black and with others for pay. Wilde wasn't like any of them. Of course, Luther also knew people could have many different sides.

He decided not to worry about Tom Wilde, but if anything made him suspicious or uneasy, he'd tell Cara.

He had a friend now, as well as a lover.

Tom Wilde knew Luther must have heard the rumors about him, but Luther never mentioned them. But then he wouldn't. It was obvious, once you got to know Luther, that he was more worldly than he first appeared. Wilde had looked into his background and even suspected he'd worked as a male prostitute in Kansas City.

Maybe it was *because* of those days and nights on the street that Luther didn't particularly care what was in Wilde's past. Wilde figured Luther was a good-size boy and strong, and with his teenager's assumption of immortality, he wouldn't be afraid of him whatever he'd heard.

Anyway, their arrangement wasn't forever. At the end of summer Luther would go to school and paint only part-time, if at all.

The summer was going very well. Wilde was getting plenty of jobs. Luther was a hard worker and a deft and steady painter on his way to becoming a craftsman. And he was a remarkably apt pupil. He'd learned quickly whatever Wilde taught him, even to the point where Wilde trusted him with jobs that required genuine artistry. Luther had talent. Wilde could spot it, because he used to teach art, and now and then one of his students displayed a gift Wilde tried to reach, tried to develop. Usually it did no good. The gifted student ignored or abused the gift and lurched ahead into a life of mundane matters and average, at best, accomplishments. It used to make Wilde sick to watch it happen. The waste. The terrible waste! A town like Hiram could suffocate an artist, and for Wilde, it was agonizing to watch art die.

Maybe that closeness and caring for some of his more talented students was what started the rumors so long ago.

Or maybe it was something else.

Wilde had become aware of the rumors early. At first they angered him. Then amused him. Because he knew they were untrue. He was sure that, being unfounded, they'd soon wither on the vine of gossip and drop off.

He'd been wrong about that. The rumors had grown and grown. The rumors had changed his life, and taken on a life of their own that persisted to this day.

The rumors were also wrong.

It wasn't boys that interested Wilde, it was girls. One girl. Which made it more difficult to fight the rumors and constant innuendo.

Wilde remembered how it had been, the sideways glances,

the lump in his stomach, the sleepless nights. The ponderous weight of it all had ground him down as if he were being milled to pulp and powder.

Finally the small-town gossip and viciousness had cost Wilde his teaching job.

He was sorry about the job, but not the girl.

When it came to the girl, he'd do it all over again.

25

New York, 2004.

Dr. Rita Maxwell sat in her leather-upholstered swivel chair and studied the open file on her desk. Her office was almost soundproof; the raucous noises of traffic ten stories below on Park Avenue barely penetrated the thick walls and were almost completely absorbed by the heavy drapes and plush carpeting.

The office was furnished in earth tones that were almost a monotone brown, but with green accents, like the throw pillows on the sofa, a leaded glass lampshade, a Chinese vase, the green desk pad, a vine cascading from its planter on a top corner of a bookcase. It all had an ordered, restful effect that seemed very professional, which was important to Dr. Maxwell. Psychoanalysis was most effective in surroundings that lent confidence.

Rita had been in her Park Avenue office for six years now, after practicing for ten years in Brooklyn. She'd gained a solid reputation and, she was sure, helped a good many of her patients. Her fee had risen to $300 per hour—an "hour" being forty-five minutes actual office time. Her patients were happy to pay it, because almost anyone in Manhattan who wanted to undergo analysis, if they were careful about whom they chose as their analyst and asked for references, would hear of Dr. Rita Maxwell. Her business depended on word-of-mouth advertising, and she received plenty of it and knew why. She got results.

Was she arrogant? She didn't think so. Not in the usual meaning of the word, anyway. She was tall, handsome rather than cute, with close-cropped blond hair and knowing green eyes. At forty-five, she was a jogger and sometimes marathon runner. She was fit and strong and appeared healthy in every way. Her broad-shouldered, almost masculine figure was made for well-cut clothes. Successful, rich enough, and as beautiful as she wanted to be, she thought she had a right to be satisfied with her personal life, but only that—satisfied.

Professional arrogance—that was something else. That kind of arrogance she possessed and even nurtured. And it worked to her advantage. Whatever the conflicts of her patients, they soon sensed in her a confidence that she could identify their problems and solve them. Something about her suggested that a violent sea might break over her calmness and reason, and as rocks they would remain.

Rita seldom disappointed.

And she wouldn't disappoint this patient, she thought, as she scanned the David Blank file on her desk.

Not that David Blank was his real name.

The questions were, who was he, really? And why was he using a false identity?

The questionnaire Blank had filled out when he arrived was either vague or unverifiable. His address was patently false, and he always paid her receptionist, Hannah, with a cashier's check. Rita never called his bluff on these falsifications. Blank's lack of confidentiality, of trust, intrigued her. What was its genesis?

Certainly, there were good reasons for many of her patients to use false names, or ascribe embarrassing problems to "friends." But that didn't seem to be the case with Blank. In fact, Rita was sure she hadn't yet touched on the reason he'd become one of her patients.

She'd made some assessments. He was fastidious, perhaps compulsive, and obviously quite secretive. He'd refused even to give his age, and had one of those faces that made it difficult to determine how old he was. Anywhere between thirty and fifty, with a shock of what was supposed to be prematurely gray hair but was unmistakably a wig. He was obviously well educated—or at least well read—and had the bearing of a professional.

And he was smart; she was sure of that.

But if he thought he was smarter than Rita Maxwell, especially playing at her game, he was doomed to disappointment. Already she was sure she could get to his core conflict, to the real reason why he came to see her, that he couldn't yet bear to talk about. She simply needed something more to grab hold of, to use as gentle leverage to get at the truth. There were layers and layers to David Blank, she was sure. And it would be her challenge to discover what lay beneath them.

Hannah was at lunch, so it was Rita who buzzed Blank up ten minutes later, precisely on time, as usual, for his appointment.

He was wearing a light tan sport jacket today, dark brown slacks, and a pale blue shirt open at the collar. There was a diamond ring that might be expensive on the middle finger of his left hand. His watch was gold, but looked antique and was of a make unfamiliar to Rita. There was no way for her to hazard an intelligent guess at David Blank's wealth, but he must be comfortably fixed or he couldn't afford her.

He gave her his warm smile and nodded. "How are you, Dr. Maxwell?"

"Fine, David. Shall we begin?"

His smile became a wide grin. "The clock is running, Doctor."

He settled into the leather recliner while she came out from around her desk and took her usual place in a nearby wing chair. Though there was a comfortable sofa in the office, Blank declined to use it, saying he didn't feel like being a stereotypical patient lying down alongside his shrink. So he used the reclining lounge chair, setting it back halfway so he was half sitting, half lying.

"Where were we," he asked, "when we were so rudely interrupted by the rush of time?"

"Montana," Rita said. She switched on her tape recorder. She taped all her sessions, with her patients' knowledge and approval. It was easier and more beneficial than taking notes.

She recited all the pertinent information, along with time and date, to catalog the tape, then began the session.

"Ah, Montana . . . ," Blank said.

Rita waited, but he didn't elaborate. "At the end of our last session," she reminded him, "you were twelve and had been sexually molested by the wife of the rancher who hired you to learn to herd cattle."

"The state agency got me away from there," Blank said, "only to place me a month later in a foster home where my guardians had the idea that any infraction of their rules meant severe punishment."

"What kind of punishment?" Rita asked dutifully. She had a notepad and pen and pretended to take notes to supplement the tapes. The note taking seemed to comfort her patients. Actually, it gave her something to do and allowed for a certain detachment that kept her patients talking.

"They denied us solid food."

"Us?"

"There were three other foster children besides myself."

"Where was this, David? You didn't mention."

"A farm in Illinois."

"What did they grow there?"

"Corn, soybeans, alfalfa."

Rita made some meaningless squiggles on her notepad.

"One time, just for skipping school, I was denied solid food for three days." Blank sounded justifiably outraged.

"Didn't you have a chance to complain to your caseworker?"

"Hah! My so-called caseworker was more interested in getting into my pants than anything else."

Ho, boy! Rita thought. And began taking her mock notes faster, feigning interest.

"Can you tell me why some women are like that?" Blank asked. "I mean, I was only thirteen at the time."

"Were you big for your age, David?"

"Jesus, Doctor!"

Rita blushed. He'd managed to embarrass her, which didn't happen often. "You know *that* wasn't what I meant, David."

"Do you know the answer to my question," he persisted, "about why some women are interested in young boys?"

"There are different reasons. Why don't you tell me about this caseworker, and maybe I can shine some light on her particular motivation. She might be a very important person in your life. You didn't mention her name."

"No, I didn't. And I wouldn't describe her as having motivation. It was more like a compulsion."

"True. You're right. It was probably a compulsion." *If it ever happened.* She locked gazes with him. "Are you interested in compulsive behavior, David?"

"Sure. You might say that's one reason I'm here."

"So tell me the other reasons."

"Let me tell you what it's like to be twelve years old and go three days living on nothing but water."

"I thought you wanted to talk about the amorous caseworker."

"This was a year before that. You can swell your stomach with water, but it isn't like food."

"I wouldn't think so."

"Oh, sure."

"Sure what?"

"The amorous caseworker."

For a few seconds he was in control of the session, and he handed control back to me.

Which means he's really in charge.

He did tell her about his relationship with the caseworker. About trysts in the barn, in the woman's car, in the farmhouse when there was no one else home. The caseworker had been interested in sadomasochism and bestiality, and forced all sorts of aberrant behavior on the young David Blank. "If it was abnormal sex, she was into it," he said bitterly.

"I don't know if there is such a thing as abnormal sex," Rita said. "There's a wide spectrum of human behavior."

He sat up slightly and gave her a sharp look. "I guess you're right, but this kind of stuff was really over the edge."

He continued telling her in minute detail about what he and the caseworker had done all those years ago in the quiet farmhouse or in the hot, buzzing barn that smelled of hay and manure. He had a great imagination.

Rita let him talk, barely listening. The recorder would pick it all up and preserve it for later contemplation. It was lies, anyway, she was sure. Camouflage for . . . something. And eventually she'd discover what.

He stayed on the subject for the rest of his appointment, playing his game with her, rambling on at $300 per hour.

Making me earn my money.

She smiled slightly. He couldn't verbally dance and dart and dodge forever. She was patient and wily. She would beat him at this nimble game of deception.

But one thing bothered her a great deal: she was sure he

knew *she* knew he was lying, and he didn't seem to care. That made it more difficult for her to figure out his reasons for coming into analysis. If he were simply going through a charade that even he knew was too obvious, why would he waste his time and hers?

Rita did know that David Blank, whoever he was, wasn't the sort to waste time or anything else.

Between appointments, or in the early-morning hours when she couldn't sleep, she found herself wondering about her mysterious patient, worrying the puzzle and getting nowhere. Sometimes it seemed he was the analyst and she the patient, though the reasons for this were just beyond her comprehension.

But Rita's confidence was unwavering.

Sooner or later she'd meet the real David Blank.

And know his reason for coming to her.

Mary Navarre and Donald Baines had just seen *Hail to the Chef* on Broadway and then had a late-night snack at a diner on West Forty-fourth Street. They were still in a good mood from the hit musical comedy when Donald keyed the apartment door, reached in, and flipped the light switch. Then he stood aside to let Mary enter first.

It was still one of her great pleasures to enter the recently decorated apartment, to see the expensive neutral leather furniture, the art on the walls, the retro slat-blinds window treatments. She would pause inside the door and let her glance take it all in before continuing her entrance.

But this time her gaze didn't stray but went directly to the white box on the sofa cushion. Not only didn't she know what it was, she was sure it hadn't been there when they left for the theater.

Donald must have somehow arranged for this; it was the only explanation.

She moved toward the large, rectangular box. Its lid was lifted on one corner and a fold of white tissue paper protruded as if testing the air.

"What the hell is that?" she heard Donald say behind her.

An act? It wasn't her birthday or their anniversary. She couldn't think of any reason she should receive a gift from her husband except for pure impulsiveness, which wasn't entirely beyond Donald.

"One way to find out," Mary said, and lifted the lid off the box.

Inside was more white tissue paper. She unfolded it and recognized the crimson silk kimono she'd admired two days ago in Bloomingdale's.

But Donald hadn't been with her. Had she mentioned the kimono?

"It's beautiful," she said, pulling the kimono from the box and holding it up so they could both admire it. "But how did you know?"

"Know what?"

"That I wanted it and decided it was too frivolous for the money."

"Why would I know?"

"Because you ordered it from Bloomingdale's."

He came over to stand next to her and reached out and touched the smooth material. "Much as I'm tempted to take credit, Mary, this isn't a gift from me."

She looked up at him. He seemed to be telling the truth. And why would he deny buying the kimono now that she'd accepted it?

"It must be from a secret admirer," he said. He didn't seem to be kidding.

"An admirer with a key?"

"Obviously. Or maybe he bribed the super to let him in." Spurred to action by that possibility, he went to the phone.

Mary laid the kimono over the box and stared at it, listening to Donald in the background as he questioned the super.

When he came back, he said, "Nobody was let into our apartment."

"If the super was bribed," Mary said, "maybe he's lying."

"He didn't sound like he was lying," Donald said. He looked hard at Mary, his brow furrowed so his eyes were squinted. "You sure you didn't order this and forget about it?"

"I wouldn't forget, Donald. Besides, that would explain the kimono, but not how it got inside the apartment." *Maybe you ordered it and forgot, like with the bouquet.* Everyone had their little mental glitches; maybe this was one of Donald's— mystery gifts. Maybe he'd instructed the super to admit the deliveryman and had only pretended to phone downstairs. Maybe the flowers had been from him, too. Roses, a silk kimono . . . There could be worse faults in a husband. "Even if you didn't give this to me," she said, "thanks."

"Don't thank me for what I didn't do." He seemed genuinely irritated. "The kimono isn't from me any more than the roses you found in here before we moved in."

"Do you think we should change the locks?"

"We should consider it." *While I bide my time and see if more mysterious gifts turn up after your shopping expeditions.* He thought he'd known everything about Mary, though they'd only been together a little over a year. Maybe he was learning something new. Maybe she was having a secret affair.

He immediately rejected the idea. After all, she'd told him about the roses.

If she had bought the kimono, or if she was some kind of kleptomaniac, sick, that could be dealt with medically.

But he had to know.

What if he hired a private detective to follow her and find

out if she behaved in any way peculiar during her shopping? It was something to consider.

If Mary was ill, he wanted to help her. And if there was some other reason for the unexplained gifts—first the flowers, now the kimono—he sure as hell wanted to know what it was.

Either way, he was afraid of what he might learn.

Renz sat on the sagging sofa, opposite Quinn in Quinn's apartment, glancing about while gnawing his lower lip.

"You've certainly done wonders with the place," he said. "With each visit I see improvement. Is that a new bent lampshade? Was that wall always a mossy green? And is it my imagination or are the roaches smaller?"

"You said you had something important to discuss," Quinn said, marveling that this was his friend and protector in the NYPD and not his enemy. What kind of dung had he gotten himself into?

"Is this what they call shabby cheap?" Renz asked, refusing to let go of his own cleverness. Then he looked sheepish, wilting beneath Quinn's baleful stare. "Oh, all right. It's this." He held up the folded newspaper he'd brought with him.

"That the *Times*?"

"The *Voice*."

"You've always struck me as a typical subscriber."

Renz shrugged. "The poetry in my soul." He dropped the paper on the glass-ringed coffee table. "What's interesting in this edition is another installment of the saga of Anna Caruso."

"The papers like her story," Quinn said. "I can understand that."

"Then you should also understand this. The more they like her story, the less they like yours. In this particular piece you are the villain. There's an old photo of you coming out of the precinct house just after your hearing. You look angry, and about to unzip your pants."

Quinn knew the shot. The photographer had caught him coming down the concrete steps and swinging his arms. His right hand, which was about two feet away from his body when the photo was taken, appeared in only two dimensions to be adjusting his fly.

For a few seconds he felt again the injustice of his situation, the old futility and rage. *I've become the victim of my own good intentions—can't the fools see that?* He'd never been naive enough to think something would inevitably right the wrong done to him, but he hadn't counted on self-pity enveloping and smothering him.

He became aware of Renz smiling at the expression on his face.

"I thought that was your end of the bargain," Quinn said. "To get me out from under the rape charge that was never filed."

"And so can't be disproved," Renz pointed out.

And Quinn knew the accusation wouldn't have been disproved if charges had been filed, even though he was innocent. Every cop knows truth is usually one of the early victims in the legal process. For a while he'd forgotten that, and it had cost him. He was still paying and, as Renz knew, was almost tapped out and dealing from desperation.

What Quinn didn't know was that Renz thought he was guilty. That was why he'd come to him. To catch a sicko like the Night Prowler, you had to think like him, get into his mind, and *be* him. And who better to do that than his spiritual brother?

Set a sicko to catch a sicko.

"I've been watching the media on this one," Renz said. "If I might brag a bit, I'm something of an expert when it comes to media in this town."

"I give you that," Quinn told him.

"What I see happening, even though it's still in the beginning stages, is you gradually morphing from heroic and beleaguered ex-cop, getting his second chance, to lecherous bully with a badge, getting a few more free whacks at the public. And all at the cost of a sweet young thing who withers at the thought of you, and is, to boot, very photogenic."

"She's withering at the thought of somebody else."

"Don't we both know it?" Renz shook his head sadly. "And don't we both know it doesn't make any difference unless you step it up and catch this loony who's offing happy couples in their prime?"

"That's why you came here? To light a fire under my ass?"

"Something like. Tell me why I shouldn't."

Quinn gave him a progress report. Though even to him it didn't sound much like progress.

"You've got shit," Renz said.

"We've got pieces—"

"Pieces of—"

"All right, all right!" Quinn waved his fist in a gesture that was threatening enough that Renz quieted down and settled back on the sofa.

"We've got pieces," Quinn continued, "that haven't yet been put together. The beginnings of a pattern. Of a picture. It's how these cases always shape up in the beginning. You're the one who knows media, Renz. I'm the one who knows police work."

Renz sighed. Made a big show of it, in fact. He picked up his *Voice* and stood up from the sofa, stretching and working one shoulder, moving his arm in a slow circle as if he were a big-league pitcher worrying about his rotator cuff.

"I'm gonna leave you with the thought that you don't have much time," he said. "Once your image is fucked, so are you. And what's happened is, your image's asshole is all greased and ready." He dropped the folded paper back on the table. "You don't believe me, read about it in the *Voice*. It'll tear your heart out. It'll make you wanna send money and flowers to little Anna Caruso."

"I already want to," Quinn said to Renz's back as he walked out the door.

He seemed not to have heard.

Or to have noticed the tears in Quinn's eyes.

26

Hiram, Missouri, 1989.

Luther had spent the last month learning more and more about what was becoming his trade, and what Tom Wilde assured him could be raised to approximate, if not *become,* art. Luther became an expert at stenciling, layering, tinting, and shading, using tone and texture and creating illusion.

His affair with Cara continued. Milford spent his evenings with his ledger books, working overtime in his office at the mine. Luther spent his evenings with Cara. She became more easily aroused and erotic under Luther's touch, and he continued to learn from her. He thought that if she loved him only a fraction of how much he loved her, he'd be happy. She couldn't love him more, because she was everything to him.

Nothing was out of bounds to the lovers. No part of either of them was secret to the other.

Which was why, when Milford unexpectedly came home from work early one evening, he walked into his bedroom and found Cara and Luther blissfully locked in mutual oral pleasure.

On Milford's side of the bed.

He stood stunned, unable to believe what he was seeing. He had to look more closely to be sure that, yes, the woman was actually Cara. Doing . . . what she chose not to do with Milford.

So engrossed were the lovers in each other that they had no idea he was there. That somehow added to Milford's astonishment and indignation—it was as if he didn't exist to them. Worst of all was his feeling that he was the interloper, the one who didn't belong here.

Here, my home, my bed, my woman . . . God, God, God . . .

Slowly he unclenched his fists, letting an inner steadiness, a solidity, focus his anger even if he couldn't control it. He went to the closet and opened its door, then began rooting around behind the hanging clothes.

He'd made enough noise to distract Luther and Cara from each other.

"Milford?" Cara's voice was choked.

Well, no wonder! Milford felt the rage in the core of him become white-hot.

"Milford!" she said again behind him, now with a curious hoarseness he'd never heard before, as if she were some other woman. "What are you doing?"

His hand closed on warm walnut. "Looking for my shotgun." How calm and matter-of-fact was *his* voice.

"Milford—Mr. Sand—wait a minute!" Luther now, talking to his back. "Let me explain how this happened. Maybe you'll understand. Honest, I'm not trying to make excuses, but this was something Cara and I didn't do on purpose. It just happened! It was nobody's fault!"

Young, so young. Milford smiled grimly. *Not going to get any older.*

He reached up on the closet shelf and found his box of shells. Then he turned and faced his wife and her lover as he broke down the double-barreled twelve-gauge and began loading it.

"No, no, Milford!" Cara retreated to the headboard and curled in the fetal position against it, as if shielding herself from an approaching tornado. Luther, the other nude figure in the disgusting scene, stood up from the bed and held out a palm in a signal for Milford to halt what he was doing.

"Give this some thought, Milford. Don't do this, please!"

He seemed afraid now, but not in the slightest embarrassed. Milford thought that was odd, thinking how devastated he'd feel in Luther's place. *How wrong.*

Well, Milford had read about Luther's background. What had the filthy animal learned during his time on the streets?

And taught Cara!

Milford finished slipping the shells into their chambers and deftly locked the shotgun closed. It made a cold metallic clucking sound—so efficient, a hard, impersonal substance forged precisely to its purpose, not like flesh.

He could smell their sex now, the heat and wetness of it. It made him more sure of what he was about to do. He thumbed off the safety.

"You can't do this, Milford!" Luther said. He was hurriedly getting dressed, already had his pants half on and was buttoning his shirt.

"Scum," Milford said calmly. "Street scum that doesn't deserve to breathe."

Cara remained curled on the bed, wrapping her bare arms about her head and whimpering.

Luther was imploring but not giving ground, as if he had a few bargaining chips left to play and might yet be persuasive. "Think about this, Milford! I mean, like, *really* think about it!"

"I am thinking about it. Are you?"

"Yes. And I'm sorry! I apologize for this. And I really

mean it! Will you give me a chance to leave? Will you promise not to hurt Cara? That's all I'm asking!"

"No and no." Milford raised the shotgun to his shoulder and sighted down its long twin barrels to the end of everything.

Luther was hobbling toward the door now, carrying his shoes in one hand and fumbling to button his jeans with the other.

"I've been a fool!" Milford screamed at him. "And you betrayed me! *You betrayed me! Scum! Street scum!*"

Milford squeezed the trigger for the left barrel. The right barrel was for Cara. The reload was going to be for him.

The hammer clicked on the shell, but the gun didn't fire.

Luther continued his flight out the door, not looking back, an absurd figure dressing and hopping and ducking simultaneously. Astonished, Milford squeezed the trigger for the right barrel.

Nothing. Another misfire.

The shells must have been on the closet shelf too long. They were too old, Milford figured.

Milford screamed and hurled the shotgun at the door Luther had slammed shut behind him.

He heard Milford's scream and what sounded like the heavy shotgun clatter off the door and drop to the floor. But Luther didn't slow down. He kept running through the house, down the stairs and toward the front door, bumping into things, brushing furniture aside. Something fell and broke behind him. Like his life.

Then he was outside, across the wood porch and down the steps and into the warm night.

Away!

Life on the streets had taught Luther some hard lessons,

and when he came across the shotgun several weeks ago, he made sure it was unloaded, then left it where he'd found it in the back of the closet. The half-dozen shells in the box on the closet shelf he didn't leave exactly as he had found them. He removed all their pellets and powder, then replaced them in their box and made sure nothing looked as if it had been disturbed.

It was a precaution that saved his life.

But now what was he going to do? It was just past dusk, and the darkening, tree-lined street was deserted and quiet, but for the ongoing scream of crickets. A car's headlights passed a block down at the intersection, but that was the only movement. Luther was sure no one had seen him leave the house, or heard the disturbance inside.

His heart was hammering and he was perspiring. Sweat stung his eyes, making it difficult to see. He dabbed at his eyes with his shirtsleeve, then wiped the back of his hand across his mouth, tasting Cara. *Cara!*

Should he go back and do what he could to protect her?

No, that might only make things worse. After dealing with the shotgun, Luther had searched the rest of the house to make sure there were no more guns. Milford wasn't armed and wouldn't shoot her. And whatever else he might do, with a knife or his bare hands . . . well, it would already have been done.

A dog began barking far away, as if to remind Luther of a wider world beyond the dark street. He noticed the smell of recently mowed grass.

The best thing he could do was get farther away from the house and neighborhood and stay away. He'd phone later, though, and make sure Cara was all right. He wouldn't give up on her. He wouldn't!

But what would he do now?

Where would he go?

What would happen to him?

It wasn't the first time in his young life he'd asked himself those same questions he couldn't answer.

Each time, the terror and loneliness were worse.

What will happen to me?

Luther awoke, slumped low on the seat of Tom Wilde's rusty pickup truck, and knuckled sleep from his eyes. The morning light flooding through the cracked windshield was blinding.

He squinted at his watch. Past ten o'clock. Unable to think of where else to go last night, he'd finally walked to Wilde's closed painting and decorating company and found a place to sleep in the cab of the old truck parked on the back corner of the lot. In the morning he'd go to work and try to figure out what he might do on a more long-term basis. As long as he had a job, he'd have some money and some options—if the state didn't send a caseworker to find him.

He thought there was a good chance Milford wouldn't bother notifying the state for a while. He'd probably prefer that Luther find his way to another part of the country. Then he could cook up some phony story as to why Luther had left, rather than admit his wife had slept with their foster child. That admission would stop the money they were receiving from the agency in exchange for their temporary care of kids adrift like Luther.

Luther looked at himself in the dirty rearview mirror and smoothed back his hair. His eyes were bloodshot and there was a look to them he hadn't seen since Kansas City. Eyes of the lost and desperate.

The afraid.

He tucked his hair back behind his ears, then opened the rusty old door and climbed down out of the truck. Tom Wilde had driven the van home yesterday, but now it was parked at the curb; Wilde would be inside the building, probably wondering where his apprentice Luther was this fine, bright morning.

There was a sharp pain in the small of Luther's back, and one of his legs was stiff. He'd only been able to get comfortable enough to sleep in short stretches on the hard, cracked vinyl of the pickup's seat.

He clenched his fists, put them behind his neck, and leaned back at the waist. Something popped in his spine, and his back felt better. He felt awake and strong enough to work today, to lug five-gallon buckets of paint and scamper up ladders. Or he was sure he'd be able to work as soon as he limbered up.

As he limped stiffly to the front of the building and its entrance, he tried not to think about what happened last night. But that was impossible.

He'd have to tell Tom Wilde, because Wilde would eventually find out about it. And before leaving for their painting job, Luther wanted to phone Cara, even if it meant he'd be talking to Milford. He wanted to make sure Cara was all right, that Milford hadn't hurt her.

If Milford *had* done something to her . . .

Luther decided not to think about that.

When he pushed open the door and stepped into the storeroom and office, there was Wilde sitting on the high stool at his workbench. He wasn't dressed for work. Instead of his paint-spattered coveralls, he was wearing faded jeans and a dark blue pullover sweater that would be way too hot in another hour. His shoulders were rounded, his head bowed as if it were too heavy for his neck to support.

"Tom?"

"Morning, Luther." But he hadn't yet looked at Luther.

When Wilde did raise his head to look, the light showed bruises on his face, and an eye that was rapidly turning dark.

"What happened?" Luther asked.

"Milford was here."

"This morning?"

"Early. He was waiting for me to show up."

"What'd he say?"

"That you were finished working here, and I didn't have any choice in the matter. He used his fists on me to make sure I understood. That was his excuse, anyway."

"What'd he have against *you*?"

"I was handy. He'd rather have been beating on you. What happened, Luther? What the hell'd you do?"

"He didn't tell you?"

"No. He was too busy pounding on me."

Luther decided to let Milford keep his embarrassing secret. And there was no reason to spread the story that Cara had slept with Luther. That would be the worst thing for Cara. So if Milford wanted to protect his reputation and wound up protecting Cara's, too, that was okay with Luther.

"We had an argument, was all. He lost his temper. Who'd have thought a worm like Milford would have a temper like that? I called him some things, said some stuff I shouldn't have."

"You must have," Wilde said. "I can tell you there won't be any making up. Not with a man like Milford. I warned you he's more dangerous than he seems." He lowered his eyes again, staring at the floor, then looked up and met Luther's gaze. "It's not just that Milford's capable of hurting people real bad; he's also got a lot of weight in this town. The folks that know him are scared to cross him, and he can make my work and my life impossible if I side with you. I've gotta do what he says, Luther. I have to let you go. I don't want to, but I have to."

"I understand," Luther said. "You been good to me, Tom, and I don't wanna cause you any more harm."

"Milford was looking for you, Luther. He won't give up till he finds you. Where'd you spend the night?"

"Here. In the cab of the pickup."

"Jesus! You were here when Milford was!"

"I guess. I musta slept through it."

"Lucky for you." Wilde dug in his jeans pocket and came up with a wad of bills. "Here's what I owe you, plus a little extra. It's all I can do for you, Luther."

Luther accepted the money and thanked Wilde.

"Where you going now?" Wilde asked.

"I don't know. I can't hang around here."

"No, I guess you can't. I'm sorry."

"That's okay, Tom. None of it's your fault." Luther moved toward the door. "See you."

"You be careful." Wilde got down off the stool and came over and shook Luther's hand, then gave him a powerful, awkward hug. "You watch out. Maybe take a bus outta here, but keep watching out the corner of your eye till you clear the town limits."

"I might do that, Tom. Thank you. You been good to me."

Luther eased out the door and walked away, not looking back. The sun was hot on his back, as if urging him on.

But he wasn't going to the bus station. He wasn't going to leave town, because that would mean leaving Cara.

Confident that Milford would be working in his office at the mine, Luther wandered around town for a while, trying to figure out where to go. If he got a motel room, Milford would eventually find him. And maybe not so eventually. Life on the streets in a place the size of Hiram was impossible. The homeless were made to move on or were arrested for vagrancy. The sheriff's department would pick him up the first day.

Luther had no idea where to go, what to do.

What now? What will happen to me now?

He found himself only a block from the Sands' big Victorian house. Maybe Cara would be there alone. He might talk to her, be sure she was all right before leaving. She might have some ideas.

He couldn't be absolutely sure Milford wasn't home. His pulse quickened as he approached the house and went up the steps to the wide front porch. He looked up and down the block. Unless someone was peeking out a window, he hadn't been seen. The only unnatural sound was a car alarm beeping insistently blocks away. A bee droned out from the branches of a nearby sweet-smelling honeysuckle and circled Luther as if sizing him up, getting up the nerve.

A few seconds after he'd rung the doorbell, Cara opened the door and stared out at him in surprise.

She looked fine, unmarked. Maybe Milford had taken it all out on Wilde.

"Cara . . . you okay?"

"I am." He saw now she'd been crying. Fresh tears glittered in her eyes. "Milford went to see Tom Wilde," she said.

"I know. I just came from there. Wilde had to fire me. Milford beat him up and didn't leave him any choice. I don't know what to do now, where to go. Listen, Milford isn't . . . ?"

"He's not here. After coming back from Wilde's, he went to work. To his office at the mine, where he's spent most of his time the past ten years."

She opened the door wider and touched Luther's arm lightly with the tips of two fingers, drawing him inside with only the slightest pressure, as if by some magnetic force that bound them with the slightest contact.

"I needed to come here and see you," Luther said. His breath caught in his throat.

He would have said more, but Cara suddenly clung to him and was kissing him hard on the mouth, grinding her lips against his. She moaned and began to tremble, digging her fingers into his back and turning their bodies so they moved back and were away from the lace-curtained window in the door and no one might notice them from outside.

When they separated, she gazed into his eyes as if at worship and said, "You came to the right place, Luther. Here's where you finally belong."

He believed her. Whatever name was on a mortgage or a marriage license, he was the one who belonged here, with Cara.

With Cara he was home.

27

New York, 2004.

He knew when she was due home from work, and he'd be watching out the window. Even from twelve stories up, he'd recognize her. He'd seen her leave for work, followed her and observed her eating lunch at an upscale restaurant on Central Park West. She was wearing a light gray dress and carrying a red purse and a folded black umbrella in case of rain. He'd know her by her clothes and by her long dark hair and by her walk, proud and erect, back slightly arched, head held high, her pace slightly faster than those around her. Almost as if she were on parade and could feel the gaze of someone watching her closely, focusing on only her out of the throngs of passing people.

Maybe she senses it already. Maybe she knows.

In the end, when destiny and time meet, they all seem to know, seem to understand that they knew all along and were betraying me. They understand the meaning and the justice and that they must pay. They're struck by the meanings of life

*and of death simultaneously and see that there is no differ-
ence. A blink, a missed heartbeat, a final exhalation, nothing
. . . the buzzing . . . color the length of light, nothing more.
Their final wisdom is the lesson and the gift.*

He glanced at his watch, then went to the window and
raised the blind. Pressing his forehead against the glass to
gain a better angle, he looked down. *Blue distance.*

And there she was!

He gasped at the beauty.

Mary Navarre strode along the sidewalk toward her West
End apartment, veering slightly now and then to navigate the
flow of pedestrian traffic and pass slower walkers. She was
wearing the leather strap of her red purse diagonally across
her torso as a precaution against snatch-and-run thieves, and
she was wielding her folded umbrella in her right hand almost like a weapon with each stride. She might have in-
timidated those walking toward her, were it not for her
smile.

She used the keypad to enter the lobby, then checked for
mail in the brass box with her apartment number above it.

Nothing but advertising circulars and a notice urging res-
idents to attend a neighborhood meeting to discuss increasing block security against the threat of terrorism.

Maybe Donald could attend, Mary thought as she relocked the box, then used her key on the door to the inner
lobby and elevators.

As she pressed the up button, she saw that one of the elevators was on the twelfth floor, the other on the fifth. The
arrow pointing to twelve didn't move, but the one resting on
five immediately began to descend. It stopped briefly on
three, then continued down to lobby level.

When the door slid open, a heavyset woman Mary had

seen before nodded to her and left the elevator in a swirl of navy blue material, trailing a long scarlet scarf. *Trying to look thinner.* Mary wondered why overweight people so often tried to hide their bulk beneath tentlike clothing that only accentuated their size. Then she remembered stepping on the bathroom scale this morning, and tried not to think about the five pounds she'd somehow gained during the past month. She and Donald, himself getting thicker through the middle, had been enjoying too many rich meals in too many good restaurants lately.

It has to stop. . . .

As she took possession of the elevator and pressed the button for the twelfth floor, Mary swore to herself again that she was going on a diet. Maybe try the Atkins. Her favorite meal was steak with a salad, rolls, and a baked potato, all washed down with a strong martini. She should be able to give up the potato, maybe a roll.

On twelve, the elevator slowed and stopped, then settled slightly as it found its proper level, and the door slid open.

As Mary stepped out into the hall, she was aware of the adjacent elevator's door sliding closed.

In the apartment she paused inside the door as she often did and admired the spaciousness and tasteful decor, reminding herself again that it was all hers and Donald's.

It wasn't until she went to the kitchen for a glass of water that she noticed the two shrink-wrapped steak filets on a corner of the kitchen table. They were prime cuts, thick and lightly marbled, the way she liked them.

She stared at the steaks, puzzled. *How on earth . . . ?*

When she'd gotten a glass of orange juice this morning, had she accidentally removed the steaks from the refrigerator and forgotten them?

But she doubted that. She was sure she hadn't even opened the refrigerator's meat compartment. She'd had no reason. Besides, she didn't remember the steaks even *being* in the refrigerator. Maybe Donald had bought them and planned for a romantic dinner at home this evening. Maybe he wanted to surprise her because they had something to celebrate. That would explain everything.

"Donald?" Her voice surprised her. It was higher than normal. Frightened.

"Donald!" *Better.*

She went into the living room and called his name again. Kept calling it as she roamed the apartment, peering into all the rooms.

She was alone.

As she walked back through the living room, she noticed one of the blinds was raised.

Something else that doesn't belong.

But she made no further connection between the blind and the steaks in the kitchen. After all, she might have raised the blind and forgotten. Or maybe Donald had done so.

Mary lowered the blind, restoring—in her mind, anyway— elegance and balance to the room. She only absently took note of the smudges on the windowpane, as if someone had leaned against it in order to peer out and down.

She went back to the kitchen and gingerly touched the shrink-wrapped steaks with the backs of her knuckles.

They were cool.

Can't have been here long.

Mary sat at the table and stared at the expensive cuts of meat she was sure she hadn't seen before.

Donald again? Playing his games?

She knew he'd deny it.

This is strange. This is goddamned strange.

She recalled stepping out of the elevator into the hall, the hiss of the adjacent elevator's door closing, what she'd felt, how the hair on the nape of her neck seemed to stir. She hadn't thought much about it at the time. And maybe she shouldn't think about it now.

Nothing . . . it means nothing. . . . Imagination . . . I am not afraid . . .

But maybe I should be!

Mary put the steaks in the refrigerator's meat compartment and left the apartment immediately. In the lobby she realized she'd forgotten her umbrella, but she decided not to go back for it.

She'd kill time down the street at Starbucks, sip a café mocha while she browsed through this morning's paper, and return to the apartment later, when she was sure Donald was home.

Definitely, they needed to talk.

The Night Prowler had stood in the elevator on the twelfth floor and waited for her, his fingertip on the button marked open so the door wouldn't close and the elevator would remain where it was.

When he heard the adjacent elevator arrive, he removed his finger from open and pressed lobby. The door slid closed just as the door next to it was opening. He actually caught a buzzing glimpse of her gray skirt—its hem, for only an instant—as she emerged into the hall.

As the elevator plunged, he leaned against its back wall and breathed in deeply. For an instant she'd been so near. The scent of her! Not of her perfume, but of *her!*

The scent of her flesh, of her color and movement and smile and glance!

She knows!

She might not realize it yet, but she knows. Somehow, on some dark level of consciousness in the ancient country of her mind, she has to be aware of what fate plans for us, of the inevitability and momentum of desire, to know how close we are, united, merged, cleaved unto each other, almost as one.

Original sin. Original betrayal.

Almost as one . . .

She knows!

28

God, this is awful!

Pearl had a terrible taste in her mouth and her teeth felt mossy. She'd fallen asleep on her sofa watching cable news, and the precarious state of just about everything seemed to have taken over her mind. She couldn't quite recall her dreams, but they'd left a residue of gloom.

She'd had dinner alone at home—a small steak, French fries, deli slaw, and a glass of cheap red wine. Satisfying. After doing the dishes at the sink, she'd put on some old jeans and a worn-out shirt and painted in the living room until she got tired. Then she did a hurried cleanup and decided to drink a soda while she watched television before going to bed.

A new reality TV show was on. Several men and women had been living together for weeks in isolation in a light-house on a small island. One of the women had finished last in a round-robin tennis match, and viewers were calling in to vote on which of the men should marry her.

Huh?

*   *   *

Pearl had dozed.

Now it was past one A.M., and on television a man in a blue suit with a red tie was arguing with another man in a blue suit with a red tie about abortion.

Pearl blinked and sat up. The TV was pulled out toward the middle of the room. Behind it, the wall was almost completely painted. This visual affirmation of accomplishment didn't afford the satisfaction Pearl had imagined. In her depressed state she wondered why she'd felt the surge of optimism and energy that prompted her to drag painting materials from the hall closet and begin rolling the wall.

She thought it might have had something to do with Quinn, but when she looked at it another way, that seemed preposterous. Quinn was old enough to be her father—biologically, anyway. Theirs would be the kind of romance you saw in old Humphrey Bogart–Lauren Bacall movies, where nobody noticed or cared that Bacall was young and Bogart was closing in on senility. Or like Fred and Ethel on *I Love Lucy.* What the hell was Ethel doing with a fossil like Fred?

On the other hand, Pearl thought, it might not be so bad to be the celluloid Lauren Bacall. Or, for that matter, Ethel. Instead of a woman on the verge of unemployment, and getting hooked on an aged ex-cop everyone thought was a child molester.

Almost everyone, anyway.

The talking heads on TV had switched subjects and were discussing the federal deficit. Pearl heard something about "sacrificing future generations."

The truth was, the future didn't look so good for Pearl, Quinn, and Fedderman. They were way out on a limb that some very important people were trying to saw off. Egan was a total asshole, and even Quinn didn't trust Renz. The local media were starting to get nasty, and Quinn was the only one who thought there'd been any actual progress on the case.

Pearl decided she'd call Quinn's sister tomorrow, maybe try to meet her someplace for coffee, and get a renewal of optimism. Michelle Quinn seemed constantly buoyed by whatever magic she worked on her computer to suggest her brother was innocent of the rape accusation. There was always the possibility she'd somehow fit together cyber pieces and make progress on the Night Prowler puzzle.

The Night Prowler. Pearl didn't want to think about that sicko tonight. She wouldn't be able to sleep. Quinn, innocent, was suffering like some poor schmuck in the Bible who'd been exiled to a far land to do penance, while the Night Prowler, a killer, took his sadistic satisfaction with impunity.

Pearl decided not to let herself get riled up. She noticed she hadn't put the lid on one of the paint cans. Oh, well. By now there was probably a skin of dried paint over the surface. As good as a lid. No need to bother with it tonight, tired as she was. In the morning she'd stuff the paint and other materials back in the closet and try to forget about them.

One of the TV pundits was waving his arms and trying to outshout the other guy, assuring everyone the future was secure. Pearl used the remote to switch him off in midsentence and went to bed.

Even in her life there were small satisfactions.

There she was. He was almost certain.

New York was big, but people still unexpectedly saw someone they knew.

She wasn't wearing the fuck-me oufit she'd had on when they first met. This morning she was dressed like a rich-bitch business broad and walking out of a building that looked like it cost a fortune every month to live there. By her actions he *knew* she lived there and hadn't been visiting.

Her hair was different, though. More fluffy or something.

He was across the street and tried to get nearer to confirm her identity, but the uniformed doorman, who acted like he knew her, hailed her a cab and she was gone before he could get close.

Not that it mattered. He was sure enough, and a closer look wouldn't have revealed all that much. The lash welts he'd laid on her were carefully applied where they'd be concealed by clothes. Same with the bruises, except maybe where he'd grabbed her by the ankles and dragged her back from the door.

She loves games, doesn't she? And doesn't it figure?

He knew how it worked with a bitch this wealthy; she had this swanky apartment, where she lived the straight life, and another apartment down in the Village, where she was the kind of woman who'd let herself be picked up by somebody who'd dish her what she needed. Someplace where she could really be herself.

He watched her cab disappear in traffic, then looked again at the tall, modern building behind the brightly uniformed doorman. He'd like to see this one again, but he'd never be able to get into her apartment here, with the kind of security this luxury fortress must have. And she probably wouldn't visit her Village apartment all that often. She must have a good job, a great one, and she'd need to be careful, so he'd have to get lucky and catch her outside. Or maybe he'd see her again in one of the clubs.

He was sure they could be happy together in their misery, at least for a while.

She could afford him and his bad habits. She had what he wanted. She'd want to give it to him.

He'd see to it.

\29

"You see the problem, Romulus," said Victory Wallace, who was decorating a brownstone on West Eighty-ninth Street. His clients were a wealthy oil wholesaler and his wife, who were relocating from Turkey. The old building would never have dreamed this could happen.

They were in the bathroom off the master bedroom on the second floor, a spacious cubicle of beige tile, with veined marble flooring and vanity tops. The shower stall, large enough to accommodate half a dozen, and with myriad gold-plated spray heads aimed in all directions, had doors with what looked like handwritten love letters pressed between layers of etched glass. Overhead was a gold chandelier that looked as if it belonged in a palatial grand hall in Saudi Arabia rather than in a West Side bathroom. Oddly, Victory Wallace (whose real name was Victor Padilla) had made it all seem right. But then, that was his talent.

Another of his talents was the grande-dame act he'd made part of his professional personality. Romulus was used to it and ignored it, though he did appreciate its marketability and Marlene Dietrich shadings.

"I mean, Romulus, my clients are under extreme pressure and determined to move in next week, and I *must* make everything tight and right. You *do* see the problem, dear man?"

Romulus flicked lint from the sleeve of his black Armani suit and nodded.

Victory, who affected the startled gaze of a deer reminded of hunting season, stared at him as if he'd expected more response. "My clients want something done with this awful steel support pole. They *insist.* And it's load bearing. It simply can't be moved!" He was a slender man, with a wasp waist, wearing tight designer jeans and a charcoal shirt with bloused sleeves. Sometimes he wore a red beret. Costume was part of the extreme shtick that was often necessary for clients at this stratospheric price level. "I mean, a big steel supporting pole in the middle of the bathroom! It looks like a drainpipe from upstairs, something human refuse gurgles through!" He made a gargoyle face, momentarily sticking out his tongue. "You *do* see what we're dealing with here?"

"Box it in," Romulus suggested.

Victory pressed a palm to his forehead as if stricken with a migraine. "No, no, we're way beyond the plaster-dust stage, Romulus. There's simply no going back. No time."

Romulus looked at the gold-plated faucets and the deliberately exposed gold plumbing beneath the marble basin. *Vulgar. Garish.* "You said the pole looks like plumbing. So don't try to hide it. Flaunt it. Make it gold-plated like the other plumbing. It would show well, but I warn you it would be expensive."

Victory waved his long right arm out to the side as if trying to flick away pesky cellophane that had stuck to his fingers. "We're way, *way* beyond expensive. Money isn't the issue at all. Simply *not* part of the equation. The problem is that the pole's surface isn't the sort of alloy that will accept gold plating." He grinned in a way he no doubt thought fetchingly at Romulus. "That's why I called you for advice, dear man. Everyone in the trade says that in a dilemma like this, call Romulus and call him first. He'll ride to the rescue like the cavalry in one of those Cinemascope Westerns, where all the colors look like they've dripped off Gauguin's palette. Well, you have *gotten* the call." Victory cupped a hand to his ear as if listening. "Do I hear a bugle playing charge?"

"I can paint the pipe and make it look like gold plating. But it will be every bit as expensive as real gold."

"Not an issue!" Victory reassured Romulus. "Now here's another request that would save my life and give my clients sheer bliss: can you, extra please, do the job *rush* rush?"

"Three days from now okay?"

Victory shook his head and brushed away the words as if they were bees swarming about him. "Two? Could you possibly make it two days? Put a rush charge on your bill. Twenty percent." He made a backhand motion. "Thirty."

"Two days," Romulus said.

"You are the *best*, dear man!"

"Of course I am."

Romulus left the brownstone and walked half a block to where his black Cadillac was parked. He knew precisely what to use on the steel pole: a special paint he'd concocted utilizing gold leaf and an off-brand primer. Neither ingredient was easy to find on short notice, but he was sure he had some among the wide array of supplies he maintained just for this kind of request. The paint had to be applied expertly in three or four coats, but the finished product looked amazingly like genuine gold plating.

Romulus settled back in the Cadillac's cool interior and pulled away from the curb. He smiled as he drove along narrow side streets, watching New York slide past outside the car's tinted windows, the tiny restaurants pretending to be sidewalk cafés, the cars double parked, the lovers walking close to each other, the life-worn and weary seated on concrete stoops, the lost wandering in slow confusion.

Life was good for Romulus and getting better. Everything was under control. For now, at least. There was order and satisfaction in this world of his own making.

He'd invented his job description: specialty painter. That was what it said on his gilded white business cards, along with his professional name: Romulus.

It hadn't been easy for him to gain the respect and admiration of those who at first regarded him as merely another subcontractor, a spreader of paint who was particularly neat in his work.

But they soon learned he wasn't an ordinary painter, which was why he now commanded such an exorbitant price from the top decorators who hired him, and who then passed on an even more exorbitant price to their wealthy clients. He matched colors precisely, shaded beveled edges and moldings so door panels appeared shadowed and deeper even in direct light, calculated colors so they best complemented furnishings. He altered texture, tinted to make rooms appear larger or smaller, created light and shadow where none really existed.

He was an artist. An original. That was what his clients wanted, just as they wanted original gowns and one-of-a-kind everything else.

He would arrive at the job in his black Cadillac, wearing an Armani suit and carrying all his supplies in a single large black suitcase. Romulus did final work after the common wall painters had left, usually letting himself in with a key provided by the decorator. He preferred to work alone, without anyone observing or interrupting him. He didn't like suggestions, or having to answer stupid questions.

Romulus wasted no time after returning to his condo,

which had been refurbished to suit his professional needs. He gathered his materials, then stood at his workbench and began to tint cautiously, adding drops at a time, stopping to clamp the gallon paint can in the electric mixer bolted to the bench. The mixer perfectly imitated the hand motion of an expert bartender shaking a martini, only with much more speed and force, churning the can's contents thoroughly. He added gold leaf, using thin latex gloves and flaking it gently and expertly with his fingertips so it drifted down like metallic snow. After each test mix he would spread a few strokes of paint on a length of pipe he was sure was the same composition as the steel support pole in the brownstone, then lay the pipe on a wooden block before a small fan that would dry it within minutes.

It took him almost three hours to find the precise formula, but the result was magical.

Romulus would bail out Victory on this job, and Victory would assume the persona that served him so well and strut and brag about the brownstone's interior to his fellow decorators—among the most sought after and expensive in New York. It would be good for Romulus' business.

For his art.

His work was done painstakingly, with tools mostly of his own making and with small, fine brushes, and it gave him the kind of visceral elation and soul-deep satisfaction da Vinci himself must have enjoyed.

It was the second highest level of elation Romulus could achieve.

Lars Svenson sat at his table in Munchen's and studied the brunette at the end of the bar. She was junkie thin and her dark eyes burned in the back-bar mirror whenever they caught him staring at her.

There were several things besides her gauntness and eyes

that he liked about the woman. Like the way she sat with her legs wrapped around each other on the high stool, one black pump about to fall off her foot. The way she gazed from time to time with such hopelessness into her drink, knowing he was watching her, *had to know*. The dark bruises on her bare arms, and on the sides of her neck.

He was especially intrigued by the neck bruises.

When he carried his drink over and sat on the stool next to her, she didn't seem surprised. And why would she be? This was why she came here. Why every woman in the place came.

Losers' lounge.

"You a regular customer here?" he asked, giving her his smile at half wattage. Not coming on too strong too fast.

"I don't know if that's precisely the word," she said, not looking over at him.

"I'm Lars."

"I'm strung out, Lars."

"Hard night?"

"Not so far. I'm still looking."

"Maybe I can help you."

"You really think you have what I need?"

He turned her on the stool so she had to look at him, then gave her the whole smile. "I know exactly what you need, and I can supply." He signaled the bartender for fresh drinks.

Her dark eyes were steady on him now. *Pools of need.* "We gonna have a few drinks now, get to know each other before we go to my place?"

"We should get to know each other," Lars said. Terribly sincere, terribly concerned Lars. "You should be careful. You might take somebody home who might really hurt you."

"I keep trying."

* * *

By midnight Lars had her tied spread-eagle and whipped to a rag. She'd never stopped liking it.

By twelve-thirty he'd found her stash in a hollowed-out romance novel. *Crap coke, but it would do.*

By three A.M. she'd showed him how she got the bruises on her neck.

By six he'd left her sleeping or unconscious or dead.

He never had learned her name.

At a little after seven A.M. he was sitting on a bench in Washington Square. Around him the city was waking up and stretching and getting into its mood.

He didn't feel good. The pressure was gone, but he knew it would return. It kept coming back after each time, sooner and sooner. And there was something odd this time. Different, anyway. He found himself wondering how the woman was. Feeling . . . what . . . sorry for her?

Not likely!

A guy across the square, big man but old, dressed in a bunch of rags, pushed himself up from where he'd been sitting on the grass and kicked at a pigeon. *Good luck with that.* He hacked and spat phlegm on the grass, then hitched up his oversize pants and limped away in the direction the pigeon had flapped.

Don't wanna be like that guy . . . not ever. . . .

Younger, stronger, employed Lars stood up shakily from the bench. He needed to get home, have some real sleep, then get to New Jersey for an afternoon move. His stomach was knotted and for some reason he felt like sobbing.

Not that he was actually going to sob. He had it under control.

He started walking toward Waverly, deciding it was probably bad drugs making him feel so down.

Where'd she buy the shit?

Maybe he should get rid of the rest of it, that he'd stolen

from the woman—*doing her a favor*—and slipped beneath his shirt before letting himself out of her apartment. Throw it down a fucking sewer someplace and forget it.

Maybe he should think about that.

30

They'd begun meeting sometimes in Quinn's apartment rather than on the park bench. Pearl's apartment was too small, and Fedderman lived in a house in Queens with his wife and kids, and wisely tried not to take his work home with him.

Pearl had helped Quinn make the place presentable, even bought some flea-market furniture and moved out the stained and sprung sofa that looked a likely place for something to nest. Some aerosol disinfectant helped, too. The various age-old cooking odors, combined with the lingering scent of the foul cigars Quinn sometimes smoked, were brought under control. The apartment smelled . . . okay.

The three detectives would sit around drinking beer or soda, Quinn in his big armchair, Pearl and Fedderman on the sofa, a large bowl of chips or pretzels before them on the coffee table. Pearl had tried to get Quinn and Fedderman to show some respect for the marred old table by putting out cork coasters, but they were ignored after the first time. When she objected, Fedderman looked at her as if she were insane. What were a few more damp rings on a table with so much character? Besides, they had much more important matters on their minds.

"What we have," Quinn said, after washing down a pretzel with a swig of diet Coke, "are two multiple murders, a husband and wife both times. The women were the primary victims, judging by the wounds. A gun was used in the first murder, a knife in the second. Both husbands and wives held jobs. But then, most households have two working partners. They were roughly in the same age group, and the women were attractive. The same could be said of thousands of couples in New York. In fact, there's nothing distinctive these couples had in common." He looked at Pearl. "You see any other similarities?"

She put down her Budweiser can. On a coaster. "You've only cited one significant difference—the murder weapon."

Quinn thought about that. It only might be significant. "The killer got rid of the gun during the first murder, planting it in Martin Elzner's hand to fake a murder-suicide, and probably had to go to a knife for his next murder because he had no second gun. Necessity over compulsion."

"Or maybe the killer's still exploring his compulsion," Fedderman said. "Finding his way by trying things out, deciding which weapon he prefers." He looked at Quinn and said, "Do you really think we're getting anywhere?"

"I don't know," Quinn said honestly. "We can tick off some common threads, but they're the kinds of similarities that can be pointed out about most couples."

"For the most part," Pearl said. "But here are some other similarities: Both couples were childless and lived in apartments. The killer was either let in or gained entry with a key. There were items that didn't seem to belong—groceries spread out on the kitchen table, duplicate items in the refrigerator. In the second murder there was a leather jacket the husband tried to return to where it wasn't bought, and he accused the salesclerk of giving it to his wife."

"Gifts," Fedderman said. "The groceries included expensive gourmet stuff the wives liked. And Marcy Graham had admired the jacket shortly before her death."

"Our guy had to know something about the wives," Pearl said. "Maybe he was in their circle of acquaintances."

"The couples didn't seem to know each other," Fedderman said, "and they moved in different circles."

Quinn swallowed a slug of Coke. "Let's stick to similarities. Pattern."

"The victims were fairly well off financially."

"You have to be, to live in Manhattan these days," Pearl said, then glanced around. "At least in the kinds of apartments they had." She stretched and reached for a pretzel. "Maybe the killer was leaving gifts for the wives, even though he didn't know them."

"A secret admirer," Fedderman said.

"Something like that. It's kinda like he was courting them, plying them with presents."

"Not many serial killers are romantics," Quinn pointed out. "If that's what we're dealing with."

"And the husbands woulda put a stop to it," Fedderman said.

"One of them tried," Pearl said. "He went to a shop where she'd admired the jacket but didn't buy it, and he raised hell trying to return it."

"So the killer at some point learned she wanted the jacket."

"Yeah, the salesclerk said she wanted it bad, but Hubby said no."

"Our killer must have seen her try on the jacket."

"Or overheard her and her husband talking about the incident," Quinn said. "Maybe even days later."

"More likely he was watching her in the shop," Fedderman said.

Quinn nodded. "Or worked there."

"The clerk, that Ira guy, is a creep," Pearl said, "but he's got an alibi you couldn't budge with dynamite." She finished her beer and placed the can back on its coaster. "The gifts—if that's what they were—are about the only pattern we have that might mean something. And the kitchens."

Quinn recalled her supposition that the killer had suffered some kind of childhood trauma involving a woman in a kitchen. The kind of speculation that was usually Freudian bullshit, but not always.

"Maybe his mother was a terrible cook," Fedderman said.

No one acknowledged him. He shrugged.

"We do know our killer has an affinity with kitchens," Pearl said.

"Like me," Fedderman said, patting his ample stomach.

Pearl ignored him. "The rest could be coincidence. We need more pattern. More commonality that looks and smells like evidence."

"We all know what we need," Fedderman said in his cop's flat voice.

At first Pearl was irked, thinking he was ragging her; then she realized what he meant. The more they learned about the Night Prowler, the sooner they'd nail him.

There was one sure way to learn more.

Quinn went ahead and said it. "We need another victim."

"Another pair of openers," Fedderman said. "When he kills, it's like dealing us more cards to play."

"And it increases the pressure on us to stop him, making our job harder. It's a trade-off and he has to know it. That's the kind of game we're playing."

Pearl gave Quinn a look he'd learned to interpret. The frustration was getting to her. She was heating up like a teakettle that bitched instead of whistled.

"Our guy's under pressure, too," Fedderman said. "He's gotta go for another double dip soon."

Pearl said, "This is becoming a crock of shit, Quinn."

"It was that from the beginning."

"This is the pressure we were talking about," Fedderman said. "Egan and the killer want us talking like you two."

Pearl said, "Feds, shut up about pressure. And kitchens and card games."

Fedderman ate a pretzel.

Pearl turned her attention back to Quinn. "So this is gonna be our strategy? We sit around like ghouls waiting for another slaughter so we can pick through the entrails?"

"Like cops," Quinn corrected her. "And we don't sit around."

Fedderman stood up and tucked his shirt in tighter, where his suspenders buttoned to his waistband.

"What the fuck are you doing?" Pearl snapped at him, surprised by his sudden movement.

"Not sitting around. Getting up to go fetch another beer. You want one?"

"I'll tell you what you can do with your can of beer—"

"Don't!" Quinn interrupted her, but he was grinning.

That made Pearl really mad.

David Blank was, as usual, punctual. But he seemed less at ease this visit as he settled into the deep leather recliner. He smiled, but not with his usual smugness, and glanced sideways expectantly at Dr. Rita Maxwell. His look said that they both knew the clock was running, time was money.

Rita decided to play on his unease, perhaps draw him out. She maintained her silence.

After almost a full minute Blank said, "Ticktock, Dr. Rita."

"That's what bombs do, David."

"Clocks too. But it's funny you should mention bombs. Time bombs."

"Did I read your mind?" *Time bombs?*

"A paragraph or two," Blank said.

"Do you feel something's ticking inside you, David?"

"As if I swallowed my watch or something?"

"You know what I mean. Something, some complex feeling, or a set of emotions that might lead to a kind of explosion."

"Explosion? No, I don't think so." He was silent for a moment. "But what if there were a certain pressure building? How would a person relieve that pressure by means other than an explosion?"

"The pressure comes from conflict, David. You share your conflict. You tell someone like me, and I can possibly help you to help yourself."

"Help me stop the ticking?"

"In a sense, yes."

"But what if the explosion's already taken place?"

"Has it?"

"What if?"

"Then it might be guilt causing your conflict and pressure. I might be able to help you there, too."

"My, aren't you versatile."

Sarcasm. I'm losing him. "You know how it works, David: confess your guilt and it lessens because it's shared."

"That isn't logical."

"I know, but it's human. That's how it works with people. Always has. Have you ever gone to confession?"

"You mean in a church? No, I'm not Catholic."

"That's what confession is for, alleviating guilt. It's a cathartic act, to unburden yourself to another. The church learned that centuries ago, and it still holds true. For Catholics, a priest might be sufficient. For others, perhaps someone like me would do."

"And I fall into the category of others."

"You said you weren't Catholic."

"The church believes confession leads to salvation," Blank said. "I'm not interested in salvation."

"Oh, David, I think we all are."

He seemed to consider that carefully. "Not all of us. Not the ones who are already lost."

"Do you consider yourself one of the irretrievably lost?"

"I must be, if I'm not interested in salvation."

"Then what is your interest? Your reason for coming to me? You must have one, or you wouldn't be here."

"I'm interested in relief. Simple relief. Because of what I might do if I don't find it."

"Then we have two questions. What do you need relief from? And what might you do if you don't find relief? I suspect if we answer the first, we can take care of the second."

Blank didn't speak or change expression.

"Are drugs involved?" Rita asked. "If so, I can—"

"Not exactly drugs."

Rita waited. She sensed Blank was on the edge, finally about to open up to her. She remained silent. Knowing when not to speak had been the hardest thing to learn in her profession. At this point there was nothing to say; Blank had to make up his own mind.

The muffled sounds of traffic below and far away filtered through the double-pane windows and heavy drapes. Faint noises from another world. They only made the office seem more quiet and isolated.

Like a confessional.

"I'm sure something is about to happen," Blank said.

Rita waited.

"It always happens sooner or later. They find out. I always know that from the beginning, but it doesn't change anything. It's part of the reason. They learn about me. And then . . ."

Rita waited.

"There are lots of reasons why people confess, Dr. Rita."

Rita waited.

"I was sixteen, living in Colorado. It was summer at a ski resort where I worked part-time. An older woman, about thirty, was a waitress at the lodge. She was a blonde and sexy. Bridget Olson was her name, but she wasn't foreign or anything; she didn't speak with a Swedish accent. I think she was from Iowa. She'd been divorced and drank too much, and she was always extra nice to me. The guy who ran the lodge made movies, but I didn't know what kind then. Bridget did, though. She asked me one night . . ."

Blank talked on while Rita sat pretending to take notes, listening to the familiar cadence of her mysterious patient's voice. There was no need to pay attention. The recorder was preserving it all on tape.

Not that it mattered.

She knew it was all lies.

I'll find out, she thought confidently, letting him talk on and on, trying to shock and divert her. She idly watched her pencil move almost of its own accord and create obscure scrawling, like messages in another language. It was as if she were making note of David Blank's earlier words that nibbled at truth and might be more prophetic than he imagined:

It always happens sooner or later. They find out. I always know that from the beginning, but it doesn't change anything. It's part of the reason. . . .

They learn about me.

Rita knew that eventually she'd learn.

If David Blank—or whatever his name was—wanted an opponent to outwit in a game of his own making, he should have gone elsewhere.

He was smart; she was learning that about him. And he was confident.

What he needed to learn was that no matter how smart he was, there was somebody who could best him. In order to reach him, to understand him, his confidence in his superiority had to be shattered.

Rita's job.

31

The apartment was quiet and dark, cool enough that the air conditioner wasn't running. A faint breeze wended through the shadowed rooms from a window that was open a crack. The bedroom seemed, like the apartment and the city around it, to be asleep itself, or at least in a state unlike complete wakefulness. It was the kind of place where dreams visited the dreamer.

Mary Navarre woke up next to Donald, who continued to sleep peacefully beside her. She was sure she'd heard a sound in the kitchen.

She prodded Donald in the ribs and whispered his name urgently.

He mumbled something and raised his head to look at her.

"I'm sure I heard a noise out in the kitchen," she said, hearing the fear in her voice.

" 'Frigerator," he said sleepily. "Icemaker or somethin'."

"It was more like somebody moving around out there, trying to keep quiet. I thought I heard the refrigerator door open and close."

He took in a deep breath, then sighed and propped himself up on his elbows. Donald was a big man, long-limbed but fleshy and with thinning blond hair. He was out of condition and not particularly strong to begin with, but his size was a comfort to her.

He cleared his throat and swallowed so he could be better understood. "So you want I should go out and talk to this hungry burglar?"

"You're not taking this seriously enough. Maybe we should call nine-eleven."

"Lotta trouble for nothing."

"Maybe not."

He wearily sat up in bed, then turned his back to her as he planted his feet on the floor. "I'll go out and look. It'll put your mind at ease, and besides, I could use a glass of water."

She wondered if he was showing off, trying to impress her with his seeming nonchalance. "Okay, you go look while I call nine-eleven."

"Don't do that, Mary. Really. All it'll be is a big pain in the ass. And next time, if something serious does happen and we call, they might not respond. I'm gonna go out there and find an ice cube on the floor, or something that fell over in a cabinet."

"It didn't sound like either of those things."

He reached back and patted her knee. "Maybe not in your sleepy mind."

"I was awake, Donald. I couldn't sleep." *A lie. I'm afraid enough to lie to him.*

He stood up and began plodding barefoot toward the bedroom door.

"Wait!" She was out of bed in a hurry, slipping on her robe. "I'll go with you."

While he waited, she went to a row of books on the windowsill and picked up one of the plaster pineapple bookends. It was painted plaster, but lead filled and plenty heavy enough if she had to use it.

Donald pried it from her rigid fingers. "I'll take it." He hefted the bookend in his right hand. "I wouldn't want you to panic at a mouse and accidentally hit me with this thing."

"We don't have mice."

Mary followed him from the bedroom. *Why am I doing this? Why don't I stay and call nine-eleven?*

But it was all happening too fast, and she couldn't let him go out there alone. Besides, he was probably right. She told herself he was probably right. Whatever she heard, or thought she heard, was probably nothing she needed to fear.

But she *was* afraid.

The kitchen was softly illuminated from the light on the stove. Mary stood just behind and to the side of Donald as he stepped through the doorway. She heard his intake of breath and saw his body stiffen, and she moved to the side so she could see around him.

A man was seated at the kitchen table. Before him was an opened milk carton, half a glass of milk, and a partly unwrapped loaf of bread. Mary realized she smelled something familiar and an instant later saw what it was—spicy lunch meat. The man was eating a pastrami sandwich. He was leaning forward over the table and had just taken a big bite when they'd interrupted him.

He seemed surprised, though not exactly. More like disappointed and angered.

What happened next took her breath away.

It was almost as if he'd expected to be discovered. He was ready to act. In one smooth and lightning motion, he was up out of his chair and around the table, wielding a long knife. Mary saw in that instant that he was wearing flesh-colored rubber gloves. The bite of pastrami remained in his mouth, forgotten and unchewed, a long red slab of the thinly sliced

meat protruding like a shredded tongue. Donald, paralyzed
with shock, had no time to react. It was as if his assailant had
rehearsed for this moment, as if it were choreographed. The
man was on him without hesitation and the knife blade flashed.

The explosive violence, the sudden blood flow and horror, rooted Mary where she stood. Donald lay folded on his
side like a full-scale, discarded doll at her feet, the plaster
pineapple still clutched in his right hand. It had all been so
fast, *so fast!*

*It has to be happening to someone else. I'm here but only
watching, like a movie. . . . Time, time for everything, about
to stop . . .*

A powerful hand gripped her hair and yanked her head
back and she knew her throat would be slashed.

Instead, the long knife blade lanced like ice low into the
softness of her belly. It took her breath away and numbed her
more than hurt. Each time she began to fall, the blade winked
in the kitchen light, piercing her and holding her up with its
force. Somewhere in her terror her mind was working. She
wanted to drop, wanted this to end, but he wouldn't let it
happen. Not yet. She couldn't die.

*He knows where to stab me where it hurts but won't kill
me!*

He'd been standing back from her and slightly to the side.
So he doesn't get too bloody. Now he shifted position and his
face was inches from hers and in brighter light.

I know him! My God, I know him!

He stabbed her differently then, harder, just beneath her
breasts and twisting up to touch and detonate her heart. The
explosion of pain turned the world white and then dim, dim-
mer. . . .

The last thing she saw was her killer's leering face, with
its lolling pastrami tongue—familiar, faint memory from a
thousand nightmares that had become real. She sank, sank,

and both her palms were flat on the floor, in warm liquid. Through silent blackness she crawled until her feeble, bloody right hand contacted something solid, a wall.

With her forefinger she blindly began to write.

32

Hiram, Missouri, 1989.

They heard his heavy footfalls on the front porch's wood floor; then the door opened and closed.

It was no surprise. As was his custom, Milford was home in time for the dinner Cara had simmering on the stove. She'd set the burners on warm and the oven's thermostat at 150 degrees; then she'd come up to the master bedroom, where Luther waited.

Luther raised his nude body off Cara and sat on the edge of the bed. He was breathing hard, watching the bulge of his slight belly go in and out like a bellows. A bead of perspiration clung to the tip of his nose, then plummeted to leave a dark, almost perfectly round spot on the carpet. He studied the spot for a moment, losing himself in it while his breathing evened out.

There was no hurry. The lovers knew Milford's habits. He'd stay downstairs and sit in his usual chair and have his usual before-dinner scotch.

Nevertheless, Cara was nervous. She climbed out of bed

and dusted herself with deodorant powder; then she slipped her dress over her head and smoothed the material. After switching the slowly rotating overhead paddle fan to a higher speed, she went to the vanity mirror and arranged her hair. Luther, who was by now back into his Levi's and holding the rest of his clothes, kissed the side of her neck. She locked gazes with him in the mirror and they exchanged smiles that were amazingly similar in their secret desires and contemplations.

Luther headed for the door.

"Luther!" she whispered in alarm.

He paused.

"Don't forget." She pointed to the covered china plate on the dresser that held a sandwich along with vegetables from the beef brisket dinner staying warm downstairs. Some of Milford's food that Milford wasn't going to eat.

Luther grinned at her and picked up the plate, his shirt draped over his wrist to free his hand that wasn't holding his shoes. Barefoot, he left the bedroom and padded down the hall to the narrow stairs in the back of the vast house. He wasn't worried about making *some* slight noise. If Milford happened to hear it downstairs, he'd attribute it to Cara moving about above him, or simply to the sounds an old house frequently made, like the creaks and groans of an old person acknowledging age.

When he reached the undecorated third floor, Luther relaxed. Milford and Cara planned on painting and furnishing the rooms on this floor, but they hadn't gotten around to starting the project and both of them knew they probably never would.

Moving more freely, Luther made his way down the hall to where a stout rope with a knot at the end dangled from the ceiling as if waiting for a hangman to tie a knot. He put down his shoes temporarily, yanked on the rope, and the folding stairs to the attic levered down from their opening in the ceiling.

Luther retrieved his shoes, climbed the stairs, then with a practiced effort raised them from above.

He was in the dim, shadowed attic, with no sign below of his passing.

Cara had fixed him up with a cot and a sleeping bag, and even an electric hot plate in case the food she gave him needed warming. He had books, most of them on painting and interior decorating, which he read by the light of one of the bare bulbs that hung from rafters by their cords. He'd removed one of the lightbulbs and replaced it with a screw-in socket, from which ran an extension cord that provided power for the hot plate and an ancient but quiet box fan. When he read at night, he usually draped the old blanket he'd cut in half over the vents at each end of the attic so no light escaped. That was when it became uncomfortably warm and he'd lie nude on top of the sleeping bag.

If he got too uncomfortable, late at night he'd venture down the back stairs into the main part of the house. Milford was no worry; he also enjoyed a nightly before-bed scotch and slept soundly.

Sometimes Luther and Cara had sex in the early-morning hours while her husband slept upstairs or, if they were in the attic, while he snored beneath them. Most of the time, however, they followed a routine of making love during the mornings or afternoons, when Milford was at the mine office and Luther had free run of the house. They could act with more abandon if they weren't afraid of waking Milford.

Occasionally Luther would sneak down from the attic and quietly slip into Milford and Cara's bedroom and watch them sleep, wondering how it would be if *he* were Milford, if Cara and the house, and being a solid citizen in Hiram, were all his to have and to hold and enjoy.

Maybe it didn't matter, he told himself. He was quite happy with things as they were, living secretly in his cozy attic nest. It was almost as if he were Cara's pet, under her protection. She'd told him once during sex that it gave her a delicious thrill knowing he was in the attic while she and Milford were living their dull lives downstairs, or while Milford was making love to her.

In a sense, Luther thought, things had worked out very well. Everyone had what they wanted. Everyone was . . . happy enough, which was about all anyone could ask of life in this hard world.

So, during the night, Luther would leave the attic only secretly, and not often. He also ventured outside occasionally in the daytime, making sure no one saw him coming or leaving the house. Though lately he hadn't gone out at all; there was always the possibility he'd draw attention, that someone would recognize him and ask where he was staying, what he was doing with himself these days.

The limited times of sunlight and fresh air weren't worth the risk, considering everything he needed was here, in the vast old house he regarded as his home. In the mornings, after Milford had left, Luther showered and brushed his teeth in the downstairs bathroom. Cara did his laundry separately, washing and drying during the day so Milford wouldn't notice extra clothing he didn't recognize. Luther had a jug of drinking water in the attic, and a chamber pot if necessary, if he couldn't wait until morning.

The best times were after Milford had left for work and the two lovers were on their own. Cara sometimes came up to the attic and told Luther how she adored him while she woke him gradually with her mouth. Usually they'd finish downstairs in the main bedroom where it was cooler. Afterward, Luther would casually get dressed, then help Cara with some of her housework. Sometimes they made love again, and sometimes they didn't. It was all up to them. Confined and secretive though they had to be, they both had more freedom than they'd ever experienced.

Luther sat down on his cot and fitted the earpiece of the battery-operated portable AM-FM radio Cara had given him. Then he stretched out on his back on top of the sleeping bag, laced his fingers behind his head, and listened to his favorite local station. He was confident no one way down on the first floor would hear his movements. And even when Milford and Cara were upstairs in their bedroom, Luther was still two stories above them. It was almost like having a private apartment in the same building, separated by more than an entire floor. Why should Luther worry in his spare but comfortable home in a corner of the Victorian's vast attic?

Roy Rabbit, a local disc jockey, was on the radio, playing the kind of music Luther liked, old songs from the 1960s. Lots of Beatles stuff. Luther especially liked the Beatles. The Monkees he thought were just okay.

When Roy Rabbit said good-bye and segued into news, Luther removed the earpiece and turned off the radio. He ate the sandwich Cara had made for him, but not the green beans and carrots, telling himself it was because they'd gotten cold but knowing he would have skipped them, anyway.

After dinner he listened to the radio some more, then read for a while, before falling asleep.

It was well after midnight when Luther awoke, warm and with a parched throat. He reached for the nearby water jug but decided a lukewarm drink wasn't what he needed. Something cold would be a lot better. And as he stood up from his cot, he realized he was hungry.

He left the attic, not raising the stairs behind him, then crept down the back steps to the third, then second floor. On the landing he stood very still, listening. He was sure he could hear Milford snoring.

Luther followed the sound down the dark hall, then peered in through the couples' half-open bedroom door.

There was Milford, a lump beneath the white sheet that Luther wouldn't have minded seeing as a shroud. Cara lay gracefully on her side next to him, one long, pale leg outside the sheet.

Luther smiled, staring at the leg. It seemed the limb of something beautiful in the act of being born. Then he returned to the landing and made his way to the first floor and the kitchen.

He got a cold can of Pepsi from the refrigerator, and then noticed a slice of peach pie on the top shelf.

Why not? Pepsi and pie. If the last piece of pie was being saved for Milford to eat tomorrow, Cara would make up some story. She was getting good at that.

He was at the table and had just finished the pie and was reaching for the Pepsi can when he heard a sound and jerked his head around so fast he felt a brief pain in the side of his neck.

Cara was standing in the doorway with her forefinger to her lips. She was wearing her pale blue silk nightgown that showed the generous contours of her breasts and her hard nipples.

"Jesus, Cara!" Luther whispered.

She walked over and picked up the pie plate, which now contained only crumbs, and carried it over and set it in the sink.

"Was that Milford's pie I ate?" he asked.

"None of it's Milford's pie." She grinned. "C'mon."

Carrying the half-full soda can, Luther stood up and followed her into the living room.

The background hum of the refrigerator receded. It was quiet and dim in the living room, but within seconds they could see by the streetlight's soft illumination filtered through the lace curtains.

"Milford's sleeping like the dead," she said. "He won't hear us." She took Luther's hand and led him to the sofa.

"Over there," he said, and pointed.

She giggled. "Milford's chair?"

"Can't think of anyplace better."

Luther took her other hand, so he was holding both, and walked backward, drawing her to the big wing chair that directly faced the TV. He placed the Pepsi can on an accounting magazine on a nearby table, then stripped off his jockey shorts and sat down. Cara removed the panties beneath her nightgown and sat on his lap. He kissed her cheek and ear and used his hand on her. It was cold from carrying the soda can, but that didn't last long.

She wriggled around so she could kiss him on the lips. They remained kissing while she adjusted her body so she faced him squarely, straddling him. Then she raised herself so he could suck her nipples. Within minutes she lowered herself onto him. She made a sound now familiar to Luther, like a soft and desperate breeze sighing through summer leaves.

Half an hour later, Cara was back in bed beside the lightly snoring Milford, and Luther was back in his corner of the attic, warmed by his love and his secret.

Sleeping the best sleep of his life.

33

New York, 2004.

Pearl and Quinn reached the scene before Fedderman.

Quinn had gotten the call from Harley Renz at eight A.M. Another married couple had been slain in their Manhattan apartment. Mary Navarre's blood had seeped through a crack in the kitchen floor and spread beneath the tiles. Some of it found its way to the apartment below, leaving a narrow, scarlet streak on the wallpaper above the stove.

The super let himself in and discovered the bodies at seven forty-five, after being shown the apartment below and recognizing that the substance on the wall was blood. He'd wisely touched nothing, locked the Navarre apartment door behind him, and called the police from his own phone. Renz, or someone in Renz's camp, had intercepted the call and gotten to Quinn immediately. The crime scene unit hadn't yet arrived. The two uniforms who'd taken the call after it had gotten past Renz were outside in the hall. It was only Pearl and Quinn in the apartment, along with the dead.

"We have our pattern now," Pearl said in a disgusted tone.

They were in the kitchen, staring at Donald Baines curled on the floor, and his wife, Mary Navarre, sprawled dead in a crusting pool of blood on the other side of the kitchen. When the super had told them the victims' names, that was all they had been—names. Now, too late, they were people. Had been people. Pearl suppressed the nausea and cold anger that built in her whenever she first came on a homicide scene. Violent death always stayed around awhile, hanging in the air like a malevolent ghost.

Quinn slipped on his latex gloves, and Pearl did the same.

"The kitchen again," Quinn said.

Moving carefully and not stepping in any blood, he and Pearl made their way over to the table. On a certain level they were both pleased. The killer was far enough along on his sick and deadly journey that it could be said he was leaving his signature at the scenes of his murders.

"Something new," Pearl said, looking at the carton of milk, unwrapped loaf of bread, and half-eaten sandwich on the table. She touched the milk carton; even through the glove she could tell immediately that it was room temperature. "It appears the killer was interrupted while having a snack." She bent low to examine the sandwich more closely. "Pastrami." She eased up the top slice of bread with her fingertip and peered beneath it. "Mustard and pickles." There was no mustard container on the table. And no pickle jar. But the sandwich was definitely homemade, not a carryout or delivery.

Quinn was stooping over Donald's body. "Stab wound." He straightened up with difficulty, a grinding cartilage sound reminding him his knees were no longer what they'd been, then went over to Mary's corpse. "Lots of stab wounds in this one. I count twelve and I probably can't see them all. Mostly around the breasts and pubic area."

"Fits our guy," Pearl said. "Focus is on the woman."

"Hubby's got something that looks like a pineapple clutched in his hand. Not a real one. Plaster or metal. As if he was going to use it as a weapon. There isn't any blood or hair on it, though."

"A shame."

Quinn twisted his body so he could scan the tabletop. He wasn't moving his feet much, what with all the mess on the floor. "Check the fridge." His own words sounded incongruous to him, as if he were asking the little lady to see if there was cold beer on hand.

Pearl opened the refrigerator door. "Well stocked, and there's a squeeze bottle of mustard and a jar of what looks like the same kind of pickles that are on the sandwich." She pulled out a deep plastic drawer lettered that it was for meat, and there was the package containing the rest of the pastrami. "Meat's in here."

"So our killer built himself a sandwich, put away the meat and condiments he used, then sat down at the table to eat."

"Like he didn't want anything perishable to spoil." Pearl felt a chill. "Maybe he planned on coming back for seconds some other night."

"Or he's compulsively neat."

"What he did here isn't neat."

"What about the milk?" Quinn asked.

"It's warm. And there's no glass. He was drinking it straight from the carton. Kind of homey and familiar. Bad mannered, though."

"Should be plenty of DNA evidence," Quinn said. "Saliva on the milk carton and sandwich."

"Maybe even tooth marks."

"It'd all be very helpful, if only we had samples to match it against."

"We will someday," Pearl said, "and we'll use them to nail this bastard to the wall."

Quinn glanced at her and smiled slightly, no longer surprised by her vehemence. *What is it, genetic?*

"What if it was one of the victims who was having the snack?" Pearl asked.

"Good question. Medical examiner can answer it later. But I don't think he'll be able to help us with what Mary tried to write on the wall."

"Huh?"

"C'mon over here," Quinn said, "and I'll show you."

Pearl followed him to where Mary Navarre lay, and they both stooped low to be closer to what she'd begun to write with her own blood on the wall.

"It looks like a caret," Pearl said.

"You kidding?" Fedderman's voice. He'd entered the apartment and come up behind them. "It's too pointy, upside down, and doesn't have any leafy stuff growing outta the top."

"She means a caret, like an *A* without a cross stroke, to show where something should be inserted in print."

"Ah," Fedderman said. "So maybe the victim was starting to print an *A* when she died. Or it could be the first part of an *M*."

"Looks like she died last," Quinn said, "like Marcy Graham. Only one or two stabs to finish the husband—I can't tell for sure and don't wanna move the body—then our killer took out all his frustration on the wife."

"He hates women, all right," Fedderman said.

Pearl gave him a look. "Don't they all? It's why the scumbags kill."

She left the kitchen and walked into the bedroom. It was restful and tastefully and expensively furnished. *Not like my bedroom.* The bed was unmade, the duvet and a blanket folded on a chair. It looked as if the victims had been sleeping with only a light sheet over them, and it was thrown back and wadded as if they'd climbed out of bed in a hurry. *Maybe somebody heard a noise.* On the windowsill was a lineup of books—mysteries, biographies, including some recent bestsellers. There was a gold-painted pineapple bookend supporting them on the left, nothing on the right. That was where Hubby found his weapon, Pearl thought. It appeared as if one or both of the victims woke up afraid of something. Hubby grabbed hold of a convenient blunt object, the pineapple bookend, and bravely went to investigate. *The alpha male.* His wife, Mary, followed and shouldn't have.

Why don't people call 911?

Pearl walked back into the kitchen and told Quinn and Fedderman what she'd observed. Then she went to the refrigerator again and looked for duplicate items or gourmet food. Nothing unusual, but if the couple got stranded in the apartment, it would be months before they'd starve.

She wandered over to the door to the hall and examined it. "No sign of forced entry."

Quinn and Fedderman didn't answer; she realized they'd both made a note of the door's condition when they entered. Pearl was a bit surprised to realize this didn't annoy her; it was great to be working with pros.

There was a crisp snapping sound as Quinn peeled off his gloves. "Egan's army's gonna be here soon. Let's get the jump on them. I'll go downstairs and talk to the super. You two start with the neighbors and the doorman. Later we'll get together at my place and compare notes."

Pearl nodded. *Maybe I'll stay the night at your place.*

Where did that come from?

She started toward the door to the hall, Fedderman close behind.

The Night Prowler stood beneath the shower and let hot needles of water drive away his thoughts. It was a time of satisfaction and peace, of triumph. When he turned off the shower, he knew he wouldn't hear the buzzing.

He'd been prepared, and his dark knowledge had been validated. He'd stood at the foot of their bed and observed them, Donald who didn't know, and Mary who knew but wouldn't admit it. They slept lightly, Mary close to Donald, as if her asleep self knew she was being watched and was disturbed. They loved each other, the Night Prowler was sure. They didn't love him and wouldn't have, even if they'd known they were two-thirds of a ménage à trois.

Mary had known, of course, but tried to hide from the knowledge.

He smoothed back his wet hair with both hands, then reached out and turned off the shower. In the white steaming bathroom he dried himself with a rough terry cloth towel; then, leaving his hair damp, he went out into the coolness on the other side of the door. He didn't bother putting on clothes; no one could see in, and he was comfortable as he was. He got a glass of ice water from the refrigerator, then sat in a corner of the sofa and used the remote to switch on the TV.

He smiled. There on cable news was a wedding photo of Mary and Donald. The caption at the bottom of the screen read, WEST SIDE SLAYINGS.

A wedding photo! Wonderful! Handsome couple.

The newlyweds in the photo disappeared and there was a blond-haired young woman in a navy blazer, standing with the victims' apartment building in the background. There were several police cars parked at the curb, and people milling about in front of the building. The journalist, whose name was Kay Kemper, wore a serious expression that didn't work because the top of her fluffy hairdo kept standing straight up in the breeze, then settling almost back down, like a lid that didn't quite fit but wouldn't stop trying. "The police aren't talking," she was saying into the microphone while staring at the camera, "but sources tell us this is almost certainly another deadly attack by the Night Prowler.

Both victims were purportedly stabbed to death, Mary Navarre and her husband, Donald Baines. The couple was childless. Neighbors say . . ."

The Night Prowler stopped listening closely; he knew all about the victims, more even than they'd known about each other, their secret places and desires. Mary he knew from reading her mail, both *snail* and *e,* from the scent of her clothes, clean and unwashed, from what she ate and liked and disliked. He knew what authors she read, what cosmetics she used, her medications and birth control pills, her breathing and scent when she slept, the up-close warmth of her flesh, her intimate thoughts murmured in her sleep. Her favorite colors.

And he knew about last night. Far more than anyone else would ever know. The way he'd possibly made enough noise to wake them. Though they *might* just as easily have slept through his secret visit as they had the others. They'd surprised him there in the kitchen, but not completely. He had, in his way, been waiting for them, sitting with his knife close at hand, sitting with a plan imprinted in his mind, a plan that required action not thought. A plan that was justice and balance and vengeance. Freedom, at least for a while. Escape and salvation, at least for a while. Oh, he was ready for surprise as he sat with his blade and his plan, eating his sandwich and drinking milk. A late-night snack, and not the first.

He was prepared, as he had been night after night. There were no real surprises in life. It was just that people had trouble reaching and touching what they knew was coming. Mary and Donald, all of them, they knew before they knew. Everything that walked or squirmed on earth knew at the end, learned at the end, welcomed the end. The terminally ill dying in hospital wards. Animals sagging limp in the jaws of predators, patient yet impatient.

Their deaths are a benediction.

Adrift on his thoughts, the Night Prowler only half heard what Kay Kemper was saying as he sat watching her glossy lips move, the way she shaped her vowels and unconsciously ran the ripe tip of her tongue, *so pink,* over her white upper incisors when she glanced down to check her notes flapping in the breeze. An errant blond strand of hair interfered with her vision and she brushed it back, almost losing the notes.

The Night Prowler wondered if the station would ever make up its mind what it wanted to do with her hair. Such indecision. *It should be shorter and closer to her head, and lose the bangs, please!* Her lips were remarkably mobile, stretching and inverting, *ideal for unnatural acts,* never still, as if they had too many nerve endings in them: ". . . had moved into their apartment only, *pink tongue,* two months ago, looking, *pink,* to . . . brutally, *pink,* murdered sometime last night . . . impacted by . . . say they heard nothing . . . any suspects . . . hopefully, *pink,* the fear . . . .Detective Frank Quinn was unavailable, for comment . . . no leads . . ."

Frank Quinn.

The Night Prowler stretched his left arm and placed his glass of water on the floor near the sofa. Quinn's name was appearing more and more in conjunction with the Night Prowler. It was becoming difficult to think of one and not the other. A team. A chess set. Adversaries.

Enemies.

The Night Prowler knew how to deal with enemies. What to expect from them. It had been his first hard lesson in life.

On the table next to the sofa was a small bottle with a rubber stopper, along with a folded white handkerchief. The Night Prowler unstopped the bottle and carefully tilted it to let a few drops fall onto the handkerchief, which he picked up and pressed lightly over his nose and mouth.

He breathed in deeply. A cool and silent wind blew somehow without motion. Walls fell away, and curtains swayed wide to reveal vistas of light and color. Truth became evident, and what wasn't evident didn't matter.

He wished now he still had his gun. He should never have used it to begin with; he should have saved it for killing from a distance.

Should he obtain another gun? It would have to be done illegally; there could be no record of a transaction, and no one must know of his possession of the gun. So there was only one way. That would be stealing. Blatantly breaking the law.

He threw back his head and laughed at the azure blue truth of it. His pursuer Quinn had broken the law, hadn't he? With that young girl, that beautiful child with flesh the hue of—

But he'd seen only photographs of the child. Anna something.

Handkerchief to nose. Breathe in, breathe in . . .

How could Quinn do such a thing? Where was honor, love, and fidelity? He was a cop! How could he betray that girl? She hadn't betrayed him. She hadn't had the opportunity.

Yesterday's Quinn.

Today's Quinn, second-chance Quinn, was a mechanical, determined hunter, a relentless agent of a god that was like Judas. The god of the girl he had raped. The Night Prowler's god of gray.

Handkerchief to nose . . .

Yes, Quinn was a dangerous man, and that was a fact the color of blood.

Quinn was a stalker who would follow and follow and *become* his prey so there would be no escape. They were, in the end, always the same, hunter and quarry, both of them diminished by either's death.

That mustn't happen. *Not to me. Us . . .*

Sleep was taking control now, a drug relaxing every muscle, comfortable and familiar, welcome as death that thwarted pain.

Mary, Mary . . .

He mustn't. Must not . . .

Enemies!

34

Renz had done his job well in stalling Egan's troops. It had been a full twenty minutes before the crime scene techs and detectives from the precinct arrived at the apartment of Donald Baines and Mary Navarre. After they arrived, information Quinn and his team hadn't had access to began flowing within the NYPD. Renz phoned Quinn that evening to bring him up to date, while Quinn was waiting for Pearl and Fedderman to arrive.

"Hubby was killed by a single stab wound to the heart. Mary Navarre had sixteen stab wounds in her. Probably the fatal one was to the heart, though several of the others would have eventually proved fatal."

"How long did she last before she died?" Quinn asked, remembering the trail of blood on the floor where Mary had crawled or pulled herself to the wall to scrawl her indecipherable message that was abbreviated by death.

"ME says it's difficult to know for sure, but after the wound to the heart, not more than a minute or so. Blood patterns indicate some of the more debilitating wounds were suffered first."

"How about prints or DNA?"

"No prints, of course. Our man favors gloves. We did pick up some DNA samples from the milk carton and the half-eaten sandwich. And we're still checking blood on the scene to make sure none of it's from the killer." Renz paused. Quinn could hear him making rhythmic little puffing sounds into the phone, a nervous habit, as if he were halfheartedly trying to whistle. "How do you read it, Quinn?"

"The bloody mark Mary made on the wall?"

"No, no, that doesn't mean shit. I mean, how do you read the situation in the apartment?"

"Something disturbed the victims' sleep and they went to investigate, Donald first. They interrupted the killer eating a sandwich and drinking milk from the carton. He had to kill them."

"Really? I've been caught drinking milk from the carton."

"Word's gotten around," Quinn said.

"Hubby was carrying a heavy bookend and primed for action." Renz, serious again.

"The killer was ready for them. Almost waiting for them."

"Whaddya mean, almost waiting?"

"He knew the risk and thought they might wake up. He had to know."

"You think he *wanted* them to wake up?"

"Maybe not last night, but sooner or later. He probably kept pushing it, increasing the risk."

"Tell you the truth, Quinn, I don't see it, but you're supposed to be the expert on how these sickos think."

"It doesn't take a psychic, Harley. After all, he was eating a sandwich while wearing rubber gloves, and he must have had his knife where he could reach it in a hurry. It doesn't look as if Donald got to use his pineapple bookend."

"He didn't. There was no trace of blood or hair on it. Quinn . . . you realize you're saying our Night Prowler did something to wake them up? That he wanted them to find him making himself at home in their apartment?"

"It reads that way. Like the way he'll eventually yearn to be caught and confess his crimes. It builds in them; they keep pressing, taking more chances. It's part of the package."

"So the shrinks say, but it doesn't make sense."

"Except in the killer's mind, and he's the one eating pastrami sandwiches with his gloves on."

"Not to mention stabbing people through the heart," Renz said.

"Not to mention. You know how it works, we have to get inside this guy's sick brain and figure out how he's thinking. Gotta *be* him, at least for a while."

That's why I hired you, baby.

"That's the only way we'll be able to predict what he might do when, where, and to who," Quinn said.

"Isn't that *to whom*?"

"Fuck youm."

Renz chuckled, pleased to have gotten to Quinn. "Well, this is his third set. If there was any doubt before, there isn't now. We've got a serial killer who does happily married couples."

"All three couples were married," Quinn said, "but two of the wives used their maiden names. There are plenty of couples living together in New York who aren't married."

"So, you're saying them being legally hitched was coincidental?"

"I'm saying if the killer knew the victims were married, he knew more about them than just their names and addresses. He couldn't have just picked them out of a crowd, or run his finger down the phone book with his eyes closed and chosen three married couples."

"Then victims and killer knew each other. That should make it easier for us."

"Or maybe they didn't know each other at all. Maybe he's somebody in a position to know people's marital status."

"Jesus! He might be employed by the state or city in some kinda record-keeping capacity."

"Or by a bank or credit bureau. Someplace where you can get real and deep information about people without them knowing about it. Or maybe someplace where you can get their keys and steal them or make copies—like a parking garage or a store where women might check their purses."

"Their keys?"

"Sure. There was no sign of forced entry into any of these apartments, but our killer came and went at will. After all, he was practically living in their apartments while his future victims were asleep." *And maybe when they weren't home.* Quinn made a mental note to have Pearl and Fedderman check the victims' neighbors to find out if anyone noticed someone coming or going during the day, work hours, in the weeks before the murders.

"Sounds to me like you're giving a two-sided problem eight sides, Quinn. Could be the killer and victims knew each other, that they were friends. Or thought they were. What's simple is usually right."

"Now you're bragging."

"Don't be such a prick. You know I'm probably right—probably correct."

Quinn knew Renz was making a classic mistake, settling on a theory too soon and ignoring other evidence. Yet he *was right* about the obvious usually being what happened in a homicide. But this killer was definitely different; Quinn had felt it from the time he'd read the Elzner murder file. "Yeah, it's possible. We still have to sort it all out."

"What about computers? These victims own one?"

Quinn remembered a laptop on a corner of the desk. "Everyone has a computer." *Except for washed-out ex-cops.*

"We'll check it and make sure it wasn't hacked. The other victims' computers were okay."

That was something Quinn hadn't thought to consider. *Slipping mentally? Or just being buried by technology like the rest of the poor schmucks my age?*

"Maybe we shouldn't be too quick to dismiss the bloody mark on the wall," he said, not wanting to come up short again.

"Egan doesn't think it's important. Poor woman just didn't get her message down in time."

"He's probably right, or the killer would have smeared it."

"Now you want some good news?" Renz asked.

"Don't tease me, Harley."

"We've made some progress tracking the silencer."

"Be still, my heart."

"We got it narrowed down some more."

"To the northern hemisphere, I'll bet."

"What with the way records are kept these days, and what you can do on the Internet, this isn't as long a shot as you think. I'll tell you, Quinn, the computer is a marvelous instrument."

Quinn wondered if Renz was jabbing at him for not factoring in what might be on the victims' computers. Or was he slyly referring to the fact that a computer had helped to set up Quinn for the rape accusation? "That's what Michelle says."

"Michelle?"

"My sister."

"Oh, yeah, the Quinn kid that turned out okay."

"Remember to let me know about the silencers, Harley."

Quinn hung up, thinking what a waste of time it was, even with the aid of computers, tracking silencers. Guns were difficult enough to trace, but mail-order silencers that had no individual serial numbers and changed hands maybe several times since their purchase . . . Quinn thought again that the only good thing about the silencer hunt was that it would help to keep Renz occupied and not ragging him and his team. Though it hadn't seemed to have that effect so far.

The intercom rasped. Pearl and Fedderman.

Quinn buzzed them up and threw the bolt on his door.

They both looked exhausted. Pearl's hair was stuck in lank bangs to her perspiring forehead, and her white blouse was patterned with wrinkles. Fedderman's eyes were bloodshot and his baggy brown suit looked as if it had been used in a tug-of-war. Pearl flopped herself down on the sofa while Fedderman trudged out to the kitchen to help himself to a beer.

"You coulda asked us," she said, irritated, when Fedderman returned carrying only one can of beer.

"Blame our host," Fedderman said. "We come in expecting a buffet, maybe some canapés, and there's *nichts*."

"Canapés and *nichts* in the same sentence. You don't hear that very often."

"Shows I'm well traveled and you're not." Fedderman popped the tab on the can and licked foam from between his thumb and forefinger.

"Shows what a *putz* you are."

"My old German grandmother would tell you who's what part of the anatomy."

"I'm going out to the kitchen and get two more beers and a bag of potato chips," Quinn told them. "Then we're gonna talk police work. Unless you two have been doing other things all day."

Neither answered as he walked into the kitchen.

When Quinn returned with the beer and chips, Fedderman said, "If memory serves, there were a couple of murders just this morning, weren't there?"

"I told you he was a *putz*," Pearl said.

Quinn said, "He didn't exactly deny it."

He yanked open the top of the potato chip bag and placed the bag on the coffee table. Then he opened the beers and handed a can to Pearl, took a swig of the other. He sat down in his chair opposite the sofa.

Fedderman sat down next to Pearl, who threw a potato chip at him. "Have a canapé."

The chip landed in Fedderman's lap. He picked it up and ate it.

Quinn told them about his phone conversation with Renz.

"You think that silencer thing will actually get anyplace?" Fedderman asked.

Quinn shrugged. "It keeps you-know-whom busy." He looked from Pearl to Fedderman. They looked as if they would have sprung at each other's throats, only they didn't have the energy. "So how was your day?"

They told him it hadn't been good. Other than the woman who'd noticed the thin trail of blood on her wall in the unit below the murder apartment, no one in the building had seen or heard anything unusual.

"What about the doorman?"

"We were including him," Pearl said. "But he admits he's not always on the door. He might have been running an errand or hailing a cab for one of the tenants. And sometimes he sneaks a smoke down in the stairwell of the building next door."

"Did anyone mention seeing something or someone unusual during the two weeks or so leading up to the murder? I mean, during daylight, working hours?"

Pearl and Fedderman stared at Quinn.

"No," Fedderman said, "but we didn't specify those hours and we didn't go back as far as two weeks."

"You will tomorrow," Quinn said.

Pearl took a pull on her beer and glanced at Fedderman. "I told you we shouldn't come here."

An incurable wiseass, Quinn thought. But so was Sherlock Holmes.

Pearl and Fedderman had left less than five minutes ago. Quinn had just finished throwing away the empty beer cans and putting the potato chip bag back in a kitchen cabinet when there was a knock on his apartment door. Someone must have bypassed the intercom and let themselves in as Pearl and Fedderman were leaving.

But when Quinn peered through the glass peephole into the hall, there was Pearl.

"I forgot my purse," she said when he'd opened the door. "My gun's in it."

Quinn stepped back so she could enter.

She went to the middle of the living room, placed her fists on her hips, and glanced around. Quinn looked, too. No purse.

Pearl went to the sofa and felt along the sides of the cushions.

"Ah!" she said, and pulled the small purse up from where it was jammed between the cushions.

She held the purse up by its strap, as if it were a fish she'd just caught, and smiled at Quinn. "You got any more beer?"

"I can get you one," Quinn said.

He went into the kitchen and came back a minute later with an opened can of Budweiser. "Tell Fedderman I'd have given one to him, only he's driving."

"Oh, he went ahead with the car. I told him I'd subway home. It's not that big a deal, and there was no point making him wait."

Quinn felt his pulse quicken. He looked closely at her.

"This apartment," she said, motioning with her arm, "probably hasn't been this neat in years."

"Pearl, you never forgot anything in your life, much less your gun."

She stooped and placed the beer can on the carpet, then came over and stood too close to him. "I can save you, Quinn."

"How is that, Pearl?"

"I can give you back your self-respect."

"You helped me clean my apartment, now you're ready to start on my life."

"Question is, are *you* ready?"

The scent of her hair, even her perspiration, was like perfume to Quinn. He remembered the way she'd looked at him as he was leaving her apartment after spending the night there and felt a tightening in his groin even as internal alarms were triggered. "Fedderman knows you didn't forget your purse."

"Piss on Fedderman. You've been friends with him a long time. You must have something on him."

Quinn grinned. "Pearl, Pearl . . ."

"I can save you," she said again, and stood high on her toes and kissed him.

He kissed her back and felt her lips part, then the warm strength of her eager tongue.

When they pulled away from each other, she smiled up at him. "I've got another side, you know."

He did know. He picked her up and carried her into his bedroom.

She seemed to like that.

Their lovemaking qualified as frenzied, Quinn surprising himself. Pearl was on top, grinning down at him, working her hips to a marvelous silent beat, her large breasts swaying with the rhythm. After a while he rolled her off and mounted her, careful to support himself with his elbows and knees. She was so small, yet there was a compact strength to her.

He was gentle but took control. She was ready for it and clamped her legs around him, somehow still managing to work her hips in response to his powerful thrusts. Her warm breath was near his ear and she made urgent, throaty sounds that grew louder and louder.

When it was finished, they lay on their backs, side by side, staring at the cracked ceiling and listening to their ragged breathing gradually even out. They'd wanted and enjoyed each other more than either of them had imagined possible. They were both still shocked and, in a way, frightened by what still gripped them. During the past half hour everything had changed for both of them, forever.

After a few minutes the only sounds in the small, warm room were of the city outside the window, the complex stage on which they would continue to act out their lives.

Where the hell . . . , Quinn wondered.

. . . is this going? Pearl asked herself.

Less than a mile from where Quinn and Pearl lay, the Night Prowler was curled in his corner with his benzene and his dreams. These were some of the best times, knowing what he was going to do next, who would be his next victims.

He wasn't completely a slave to his compulsion. He had free will. He knew the actress would be perfect, with the graceful, practiced music of her every move, as if her walk drew energy from the ground. But she wasn't married and so wouldn't do and couldn't do. Living together in sin, delicious sin, that wasn't like marriage, no matter how hard people pretended.

The actress had called to him without knowing. She was unaware of her own silent voice and that she was an actress in more ways than she suspected. Yet she wasn't one of them, one of his, so he'd decided to forget her, as he had so many others. They were like bright coins of little value that he hadn't bothered stooping to pick up.

He closed his eyes and pushed all thoughts of the actress away, and lovely Lisa strode toward him across vistas like a high-fashion model on a celestial runway. She emerged from shadow into light and into focus. Staring inward, he marveled at her beauty.

My God!

Tears tracked down his stiffened cheeks. There was no need for the actress. Not if he had Lisa.

He could see her clearly now in every detail. Such was the power of his mind to re-create beauty and essence. Lisa tucking in her chin and giving him a flirtatious look. Lisa smiling. Lisa whirling. Lisa complete.

He rewound time and there she was, Lisa Ide, manager of the jewelry store she and her husband, Leon Holtzman, owned on West Forty-seventh Street. Lisa working behind the glittering showcases. Lisa in her kitchen, *yellow,* at the big white stove, *hot grease smell,* stretching and reaching to get something from the back of the refrigerator, *white blue,* doing dishes by hand, *suds yellow rubber fingers,* facing away from him, wearing the tight, tight black slacks he'd seen her in, *her flesh, her flesh.* She had her auburn hair swirled high and piled jauntily toward the back of her head, precisely the way she'd worn it when he'd watched her leave the jewelry store and stride along the crowded sidewalk.

Fading . . .

He raised the folded cloth to his face and inhaled, smiling but still crying.

There she was! In focus, in color . . .

He could dial in on her much faster now, the way he needed to, the way he needed her. Lisa Ide, with her bright blue eyes so widely spaced, *ocean,* and her wide mouth with its full lips, *wet red,* and slight overbite. Lisa Ide dining at the sidewalk café across from Lincoln Center with her husband Leon, raising her coffee cup to her mouth, pursing her lips so softly. A small woman but so complete, so perfect in so many ways. Her lushness, the endless and wonderful spectrum of her coloring. A man like Leon, a simple merchant whose work was his life, would never in a thousand years understand Lisa. He dealt in precious stones and yet was unaware of what was precious and so near him.

A man like that deserved nothing but death.

Yes, there was no doubt who was next. The Night Prowler could feel the fatal knowledge stirring in him like a thing aborning that would begin its rapid and relentless growth. It was barely potent now, harmless, but it would grow teeth and claws. And it would have its way.

He pressed the folded cloth hard to his nose and inhaled deeply, but the benzene was losing its effect and he felt himself simply falling asleep.

The buzzing, briefly, but fading away . . .

And he dreamed, unable now to escape from her: Lisa standing in the bathtub, about to lower herself into the warm water. Lisa pausing nude on the stairs, like Picasso's painting somehow unscrambled and made whole woman. Lisa watering flowers. Lisa in bed asleep and almost smiling. Lisa's hair and eyes and flesh and lips and glance and smile . . . the music of her colors and her walk. Of her pain to be. *Moana Lisa . . .*

He understood that destiny and dream were one.

Detective Quinn, Lisa Ide. What I know and you don't. Soon-to-be-famous Lisa.

35

Quinn awoke to the scent of coffee and frying bacon.

He suddenly recalled last night—Pearl.

Now she was in his kitchen preparing breakfast. Where had this domestic Pearl come from? For that matter, the Pearl she'd displayed last night had been quite a surprise.

He climbed out of bed nude and trod heavily into the bathroom.

"Quinn?" Pearl's voice from the kitchen stopped him. *Must have heard the floor creak.*

"Yeah?" His sleep-thickened voice came out as a growl. "Yes?" *Better. Civilized.*

"You have time to shower and shave before breakfast."

"Uh-huh." He continued on his way to the bathroom.

When he was clean and shaven, he slicked back his wet hair, then returned to the bedroom and rummaged through his dresser drawers until he found an old robe he hadn't worn in over a year. *The gentleman in his dressing gown.* He put on the robe but couldn't locate his slippers, so he padded barefoot into the kitchen.

Pearl was standing at the stove holding a spatula. She'd

made a pass at combing her thick hair, but it was still flat where she'd slept on it. She was wearing the clothes she'd had on yesterday. They looked as if she'd been wearing them for a week. Her blouse had wrinkles that might never iron out. This was not a woman who looked as if she belonged in a kitchen, yet she had the table neatly set, crisp bacon already on plates, and eggs sizzling in a frying pan.

"I thought you might want to go out for breakfast," he said.

The coffeemaker's glass pot was full. Two clean cups sat nearby. He went over and poured himself a cup of the strong black brew. There was no cream in sight. *How did she know I like my bacon crisp, my coffee black? She must have been observing all this time.*

Pearl was smiling at him. "Eating at home'll be better."

Home? "What I thought," Quinn said, "was we might have breakfast at the diner down the street, then take a walk. Maybe you could pick up some clothes at one of the shops near there."

She raised her eyebrows, puzzled. "Why would I want to buy clothes?"

"Fedderman'll be here sooner or later this morning. He'll see you're wearing the same clothes from yesterday. He'll know you spent the night."

Careful . . . don't break what happened last night like the eggs. "Makes no difference to me. Sunny-side up?"

"Over well. It does make a difference to me."

"If that's how you feel about it. . . . Break the yellow?"

"No."

She used the spatula to slide one egg onto a plate with the bacon, then deftly flipped the egg remaining in the skillet.

"I don't think it's such a good idea, Pearl, advertising that we slept together."

She motioned with her head at the egg. "Hard enough?"

"Sure."

"Fedderman left a message on my machine at home this morning. He said since I didn't pick up, he assumes I left and took the subway here and we can meet later. He won't be here for another hour. I'll go out after breakfast and find something else to wear." She transferred his egg from skillet to plate and grinned at him. "Not that Fedderman will be fooled."

Quinn knew she was right, but he still wanted to maintain deniability. If it was important to presidents, why not to Quinn? "It's possible that someday he might have to testify about our relationship under oath."

"You have a point there," Pearl said, but she seemed amused by the idea. Toast sprang to attention from the old toaster with a sound like a sledgehammer striking a sack full of steel springs, startling Quinn. Pearl plopped each slice of hot toast on a saucer and placed the saucers on the table, then sat down to eat.

Quinn sat across from her, watching her carefully butter a piece of toast. He sprinkled salt and pepper on his egg. *What the hell am I doing here? How did this happen?* "Pearl—"

She passed him the butter. "You rather have jelly?"

"Butter'll do."

"What about last night, Quinn?" Pearl taking the offensive.

"It was fantastic," Quinn said, and meant it. He found it wonderful watching her smile from across the table.

Easy . . . don't fish for an answer you don't want. . . . "I need to know if it was a onetime thing."

"I don't see how it can be, Pearl. You're already an addiction."

She stood up and walked around the table, swallowing a bite of toast, then leaned down and planted a buttery kiss on his cheek.

"This . . . us . . . it won't interfere with the job. I promise." She sat back down.

"I won't let it," Quinn told her.

After breakfast he fished in his wallet and gave her a hundred-dollar bill from the money Renz had paid him.

"Quinn—"

"Jesus, Pearl, it's for clothes! A change of clothes was my idea, so at least let me buy them for you."

"Why should you?"

"Because I'm the one worried about Fedderman."

She was quiet for a while, still not liking even the faintest notion that he was treating her like a hooker. Last night must not be tainted.

"I've got my own money," she said.

Quinn gave up. He cleaned up the kitchen while she went shopping.

She came back half an hour later carrying a single paper sack, then went into the bedroom to change.

She emerged in the same wrinkled slacks but with a new black T-shirt lettered GIANTS across her oversize breasts.

"There aren't any decent places to shop around here; this was all I could find. It's a boy's medium."

The T-shirt fit fine everywhere other than the chest. A boy, medium, wouldn't have put that kind of strain on the material. The dark blue blazer she'd worn yesterday had been draped over the back of a chair and wasn't so wrinkled. When she put it on over the T-shirt, GIANTS was still visible in convex yellow lettering.

"Best I could do on short notice," she said.

"Was that the only team they had?"

She started to answer, but the intercom interrupted her. Quinn walked over and buzzed Fedderman up.

As soon as Fedderman stepped into the apartment, he stood still and looked at Pearl, then at Quinn. "Pathetic." Back at Pearl. "Couldn't you find a Yankees shirt?"

"Why Yankees?"

"You know. . . . 'Whatever Lola wants . . . ' "

"What the hell's that supposed to mean?"

"It's a song from a Broadway play. *Damn Yankees.*"

"I can't afford Broadway plays on a cop's salary."

"I know. I'm rubbing it in."

"You are such a prick, Fedderman."

Quinn held out an arm to stop Pearl in case she decided to advance on Fedderman. This was going to be a big problem. He'd really screwed up last night. Complicated things. "Okay, okay! It's time for us to get to work."

Pearl was glaring at Fedderman, who was smirking.

"Everybody pretend," Quinn said, and strapped on his shoulder holster. "Please."

"The whole world pretends," Pearl muttered as they were walking toward the elevator.

"Keeps us employed," Fedderman said.

Quinn wondered for how long.

36

"You seem relaxed today," Rita Maxwell said to David Blank.

Blank sat back in the recliner's soft leather and closed his eyes. "You seem surprised. Even your most troubled patients must have a good day now and then."

Rita decided to work with what he'd given her. "What in particular is making you feel good today?"

"Fit and finish."

"Can you be more specific, or are you talking about your car?"

"I'm talking about the cosmos. Today everything seems to fit together precisely in its proper place."

"And the finish?"

"The colors are perfect."

"You refer to colors often."

"That's because I paint. Landscapes, mostly. Though sometimes figures. Nudes. The different hues on a human body are amazing in their number and subtlety."

"You mean eyes, hair . . . ?"

"That too. Human flesh, though, if you look closely, if you listen . . ."

Listen? Color and sound mingled. Cross-sensory perception. Not unusual in a talented artist, though not to such a degree. "What do you hear if you listen, David?"

"Sometimes beautiful sounds. On bad days, when the colors fade or run together, a gray buzzing. Not today, though. I hear a humming like soft music, different with every woman."

"Only women?"

"I'm not sure. Are you suggesting I'm a repressed homosexual?"

Huh? "No, I'm not." Blank didn't seem angry. More as if he were amused. "Do you have issues concerning your sexuality?"

He opened his eyes and laughed loudly. "Issues . . . I love that! Isn't that a term for what you've given birth to?"

"It can be." Rita put a touch of amusement in her voice so he'd know she wasn't serious. He was loose today, all right. In a good enough mood to joke with, and where might that lead? "I think we can assume you haven't given birth."

"No, not to anything." He laced his fingers together. "Not in the conventional sense, anyway."

She was puzzled. "You mean your art?"

"Of course. There was a woman who posed nude for me, a model named Carol. So beautiful. I worked so hard to capture her tension and all her hues."

"Tension?"

"In a physical sense. Angle and muscle tension. Not everyone can be a good artist's model."

"I wouldn't think so."

"An artist and his model are usually in a strictly business relationship. And that's how we started out. Then one day, in my apartment studio in the Village, she fainted. I thought I'd demanded too much of her, trying to use every second of the rare and perfect light. . . . It was golden; you could hear and touch it."

He gave Rita a sideways glance to make sure she was paying attention. She nodded and wriggled her pencil.

"I felt guilty," Blank continued. "I was sorry for her. So I picked her up and carried her to my bed, where she could rest, and as I laid her down, she opened her eyes, and the way she looked at me and smiled, I knew. . . ."

He continued his tale of seduction and sexual adventure while Rita pretended to take notes.

"Two people were never closer than we were," Blank was saying. "We hardly ever went outside the apartment for the next month, only sending out for . . ."

Rita moved the pencil steadily, noticing that her squiggling, meaningless marks were for some reason beginning to resemble Arabic script. The session with David Blank had settled into its usual pattern, and she was only half listening to him, thinking *lies, lies, lies. . . .*

Except for the first ten minutes.

When he'd gone, she would rewind the tape and listen to the first part of the session carefully. It hadn't been so much what he was talking about, but rather the relieved, buoyant tone of his voice, as if some great pressure were no longer exerting its force on him.

Blank still hadn't revealed the real reason why he was coming to see her, his actual problem. But his wasn't the usual game of diversion and deflection that tentative patients played. She understood what he was doing: He was setting the riddle out there for her to unravel. And a part of him wanted desperately for her to succeed, because he understood the terrible pressure would return and he was afraid. Buzzing. Order and color. Fit and finish. The psychosis as car. And David Blank knew he was speeding toward another collision.

The cross-sensory perception, now *that* was interesting. If true.

He did seem sure that Dr. Rita Maxwell was his answer, that she could and would eventually help him, perhaps save him. But first she had to know what he was concealing. *Who was Carol?*

Sooner or later, Rita would know. However and why ever he'd found his way to her, David Blank—whoever he was—whoever Carol was—had chosen the right analyst.

Patience was in order. Progress was being made. Rita was slowly learning, always learning, and would find the answer to the riddle of David Blank.

Quinn sat on the hard wood and concrete bench just inside Central Park and watched the joggers and cyclists. An attractive woman in her early twenties pedaled past on a mountain bike, something everyone needed in a city as flat as a Monopoly board. Quinn watched her graceful form recede as she stood high on the pedals to pick up speed, her hips swaying with her effort, her long brown hair catching the sunlight. He wondered about her life. She might be a student at NYU, or a young professional, a wife, a mother, an actress, a musician or artist, a hooker or an off-duty cop. The human mystery.

He decided maybe it was time to use the media.

Dave Everson was a journalist with the *Times* who had long ago given Quinn his direct-line number at the paper. Everson was a journalist Quinn trusted, and he remembered the number. Quinn drew out his cell phone from the pocket of his sport jacket folded on the bench, and for the first time in years he called it.

"I'll be damned," Everson said when Quinn had identified himself. "It's been a while."

"Too long," Quinn said.

Everson was no fool; he knew Quinn had something in mind. "So what do you need?" There was the slightest tremor of excitement in his voice.

"Heat."

Everson laughed. "You've already got that, Quinn."

"For somebody else," Quinn said.

"Ah. . . . With conditions, I assume."

"You'll be first in line as things break, Dave."

"And you want to be an anonymous source."

"No, I want the bastard to know I'm at his heels."

"Hey, that'll be a much better story. *Mano a mano.* I do like you, Quinn."

"I can be a likable sort. We dealing?"

"Proceed."

Claire Briggs frowned and checked again for the chemical reaction.

Blue. Again. No mistake.

She was pregnant. So said her home-testing kit.

She had to tell someone, but not before Jubal. He must be the next to know.

At four o'clock Jubal was back from his two o'clock audition for the role of the sensitive hero in the Lincoln Center production of the Vietnam play *Winding Road,* which was set to open in three months.

"So how'd it go?" she asked, but she knew from his expression how it had gone.

He wore a light blue sweater like a cape, its arms knotted at his chest, though the weather had been too warm for a sweater when he'd left the apartment. Now he unfastened the loose knot and tossed the sweater onto the sofa in a heap.

"It went like shit!" He flung himself down next to the sweater in a similar heap and sat frowning.

"Jubal . . ." Claire moved toward him as he hung his head and his shoulders began to quake.

Then he looked up at her, grinning. "I got the part!"

Claire stood still and took a deep breath. "Oh, damn, you had me!"

Jubal shrugged, still with the grin. "Well, I can act!" He jumped up and hugged her, lifting her off the floor and spinning her in a dance across the room.

When he put her down, she was almost too dizzy to make her way to a chair and fall into it, gasping and laughing.

"It's a day for good news," she said when she could talk without choking or coughing.

Jubal was pacing, too excited to sit. "Actually, it's only a callback, but I can be sure of the outcome. Everything fell into place, as if I trained all those years just for the part. I was last to audition. I'm one of three choices and the other two aren't even close. One's Victor Valentino."

"Never heard of him."

"He was in *Back Alley* last year. Guy looks like a thug, but he can act. He might wind up playing the tough sergeant."

"Who's the other guy?"

"Randy Rallison."

Claire had acted with Rallison. He had difficulty remembering his lines, and many in the cast suspected he had a drug or drinking problem. "A zombie onstage compared to Jubal Day."

"I'm positive the producer feels the same way. He gave me the wink as I was leaving. I'm sure he gave me the wink."

Claire sighed and rested a hand on her stomach. She couldn't stop smiling.

"We're going out for dinner and celebrate!" Jubal said.

"We have more than one thing to celebrate."

"I know we do! The way your career's going. And this apartment is great! We're lucky, Claire. Damned lucky!"

"I'm glad you think so, Jubal. But we're luckier than you know. I'm pregnant."

He stopped pacing and stood still. His features re-arranged themselves into a mask. She had no idea what he was thinking. Doubt flashed through her mind like a light-ning bolt.

"I shouldn't have surprised you like that." She heard the quaver in her voice and hated it. Her stomach began to ache. She knew then what she needed, what she had to have.

"You know this for sure?"

"I've missed two periods and my home test says I'm preg-nant. I'm sure. I feel . . . different. There isn't any doubt."

Now he was grinning. "My God! You're *pregnant*!"

He came to her, lifted her gently to her feet, and kissed her.

"We can turn the spare room into the baby's room," he said. "We can spoon-feed the kid and change his diapers—"

"Or hers."

"Hers. And push him-her in the park in a stroller."

"We can watch her-him take her-his first step."

"Teach him-her how to grip a baseball."

"And how to say *please* and *thank you*."

"And not spit the spinach."

"We can get married," Claire said.

37

"New computers," said Sergeant Rudd, who was manning the precinct desk when Pearl walked in. He was an aging, broad-shouldered man, with white hair, a whiskey nose, and eyes the color of lead bullets. "We need to keep up with the feds when it comes to technology."

Pearl looked over to where the clerk sat and saw him wrestling a keyboard out of a box. The computer on his desk did indeed look new, and had a monitor featuring an impressively large flat screen.

"How are they preserving our information?" Pearl asked.

Rudd stared at her.

"I mean, are they transferring all the data from the old computers to the new ones?"

"Oh, sure. I overheard the technicians talking about some kind of ZIP drive thing. Nothing to it, according to them. But far as an old cop like me's concerned, a computer makes a good boat anchor."

"Dinosaur," Pearl said, walking on toward the squad room.

"You too," Rudd said behind her. "You're just a smaller, prettier one. 'Specially this morning." She turned and saw his seamed face split into a grin. "There some kinda reason for that?"

Holy Christ! Was it that obvious to the trained eye? Pearl felt herself blush and pressed on, ignoring Rudd's chuckle.

The squad room was a mess. Half a dozen technicians who looked like teenagers in pale blue blazers were setting up new computers on the old steel gray desks, or on typing tables beside the desks. The twentieth and twenty-first centuries were colliding here. There were only two detectives around, a smarmy little creep named Weatherington, and a large, potbellied man she knew only as "Big Mike." They were both undercover vice, which as far as Pearl was concerned was exactly where they belonged.

She stood still for a moment, taking in the electronic carnage. Then she went back to the booking area.

"Looks like some kinda college frat prank goin' on in there, don't it?" Rudd said.

"Maybe it is." Pearl motioned toward the squad room with her thumb. "Which of those desks used to be Quinn's?"

Rudd returned his attention to the paperwork that occupied him. It was almost as if he expected the question; he'd been day desk sergeant for over five years and had the answers. "Second on the left as you walk in the door."

He didn't ask Pearl why she'd asked. She thanked him and returned to the squad room.

She went to the second desk and saw the new computer on it, but there was no old one sitting on the floor to be removed later.

"What happened to the computer that was on this desk?" she asked the young technician who was working at the desk two over.

"Didn't replace that one," the young woman said. She weighed about seventy pounds and had glasses the size of CD-ROMs. "It was new enough that we just ramped up the memory. Five-twelve RAM now."

"Wow," Pearl said. "How new?"

"Three or four years old is all."

"Any of the others like that? New enough they were kept?"

"Not to my knowledge," the young woman said, and began undoing a tangle of cables.

Pearl thought about going back and asking Rudd where Quinn's old computer might be, but she decided against it. She had a pretty good idea.

She sat down at one of the new computers and booted it up. "Programs the same on all of these?" she asked another of the teenage techies. This one was a boy with a bad complexion and a bushy unibrow over watery brown eyes.

"Just like your old one only bigger and faster, ma'am. Sort of like a second marriage to a younger man."

Pearl looked at the pimply punk, wondering if he might be coming on to her. But he seemed oblivious as he did something to the back of one of the tower units with a screwdriver. He removed the cream-colored metal shell case which was apparently attached only by a few small screws, then began tinkering with the computer's electronic guts.

Pearl leaned to the side so she could see. "That the hard drive?"

"Hard as you like it, ma'am."

Pearl stared at the kid. He smiled and went back to his work.

What's with me this morning? Does the male sex somehow smell recent activity?

Pearl keyed in her PIN and went to the software program that matched items in the evidence room with dates and case numbers. As soon as she typed in Quinn's name, a reference number came up that would act as a guide, much as the Dewey decimal system helped to locate library books.

She copied the number on a Post-it, then shut down the computer and walked back to the evidence room.

A sleepy-eyed sergeant was on duty behind a counter, sitting down and engrossed in a *New York Post*. Pearl flashed her shield and logged in, and the sergeant went back to reading what looked like yet another piece on Anna Caruso.

Pearl pushed through a wooden swing gate and entered a caged-in area in a windowless room built onto the back of the precinct house over twenty years ago.

It wasn't hard to find the computer, wrapped in plastic on the second shelf of a tier of metal shelves. Pearl glanced around. At this hour she was alone. She had privacy.

She made sure the tag on the computer matched the reference number, then dragged it over to the edge of the shelf and turned it around. After peeling back about a yard of masking tape, she slipped the plastic wrapping from the computer.

Pearl had been afraid to borrow a screwdriver from one of the techies, but she'd brought the Swiss Army knife she carried in her purse.

Its screwdriver worked just fine. It took her less than ten minutes by her watch to detach and lift off the computer's rectangular metal case, remove the hard drive, then replace the case. Within another few minutes she had the computer rewrapped and taped, and back in its original spot on the steel shelf.

The hard drive was shiny steel and about the size and shape of a paperback book. She tucked it into her waistband beneath her blouse, then returned to the squad room.

"Going out," she said to Sergeant Rudd, who was still busy with his paperwork.

"Why? Those kids making you feel dumb?"

" 'Fraid so." She grinned.

"Used to be," Rudd said, "people got smarter as they got older."

"That was always just a rumor," Pearl told him as she pushed open the heavy door and went out into the morning heat.

As she walked toward her unmarked, she glanced at her watch. Not yet eight o'clock. If she remembered correctly, the stock market didn't open till nine-thirty. If she drove fast and didn't get bogged down in traffic, she should have time.

Of course she could make her destination in plenty of time if she used the light and siren. Trouble was, she wasn't on a call, and it wasn't an emergency, so strictly speaking, it was against regulations.

Pearl decided to use the light and siren.

When she turned the car onto Michelle Quinn's block, the dashboard clock said it was eight-fifty. The stock market wouldn't open for another forty minutes, so it was possible that Michelle was still in her apartment.

Pearl left the unmarked in a no-parking zone and jogged across the street toward Michelle's building. It was the first time she'd seen it. Her other meetings with Michelle had been at a coffee shop near her office in the financial district. It was an obviously expensive building, with a uniformed doorman who looked like the dictator of a small country. Michelle must know her stuff as a stock analyst. In fact, from what Pearl had heard, any analyst out of prison and still employed after the recent bear market must know his or her stuff.

She gave the doorman her name and told him who she was here to see. He studied the tiny screen of a personal digital assistant he produced from a secret pocket in his tunic. One of his eyebrows arched.

"She isn't expecting me," Pearl said.

She stood back and admired his epaulets as he phoned upstairs to see if Michelle Quinn was home and receiving visitors dressed like Pearl.

She was, and she was.

Quinn's sister was standing with her door open so Pearl

would locate the apartment easier. Michelle was dressed for work in a pinstripe gray skirt and blazer, a lighter gray blouse, with a red-and-gray tie—or rather dressed for *going* to work, with her white sneakers sharply contrasting with the somber outfit. Pearl knew that like many New York career women, Michelle would carry her conservative, uncomfortable shoes in her purse until she reached her office.

When Pearl approached, Michelle smiled and extended her hand. "Something important?"

"Maybe. I don't want to take up a lot of your time," Pearl said as they shared a handshake.

"If it's about Frank, go ahead and take it up." Michelle ushered her into a spacious and tastefully furnished apartment with a magnificent sun-touched vista of the city and the Hudson River beyond. The air, which seemed fractured by the crystalline light made somehow more intense by passing through the slanted panes, carried a faint, pleasant lilac scent.

"Nice place," Pearl said, wincing inwardly at her understatement. Most people in Manhattan would kill to live here. Pearl, maybe.

Michelle offered her coffee, which Pearl declined; neither woman had time to waste.

They went through the living room into a book-lined den furnished in rich wood and soft leather of the sort that looks worn-out the day it's bought. On a wide walnut desk sat a blue-and-gray computer—it might have been lifted from the control panel of the starship *Enterprise*. Michelle motioned toward a chair, but Pearl declined again and reached into her purse. She drew out the hard-disk drive she'd removed from Quinn's old computer. "This is—"

"I know what it is," Michelle interrupted. Caution had crept into her voice. She gave Pearl a look, something like the one Quinn sometimes gave her.

"I won't tell you how it came into my hands," Pearl said, seeing Michelle's problem, "but I will tell you where it's from. It was part of the computer that was on your brother's desk in the squad room when he had his problem."

Michelle stared at the tiny steel rectangular box and frowned. Pearl wasn't sure what she was thinking, but she felt like telling Michelle not to fret so much. This was something she was getting from a cop; it wasn't Enron all over again.

Of course, on a personal level, it might be worse.

Michelle moved closer and reached out and accepted the hard drive, gripping it firmly, obviously keenly aware that her fingerprints were now on it. This was a woman who sized up the game and didn't make a move lightly.

"I'm sure a lot's been deleted," Pearl said, feeling better about Michelle now. Quinn said she could be trusted all the way, his good true friend as well as his sister.

"Not much actually gets deleted," Michelle said, "unless whoever's doing it really knows how. Or whoever's trying to recover it *doesn't* know. Prisons are full of people who mistakenly thought they deleted incriminating evidence on computers."

"I remember from seeing on my own computer how it keeps a kind of log—times and sites visited on the Internet. A chronological record of where I've been. If you were to arrange them chronologically . . ." Pearl was increasingly aware that she didn't know what she was talking about. Not enough, anyway. But then, wasn't that why she was here?

Michelle was staring at her, waiting.

Pearl pressed on. "If you could somehow recover those times, dates, and places on the Internet, the child porn sites, and compare them with when your brother was on duty, we might be able to prove he was somewhere else when at least some of those sites were visited." Pearl gave her a level look, trying to appear intelligent. This Michelle was intimidating. "Is any of this even remotely possible? Might that information still be accessible?"

"It probably is."

The woman's face didn't give away much, Pearl thought. Mount Rushmore with makeup. "So what would you have to do to get to it?"

"Risk my career."

"Like I'm risking mine," Pearl said. "And Quinn's not even my brother."

Michelle smiled. And in that instant Pearl knew her romantic relationship with Quinn was no secret. Maybe Michelle had talked to Quinn. Or Sergeant Rudd. Or maybe Michelle somehow had read her, simply figured it out. Maybe it had been on the damned radio.

"Good point," Michelle said. She examined the disk drive more closely. "It's an internal drive, so it doesn't simply slide in a computer bay ready to go. Somebody must have used a screwdriver to remove it."

"You're the expert," Pearl said.

"I can reinstall it in another computer and examine it. There are ways, software programs, that can retrieve almost anything supposedly deleted. And most people—probably the ones we're dealing with—think once they've pressed the delete key, they've actually irretrievably deleted whatever it is they want to get rid of."

"You have this software?"

"If I need it, I can obtain it. But I might be able to get to what we need using another computer's system programs. It might take some time."

"When can you start?"

Michelle removed her blazer and carefully folded it inside out and draped it over the back of a chair. "Now. This morning. It promises to be a quiet day in the markets. Money's on the sidelines waiting to see what the Fed's going to do."

"Yeah," Pearl said, "the feds."

Michelle grinned. "I'll make a few phone calls, then set to work on this. Don't expect anything right away—like today. Where can I get in touch with you?"

Pearl leaned over the wide, polished desk and wrote her name and cell phone number on a tablet. "Here, or you can try Quinn's number."

"Uh-huh." But while her tone was dubious, Michelle appeared secretly pleased. Pearl thought it was nice to be approved of.

"You have my word the source of any information you come up with will remain confidential if at all possible. But the truth is, that's all I can promise."

"I understand. Your word's good enough."

"Thanks," Pearl said. "I mean, really thanks."

She thought Michelle was going to say she was welcome, but instead she said simply, "He's my brother."

"One other thing," Pearl said. "Unless you come up with something we can use, there's no need to tell Quinn about any of this."

"Unless for some reason he asks. I'm not going to lie to him. He's had enough of that."

"So he has," Pearl said. "I'll quit using up your morning and find my own way out."

Michelle didn't waste time on amenities. She was already sitting down at her desk as Pearl was leaving.

Back down on the sun-warmed sidewalk, Pearl thought about what she'd done: stolen police property from the evidence room and involved Quinn's sister. And undoubtedly Quinn himself, if the theft came to light and there was nothing exculpatory on the hard drive.

Everyone involved might take a big hit, even Fedderman. None of them would be trusted again. The law had been broken. Loss of careers would be the least of their problems.

Computers, Pearl decided, were dangerous instruments.

* * *

Lars Svenson writhed around in his bed for several hours, but sleep never came. He considered using more of the stash he'd stolen from his latest conquest, but that was what had probably put him on edge in the first place.

He sat straight up in bed, sweating and trembling. This was pure shit. It felt like there were bugs crawling around just beneath his skin.

He was never going to get to sleep, and he'd be like he was dead when he started work this afternoon.

If he was going into work. The way the day was shaping up, he might call in sick. Or take a vacation day.

Right now he was going to climb out of bed and get dressed. Get out of the apartment and take a walk. Maybe have a drink or two somewhere and try to numb himself, relieve the pressure that was building and building in him.

Walk some more. Maybe for hours.

Sometimes, if he walked far enough, walking helped.

Sometimes it didn't.

38

Lisa Ide realized she'd forgotten her glasses. She'd need them to read the tiny ornate print of the menu at Petit Poisson, where she was due in half an hour to meet two old friends from college. Over lunch and pastries they would have a grand time talking about long-ago allies and enemies. Maybe there'd be photographs to examine, old and recent. Lisa was looking forward to this lunch; it held the promise of being a real bitchfest.

She stopped walking and moved back against a building to avoid the flow of pedestrians. She was less than halfway to her subway stop. There was still time for her to return to the apartment, get her glasses, then take a cab to the restaurant.

Her mind made up, she began striding hurriedly back the way she'd come, breaking into a graceful half walk and half run to make the blinking walk signal at the intersection.

In the hall outside her apartment door, she fumbled with her keys and dropped them. Reminding herself she had plenty of time, she bent over and picked them up, then keyed the lock and opened the door. Within seconds she should be leaving with glasses in hand.

Where are they?

She'd read herself to sleep last night, a Michael Connelly thriller, and probably placed the glasses on top of the book on the nightstand before switching off the light on her side of the bed and dozing off.

But she'd taken only a few steps toward the bedroom when she recalled wearing the glasses in the kitchen this morning to read the calorie count on the cereal box. And later when she'd looked up a phone number in her address book.

She went to the phone on its table near the door.

No glasses.

The kitchen, then. I probably carried them back into the kitchen an hour ago when I got bottled water from the refrigerator. Of course! I must have set the glasses down when I used both hands to loosen the cap on the plastic bottle.

As she was moving toward the kitchen, she heard a slight sound from the bedroom, perhaps something falling.

She stopped. Leon must have taken ill and come home.

No, that wasn't like Leon.

But if it's anyone, it must be Leon.

Maybe he'd returned from the shop for something he forgot. She was here because she was absentminded, so why not Leon?

"Leon?"

She waited for an answer in the heavy silence of the still apartment. There was none. She called louder: "Leon!"

Okay, he must not be home. The sound from the bedroom had simply been something falling over—a picture frame, maybe—or had been from the apartment upstairs. Or perhaps the faint noise had been only in her imagination. Lots of possibilities. She didn't have time to worry about them now.

Lisa continued on her way to the kitchen. As she walked through the door, she immediately saw her glasses lying next to a folded dish towel on the sink counter.

Great! Nothing to do now but snatch up the glasses and be on my way again.

As her fingers closed on the thin steel frames, she glanced at the digital clock on the stove. *Still plenty of time.*

She was leaving the kitchen when she noticed the bouquet of yellow roses in the center of the table.

She stopped cold, then went over to look at them. There were half a dozen of the freshly bloomed, cut yellow roses in a plain glass vase with water in it, no card. Quite beautiful. She couldn't resist leaning over the table and sniffing the nearest blossom, enjoying its fragrance.

Leon again? Another of his mystery gifts? Like the strange earrings I discovered in my jewelry box, the ones he's pretending I had for years and forgot about?

If so, she wasn't supposed to find the roses yet; they were a surprise for this evening. Did he think it was their anniversary or her birthday? Either was possible. He'd gotten the dates of important occasions wrong before. Lisa remembered when the shop had been forty-eight hours early for Valentine's Day, which the sale sign Leon had placed in the window proclaimed as TOMORROW. Lisa had to smile.

She thought about calling her husband's name again, or double-checking to make sure he wasn't in the bedroom.

But if he was in the bedroom, it was because she'd surprised him by coming back to the apartment unexpectedly, and he didn't want her to know he was home. He was hiding, hoping she wouldn't discover him or the roses.

Lisa stood wondering what to do, then decided she should do nothing.

Let Leon have his fun. Maybe he knows what he's doing. He might be leading up to something. Like a European vacation or a Caribbean cruise.

Lisa left the apartment, making sure the door was dead-bolted behind her. This evening she'd pretend the roses were a big surprise. Whatever was going on was weird, but there was nothing to do but roll with it.

Only when she was back on the crowded sidewalk, waiting for the traffic signal to change so she could cross a busy intersection, did she let the thought occur to her fully: *What if somebody else put the roses in the kitchen and went into the bedroom when I returned home unexpectedly?*

Somebody not *Leon!*

"Move it or lose it, lady!"

The light had changed to a walk signal. A florid-faced little man was trying to get around her, bumping her hip with his attaché case. Threads of sparse black hair were plastered across his otherwise bald scalp, and he was wearing a natty gray suit and what looked like a blue ascot.

"Move it or—"

"I never heard that one before," Lisa said. "Is it copyrighted?"

The fussy little guy did what she should have done—ignored the remark.

She let him pass and stride out ahead of her as they crossed the street.

Beyond him Lisa could see Petit Poisson's sign.

And was that woman in the blue dress Abby? The pudgy one hurrying into the restaurant?

If so, she's put on weight. Lots of weight.

Lisa forgot all about the yellow roses as she quickened her pace. She didn't want to be the last to arrive at the restaurant.

A person could get talked about.

39

Luther watched them sleep. Milford had drunk more than his share of scotch after dinner and seemed almost unconscious, too deep in his slumber even to snore. His breathing was as persistent and rhythmic as the sea. Cara slept more lightly beside him.

Luther, moving closer, could see the delicate flesh of her closed eyelids responding as her pupils shifted beneath them.

She's dreaming. Maybe about me.

He might wake her and they could go downstairs, or up to his attic nest. Or—and this they had never dared—they could have sex right there in bed beside Milford, to the regular beat of Milford's own breathing and ignorance. Luther considered it; Milford hadn't budged since he'd entered the bedroom, and probably since long before that. His hair wasn't even mussed. Luther could wake Cara with a kiss, place a palm over her mouth to quiet her if necessary, and then . . .

Don't be an idiot!

Realizing he was breathing hard enough to hear, Luther

backed away from the bed. As if sensing his presence, Cara raised a hand lightly to her forehead, then lowered it. Her eyes remained closed.

Let the Sands sleep for now. Luther would prowl his secret domain.

He left the bedroom and closed, but didn't latch, its door behind him. After only a few steps he felt safe. Sound wouldn't carry through the thick walls. Not bothering to be quiet, he descended the creaking stairs to the first floor.

This was his time, his own dim world where he could indulge himself with whatever he needed at the moment—food, drink, shelter, woman. . . .

At the moment he was hungry. Maybe because of the benzene he'd been inhaling in the attic; it did that sometimes, made him want sex or food later. It could also affect his judgment, something he realized only in retrospect.

Luther made his way into the kitchen, which was illuminated by the night-light on the stove and moonlight filtering through the curtained window. He remembered the scent of dinner a few hours before when he was lying on his cot reading in the attic, almost the taste itself, rising all the way through the vents and cracks and air spaces of the old house to its highest regions. The Sands were having turkey, one of Milford's favorites that Cara prepared regularly. *Thanksgiving at least once a week*. There were always leftovers, and she would make sure there was plenty of white meat for Luther.

He smelled something else when he entered the kitchen. Roses. There was a clear glass vase in the center of the table containing half a dozen yellow roses Cara had brought in from the garden. She loved roses, especially the yellow ones. The scent of roses reminded Luther of Cara, and he knew it always would.

He opened the refrigerator and there was a large remaining portion of the bird on a platter and covered with alu-

minum foil. He removed the platter and placed it on the
Formica table.

When he pulled back the foil, he was pleased to find more
than half of a good-size turkey, baked to a perfect golden
brown. Even one of the drumsticks remained, but Luther
knew he couldn't chance eating it. Milford liked drumsticks
and would wonder. Luther would satisfy himself with a few
thick slices of white meat for a sandwich, washed down with
milk from the carton. Afterward, he'd rinse off the knife he'd
used to carve the meat and replace it in its drawer. Then he'd
return the turkey, milk, and condiments to the refrigerator,
making sure there were no telltale crumbs, and creep back to
his cot in his secret space above.

He found half a loaf of bread in the metal box with the
yellow rose decal on it, and laid it next to the turkey and
milk on the table. Back to the refrigerator for the milk carton, a jar of mustard, and another of pickles. On impulse he
took a jar of olives, too, to eat on the side.

Before sitting down to his feast he glanced at the stove
clock. It was three A.M. The time of deepest sleep. Or so he'd
read in a recent copy of *Psychology Today*.

Luther had finished all but a few bites of his sandwich
and was considering another when he heard something off to
the side and behind him. He knew what it was immediately—someone's sharp intake of breath.

He stopped chewing and turned his head slowly, not really wanting to look, to find out who'd made the sound, pray-
ing it was Cara so his heart could start to beat again.

Cara! Please, Cara!

His prayer was only half answered.

Milford stood in the doorway, Cara behind him and peering around his shoulder. Milford appeared stunned. Cara
looked horrified. Time itself paused. Luther knew they were
all like figures in a painting, no one moving.

He wished it could stay a painting forever.

Milford moved first, lurching toward Luther, only to stop short, as if he hadn't quite gotten over his surprise enough to change direction and go around the table. "What the fuck are *you* doing here?"

His hesitancy gave Luther courage. "I live here."

Milford appeared more puzzled than enraged. "You *what*?"

Luther looked past him at Cara, who still hadn't moved or changed expression. She obviously wanted nothing so much as to whirl and run, only there was no place to go.

"I live here," Luther repeated, wondering himself where he was finding the courage. *Love. It must be love for Cara.*

Milford put his fists on his hips. He was wearing only his Jockey shorts and his musculature was evident. He was thin, even skinny, except for a small pad of flesh that hung over his elastic waistband, but there was a reedy look of strength about him. "Well, now, you little jack-off, if you live here, how come I haven't noticed you around?"

"Maybe you haven't looked close enough."

"And maybe you better explain what's going on here with the one chance I'm gonna give you before tearing you apart so you look something like that turkey. You can start by telling me how the hell you got in here."

"I've been in here." Luther noticed his heart rate had decreased, but he was still frightened. In control, though. Claiming what was his. Or what he wanted so badly that it should be his. "I come and go through the door, just like you do."

"Without a key?"

"I have a key."

Milford peered up at the ceiling, as if for some message written there, then back down at Luther. "You're doing a piss-poor job."

"Of what?"

"Explaining."

Luther glanced at Cara. Her eyes were wide and disbelieving, dark and deep in their shadowed sockets. This was the time they knew would come—both of them—though they'd never spoken of it. He had to be strong.

He faced Milford. "I'm . . . Cara and I love each other." In the corner of his vision he saw Cara bend forward with the force of his words, as if she'd suffered a blow to the stomach.

Milford was stupefied. His eyes widened like Cara's and he looked at her, then back at Luther. There was a click, then a low humming. The refrigerator coming on. Its soft, steady sound only served to intensify the silence.

"I've been living in the attic for over a month," Luther said. "Cara's been taking care of me. She loves me, not you."

Milford laughed, but it was an ugly sound, more like a bark. "In the attic, huh?" He placed both palms on the table and leaned forward. "Listen, Luther, you are one stupid kid. I ask you for the truth and you hand me this fantastic bullshit nobody'd believe. You shoulda made up something better than that, something that could be taken seriously, because—"

"Ask Cara."

"I don't have to."

"You don't want to."

That stopped Milford. He stood up straight and looked over at Cara.

She bowed her head and stared at the floor. "It's true."

Milford actually staggered back a step. *"What?"*

"It's true about the affair."

"You've been fucking this . . . this *kid?*"

She nodded, afraid to look at him.

"A pattern of lies," he said softly. "A lie in every look you gave me, in every word you spoke. . . ."

"I guess that's so."

"You are a cheating, deceiving whore!"

"Maybe I am, Milford. Yes. Yes, I am."

Milford roared and slammed his fist down on the table. Luther's body jerked. The carving knife clattered off the platter. "You two have been making a fool of me for a month?"

"I didn't say we were making a fool of you."

"Now we'll see what kind of fool *you* are," Milford said, glaring at Cara. "Look at me, goddamn you!"

She managed to do that, her lower lip trembling.

"Don't hurt her," Luther warned. "Don't you hurt her."

Milford ignored him. He and his wife might as well have been in the kitchen alone. "You have a choice to make, Cara, and by God it'll be final! You understand what I'm saying?"

She nodded. Now that she'd managed to meet Milford's eyes, she couldn't turn away from their pain and accusation.

Luther stared at Cara, but she wouldn't look at him. He knew this was the balance point—the beginning or the end. Cara held everyone's future in her hands.

Tell him, Cara! Tell him! If only you're not too afraid! Don't be afraid, please!

But she was too afraid.

"It only happened twice, Milford, and I'm sorry. I do beg your forgiveness. If Luther's been living in the attic, I swear to you I don't know anything about it."

Luther felt the floor drop out from beneath him.

Black air rushed past him, roaring in his ears. He was betrayed, crushed inside, and unbelieving at least for a few seconds.

Then the reality of what Cara had said exploded in him.

It was his only reality.

He was floating, standing up but floating, the carving knife gripped tightly in his right hand, feeling a hot rage rising within him like a red rush of hatred, a red flood of vengeance, a red tide of blood that rose and crashed like an ocean. . . .

* * *

When he awoke, he was perspiring heavily and thought he'd been dreaming, that he was on his cot in the attic and he'd had a nightmare.

Whew! Awake! Everything's okay, okay. . . .

Only it hadn't been a dream and it wasn't okay.

Luther wasn't lying on his cot. He was on the kitchen floor, slumped awkwardly with his back against the wall. There was something in his mind, a dark dread he couldn't name.

He was terrified of looking to his left, but he looked.

Milford was sprawled in a scarlet pool of blood near the table. Cara was on the floor just inside the door, lying on her stomach with her head turned so Luther could see one open eye. The other eye was beneath the level of the thick blood that had collected and crusted where the side of her face was pressed against the floor. *Red, so red. . . .* Her nightgown was torn, slashed. *She* was slashed!

Oh, God, God, God!

Luther made himself look again at Milford. Plenty of blood, but not like with Cara. Milford had simply been stabbed. Her flesh was sliced, in tatters.

Cara! Cara!

Suddenly Luther thought about the turkey above him on the table, the turkey he'd carved and had been eating, the white bones, the white meat sliced, *the white flesh,* and the shreds of skin dangling.

He slid all the way to the floor, propping himself on his elbows, and began to vomit.

It was a long time before he stopped.

40

New York, 2004.

The Night Prowler read the quote again, feeling his anger build, and perhaps his fear. It was right there for the world to see on the front page of the *Times,* and attributed to the bastard Quinn:

> *He has some way of knowing whether his victims are married, even if the wife is using her maiden name. Which means he either has access to and knows how to use public records, or he and the victims had previous contact, possibly knew each other well.*

The Night Prowler wadded the front section of the paper and hurled it toward a wastebasket. It missed. It didn't matter. He didn't believe in omens; he believed in destiny.

He stood up, walked to the window, and looked out into the night that belonged to him. The city was darkness and scattered points of light, each a false promise. There was little color in the night, but there was security.

According to all the literature, he was at the point in his "career" where he should be feeling intense pressure to kill more and more often, while he secretly yearned to be caught. He laughed out loud and didn't like the way it sounded, almost like a cawing, and clamped his lips together.

The literature was only half-right. He didn't at all wish to be caught. He'd anticipated the natural reactions within his mind and body, and the tricks of the mind the hunters tried to get you to play on yourself. Oh, he knew how to deal with them!

He was always mindful of the hunters, of Quinn. But he had to be. That was logical. It was caution, not stress.

He observed his reflection in the glass between himself and the night and a world that was mad. He smiled. After a pause his reflection smiled back. Everything was under control.

He turned away from the window and his gaze fell on the wadded newspaper on the floor near the wastebasket.

The media had their story line: Quinn, the hunter, versus the Night Prowler, the prey. And the prey should be feeling the pressure. Quinn had figured out something, so he must be closing in. Since he must be closing in, he must ultimately be successful. It worked out that way in movies, on TV, and in books.

But that was a scripted, different sort of destiny.

The Night Prowler smiled. Real life wasn't that simple.

Neither was real death.

Death from a distance.

He'd figured out where to get a gun.

Lisa had put the yellow roses in a better vase and set them on the buffet in the dining room. She rearranged them carefully, until they were just right.

When Leon came home from the shop, where he'd worked

later than she had, he glanced at them and smiled. "Beautiful," he said. He took a more careful look at the *Post* folded beneath his arm, then tossed the paper on the coffee table. "So how was lunch with your old college pals?"

"Fine. Everyone still looks good. Janet is still beautiful, but Abby's put on lots of weight."

"She's fat?"

"Some people might think so."

"You always liked Janet better than Abby, didn't you? I mean, from what you told me about them."

"Janet was my roommate. She's only in town visiting. She and her husband John live someplace called Morristown."

"Sure. In New Jersey."

"No. This one's in Tennessee. She's acquired this funny accent."

Leon smiled. "I bet you sounded funny to her. She here on business?"

"Partly. She's leaving in a few days."

"Too bad." Leon absently picked up the paper he'd tossed on the table. "Night Prowler. That's all you read about or see on TV. Nothing but gossip that turns out next day or week not to be true. Where the hell is Walter Cronkite?"

"Somewhere on his sailboat, I imagine. And good for him."

"The news is all sensationalism." Back on the table went the paper.

"All about money."

"Yeah, isn't everything?" Leon didn't sound unhappy about it. "You three girls talk about your love lives?"

"Leon! Of course we did."

"So what'd you say about me?"

"Everything." Lisa managed to get it out without laughing.

"Know what that means?"

"We have dinner out at the restaurant of my choice?"

"You got it," Leon said. But he sat back on the sofa and worked his loafers off, using only his feet. Lisa wished he wouldn't do that. It was hard on his shoes. One of them, anyway. "Before we leave, let's have a drink."

"I don't want one," Lisa said, "but I'll get you one. There are martinis mixed in the refrigerator."

"Thanks," Leon said. "Straight up."

So that was it for the roses. He didn't ask about them, so he probably did buy them for me and secretly had the super let himself in and place them on the table. Well, if he doesn't want to discuss them, neither do I. We can play this game forever. There are worse kinds of husbands than the sort who leave gifts lying around. Janet and Abby can eat their hearts out. Though Janet's husband in that photograph is a nice-looking guy, some kind of war hero and engineer. He looks like a winner. The guy Abby's living with is a geek who looks like he lost most of his hair to the mange.

Lisa decided to join Leon in a before-dinner cocktail, so she got two stemmed martini glasses down from the cabinet near the stove.

As soon as she opened the refrigerator door to get out the half-full mixer, she saw the decorative box of Godiva light chocolates, her favorite candy. There was a small red bow on the box, but no card.

She smiled and shook her head.

Oh, Leon . . .

Anna had been reading in bed, Bradlee's unauthorized biography of Yehudi Menuhin, but she'd become restless and put down the book. Then she'd gotten up, paced awhile, and gone to the closet to get down her father's gun that she'd sneaked from the house in Queens.

Back in bed, she lay again propped on her pillow, but instead of a book, it was the gun that rested heavily in her lap.

Anna had read the day's papers, all of them. *Quinn, Quinn, Quinn.* His photo, his words, his lies, were everywhere. They were starting to make him a hero again. And his victim, whom they barely mentioned if at all. . . . Well, that was a long time ago.

To everyone else, anyway. Not to Anna.

She absently began stroking the gun, then realized what she was doing and stopped. According to the pop psychologists, a gun was supposed to be a penis substitute. Maybe it could be, but it was the deadly mechanical aspect of the pistol that intrigued Anna. She began squeezing the trigger over and over, letting the firing pin fall on empty chambers as the cylinder rotated. The mechanism sounded precisely the same each time—a muted, substantial metallic click.

This is one of the few things in life that works as it should, each time, every time, until time itself wears it out.

The gun was such an impersonal instrument—heavy for its size, precise in design and construction, oiled, smooth, efficient and deadly in its purpose. It didn't know shooter from victim, right from wrong, justice from injustice. It simply fulfilled its purpose. Mechanical, irrevocable, it promised a trip to eternity, one-way, nonrefundable.

Eternity was where Quinn belonged, if for no other reason than that it was somewhere else. Somewhere Anna was not.

She climbed out of bed again, got the box of bullets down from the closet shelf, and carefully loaded the gun.

It felt better loaded, even heavier and more potent.

It felt serious.

Holding its cool bulk in both hands was definitely reassuring. She decided to start carrying it in her purse, or tucked in her belt beneath her blouse or raincoat. She knew it was illegal to carry a gun without a permit, but it made her feel safer. And it wasn't just a feeling. Anna was sure that with it she *was* safer.

She reluctantly put the gun and the box of cartridges in the drawer of her nightstand. In doing so, she looked at the clock radio and saw that it was almost midnight. She wouldn't get much sleep before subwaying into the city tomorrow morning. She wouldn't be at her best for her lessons.

But that didn't have to matter. Anna decided to get up at the usual time, dress, and go into the city, but she'd skip Juilliard tomorrow. She'd take a walk and enjoy the park or the city streets. When she went out now, she usually wore sunglasses so people wouldn't recognize her. Not that most of them would, anyway. But if they did, she knew what they must be thinking, how they must be seeing her.

Her mind was made up; there would be no music tomorrow. She'd take a walk.

She'd find something to do.

She switched off her reading lamp, fluffed her pillow, and rolled onto her stomach.

If only I could switch off my mind!

She closed her eyes in the dark and found more darkness.

After a while she dozed off, hearing the music she wasn't going to play, terrified of sleep.

41

Hiram, Missouri, 1989.

Oh, Christ! I killed them! I killed them both!
Cara!
Christ! Christ! Christ!
Luther pressed his back hard against the kitchen wall, scooting and digging in his heels, as if he might make himself a part of the wall, or be somewhere or something else.

Still with his shoulders against the wall, he slowly worked his way to a standing position. He was unable to look at Cara or Milford. The bloody knife he'd been gripping lay at his feet and kept drawing his gaze, as if by some kind of unnatural force. The kitchen was so hot it was dizzying. And there was the blood with its coppery sweet scent, the vomit on the floor, on Milford's white T-shirt. And already the stench of the dead, Luther was sure.

The dead!
Hearing himself whimper, Luther carefully found his way across the kitchen without stepping in any blood. Trembling, he worked his body around Cara and through the doorway to

the hall. He went to the bathroom and stripped off his bloody Jockey shorts and T-shirt and let them lie in a heap in a corner. Then he stepped into the claw-footed iron tub and turned the shower on cold, then warmer. He began to scrub with the soap, cleansing the blood from his face and neck, his arms and chest and stomach, his hands, his hands, his hands. He scrubbed his hands with a stiff-bristled brush until they were chafed and sore, long after the blood of Cara and Milford had disappeared from his reddened flesh.

Then he toweled dry, naked and shivering, and went up to the attic.

If only I could lie down here, be safe here forever.

But he knew better. He was thinking *that* clearly.

Quickly he dressed in his jeans, sneakers, and a blue pullover shirt with a collar, a recent gift from Cara. His mind and body seemed oddly detached from each other. He only knew he had to get out of the house, to get far away.

After leaving the attic, he went into the master bedroom on the second floor and found Milford's wallet on the dresser. And there were Milford's keys alongside some loose change. *His car key!* Luther slipped the bills—a little over $50—into his own wallet, then slid the change and keys into his jeans' tight side pocket.

It was almost four A.M., in the still moonlight, when he opened the garage door and backed Milford's midnight blue Ford Fairlane, with its headlights off, down the long gravel driveway and out into the street.

At first he had a little trouble getting used to the car, but it was an automatic shift and he was soon comfortable enough driving. A block away from the house, he turned on the car's lights.

Luther understood he was in trouble—major trouble—and that even beginning to cope with it was beyond him. He was making one mistake after another; he was aware of it but knew nothing else to do. He was running on fear and instinct, and not reason. Soon Milford and Cara's bodies would be discovered, and everyone would be searching for Luther. *Everyone!*

He knew only that he had to gain distance as fast as possible. Distance might somehow make him safe. At least give him time to think. Distance, in time and miles, had always been his ally. It might save him again.

Careful not to drive too fast and draw the attention of any sheriff's car or highway patrol cruiser that might be prowling the deserted streets, he rolled down Main toward the highway out of town. The highway he wanted to drive forever.

Luther wasn't much worried about the sheriff; he was probably at that all-night truck stop, if he wasn't home in bed asleep. But Nester, that creepy deputy, might be driving around town, working the graveyard shift.

When Luther was passing Wilde's Painting Company, he saw that the lights were on in the office and storeroom.

Wilde! Tom might know what to do! Tom Wilde might help him! The one person he trusted!

Help close to home!

Luther slowed the big Ford, turned the corner, and pulled into the rear drive, where the van was backed close to the overhead door. He parked tight alongside the van, then got out of the car. The small passage door near the overhead was unlocked. Luther looked up and down the dark street before he ducked inside.

Tom Wilde was standing at his workbench, going through his familiar routine of assembling materials: paint cans, buckets, and scrapers. Getting ready for today's job, which would start later this morning. Luther knew the job would be a long drive's distance; Tom meant to get an early start and use the morning light.

He stood watching Wilde from behind, feeling an unexpected flood of affection for him. The familiar, slightly round-shouldered figure in comfort-cut baggy jeans and a speckled white paint shirt, with a bush of unkempt hair and ears that stuck out a bit too far, somehow inspired confidence and trust.

Wilde sensed someone was there and turned, startled.

"Luther! God, boy, you scared the crap outta me." Wild looked more closely at him. "What are you doing here at this hour? Something wrong?"

"Something's plenty wrong, Tom!"

Luther tried to explain everything to Wilde, but he soon began to cry. Ashamed, embarrassed, afraid, he sat down on a five-gallon paint pail and sobbed.

Wilde let him cry. He placed a hand gently on Luther's shoulder, a reminder that he was there, that he cared, and waited patiently, giving Luther all the time and tears in the world.

When Luther's raking sobs became less violent and frequent, Wilde walked over to a cabinet above the workbench and got down a bottle of Four Roses bourbon and an eight-ounce water glass. He poured about two fingers into the glass, then brought it to Luther. "Drink this. Gulp it down without breathing in."

Luther did as he was told, and the liquor hit him with a warm force that jolted his thoughts. He did breathe in now and immediately regretted it, inhaling the alcohol fumes and almost choking.

"Keep breathing deep, Luther." Wilde's hand was back on his shoulder. "You gotta show 'old man booze' who's in charge."

Luther sat with his elbows on his knees, his head bowed, breathing as Wilde had instructed. Gradually the choking sensation went away as he sucked in the cooling scent of the bourbon. It was clearing his head like a breeze on a warm night.

He was better now, had his self-control back. Control. Control was so important. "I'm okay now, Tom."

"Good. Let's talk. Things usually aren't as bad as they first appear. And whatever's wrong, maybe I can help."

"Nobody can help me now," Luther said in a flat voice.

"Lots of times people think that and they're wrong. I'm your friend. Try me. See if I can help. You've got nothing to lose. Where've you been staying since you had your falling-out with Milford?"

"I been with Cara."

"Cara? You mean Cara Sand?"

Luther nodded.

"I don't quite understand," Wilde said.

Luther watched him walk over to the workbench, pour some bourbon into a glass for himself, and down it in one gulp. It didn't seem to affect his breathing. He gave Luther his worn, wise smile.

"Cara Sand, huh? Okay, I'm ready. You can tell me, Luther."

And Luther did, in his new, flat, so very calm voice.

When Luther was finished talking, Wilde went over to the workbench and had a second drink.

"I don't wanna doubt you, Luther, but you sure you didn't dream all this?"

"I'm sure."

"How about we drive back to the Sand place and you can show me?"

Luther stood up. "I don't wanna go back there! I can't!"

Wilde looked at him and nodded. "Okay. Mind if I give them a call?"

"Go ahead. They won't answer."

Wilde used the phone on his cluttered desk and stood listening to the ringing on the other end of the connection, looking at Luther.

"They oughta be home, this time of morning when it's not even light out."

"They're home," Luther said.

After a good three or four minutes, Wilde hung up the phone.

He stood chewing on the inside of his cheek for a while, the way he did when he was thinking hard. Then he rolled the desk chair over near Luther and sat down in it so they were close and facing each other.

"You need to go to the police and turn yourself in," Wilde said. "I'll go with you, and I'll see you get a good lawyer."

"I can't. I told you what I did. They'll execute me or I'll spend the rest of my life in prison. You know that's true, Tom. You promised you'd be honest with me."

"Yeah, you're right, that's what'd happen if all you told me's true."

"It's all true. I'm not giving myself up!"

"Then what you've gotta do," Wilde said, "is get outta Hiram, go far away. You won't do that in Milford's car. The highway patrol'll be looking for it and nail you within hours of the bodies being found." He shook his head as if trying to clear it of unwelcome thoughts. "You need to go to a big city in another state, where you can change your name and make a new life. I know that won't be easy, but unless you want to turn yourself in to the law, that's your one and only chance. You've gotta become somebody else. A different you. It might not be much of a life, after what's happened, but at least it's something."

"That's all I'm looking for, a chance. Something. Because right now I've got nothing. I don't care what the odds are, Tom. Worse comes to worse, they'll catch me and I'll be right where I'd be if I gave up now."

Wilde smiled sadly. "Very logical, Luther."

"Ain't it?"

"It'll be dark for a while yet. You drive Milford's car a few miles outside of town and park it well off the road. I'll follow in the pickup and drive us both the rest of the way."

"Rest of the way where?"

"To where my fishing boat's tied up. They'll be looking for Milford's car, but not a boat."

Luther didn't like the idea of being all alone in a small boat out on the wide, dark river. Still, he'd be safe there from everything *but* the river.

"You take the boat downstream. I'll give you some tackle and a casting rod so it'll look like you're fishing, if anybody takes note of you."

A boat. . . . The idea was growing on Luther. For the first time he felt a twinge of hope. Maybe he could escape this, after all, get away clean from what he'd done, somehow start over, make it right. Make his whole life right.

"You'll be with the current, so you can get pretty far downriver before daylight. Then, when it's light, when you see a likely spot, you dock the boat and . . ."

"What?"

"Then you're on your own, Luther. I'll have helped you all I can."

"What about you, Tom? I don't wanna get you in any trouble. Won't you be suspected as an accomplice?"

"I don't think so. Nobody'll notice my old boat's missing. And I sure won't bring it to their attention. If it is found downstream, it'll look like it came untied and drifted away. Wouldn't be the first time."

Luther swallowed. He looked ready to begin sobbing again. "Tom—"

"Don't thank me, Luther. Do it by going somewhere and creating a good life for yourself. That'll be my thanks."

Wilde stood up from the desk chair.

"It's not the end of the world, if we won't let it be, Luther. Let's get moving while it's still dark out."

Wilde kept his small wooden rowboat pulled up on the bank, near a deserted A-frame cabin built by a weekend fisherman years ago. The cabin had been abandoned after flood damage. The receding water left what remained of a small wooden dock, and a narrow, rutted dirt road that ran from the county highway almost to river's edge. The road was overgrown and disappeared in spots, and even after a light rain, it was muddy and almost impassable.

As Wilde parked the pickup near the A-frame, Luther could see why nobody would notice the boat was missing. Hardly anyone other than Tom must come back here. The only place that there was a break in the trees was a low, marshy stretch of ground that was a breeding pool for the mosquitoes that closed in on the two men as soon as they got down out of the truck.

Wilde slapped at one of the voracious insects on his arm and reached into the pickup's rusty bed for his heavy metal tackle box.

Luther went to the back of the truck and got the casting rod, another tackle box, and a net. With both hands full, he felt a mosquito sting the back of his neck but couldn't slap at it. "Damned bloodsuckers!"

"Aren't they, though?" Wilde said, and led the way down the steep mud path toward the boat and the sloping river-bank.

The boat was pulled up about twenty feet from the water. It was a wooden fourteen-footer with a couple of oars lying in the bottom beneath three plank seats. Its hull was mud-streaked and rotted in places and had once been a light green with a red stripe around the waterline. Now it was mostly a weathered gray color, and the waterline stripe was hard to make out except near the bow. Though it was far from the water, this was flood country and sometimes inaccessible, so a thick, slack rope ran from a cleat on the bow and was knotted around what looked like an old automobile axle driven into the bank.

"You sure this thing floats?" Luther asked seriously.

Wilde laughed softly. "It's like you, Luther, more seaworthy than it looks."

"I don't plan on going all the way downriver to the sea," Luther said.

Wilde untied the boat and tossed the rope into the bow. Luther pushed while Tom Wilde pulled, and together they slid the boat along grass and mud and into the water. Standing knee deep, Wilde wrapped the bowline around a slimy branch that extended out low from the bank.

Luther and Wilde went back to where they'd left the fishing tackle and carried everything down and loaded it into the boat. Moonlight glanced dully off the water. They were in a small cove, and though a stretch of the black, tree-lined opposite bank was visible, Luther was sure no one was observing them. He slapped at a mosquito, this one trying to lance blood from the back of his wrist, and felt the insect mash beneath his hand.

"Once you get out on the river," Wilde said, "they won't be bothering you. They can't abide the current."

Both men were breathing hard from their efforts with the boat and heavy fishing tackle. They stood silently for a while, catching their breaths, trying to figure out how to say good-bye.

For the first time escape seemed not only possible to Luther, it seemed likely. He might actually take the boat downriver, sink it or dock it in some secluded spot, then make his way to safety and another chance, another life. He could be someone else entirely, *the person I want to be,* as Tom Wilde suggested.

Tom Wilde, who'd been like a father to him, but who was also the only one who could implicate him in the murder of Milford and Cara.

Luther, his head cleared by passing time, had been thinking about that. There was plenty to indicate he'd been in the house at the time of the killings, but if caught, he could always say he was also an intended victim of an intruder who'd murdered the Sands. He'd claim he defended himself with the kitchen knife, then dashed through the house and outside and escaped. He knew how it would look for him, so, of course, he ran away. In that situation anyone would have run.

His life on the streets had taught him the value of having a cover story in case he needed one.

But it was a cover story Tom Wilde could contradict, and would, if he was under oath in a court of law.

Luther looked at the heavy steel tackle box in the boat, and the thick bowline. He realized he was different now. Someone else. Someone harder. He'd gone through a door and now he was confronted by another. Whether to open it was his choice.

"I guess this is good-bye, then," Wilde was saying.

Tom Wilde, who'd been kind to him and taught him a craft—an art. His mentor and only friend.

His greatest danger.

"I guess it has to be," Luther said.

Neither Wilde nor Luther ever returned to Hiram. Milford Sand's Ford Fairlane was found parked among some cotton-wood trees off the highway outside of town. It was assumed Luther had murdered the Sands and made his getaway in the car. But without Luther, how the murders occurred was only speculation, and Luther was never seen again.

Tom Wilde's old pickup truck was found parked next to the ruined A-frame near the riverbank. A week later his boat was discovered capsized in the weeds five miles downriver.

It was assumed he'd been fishing and perhaps struck his head while falling from the boat and drowned.

Every so often, the river claimed a life that way.

42

New York, 2004.

Finding out where he lived had been easy. He was in the phone book.

It was the first place Anna thought to look, but she'd been surprised to find Quinn's name, address, and phone number. It was unsettling, how simple it had been. As if he might also be in the Yellow Pages under RAPISTS.

So here she was this morning, not at Juilliard with her viola, but across the street from Quinn's apartment with her gun.

What's a nice girl like you . . . ?

She wasn't sure herself.

Anna was running on pure emotion now and knew it. This wasn't smart. In fact, this was totally dumb, what she was doing. But something in her was making her do it; to resist it would have been to escape something that had the most powerful hold on her she could imagine. That, too, was unsettling, that people could be made captive and controlled by something inside themselves. One of the reasons it was disturbing was that it explained in part why Quinn had raped her, almost provided him with an excuse.

There is no excuse for evil. It has to be—

There was Quinn, emerging from his apartment building! Quinn in the flesh!

Anna felt dizzy; for the first time in years, she laid eyes on the monster of her memory. He was big, but not as big as in her fearful thoughts and terrifying dreams. She knew larger, more ominous-looking men. Her friend Agatha's father, and Professor Fishbien at Juilliard. But Quinn did look like what he was—a thug, a rapist, a liar. Not that he wasn't dressed respectably enough, in brown slacks and a tan sport coat. He was even wearing a tie.

Sheep's clothing . . .

As Quinn buttoned his jacket, Anna caught a glimpse of a leather strap and knew it was part of a shoulder holster.

I have a gun, too! I have a gun, you bastard!

Quinn glanced up at the sky as if checking for rain, then began walking. He had a lumbering yet athletic gait, relaxed but poised to move fast on short notice. He seemed amiable but at the same time dangerous, a man who would enjoy a cruel joke. Staying on the opposite side of the street and well back from him, Anna began to follow.

Quinn walked only a few blocks and entered a diner, where he no doubt would have breakfast.

Anna decided to wait for him.

She found a spot across the street and moved back into a shadowed stone angle at the base of an office building. Hardly anyone paid attention to her as they hurried past. If they did happen to glance at her, as far as they were concerned, she was just another young woman waiting for a friend or a lover, or she was building up nerve to go for a job interview. She was like thousands of others who were tending to business, professional or personal, in the city.

Still, Anna felt as if she were being stared at, maybe because of the gun in her purse. She pretended to be bored, and now and then, more for herself than for anyone who might be observing her, she glanced at her watch as if concerned with the time. *Waiting for someone . . . that's what I'm doing. . . .*

Anna watched people coming and going at the diner for almost an hour. Then Quinn emerged, with two people she'd seen go inside not long after she'd taken up position across the street. One was a balding, middle-aged man in a horribly wrinkled brown suit that emphasized his stomach paunch. The other was a short, dark-haired woman with vivid features, even from this distance, wearing a conservatively tailored gray skirt and dark blazer that didn't disguise her curves.

They must be the other detectives Anna had read about in the papers. "Team Quinn." The rapist's friends and helpers.

Anna felt an overwhelming curiosity about Team Quinn. She wanted to know where they went on days off from work, what food they liked, which TV shows, what were their hobbies. How did they spend their free time, the time when she was trying to think about anything other than Quinn and what he had done to her? What did the other two think about Quinn's second chance? Quinn, who had never seen the inside of a courtroom as a defendant, much less spend a day in confinement. They were supposed to be hunting a killer, and catching him would somehow—at least in the minds of some—rehabilitate Quinn.

A real rapist. Real detectives. How will they spend their workday?

The three detectives walked slowly and casually along the sidewalk, talking and gesticulating to each other. Then they stopped near a plain white car and chatted a few minutes more. Quinn stood with both hands in his pockets and seemed to be doing most of the talking now.

The baggy-suited man got into the car, and the dark-haired woman walked around to the driver's side. But before she did, in the brief time the other man was in the car and she and Quinn were alone on the sidewalk, she dragged her fingertips lightly along Quinn's arm and smiled at him.

Interesting . . .

Still smiling slightly at Quinn, who stood motionless watching her, the woman slid into the car behind the steering wheel.

Quinn still didn't move as the car waited for a break in traffic, then pulled away from the curb. Several pigeons, which had been pecking away in the gutter, flapped into the air to get out of the way, then circled and settled back down exactly where they'd been.

When the vehicle—probably an unmarked police car—had rounded the corner, Quinn began walking. He moved easily, with one hand still in a pants pocket, not in any rush. At a magazine kiosk near the corner, he stopped. The hand came out of the pocket and deposited some change on a stack of magazines, and he picked up a newspaper. After a glance at the paper, he tucked it under his arm and continued on his way.

There was no doubt in Anna's mind what she should do. She had no car, so obviously she couldn't have followed the other two detectives.

That left Quinn.

Don't do it. Turn around and go home. Dumb, dumb . . .

But here she was and she had nothing to do but follow him.

Anna gave up trying to talk herself out of it. She was already walking behind Quinn, anyway, though she hadn't made the conscious decision to do so. It was as if choices were being made for her by some higher power.

She was sure it had something to do with the gun, but she didn't understand the connection.

* * *

Leon Holtzman was hungry.

The illuminated red numerals on the bedroom clock indicated it was two forty-five A.M. Leon's stomach had been upset that evening and he'd eaten light when he and Lisa met friends at the French Affaire for drinks and dinner. The mint cappuccino he'd had for dessert hadn't helped his digestion, as he'd foolishly claimed it would. Lisa had warned him about drinking coffee to medicate a dyspeptic stomach: *So what are you, Leon, a doctor?* He wasn't. He should have listened.

After parting with the other couple outside the restaurant, Leon and Lisa cabbed back to the apartment, bouncing over what seemed like dozens of potholes. Each crevice caused the driver to accelerate and then brake suddenly, as if he were in a series of hundred-foot drag races. At times Leon thought he might lose his small but excellent dinner in the back of the taxi. Once, grim-faced, he'd suggested to the driver that the cab should be equipped with a barf bag.

It was past eleven o'clock when they arrived home, so he'd taken some expired prescription medicine of Lisa's to calm his stomach and gone straight to bed.

Now, less than four hours later, whatever was bothering Leon seemed to have left him, possibly due to the medicine whose brand or generic name he'd have to remember. His normally healthy appetite had returned.

He glanced over at Lisa's shadowed form and listened to her breathing. She was obviously sleeping well, and Leon didn't want to disturb her. He held his breath as he climbed out of bed and located his pants on the chair where he'd folded them the night before.

The bedroom was dim and he was still disoriented; he had to brace himself with one hand on the dresser as he slipped his left leg into the pants and his big toe found resistance. Almost falling, he cursed under his breath. Fifteen—no, ten!—years ago, he could have put on his pants in a dark room while running. Jumped into his damned pants! That was the young Leon Holtzman!

Standing up straight, he fastened his belt rather than let it dangle, took another look at Lisa to make sure he hadn't awakened her, then quietly made his way toward the kitchen.

He saw right away that the hall was brighter than it should be. Lisa must have forgotten to switch off the kitchen light when she came to bed—again. With what the utilities charged these days! What if he gently woke her up, talking to her nicely, of course: *Lisa, honey, I just wanted to tell you, so maybe you won't forget next time, that you went to bed and left the kitchen light on—again.*

No, that was probably a bad idea.

Leon was still slightly irritated by his wife's forgetfulness, distracted as he entered the kitchen.

He stopped short just inside the door.

Incredible!

His mind tried to catch up, tried to figure out if he should be terrified, angry, or both at the sight of the strange man seated at his kitchen table and sipping milk from the carton. *Unsanitary!* Leon inanely wondered if he should berate the stranger for his thoughtlessness and lack of manners. He heard his mother's long-ago words: *This is how disease spreads, Leon.*

He began to recover from his surprise and stammered incoherently as he took a few steps toward the stranger in his kitchen, who was casually placing the milk carton on the table.

The man rose to greet him, as if to shake hands.

Lisa awoke.
Leon?

She sensed that her husband was gone even before she reached an arm over to check and felt only cool linen.

Was he ill?

He hadn't felt well most of last night at the restaurant, and the cab ride had made him worse. *Cab ride from hell! The subway would have been better!*

She recalled now what had awakened her, a noise from the hall bathroom, or maybe the kitchen.

So Leon had gotten up and was either trying to find something to ease his discomfort, or he was feeling better and was in the kitchen rummaging about for something to eat. It would be one or the other.

Lisa decided to get out of bed and go find out which.

43

Quinn was on his way to meet Pearl and Fedderman at the park entrance the next morning when his cell phone beeped.

He slowed his pace but continued walking as he drew the phone from his pocket and held it to his ear.

Harley Renz answered his hello with "You up for another one this morning, Quinn?"

At first Quinn thought Renz had somehow found out about him and Pearl and was being a wiseass. Then he realized what he must mean and stood still. "You sure it's our guy?"

"That's *your* job, isn't it?"

A woman danced around Quinn, deliberately grazing his hip, and glared at him for taking up sidewalk space to have a phone conversation.

Screw you, lady. "Don't waste my time, Harley."

"Waste time? The principals in this little drama aren't going anywhere. A man and his wife, dead in their apartment on the West Side."

"You sure it's his wife?"

"What are you, the morality police?"

"Harley . . ."

"Okay, I'm assuming," Renz admitted. And he gave Quinn an address in the seventies.

As soon as the connection was broken, Quinn called Pearl and told her his location, then called Fedderman, who was already driving in from Queens in the unmarked to pick up Pearl. The morning was moving fast.

After replacing the phone in his pocket, Quinn made his way to some shade beneath an awning in front of a luggage shop and waited. There had been no point in walking the rest of the way to the park.

Which was a shame, he thought; it was a beautiful day in the neighborhood.

Renz hadn't been quick enough this time. When Quinn, Pearl, and Fedderman arrived, there were already half a dozen police cars and an ambulance positioned in front of the victims' building.

Pearl parked the car half a block down and they walked back.

"The uniform on the door," Fedderman said, "I know him. Name's Mehan and he'll talk to me if I ask."

"Go ahead and ask," Quinn said. "Pearl and I will go up to the apartment and get started."

Mehan was one of those beefy, redheaded guys with a pink complexion that made him look as if he'd burn if he even got near a beach. He saw them approach and without moving anything but his eyes gave them a look—not curious, not even interested, just a look.

But there was a flash of recognition when he saw Fedderman. "Wha' say, Feds?"

"Not much." Fedderman moved off to the side so Mehan could get a clear look at Quinn and Pearl.

Quinn flashed his new shield to be polite and Mehan nodded.

Pearl followed Quinn into the lobby. It was an impressive vista of marble, mirrors, and oak paneling, but there was a faint ammonia scent, as if the floor had just been mopped and disinfected. Another uniform was standing like a good soldier by the elevator. He was compliant; if Quinn and Pearl had made it past Mehan, they were okay to go farther. Security folding like an accordion.

"You're lookin' for fourteen B," he said to Quinn.

Quinn thanked him.

The uniform smiled and nodded to Pearl as she and Quinn waited for the elevator.

On the fourteenth floor there was another uniformed cop posted outside an apartment with its door wide open like an invitation to the hospitality suite at a convention. This cop, a big curly-haired guy who looked like he should be a country-western singer, recognized Pearl.

"Stayin' outta trouble, Pug?" he asked with a grin.

"You better watch out that I'm not," Pearl said as she and Quinn moved past him into the apartment. She might have been joking; Quinn never knew for sure.

Great place, Pearl thought, looking around the living room. Lots of space, high ceilings, new-looking furniture, and the flawlessness of fresh, cream-colored paint. *I've gotta get painting again in my apartment.* The drapes were a pale blue that complemented furniture upholstered a darker blue, where it wasn't brushed steel. Pearl wasn't one for the modern look, but this place she could live in.

What she was wondering now was, *who died in it?*

Nift, the Napoleonic little ME, was standing off to the side in the living room, ignoring a couple of techs dusting everything for prints. As usual, Nift was nattily dressed, this time in a chalk-stripe black suit that would shame Fedderman when he came upstairs. Of course Fedderman wouldn't notice. Nor would he notice Nift's white-on-white shirt and improbably lush silk tie. Fedderman bought his ties in drugstores.

"Guy looks like a Wall Street asshole," Pearl whispered to Quinn as they approached.

Nift had just finished peeling off his rubber gloves. He looked over at Quinn and Pearl and smiled. "Ah, even more detectives."

"Fill us in," Quinn said.

"Why? Are you hollowed out?"

"Don't be such a prick," Pearl said.

Nift gave her his imperious look, as if to say, *yes, the peasants are still revolting.* "You gonna report me for insubordination, Sugar Ray?"

"She's gonna report me," Quinn said, "for dropping you out a window. Don't waste our time—do your job and give with what you've got."

Nift grinned at Quinn to let him know he wasn't afraid. "Didn't you threaten to do that window thing to me before?"

"Yeah, but you came around."

Nift appeared unfazed, but he did get cooperative. "Two dead in the kitchen, a Lisa Ide and one Leon Holtzman. Husband and wife, or so I was told by others of your ilk. Leon was stabbed three times, Lisa approximately twenty, many of the wounds in erogenous zones."

"On both bodies?" Quinn asked.

Nift seemed to consider going smart-mouth again, then changed his mind. "Only on Lisa. Leon got it in the heart, as she did. But he died fast, and my guess is her other stab wounds were inflicted first."

"The killer enjoyed his work," Pearl said.

"And who wouldn't? Anyway, this all seemed to transpire this morning, sometime between two and four o'clock." Nift absently smoothed his wonderful maroon-and-black tie. Quinn noticed he wore a gold clasp to keep the tie from dangling and getting bloody. "That's about all I can tell you for sure, until after the postmortem."

"Any signs they resisted?" Pearl asked.

"To speculate would be playing detective, Detective."

"Nift, how would you like—"

"There are only a few defensive wounds on the victims' hands and arms, not as if they put up what you'd describe as a struggle."

"I'd describe talking to you as a struggle. In fact—"

"Look like the same knife that killed the other married couples?" Quinn interrupted. Sometimes it was difficult to maintain a businesslike atmosphere with Pearl around.

"The Night Prowler's knife? Yeah, it could have been. Remember, I've only done the prelim, so that's all I can tell you right now."

"Nift—"

"Let's go," Quinn said, gripping Pearl's elbow and steering her away. After a few steps she jerked her arm out of his grasp and gave him a look he felt bounce off the back of his skull.

They went into the kitchen to examine the carnage.

There was the husband on the floor, dead with his eyes open in suspended surprise. There was the wife about five feet away from him, lying on her back in a bed of blood, with her legs splayed and her bared breasts carved by a madman. Her left nipple was missing. Pearl thought she saw it on the floor near the woman's hip, but it was difficult to know for sure, the way it was coated with dried blood.

"He's getting more violent," Pearl said, feeling bile rise in her throat. *Don't get sick and lose it. Not in front of Quinn. Or Nift. Can't be weak. . . .*

"Check out the table," Quinn said.

Pearl looked to her left and saw an open milk carton.

She went over and peered closely at it without touching it. "Expiration date's not for another three days." She touched the carton lightly now with the inside of her bare wrist. "Room temperature."

Two detectives who'd been in a back room, apparently the bedroom, entered the kitchen. One was a seriously over-weight guy with a shaved head. His partner was a handsome African American in his forties who looked as if he worked out and lived in a health store. They were Egan's troops.

Quinn and Pearl reached for their shields. "We're—"

"We know who you are," the bald one said. He gave Quinn a nasty grin. "I thought you were assigned to juvenile."

"I'm Lou Jefferson," said the black cop. "My partner's Wayne Frist."

Pearl was giving Frist a dead-eyed look. "We all going to cooperate?" she asked.

Frist looked away as if dismissing her.

"As long as we're here together," Jefferson said, "we might as well make nice."

"We already got the victims' names," Quinn said, trying to prime the pump.

"Here's some more on them." Jefferson was referring to his notepad. "They owned a jewelry store on Forty-seventh, L and L's Diamond Emporium. I know it; it's one of those long, narrow places lined with showcases. They sell mostly diamonds, but also other kinds of gems and jewelry. There are a couple of valuable pieces laying around the apartment, but Wayne and I just finished tossing the bedroom. Nothing seems to have been stolen, but we'll try to get an inventory from somebody who'll know."

"Lou . . . ," Frist said, sending an angry look Jefferson's way. Clearly, he thought Jefferson was being too coopera-tive.

"Anybody see or hear anything suspicious?" Quinn asked.

"We haven't talked to the neighbors or doorman yet. We just got here about twenty minutes ago."

"I've gotta get some air before I puke," Frist said with a sideways glance at Quinn. He eased around a puddle of blood and out the door.

"He seems so sensitive," Pearl said.

Jefferson paid her no attention and addressed Quinn. "You talked to the ME, so he told you about stab wounds and such?"

"Yeah, he was very cooperative."

"For such a dickhead," Pearl added.

Jefferson grinned and flipped his notepad closed. "I heard she was kinda rowdy," he said to Quinn.

"Oh, she is."

Not giving up his grin, Jefferson gave them a little half salute and left the kitchen to join his partner.

"What a putz," Pearl said.

"Forget being testy for a while. What do you think here?"

"Gotta be our guy," Pearl said.

Quinn stooped low and looked at the couple whose marriage had ended so suddenly and unexpectedly. Lisa had been quite beautiful. Leon, the older of the two, with gray hair and beard stubble, had been a lucky man.

Pearl went to the refrigerator and opened it. "Gift box of chocolates," she said. "Expensive. Any woman would appreciate a present like that."

Quinn stood up, hearing the cartilage in his knees crack. "I'm sure we'll learn that Lisa loved chocolate."

"And she loved jewelry, judging by the wedding ring she slept in and those diamond stud earrings she must have been too tired to remove when she went to bed last night. They look like they cost what a cop makes in a year."

"She and Hubby owned the shop," Quinn said, "so why not?"

"I wasn't criticizing," Pearl said. "I was complaining."

There was nothing unexpected in the bedroom. The king-size bed was unmade, two pillows obviously used and the covers thrown back. It looked as if the bed's occupants had gotten up in mild haste and expected to return.

Pearl and Quinn didn't spend a lot of time there.

When they returned to the living room, the techs were still busy and Nift hadn't left. He was talking on the phone near the door. Pearl drifted away and took a short tour of the rest of the apartment, in part to admire the decor.

When she got back, Quinn was standing by the window. Pearl went over and stood next to him, then looked down to see what he was staring at.

Jefferson and Frist were below, talking to the uniformed doorman, who must have just come on duty, his schedule altered by the murders.

"I went into the dining room," Pearl said softly. "There's a vase of yellow roses in there. Fresh ones."

Quinn looked over at her.

"This is the third murder with at least one yellow rose present someplace in the apartment."

"More pattern, huh?"

"I'd say so. And it's always possible Mary Navarre, the only roseless victim, received roses earlier and they wilted and she threw them out. I know they weren't in her trash, but she might have dropped them down to the incinerator."

Fedderman entered and walked over to join them.

"Let's go," Quinn said, sounding businesslike.

"Where?" Fedderman asked.

"It's ten o'clock. Frist and Jefferson are down there interviewing the doorman, who was no doubt asleep at the time of the murders and doesn't know anything. You two start with the neighbors. By the time Frist and Jefferson get done jerking around outside, you'll be a couple of apartments ahead of them."

"Sounds right," Pearl said.

The three of them moved toward the door. Nift had just hung up the phone and was standing there.

Pearl paused in front of him. "Leonard or Robinson?" she asked.

Nift stared at her. "Huh?"

"You called me Sugar Ray. Which Sugar Ray?"

"Oh. I don't know. Who the fuck cares? Only Sugar Ray I know is Leonard."

"I'm Robinson," Pearl said, and gave his tie a sharp yank so the gold clasp popped off and bounced on the carpet. "Find that or you'll be a suspect."

She was out the door and gone before Nift could get over his shocked anger and think of a counterpunch.

Anna Caruso stood across the street from the apartment building Quinn and his detectives had entered. She wasn't noticeable because she was only one of several dozen people gathered in a knot of onlookers that shrank and grew as passersby joined the group and others left.

There really wasn't much to see except parked police and emergency vehicles, including an ambulance. What people were waiting to see, Anna knew, was if someone would be carted out and placed in the ambulance either alive or dead. That was how people were. Since the ambulance had been there for some time and there was obviously no rush, the odds were improved that someone inside the building was dead. Anna had heard several of her fellow gawkers speculate that this might be another Night Prowler murder.

Anna shrank back a few feet to be less noticeable as her interest increased. The two guys in suits who had to be cops had left after talking with the doorman, and now Quinn emerged from the building.

He, too, walked over to accost the doorman, who excused

himself for a moment to hold the door open for one of the building's tenants. The doorman seemed a little annoyed, as if murder shouldn't interfere with his job. There were doors to open, packages to sign for, cabs to hail.

After about five minutes Quinn left the beleaguered doorman alone and walked toward the corner.

Anna followed, hanging back and staying, as was her strategy from watching movies and TV, on the opposite side of the street. Tailing somebody really wasn't all that difficult. For Anna, it had become an obsession.

What would it be like to be a cop, instead of playing music?

At the intersection a cab pulled over near a fire hydrant and a woman laden with shopping bags struggled out from the backseat.

Quinn picked up his pace and retrieved one of the plastic bags the woman had dropped, then exchanged a few words with her and took over the cab. Anna saw him in sharp profile as he leaned forward in the back of the cab and told the driver their destination.

She decided not to try to follow. What was the use? By the time she found a cab herself, Quinn would be well out of sight. The "follow that cab" method seemed to work only in fiction.

She stood rooted by anger as she watched the cab drive away. Usually she rode the bus or took the subway. Quinn could afford cab fare these days, on the money the city was paying him—the city that should have prosecuted him.

Anna wandered back to the building, where she knew two more Night Prowler victims probably lay dead.

Her thoughts were jumbled by her insistent rage. She should feel sorry for the victims, but she could only feel sorry for herself. After all, if it weren't for the Night Prowler and his victims, Quinn would still be under whatever rock he'd retreated to in order to escape a trial and prison.

While Anna lived with her rage and shame, circumstances had worked in her attacker's favor. A serial killer roamed the city, and the police thought Quinn was their best chance to stop him. The city needed Quinn, so the city embraced him—after discarding Anna.

It isn't fair! she kept repeating to herself as she walked faster and faster.

Her anger was a driving force she could no longer control.

It isn't fair!

44

Seated in the back of the cab, Quinn called Harley Renz on his cell phone and gave him the details of the latest Night Prowler killings.

He slipped easily into cop talk, clipped, incisive, and impersonal.

"It's gonna get even stickier," Renz said when Quinn was finished. "The public'll be leaning on the pols, who're already leaning on the department higher-ups, who're leaning on folks like me. Shit rolls downhill and picks up speed, Quinn, and that's where you are, at the very bottom of the hill."

"Well, let's hope it hits the fan before it reaches me. You got anything I should know?"

"Only that Egan and his pals are saying bad things about you. Off the record, of course."

"Off the record to the media."

"So astute you are sometimes."

"Maybe I can be astute and deduce something before Egan's troops do."

"They sense a shift in the balance, Quinn; innocent Anna

is becoming the seriously wronged and sympathetic party, and you're on your way to becoming the villain again."

"I sense it, too," Quinn said. "We'll just have to work through it. When you can, let me know what the postmortems reveal."

"Okay. Speaking of Egan's troops, who drew the case?"

"Couple of guys named Frist and Jefferson."

"Both deep in hock to Egan. Jefferson's okay, just in a bind and covering his ass. Frist is a jack-off under the best of circumstances."

"That's kind of how I read them. Frist is afraid of Pearl."

"Who isn't?"

"Anything new on the silencer?" Quinn asked, getting in a dig.

"You laugh about the silencer, but we're narrowing it down. It's the kinda police work you never did grow into, Quinn, which is why your career turned to garbage."

Quinn thought Renz might have a point.

"Where you going now?" Renz asked.

"How'd you know I'm going someplace?"

"I deduced from the car engine and traffic noise, plus the rattling when you hit potholes indicates a New York cab."

"That's good deducing."

"I'm a policeman, you know."

"I didn't. I'm on my way to my place to reexamine the murder files. I want to make sure of something."

"What would that be?"

"Deduce," Quinn said, and cut the connection.

The buzzing had abated.

The Night Prowler sat at an outdoor table at a restaurant on Amsterdam and ate eggs over easy while enjoying the beautiful morning. It was the beginning of another warm day, but with a gentle breeze that made being outside comfortable and chased away exhaust fumes.

Three tables away sat a woman with long brown hair, sipping coffee and studying papers she'd removed from a briefcase that was alongside her chair. She had striking blue eyes and slender, delicate features. The expanse of nyloned leg visible between black high-heeled pumps and the hem of her blue skirt was difficult not to keep glancing at, and she knew he was watching her—he was sure of it.

You like being observed, studied. You like it very much.

Are you feeling between your thighs, in the core of you and in your heart, what I'm feeling? Are you?

Sensing his thoughts, he was sure, she looked over at him, then quickly back down at her papers on the table. No change of expression. But he'd seen her blush, caught the subtle alteration of color in her flesh, the soft rose hue that came and went with emotional tide.

The Night Prowler didn't change expression, either. He simply looked slightly away and took a sip of his own coffee, talking to her in his mind.

You're not as untouchable as you'd like to think. You can be touched, so pink and red and brown. You're a confection. What color are your nipples? You can be had. You can be had by me.

She used a pen to make a notation on one of the papers, not looking over at him. But he knew she'd heard in her mind the message of his own.

A man in his thirties, with wind-mussed blond hair and carrying his suit coat slung over his shoulder, entered the restaurant's cordoned-off seating area and sat down across from the woman. She smiled at him and immediately tapped the edges of her papers on the table to align them, then leaned sideways gracefully and slid them back into her briefcase.

The Night Prowler made it a point to ignore her now, not wanting to be noticed and outnumbered. He tried to avoid scenes.

But I haven't forgotten you. I put you away in my mind and I'll get you out later, when I need you.

Nothing will come of it.

Or maybe something will.

He looked down and saw that he was gripping his spoon almost hard enough to bend it. Lowering the spoon to the table, he felt a sudden chill, as if the morning had cooled abruptly.

This woman was a total stranger, he cautioned himself. They had never spoken. He knew nothing about her other than how she looked. How she held herself in repose. How she moved.

But wasn't that enough? Wasn't that how it was supposed to work, according to the literature, to the police, to the hunter Quinn? Compulsion. *Something distinctive about the woman might have triggered my compulsion!*

The cops, the FBI, assumed that after a certain amount of blood and benediction, the serial killer's compulsion would become stronger and seize complete control of him, and eventually force mistakes.

Control was something the Night Prowler refused to relinquish. Powerful hidden desires could be coped with and managed. They could be channeled and fulfilled. That was something the so-called experts were afraid to acknowledge. But they knew it. And if they didn't, they were learning. He was teaching them.

He finished his eggs, which were cooling in the breeze, then signaled the waiter for a refill on his coffee and began reading the newspapers he'd bought at two separate kiosks. This was enjoyable, sitting in the sun and at his leisure leafing through the papers for news of himself. His anonymous, famous self.

His gaze fell on a name he recognized. In a weekly celebrity feature called "Showbiz Shebangs," halfway down an inside page. Claire Briggs.

But what made him sit up straight was the information that surrounded her boldly printed name. He read the paragraph again:

> Actress **Claire Briggs**, *currently charming Broadway audiences in* Hail to the Chef, *will be married next week to her longtime love interest, actor* **Jubal Day**. *Time and place are of course a secret, now that Claire glitters as a major Broadway star. Congrats to the happy couple.*

The Night Prowler read the paragraph several times, completely forgetting about the woman three tables away. He couldn't help smiling as he added cream to his coffee and stirred. He watched as the marbled liquid absorbed the whirlpooled white strands and became a uniformly rich but light caramel color. *What color are your nipples?* Then he turned his attention yet again to the show business gossip column. He couldn't stop reading it.

Compulsion? Maybe. But surely there's a proper time for compulsion if it's controlled. If it's focused. So enjoy, enjoy. . . .

Who said the papers never printed good news? Claire Briggs was getting married. She of the braided hair and beguiling grace.

Claire Briggs!

Congrats to the happy couple!

45

When Quinn climbed out of the cab in front of his apartment building, he saw a gray-haired man about sixty sitting slumped on the concrete stoop.

Future me, if this investigation doesn't work out.

The man's bearing suggested he'd been there awhile but was prepared to wait longer. He was wearing gray slacks and an untucked tropical print shirt. When he saw Quinn, he became more alert and removed his sunglasses, then stood up stiffly, as if his back ached.

As Quinn approached, he saw that the shirt had a colorful ornate design of parrots and exotic blossoms. The man was older and taller than he first appeared, and there was something in his patient stance and in his eyes that said he was a cop.

He smiled, just a bit, and asked curiously, "Quinn?"

"Quinn," Quinn said, and shook the man's proffered hand.

His grip was firm and dry, and he didn't make the handshake a contest. "Name's Nester Brothers. I'm here about the Night Prowler murders. There somewheres we can talk?"

"We can go upstairs to my place, or there's a bar a few blocks over." Quinn glanced at his watch. "I know it's only eleven o'clock, but—"

"Bar," Nester said.

Ten minutes later they were seated in a front booth of Whichi Woman, a small lounge that served almost inedible sandwiches along with booze, and featured bad music on weekends. It was a pickup parlor for mostly legitimate singles on the prowl, but occasionally vice cleared away the hookers. The bland-featured, overweight bartender had the door propped open as an invitation to fresh air, but the place still smelled of last night's stale beer and disappointment.

There was only one other customer in Whichi Woman, a despondent-looking business type hunched over what looked like a martini at the far end of the bar. Quinn wondered if the poor bastard had just been fired. Every inch of his elegantly hunkered form suggested it was a miserable world and he was miserable in it.

When Nester had a beer in front of him, and Quinn a club soda with a twist, Nester looked outside the spotted window at the cars creeping along and being left behind by the flow of pedestrians. "Shit pot fulla traffic," he said, "but it looks like it's goin' no place fast."

"It mostly is," Quinn said. *Isn't?* "First time in New York?"

"Yep." Nester took such a big, hearty swallow of beer from his frosted mug that it might have hurt him.

"Business or pleasure?"

"Business. You. I came here to see you about this Night Prowler asshole." Another long pull of beer. Nester was some robust drinker, considering it wasn't yet noon. "I used to be a cop."

"It shows."

"I s'pose it does. I was a sergeant in the Saint Louis Police Department. I'm retired now. Got pensioned off after a back injury few years ago. Before the Saint Louis job, I was a sheriff's deputy in a little river town in Missouri. Place called Hiram. What I do now that I'm not workin' is sit on my ass and read the paper, watch TV news, an generally try an' stay outta the wife's way. 'Nother thing I do is spend time online. You ever get online, Quinn?"

"Not much anymore."

"Most everything ever printed about the Night Prowler killin's is online. While I was readin' about 'em, somethin' started to bother me, an old cop's kinda hunch that starts in the gut instead of the brain. You fathom what I mean?"

"I fathom." Quinn sipped his club soda to be sociable and signaled the bartender for another beer for Nester, whose mug was almost empty. The bartender was busy hoisting a metal barrel out from behind the taps and simply nodded to show he'd seen Quinn.

"I thought you oughta know about the Sand case."

"Never heard of it," Quinn said.

"No reason you shoulda. It happened in Hiram back in '89, half a continent away."

Both men were silent while a hard-looking waitress, who'd just come on duty, placed a fresh beer on the table and withdrew.

"That woman have a cussword tattooed just below her left eye?" Nester asked.

"She did," Quinn said. "New York."

"Back to Hiram in '89," Nester said, "where you never saw that kinda tattoo and probably still don't. Fella and his wife, name of Milford and Cara Sand, were found stabbed to death in their kitchen. Ugly scene, 'specially the way the wife was carved up, round the crotch and tits. Ordinary enough couple, though Milford could be a bit of a shit. Sometimes they were foster parents, and they had this sixteen-year-old boy, Luther Lunt, stayin' with 'em at the time."

Quinn got his notepad from his pocket and found that

he'd used the last sheet of paper. He pulled a napkin from a holder on the table and began making notes on it.

Nester waited patiently until Quinn had caught up. "'Bout three in the mornin'," he continued, "young Luther stabbed the both of 'em to death in their kitchen, then hightailed it outta town. Nobody in Hiram ever seen him again. What made me come see you is I noticed a lotta similarities in the Sand murder, which I helped investigate, and these Night Prowler killins of yours."

"Such as?"

"They all but one took place in kitchens in the early-mornin' hours, all the victims were married couples, all stabbed to death but for that pair that got themselves shot, all with food layin' around like somebody'd been snackin' or grocery shoppin' recently."

"Did there happen to be fresh-cut flowers at the crime scene?" Quinn asked.

"Sure were. Half a dozen roses right there in a vase on the kitchen table."

"Remember what color they were?"

"Yellow."

Quinn felt his blood begin to rush. "Any doubt the kid did the deed?"

"None whatsoever. His prints were on the knife, autopsy showed he'd likely had recent sex with the wife, and he bolted like a scalded rabbit. He stole the Sands' car and used it to get outta town. His prints and some of the family's blood was all over it when we found it parked off the road outta sight among some trees."

"This Luther have any priors?"

"Nothin' violent, and only one conviction, but he was a rough number with several arrests. Vagrancy, male prostitution, theft. He'd been a street kid in Kansas City."

"Working his way up to murder," Quinn said, sipping his drink.

"Well, he made it all the way. It looked like he'd been secretly livin' in the Sands' attic for a while, ballin' the wife and havin' a grand old time, till old Milford caught 'em together. Least that's the theory."

"You buy into it?"

"Sure, there's nothin' else." Nester was already halfway through his second beer. "An' Luther ain't been seen nor heard of since the murders."

Quinn thought about what he'd just heard. "I'm glad you came to see me, Nester. I'll find out more about this Luther Lunt. Sic the feds and their computers on him."

"I done that already," Nester said with a note of pride. "I still got connections, friends in high-tech places."

"Great. Will you copy me what you have?"

"No need. Got it all in my pocket. An' you can have it after only one more beer."

Quinn laughed and signaled the woman with the bold tattoo. "Nester, I bet you were one hell of a good cop."

"Still am," Nester said. "It ain't the kinda profession you ever really retire from."

"That's something we can drink to," Quinn said.

Claire Briggs stood with her arms crossed in the center of the bare bedroom and looked around with satisfaction.

This was to be the baby's room, and would look like it as soon as it was decorated. Right now it wasn't very impressive. The absence of furniture revealed cracks in the plaster walls, and there were scrapes and gouges in the paint from when the movers took out the furniture, knowing the room was going to be redone and they didn't have to be careful. The windows were dirty and the old blinds didn't admit enough light. The tarnished brass ceiling fixture, which might have been original to the 1920s building, cast barely enough illumination to chase away the pale shadows.

But Claire had a vision for the room: bright yellow paint, a white picket fence flush with one of the walls, with stenciled daisies and red geraniums peeking through the slats. There would be new blinds and white curtains. It would be a well-lit, cheerful room, a place of optimism and beginnings. And at night, when the switch was thrown and the new ceiling fixture winked out, artificial stars—invisible during the day—would twinkle across the ceiling in an accurate representation of the heavens. Something for her baby to gaze at from earliest infancy.

Her baby.

Her child—hers and Jubal's—was beginning to occupy her thoughts more and more, even though she also had her wedding to think about. At the oddest, most unlikely times during the day, she would dream or wonder about the child she would bear. These thoughts of the baby and its future had even begun happening onstage, though thank God they hadn't interfered with her performance.

Her pregnancy didn't show yet. If she had to get pregnant, her timing couldn't have been better. She could act weeks longer in *Hail to the Chef,* she was sure, maybe even for a while after the baby began to show. Her reviews had been that good and the box office was holding up. Then a long break from show business would be welcome. Time to play mommy.

Sometimes she could hardly wait for her pregnancy to be far enough along that she might have an ultrasound done and could determine the baby's sex.

Or did she and Jubal really want that information?

It was something to be decided later. Claire was happy now and she lived for now; that was the important, overriding thing. She hadn't dreamed her pregnancy would mean so much to her. There must be something in all that talk about hormonal behavior.

Sometimes she felt guilty for not looking forward more

to her and Jubal's wedding. It was going to be a small, brief ceremony in a church in the West Village, and would be attended only by a few friends and family. Claire's longtime friend from Wisconsin, Sophie Murray, was flying to New York and would be her maid of honor, and a fellow actor of Jubal's, Clay Simms, was to be best man. It wasn't that Claire felt blasé about the wedding; it was just that the ceremony was only a formality. She and Jubal might as well have been married the past four years.

It was the baby that was everything to Claire now. Even more than her career. (And that was something she *never* would have predicted!) She knew she couldn't explain that adequately to Jubal. He wouldn't understand. But he might after the baby was born. In fact, she was sure he would.

That certainty was something else that made her happier than she'd ever been. Her acting, her relationship with Jubal, her pregnancy. Everything in her life seemed to be falling into place.

All the way across the board, Claire was on a gambler's roll.

Time after time, coming up roses.

46

Somewhere in the chaos must be something useful.

Quinn sat back in his kitchen chair and looked at the spread of handwritten notes, computer printouts, and copies of forms and records Nester had given him. What was laid out on the table had all been contained in a large folded brown envelope the retired cop and sheriff's deputy wrestled out of a back pocket.

An envelope content that hadn't been wrinkled or folded, though, was a copy of a black-and-white snapshot of Luther Lunt taken by Cara Sand. It had been discovered in the bottom of one of her dresser drawers when the Hiram police searched the house after the murders. Luther was outdoors, barefoot, wearing faded jeans and a white T-shirt, a slender but muscular kid with tousled hair, leaning with one hand against the trunk of a large tree and smiling at the lens. He looked wholesome and innocent. While his body might have passed for twenty-one, his face could have been fourteen. Cara Sand must have known what she was doing when she'd decided to have an affair with him.

Quinn stretched out an arm and reached for the diet Coke

on the table. He sipped and thought. This Luther Lunt was some pumpkin despite his appearance of naïveté. He'd led a tough, impoverished life, which must have suddenly become heaven when he moved in with the Sands and had his way with the willing wife. And from reading newspaper clippings and Nester's notes, Quinn was sure Luther had indeed led a phantom life in the attic, descending into the real world only when the master was away, or occasionally at night for a secret tryst with Cara or for food. Food in the kitchen, where he'd apparently been interrupted around three A.M. while eating a sandwich and drinking milk from the carton.

Domestic murder in the early-morning hours. Every cop knew that was the prime time for it, if not in the bedroom, in the kitchen. *Home, sweet . . . yeah.*

Murder could be prosaic, so why not in the middle of a late-night snack?

Quinn let his chair tilt forward so its front legs contacted the floor, then looked again at the photograph of Luther Lunt. The boy standing and smiling, in what was probably his victims' backyard, would look much different now. He might have gained weight, lost some or all of his hair, grown a mustache or beard. The subtle rearrangements of time.

But whatever his appearance, Luther was out there somewhere in New York.

Staring hard at the photograph, Quinn could feel his presence. There was always a moment when hunter somehow made a mysterious connection with quarry, whether each or only one of them realized it. This was the moment for Quinn, the instant he'd been waiting for, perhaps prompted by Nester's visit and Luther's photograph. Quinn was now locked on to Luther in a way he hadn't been before. Luther grown older . . . thirty-one now, if his recorded birth date was correct. Luther an adult and a fugitive who'd adapted and led what might seem an outwardly normal life.

Quinn knew he was out there, and knew he was feeling

the vise tighten as he killed more often, and increased with each murder the odds of his being caught. Luther Lunt, feeling the pressure, irritable, not sleeping well lately, off his appetite because of the ache in the pit of his stomach.

And there was no reason he shouldn't feel even more pressure.

Quinn decided to give Dave Everson a call at the *Times*. The Luther Lunt photo should be in the papers and on TV news. The media would make sure the prime suspect in the Night Prowler murders would have his photograph appear all over the city and beyond. They'd do a better job than a police artist in aging Luther, giving him no hair or shorter or longer hair, facial hair, a double chin, lines in his face, experience in his gaze. Though still a young man, his hard years would show on him, scars inside and out.

Quinn knew this kind of media blitz worked sometimes. Someone out there would see the original photographic image or one of the artists' renderings and decide maybe they did know Luther Lunt, though that wasn't what he'd be calling himself these days. They wouldn't be sure at first; then they'd think about it—whether they wanted to or not— and eventually they'd phone the police.

Usually they'd be wrong about whoever it was they suspected; any photograph, especially an old one in black and white, resembled a lot of people.

Then one day one of the callers would be right. The adult Luther Lunt would be identified. And at Quinn's convenience, he and Luther would meet.

Quinn stood up and stretched until his aching spine made a soft popping sound and he felt better. Then he went to the phone in the living room, where he could sit down again but in a softer chair.

It was time for Luther Lunt to become a celebrity.

* * *

The Night Prowler watched the television screen in horror and rage. First the photograph had been in the newspapers, stopping and momentarily paralyzing him as he walked past a news and magazine kiosk on Broadway. Now the long-ago image was on seemingly every channel broadcasting the evening news. There stood a young Luther Lunt, leaning against the tree in the backyard that had been part of his home. Time made it seem like a photo of someone else, all part of a world the Night Prowler wanted to remain in the past. The photo had been taken by Cara, obviously on the spur of the moment, then put somewhere and forgotten.

And now here it was, an instant, a reality, preserved and displayed years and years later, as if a page in an album had been turned. *Photo by Cara, a fraction of time in our bubble of time, in which we lived, loved, feared. . . .*

The buzzing began again, a gray cacophony of every color, not loud now, but growing louder.

As the Night Prowler watched the TV, a retired FBI profiler was explaining Luther's mental illness in pseudomedical terms and talking about what kind of man he'd be now. An artist's conception of how Luther might appear at different weights and with varying hairstyles and beard and mustache styles showed on split screen while the former profiler yammered away in her strange combination of scientific and media speak.

She knows nothing about her subject! Nothing!

Neither does the pathetically untalented artist!

Some of the media gave credit to the journalist who "broke" the story, a man named Everson. But the Night Prowler knew who really found and loosed the relentless demons from the past. It was the demon of the present—Quinn!

Of course the Night Prowler knew why. He was supposed to think now that Quinn was on his heels, ready to run up his back if he made the slightest mistake.

Or if he *had* made a mistake!

Quinn was a tracker, a stalker who dealt in the past and eventually closed on a present where he and his prey would meet. And it was the pressure he could exert that made his prey slow down, hesitate, and make a seemingly innocuous wrong move that could lead to disaster. It was like an obscure code, the rules of this game, which Quinn assumed he knew better than his quarry. Advantage, Quinn: The pursuer could make many mistakes and the game would continue, while the pursued could afford only one miscue and it would be game over. The increasing pressure on the hunted would inevitably lead to that fatal oversight or miscalculation.

So Quinn thinks.

The Night Prowler used the remote to switch off the TV. He smiled grimly. Different people felt pressure in different ways, and found different ways to relieve it. *White powder, pink sex, green money, red vengeance, the blue eyes of the gods . . .*

The Night Prowler went to the cabinet beneath the kitchen sink and groped in darkness for the handgun that was hidden behind the plumbing and wrapped in an oily rag.

He got the gun out and stared at it. An ugly, functional thing, manufactured to kill. *Black forever. . . .* It had belonged to a man the Night Prowler knew sold drugs and would not report its theft. He absently ran a fingertip over the rough texture of its checkered grip, an indecipherable topography of its past.

A gun like this, who knew its history?

Who knew its future?

He rewrapped the gun and carefully wedged it back in its hiding place beneath the sink.

But out of sight wasn't necessarily out of mind. Just as Quinn was now never completely out of the Night Prowler's thoughts, which condition was certainly and precisely what Quinn intended. That was his strategy. That was part of how the pressure was applied.

That was how it was *supposed* to work. Ask any TV pundit or armchair psychologist who'd never shed anyone's blood and who never dreamed their own might be shed. There were well-documented ways to understand and hunt down the serial killer. Millions of words had explained the who and how of the phenomenon and even the why. Book after book had been written on the subject.

But not all prey were alike. Sometimes the hunter wasn't fully aware of what he was tracking.

Sometimes the hunter wished that somewhere along the trail, he'd missed a turn.

Black forever . . .

Lisa Ide's Visa card showed a charge for lunch the afternoon before her murder. She'd dined at an East Side restaurant Quinn had never heard of, Petit Poisson. Fifty-nine dollars with tip for a salad, pastry, and drinks. Nothing petite about the price.

He doubted that Lisa had dined alone, so he sent Pearl to see what she might learn from the restaurant's staff.

47

When Quinn had first brought up the subject of Petit Poisson, Pearl assumed he was inviting her to lunch, and someplace expensive. But this was work, the Job. They were being colleagues, not lovers. She wondered if it was possible to be both.

When she walked into the restaurant, she understood why the prices were high. This was a premier rent area, and there was room for only about a dozen tables.

What Petit Poisson lacked in size, it made up for in elegance. Pearl could imagine sitting at one of the smaller round tables with Quinn, next to thick red drapes over leaded windows facing the street. Chairs and a large sideboard were elaborate and gilded. Light was furnished mainly by candles and an ornate brass chandelier dangling low on a thick chain from the center of the beamed ceiling. The restaurant tried, but it wasn't a cute place as its name suggested; it was more as if a rowdy peasant tavern had been bought and redecorated by decadent dandies just in time to beat the revolution.

Pearl dealt firmly with the imperious maître d', who referred her to a waiter named Chan, who pronounced his name as "Shawn." He spoke with what sounded like a genuine French accent.

Chan was amiable and cooperative and of indeterminate lineage. Yes, he must have waited on that table at the time on the charge receipt. Yes, he recognized the charming woman in the photograph Pearl showed him. (Here if he had a mustache, Pearl was sure he would have twirled it.) No, he hadn't realized she was the latest victim of the Night Prowler. He shook his head sadly at the waste and the pity. No, she hadn't dined alone. There were two women with her, approximately her age. Of course there would be a record of their presence if they paid by charge, and who paid with cash these days?

The restaurant manager, who wore a silky, flawlessly tailored blue suit, sashayed over and introduced himself as Yves with a silent *S*. He politely inquired if there was a problem. When Pearl flashed her ID and explained that the problem was a homicide, he guided them to a far corner of the restaurant in case one of the few early diners might glance over and be gastronomically upset by police presence.

Pearl was polite but gave the impression she might any second draw her weapon and shout "Freeze!" Yves was cooperative, though not as friendly as Chan, and without nearly as convincing an accent.

He used the accent to instruct the waiter to return to his station. Yves said it as if he meant Chan's station in life.

When Chan had departed, Yves ushered Pearl into a tiny, cluttered office. It wasn't nearly as elegant as the dining area, or as Gallic, though there was a big color photo of the Eiffel Tower framed and mounted on the wall behind the desk. It was taken on a misty night starred by the many lights of Paris, and the famous landmark had probably never looked better.

Yves said the charge and debit forms from the date of

Lisa Ide's lunch hadn't yet been transferred to the bank, so there should be a record of who shared the table with her, assuming of course they paid separately by card.

He got several banded reams of receipts from a safe alongside his desk and sat rummaging through them, flicking them rapidly with his thumb like a gambler counting money. The receipts were apparently in chronological order, because when he got to the desired date and time, he slowed his rampage through the forms and settled on one, then two more, and separated them from the others.

Pearl already had a copy of Lisa Ide's signed receipt, so she waited while Yves duplicated the other two forms on a printer hooked up to his computer.

She looked at the copies after he handed them to her. Chan's name and the same table number were at the top of each copy, along with the printed date and time. And there were the signatures of the women who'd dined with the dead: Abby Koop and Janet Hofer.

Pearl thought Chan should have drawn a smiley face alongside his signatures—lent some cheer to the place. But it wasn't that kind of restaurant. Pearl smiled and thanked Yves as she stood up and shook his hand. "Montand," she said.

He appeared puzzled.

"That's why your name was familiar to me. The famous French actor, Yves Montand. He starred with Marilyn Monroe in something or other."

"I'm afraid I never heard of the man," Yves said. "Marilyn Monroe, though."

"Are you or were you ever French? This is the police asking."

"Not really." Yves smiled, but the admission seemed to pain him.

"It doesn't matter," Pearl said.

And she meant it. She was happy. She had names. Soon

she would have addresses. Soon she would talk to the two women who were friends, or at least acquaintances, of Lisa Ide.

Wouldn't Quinn be pleased? *Mon Dieu!*

At the office door she turned and said, *"Au revoir."*

"I hear that all the time," Yves said.

Quinn agreed to meet Pearl at the Nations Café, a multi-cultural eatery on First Avenue near the UN Building. She'd phoned and told him she had the information she needed and they could question the two women who'd lunched with Lisa Ide at the West Side French restaurant near the time of her and her husband's murders. They were, as it turned out, old college chums of Lisa.

Quinn thought the three women probably spent most of their lunch conversation reliving the past, unaware of how short Lisa's future was, and would have little to add to the investigation. But Pearl seemed proud, and she had a right. There was real satisfaction in doing detective work and knowing you'd inched forward. And talking with the two women would explore a lead that should be investigated, even if it came to nothing.

The more Quinn saw of Pearl's work, the more impressed he was by her insight and thoroughness. And the more he understood the underlying fear and loneliness that had created her protective shell. Or might his newfound emotions be affecting his judgment? Might Pearl be deliberately playing him? It had been so long since Quinn felt this way about a woman.

How the hell could a man know?

Quinn did know Pearl played hard and for keeps. And Pearl could be tricky. That was what attracted him to her in the first place. Well, maybe not in the first place. . . .

Such were Quinn's thoughts as he waited for the traffic

signal to change, then crossed East Fifty-sixth and continued strolling along First Avenue toward the diner. He wasn't in any hurry. He was only a short block away from his meeting with Pearl and was fifteen minutes early.

It was a warm evening but cooling down. Good weather for walking in the city he loved despite its warts. As usual there was plenty of traffic on First, all heading north at a fast clip. He breathed in diesel exhaust as a truck pulled away from a loading area. The lumbering vehicle drew angry horn blasts as it edged into a convoy of taxis cruising the curb lane for fares.

Quinn didn't mind the mingled exhaust fumes, maybe because they reminded him of the city and cars. He liked cars, though owning one in Manhattan hadn't made sense to him even when he could afford it. But he felt good standing near the rush of traffic and hearing its constant, growling din.

Later, if he *could* afford it again, maybe a car.

A photo clipped from the newspaper and taped to the inside of a florist's shop window caught his eye. The shop was closed and dim inside, so the rectangle of newsprint on white was particularly noticeable. He walked closer to examine it.

What he'd thought at first glance turned out to be true. The photo in the clipping was that of Luther Lunt, along with a rendition of a projected older Luther with less hair and heavier features. The present Luther. Approximately.

The city was spooked, Quinn thought, standing and staring at the clipping. Then he noticed the decal or etching just above it, a spiderweb of what looked like cracks in the glass.

As he watched, another web appeared, along with a white-edged hole in its center.

Not decals or etchings at all.

There was no sound of shots over the noise of the traffic, so it took Quinn a few seconds to realize the significance of what he was looking at—bullet holes!

Someone's shooting at me!

He crouched low and ran for the cover of a parked car, peering through its windows at the people on the opposite sidewalk. No one seemed to have noticed anything unusual. Had the shots come from a window?

He was about to look up when he caught movement in a passageway between two buildings across the street. A dark shape moving fast. The flit of a sneaker sole, rising, disappearing. *Running!*

Getting away!

Like hell!

Quinn was out from behind the car and dashing across the street. Horns blared and someone shouted; he heard the screech of brakes an instant after a front bumper brushed his pants leg. He zigzagged to avoid another oncoming car, stopped cold to let another pass, then was up on the sidewalk and running hard toward the passageway where he'd seen the dark figure disappear. The Night Prowler—he could feel it!

He bumped someone walking along the sidewalk and heard the man's expulsion of breath. Then he was in the darkness of the passageway, running toward faint light at the opposite end.

For an instant he glimpsed movement and was sure the Night Prowler was still in the passageway, moving as if picking up speed. Perhaps he'd paused halfway and begun to walk, thinking he hadn't been seen, that he was safe.

Quinn ran faster, seeing movement again, this time to the left, as his quarry reached the next block. All right, he knew which way the figure had turned; he had direction. His side ached and he was breathing in fire, but he kept his legs pumping, lifting his knees higher.

At the end of the passageway Quinn slowed, gripped rough brick wall, and half ran, half swung around the corner.

Gasping for breath, he smelled the East River. He was on

a street running parallel to its bank. Sutton Place. Again he saw movement, ahead of him, more than one figure.

No one behind him.

Then up ahead, faster movement, and he saw the figure he'd been pursuing turn onto East Fifty-seventh Street.

Good! As he approached the corner, Quinn saw the sign at East Fifty-seventh: DEAD END.

Thank God!

He ran down the short block to a concrete ramp with a black iron handrail. In the corner of his vision he saw NO DOGS ALLOWED as he negotiated the ramp and found himself in a small parklike area where neighborhood pet owners walked their dogs, despite the sign, or wandered down to the river's edge and stared at the listless slide of gray water.

There was a brick surface lined with benches, some large trees in grassy rectangles, a sandbox where the kids could play, and a statue of a wild boar to disturb their dreams. On his right was a raised brick walkway. A low concrete wall topped with a curved iron rail faced the murky water.

Half a dozen people were in the park. All were walking dogs, except for a couple leaning on the iron rail and watching the river while they held hands. *No Night Prowler. . . .*

A tall woman wearing a ball cap, tank top, and jeans was standing off by herself, but her animal, a large black Lab, was off leash and bounding around. The woman had a clear plastic bag over her hand like a glove and was calling, "Jeb! Jeb!" Presumably the Lab. The dog skidded to a halt, then stood gazing back at her in a calculating way, then in the direction it had been running. It yearned to go but was frozen by command. "Jeb! C'mere, baby!"

The conflicted Jeb reluctantly turned around and began slouching toward his owner.

Had Jeb been chasing someone?

It was possible to scale a fence and escape from the park through the grounds of the building next to it.

Quinn sucked in air and began running again, in the direction the dog had strained to go.

As he passed the crouching, resigned dog, he saw it glance up at him.

A few seconds later he heard the scratching and clatter of paws. Jeb, running behind him, gaining ground.

"Jeb! You get back here!"

Quinn saw a low dark streak flash past him. Jeb, rocketing out on four good legs and with sound canine lungs. Jeb with a solid sense of purpose at last.

He's chasing something, all right! He's—

Everything heavy on earth slammed into Quinn's chest.

He stumbled, stopped running, and stood bent over, trying to endure the pain that was tightening around him. His left arm was stiff, aching.

Heart attack!

"You okay, bud?" A man's voice.

Quinn tried to say he wasn't, but he couldn't speak. Couldn't even croak. He sank to his knees, then went all the way down. A small brindled dachshund stared at him in watery brown-eyed sympathy.

"Is he all right, you think?" A woman. Jeb's owner.

Quinn saw lower legs, shoes, men's and women's, a pair of dark pants with cuffs. Lying doubled up on the ground, he couldn't lift his head to see higher.

"Guy looks plenty sick." The man. The dachshund was yanked back on its leash, as if its owner feared Quinn might be contagious. "Anybody got a cell phone to call nine-eleven?"

"I do!" answered several voices.

Shit! An ambulance . . . emergency room. Well, maybe not a bad idea. Steel bands contracting around my chest . . . that's how it's supposed to feel and it does. . . .

"*There* you are, you bad dog!"

Something pink and wet and warm was suddenly on Quinn's cheek and nose, then all over his face.

Don't ever be a police dog, Jeb.

The Night Prowler stood in the steel and Plexiglas bus stop shelter, but he didn't board either of the buses that pulled to the curb near him to take on or let off passengers. He was able to lean in a corner of the kiosk and gaze through the clear plastic over the top of an advertising poster touting a Broadway play about marriage and infidelity. Apropos, thought the Night Prowler.

What he could see over the top of the poster were the twin wooden green doors of the small brick church that had been in the Village for years. There were more than the usual number of cars parked nearby, and half a block down from the church a white limo sat at the curb, its uniformed chauffeur waiting patiently behind the steering wheel. But those were the only signs that a wedding was taking place inside. The chauffeur was busy studying a newspaper, and the Night Prowler was certain the man hadn't noticed anyone letting buses pass by at the stop half a block away on the other side of the street.

It was a beautiful morning for a wedding. A gold-and-blue day. The sun was no captive of clouds, and its pure light illuminated the white wooden cross on the church's roof as if to shout, *She's here! She's here! Claire Briggs in white, with eyes like the blue mystery of oceans, so alluring, so deep, about life, about death . . . the old knowledge . . . blue and deep unto darkness. . . .*

Both church doors opened at the same time, and tuxedoed ushers leaned down and fixed kick-plates so they wouldn't swing closed. Claire would be coming out! The Night Prowler swallowed his breath, a bubble of life.

People began filing out of the church. Some were dressed in suits with ties, others more informally, a few even in jeans. Friends from the theater world. Most of the women were dressed up. Everyone was smiling as they tried to obey the frenetic, arm-waving instructions of a skeletal-thin man in a gray suit. They milled about, then formed lines down each side of the dozen or so concrete steps. The steps didn't allow enough room, so the lines extended along the sidewalk. Several people not connected to the wedding stopped on the Night Prowler's side of the street and stood waiting to see what was happening. Wedding? Or funeral?

There she is!

Claire in a wedding white dress, standing next to her new and not-so-handsome husband Jubal Day! Putting on a little weight around the middle lately, Jubal?

The Night Prowler stood transfixed, his breathing shallow, as bride and groom made their way down the church steps beneath a shower of birdseed (rice being prohibited at the church, as it was harmful to the birds as well as a waste of human sustenance), running a gauntlet of grins and good lucks.

Claire smiled and gracefully used her left hand to brush the shower of airborne well wishes out of her hair, then adjusted her turned-back veil. Over the distance the Night Prowler could smell the fresh white shampoo scent of her hair, could hear the music of her happiness. It was amazing, the force and foresight of his mind!

Astounding! I'm with her, seeing her from here and beside her! Now and later. Two places at once? Why not? It's called objectivity. It's called destiny. And it's there to see, if you can see it. What's the future but the present roaring toward us?

He realized the doctor would have a medical term for what he was thinking, the priest a religious term, yet they wouldn't believe, not really. It distressed him sometimes, the failure of imagination in the highly educated.

They're fools hamstrung by their torrent of facts and fears, their comforting black-and-white delusions. Like. . . . Well, never mind that now.

Claire!

She tossed her bouquet high into the air, and a girl about twelve who would never be pretty caught it and hugged it to her spindly body as if a prince might spring from it.

Claire laughing . . . mouth wide, throwing her head back the way she does. . . .

Into the limo . . . new car smell, slick leather seats . . . slide, slide . . . the door shuts; then the chauffeur's door up front . . . the smooth vibrant power of the engine, the engine, the faces at the windows, all smiling in, shouting silently . . . our wedding guests. . . . The wedding, the engine, the blue-gold day beyond the tinted glass, running figures like the palest of shadows, life, sliding, sliding away outside the window as the limo gains speed. . . .

The kiss to the clean white future! Lips, teeth touch . . . the cleaving unto the husband . . . white and flesh . . .

Happy Wedding Day, Claire!

Yours and mine.

48

They were in the doctor's antiseptically clean, neatly arranged office in Roosevelt Hospital. Quinn sat in an uncomfortable wooden chair with upholstered arms, facing the desk at an angle. There were no windows, but the room was so bright from fluorescent lighting set behind frosted panels that there was an impression of natural light. On a shelf along with some medical reference books sat a small glass vase with a rose in it, which Quinn was sure was plastic. In the air was a faint scent of peppermint.

The doctor's name was Liran. He was a small, effeminate man, with dark eyes, thick black hair, and the kind of slender, long-fingered hands Quinn thought a surgeon should possess. On the wall behind him hung an improbable number of framed diplomas and certifications. Before him on his desk were spread various black-and-white images and printed-out results of tests done on Quinn.

Quinn was optimistic. The pain in his chest had receded in the ambulance and was almost gone completely by the time they'd arrived at the hospital's emergency entrance. He'd wanted to leave, and it was only reluctantly that he agreed to undergo a series of diagnostic procedures and spend the night. When the nurse had asked him who they might contact about his condition, he'd thought about giving them Pearl's name and phone number, then decided against it. He could imagine Pearl barging in and taking charge, possibly irritating the staff to the extent that they might recommend a transplant.

"We'll wait to see how I am in the morning before we call anyone," Quinn told the nurses.

They made it clear they didn't like that idea, even if they had to go along with it.

He heard them talking about him out in the hall when they left. "So let him die alone," one of them said. He liked a nurse with a sense of humor.

They left him alone until they returned with a young doctor, who began questioning him about his "event" and eventually recommended what needed to be done to gain further information about his symptoms. Through most of the night Quinn was poked, probed, made to drink foul liquids, scanned, X-rayed, and had his molecules jangled by an MRI machine, until finally he was given a sedative that didn't work very well.

Morning had been a long time dawning.

"We detect no damage to the heart," Dr. Liran said with an Indian accent, "but the images show considerable arterial blockage."

Quinn asked what that meant.

Dr. Liran shrugged behind his desk. "That you've lived as long as you have, even though you've eaten too much fatty food, and inherited a predisposition for plaque buildup on arterial walls." He smiled softly. "You'll be glad to know you're rather typical in that regard, Mr. Quinn."

Quinn decided to drive to the point. "Did I have a heart attack?"

"A mild one, perhaps, that left no visible damage."

"Or it might have been indigestion?"

Dr. Liran laughed merrily. "Oh, only if you're an incurable optimist. You are only slightly away from being a prime candidate for angioplasty, Mr. Quinn." The doctor regarded his test results, drumming his manicured nails on an opened file folder. "I see that you are a police officer. Do you get adequate exercise?"

"No."

"Control your diet?"

"No."

"Smoke or drink?"

"A cigar or a glass of scotch now and then. Occasionally both at the same time."

The doctor gave Quinn a look that might have carried mild disdain, then peered down again at the clutter of material on his desk. "You had been running when you were stricken?"

"Yes, I was chasing someone."

"Uh-hm." That seemed to satisfy Dr. Liran. He let the subject drop. If he recognized Quinn from newspapers or TV, he gave no indication. Probably he was too busy saving lives to follow the news. He had his own serial killers to deal with.

"So what happened is nothing to worry about?" Quinn asked hopefully.

Dr. Liran looked pained. "I would say it's definitely something to be concerned about. It was your body demonstrating to you the direction in which you're going, which is toward a severe heart attack if you don't take proper and reasonable precautions. I would like to impress upon you that despite lack of detectable damage to the heart, what happened to you is in itself quite serious."

"A wake-up call," Quinn said.

"That's not the medical term, but it will do. I'm going to prescribe some pills to help lower both your blood pressure and your cholesterol count, but they won't lower them enough by themselves. Much of this is up to you, Mr. Quinn. Here with your prescriptions is a suggested diet. Follow it, and avoid strenuous physical activity until we place you on an exercise program. I want to see you again approximately one month from today. When you know your schedule, call and make an appointment. If you don't call us, we'll call you."

Quinn accepted the papers the doctor was holding out for him, then stood up and thanked him. "Don't worry, Doctor, I'll call."

Dr. Liran smiled. "They all say that. Either way, I suspect we'll be seeing each other again."

"Acid reflux," Pearl said later that morning, after Quinn explained to her—with some modification—why he hadn't appeared for their meeting last night. "That's acid bullshit, Quinn, and we both know it."

They were in the unmarked, Pearl driving, on their way to talk to Abigail Koop. Fedderman was on his way to question Janet Hofer, the other woman who'd had lunch with Lisa Ide shortly before she died. Hofer was still in New York on an extended vacation.

"The important thing is, I almost caught the bastard," Quinn said. They'd stopped at Krispy Kreme five minutes ago. He opened the paper sack as Pearl jockeyed the car too fast around a corner.

"The important thing is, you had a heart attack."

"There was no heart attack. I told you, the hospital said I was fine. It could have been simple acid reflux causing chest pains." He'd heard somewhere of people having acid reflux and thinking it was a heart attack, so why wouldn't she believe him?

Pearl said nothing and stared straight ahead as she drove, letting Quinn know she was plenty ticked off and not buying what she was selling.

"If I'd been ten years younger, I would have worn him down," Quinn said. "We almost had him."

"How can you be so sure it was the Night Prowler?"

"He shot at me."

"What?"

He told her about the bullet holes appearing in the shop window.

She drove for a while without saying anything.

Then: "He's stalking you, Quinn."

"Us, maybe."

"More likely just you. That macho thing."

"Yeah, you're probably right, but we can't be sure. The three of us need to be careful."

"You're just the guy to talk about being careful."

"Put it away, Pearl."

"God! A heart attack." *Afraid again. He's made me afraid of losing something again.* "Did they give you any medicine or instructions?"

"Some pills. Put me on a low-fat, low-cholesterol diet. That means low food."

"Jesus, Quinn! You're eating a doughnut!"

"I'm a cop, Pearl. I've got a right."

"Don't you make light of this, Quinn!"

"I'm starving, Pearl. This is breakfast. It's all I'm going to eat."

"Believe it," Pearl said.

Quinn decided to be quiet the rest of the way to Abigail Koop's apartment.

"Acid reflux, my foot . . . ," Pearl said under her breath.

Koop was a fleshy but attractive woman with beseeching brown eyes peering out from beneath dark bangs. Quinn wondered where he'd seen such soft eyes before, then remembered a dachshund gazing at him when he was on the ground with his heart . . . event. Unlike the dachshund, Koop had a slightly crooked nose, an uncertain smile, lots of jewelry, and a manner suggesting she yearned desperately to be liked.

Her West Side apartment was like her, overfurnished and with a tentative decor that didn't know quite what it wanted to be. A traditional gray sofa squatted on a maroon-and-black Persian carpet and faced an Early American TV hutch on top of which was a lineup of Harry Potter novels anchored by large bookends that were busts of Lincoln. Everything in the room seemed to be of different heights and placed next to everything drastically shorter or taller than itself. A small, bucolic landscape was mounted on one wall, a large, modern museum print on another. Please like *something* about me, implored the room. Or maybe Quinn thought that because of how he'd sized up Abigail Koop.

"Please call me Abby," she told them as soon as he'd announced they were the police detectives who'd phoned for an appointment.

They agreed to do that, then sat side by side on the gray sofa while Abby sat down on a delicate little chair that was possibly French Provincial. Abby perched with her thighs pressed tightly together beneath the skirt of her gray business suit. Her hands were folded in her lap. She stole a glance at a clock on a table, then seemed sorry about it. Pearl figured Abby was going in late to work in order to have this conversation.

"We won't take up much of your time," Pearl said.

"It was a shock, what happened to Lisa." Abby began nervously twisting the forefinger of her left hand with the thumb and forefinger of her right, as if testing to see how firmly the finger was screwed into its socket.

"You were good friends?" Quinn asked.

"I suppose you'd say so. We were good friends in college, anyway. But time passed and we lost touch. I moved back to

New York from Connecticut last year and didn't even know Lisa was in town until we ran into each other about a month ago and exchanged phone numbers."

"The other woman you had lunch with, Janet Hofer, did you know her the same way?"

"Yes, I did. In college. Janet and I kept in touch enough to exchange Christmas cards, photographs, that sort of thing. Then she called and told me she was coming in to the city for a jewelry convention and I suggested we have lunch with Lisa and talk about the old days."

Quinn and Pearl glanced at each other. Jewelry. Like Leon and Lisa. "What kind of jewelry?" Pearl asked.

"Nothing expensive. Janet sells it part-time, sets up a booth at shows, holds jewelry parties, that kind of thing."

"Paste?"

Abby looked at him, not understanding at first. "Oh! Yes, I suppose. Nothing with real stones in it, or real gold or silver, unless it's plated. She and Lisa joked about that at lunch, how they had the high and low ends of the market covered. Not that Janet didn't carry some very attractive items. I bought some from her." She held up an arm on which dangled several gold hoops. "These bracelets."

"Nice," Pearl said. Pearl, who thought of bracelets as handcuffs.

"Did Lisa tell you anything that suggested she or her husband might be in any kind of danger?" Quinn asked. It was probably only a coincidence that both women dealt in different sorts of jewelry. And it wasn't as if Janet Hofer had been murdered. Now, if any of the other victims had sold jewelry . . .

"No," Abby said. "Lisa talked as if everything in her life was going well. She showed us pictures of her husband, her apartment—showed Janet, anyway, since I'd seen them when we'd run into each other last month. She seemed . . . oh, I would say, well, normal." Twist, twist went the finger. Must hurt, Pearl thought.

"You never met Leon?" Quinn asked.

"Never. Just saw his photo. Nice-looking man, but older than Lisa. Not that that isn't okay . . . with me. Especially since he seems—seemed—to be something of a romantic."

"How so?" Quinn asked.

"Lisa said he'd been leaving her presents, but not letting on they were from him. Playing games with her, in fact. Sex, love, were all about games, she said." Abby was looking away from Quinn and directly at Pearl. Woman to woman.

Pearl nodded. *Lisa was right about that. She hadn't known how right.*

"What kinds of gifts?" Quinn asked, not letting on that he felt like grabbing Abby and shaking the information out of her.

"Oh, candy. A blouse she'd admired once when they were shopping together for something else. Caviar real recently. Lisa was wild about caviar. Myself, I just see it as fish eggs."

Quinn didn't recall seeing caviar or an empty caviar container in Lisa and Leon's kitchen.

"Flowers—"

"What?" Pearl asked sharply.

Abby stared at her. "Flowers. Lisa said Leon had given her flowers. Not officially from him, of course. Like he was a secret admirer. Playing his romantic games."

"What kind of flowers?"

"Roses, I think she said."

"Yellow ones?" Quinn asked almost lazily, not wanting to lead her.

"They might have been yellow."

Abby absently twisted her finger harder, then must have hurt herself, the way she looked down and stopped and folded her hands in her lap.

"Yellow. Uh-huh. In fact, I'm pretty sure she said they were yellow."

* * *

Back down in the unmarked, Pearl started the engine and switched on the air conditioner while Quinn used the cell phone.

"I'm busy this morning," Harley Renz said when Quinn had identified himself. "Everybody's on my ass from the mayor to the guy who can't get close enough to kiss the mayor's ass. Say you got something for me, Quinn."

"Stomach contents," Quinn said.

"Jesus, I just ate. Talk plain."

"Did the ME list the postmortem contents of Lisa Ide's stomach?"

"Yeah. Sure."

"Caviar?"

"Among other things. How'd you know?"

"I'm a detective. It's my job to find out things. You told me that yourself."

"About the caviar?"

"About finding out things."

"Dammit, Quinn!"

Quinn waited.

"All right, all right, maybe I rag you too hard. It's in me, and you sure as hell deserve it. What does this caviar mean, other than the late Lisa had a hoity-toity dinner before she died?"

"It means she really did love caviar and that she and Leon were definitely done by our guy. He left caviar in their apartment recently, somehow knew Lisa was crazy about it and made it one of his gifts to her. He also gave her yellow roses. This makes three out of four Night Prowler murders where yellow roses were or had been somewhere around."

"Maybe the husband, Leon, really left her the gifts. He musta known she liked caviar, and he mighta given her the roses."

"Not the husband."

"Why not?"

"He and Lisa are dead."

"Yeah. That might be convincing to a jury."

Quinn related what else they'd learned from Abby Koop.

"So now we got our solid link," Renz said, warming to the information and obviously pleased. "Think we should feed the information to the media? It'd take some pressure off me."

"And put more on the Night Prowler," Quinn said. He made a mental note to call Everson and give him a heads-up on the information Renz was going to give out. "Make sure the media know about the other anonymous gifts, too. I want this asshole to think we're pounding at his heels."

"Like you were last night?"

"How'd you find out about that?"

"I got a connection at the hospital who saw your name on the patient list and did some checking. But don't worry about it, Quinn, my source won't say anything if he doesn't wanna go to prison for drug theft. And I'm not gonna pull you off this case. By the way, we recovered the bullets."

"What bullets?"

"The ones that were fired at you last night on First Avenue. Thirty-two caliber. I sent somebody around to recover them and had ballistics run a quick, confidential test. In case we might wanna make a match in the future when he tries for you again, or maybe shoots somebody else."

"But he's still using a knife on his victims."

"He won't try to use one on you. He doesn't wanna get close enough. And he almost got you last night. You mighta died from a heart attack, even though he missed you. You hear the shots?"

"No, but that's not surprising. He fired from across the street—maybe even out a window—and there was a lot of traffic noise."

"So he mighta used a silencer."

"I suppose." *The silencer again.* "But like I said, it was noisy on the street, and I took right after him. The people on the other side of the street might have heard a shot. I didn't take time to ask."

"I still say he's using his silencer. Speaking of which, the only silencer of that model unaccounted for in our neck of the woods was bought three years ago by a Wilhelm Whitmire, eighty-nine years old, who lives on West Eighty-seventh. He said he decided last year he was too old and shaky to have guns around, so he sold all his. Nobody wanted the cheap-ass silencer, so he tossed it in the trash five or six months ago."

"So you hit a dead end."

"Not necessarily. One of the other silencers might have been bought somewhere else and transported to the New York area. Maybe even from another country."

Quinn didn't bother to say he'd pointed that out to Renz weeks ago. *Enough about the silencer.*

"You sure nobody else knows about my hospital stay?" Quinn asked.

"Not in the department, no. And I won't tell anyone. It's not that I don't have a heart myself, but I'm thinking of the greater good. It's my duty to protect the public, and you're our best bet to nail this fucking Night Prowler."

"You were born to command, Harley."

Renz chuckled. "To serve, you mean."

"Whatever you're doing, the condition of my heart's the last thing you better discuss with the media or anybody else."

"Not to worry, Quinn. It's between you, me, and your arteries."

Quinn broke the connection.

Pearl looked over at him. "What was all that heart talk?"

"Renz knows about my night in the hospital. He's got a connection there who told him."

"Is he pulling you off the case?"

"No."

"I didn't think so. He doesn't know what a heart is, because he doesn't have one."

"He's not going any further with the information," Quinn said. He gave Pearl a look she hadn't seen before. One that scared her. "And neither are you."

Pearl nodded and put the car in drive.

She thought about the expression on Quinn's face, what was in his eyes. Her breathing was coming a little hard. She'd been on the Job long enough to know people, and men in particular. The genuinely bad guys. The flip side. This Quinn had healed stronger where he'd been broken and was not a man to be messed with. The real and dangerous deal.

Pearl rather liked that about him, but she decided it would be wise to pull in her horns.

Until he loosened up, anyway, with her help. And she *could* help him because she knew how guys like him thought, and they all thought the same way. Quinn couldn't throw away the rage because he thought it made him strong.

It was something she'd have to change.

That and some other things.

49

Fedderman joined Quinn and Pearl for lunch at the Diner on Amsterdam. They had a booth that looked out on the street. The sun blasting through the spotted window made the place too warm. It was also noisy and the food wasn't very good. There were dead flies on the windowsill.

Pearl was afraid to eat the tuna sandwich she'd ordered. Quinn picked at his egg-white omelette. Fedderman voiced doubts about his meat loaf sandwich but devoured it, anyway. Pearl suspected it would make him sick. She said they weren't coming back here—ever. Neither man disagreed with her.

"So what'd you get out of Janet Hofer?" Quinn asked Fedderman, sipping diet Pepsi through a straw, certain the guy behind the counter had screwed up and given him the real stuff.

"Nice woman, sells jewelry. I bought this from her." Fedderman lifted his wadded brown suit coat from the seat beside him and held it out to show a bejeweled red, white and blue top hat pinned to the lapel.

"Patriotic," Pearl said.

"It cost less than you think."

"You have no idea what I think."

"Hey! Easy, Pearl."

"Stick to the job, Feds, so we can get outta this shit hole as soon as possible. I don't wanna hear about goddamn lapel pins." She looked at Quinn, who was obviously struggling not to laugh. Pearl frowned.

"She's right," Quinn told Fedderman. The wink was in his voice, and it made Pearl even madder, but she said nothing.

Fedderman told them about his interview with Janet Hofer. It didn't add anything, but it corroborated Abby Koop's account of the conversation the three women had at lunch. Lisa Ide had been receiving anonymous gifts, including expensive jewelry and her beloved caviar. Lisa Ide had received yellow roses. Lisa Ide was dead, along with her husband.

Since it was no secret, and was going to be in the news if it wasn't already, Quinn told Fedderman about the shots that had been fired, and how he'd almost caught up with Luther Lunt last night. He didn't mention the chest pains or the night in the hospital. Neither did Pearl.

"Renz is feeding the information to the media," Quinn said. "Along with details about clues left behind in the Lisa and Leon murders."

"That's gonna pressure Lunt," Fedderman said in a concerned voice, "and he's already hunting for you."

"That's another way of saying he's being flushed out into the open."

"Or that he's doubled back on his trail like a tiger and is about to ambush the hunter."

Pearl looked at Fedderman. "I didn't know you knew anything about hunting."

"I do about hunting people," Fedderman said, "and the people I hunt. And our Night Prowler's about ready to crack. News reports that we're practically inside his clothes with him are gonna drive him up the wall."

"Nothing there but the ceiling," Quinn said.

Fedderman nodded. "That's my point. No place to go next but out the door, and we're between him and it. Especially you, Quinn."

"That's the idea," Quinn said, "to bring him and us together."

"I hear you," Fedderman said. "And for the first time I think it's really gonna happen." He shook his head. "But, at this point, who can predict what this sick freak is gonna do? All that pressure—"

"On everybody involved," Pearl said. She took a sip of her iceless iced tea and made a face. "Something's gotta crack someplace soon."

"Or somebody," Fedderman said, giving her an appraising look.

Another of those composite drawings, all distressingly black and white. They thought they knew everything about him now, Quinn and his loathsome companions. They did know about the anonymous gifts, what the anchorwoman called my—*his*—sick obsession. The Night Prowler made a mental note of the woman's name and the local channel she appeared on, and the red, red of her full lips carefully shaping her black vowels. Maybe someday he'd demonstrate to her about obsessions, make her obsessive about dying because it was better than living another moment under his hand.

He knew what Quinn was doing, trying to increase the pressure on him to crack, like those serial killers in all the films and novels. Didn't the fools ever stop to think it seldom happened in real life? Almost always it was chance that led to such a killer being caught—unpaid traffic tickets, *official black on white,* an improbable crossing of paths with an unknown witness, a call to jury duty, a neighbor's complaint about noise. . . . Minimize those kinds of risks and the police might chase their blue tails forever.

But he knew it was true that the dark, cold pressure, the unreasonable fear that was being brought to bear, might lead to one of those minimal risks actually working for the law. What might not have been a mistake early in his magnificent run of victims might be a fatal error further down the road of rage and redemption.

And maybe it didn't have to be a mistake. Yesterday on Columbus Avenue the Night Prowler had encountered an old man he used to play chess with in Central Park. Wilhelm Whitmire had been old when they'd first met, and seemed ancient now. In their conversation he mentioned that the police had talked to him recently about a silencer he'd bought and then thrown away months ago.

The Night Prowler recalled hearing about the silencer when it had been discarded, then secretly digging it out of Whitmire's trash still piled at the curb. It was the silencer he'd used when he'd shot the Elzners. He was sure it wasn't traceable, but still the law had talked to Whitmire. They'd gotten that far. They were in the neighborhood.

Quinn again, getting closer, turning the screws.

He suddenly found himself yearning for an end, for green closure.

God! Not closure*!* How he hated that overused and abused word! When would people learn that closure was a temporary state? That people never "got on with their lives" except in the sense that they had no choice? Time would pass; they would grow old and overwhelmed and die along with their fears and dreams and become dust.

The Night Prowler wasn't dust and didn't intend to become it anytime soon. He knew what he had to do, what time and events demanded.

There were many ways to deal with pressure. He liked his way best.

Claire?

No, the time isn't right; the fruit isn't ripe. There's a critical point in every marriage. A testing point. Time like a blade. Everything in the balance. Both parties know it. On the edge of the knife . . .

He reached for the folded cloth at his side, then held it expertly to his nose, little finger extended, and breathed in deeply.

White! White to the horizon . . . the narrow fine line of the horizon cleaving earth from sky, bone from flesh, present from past, one world from another . . .

The fire in the marrow, the edge of the knife.

50

Ready for the chess game.

Dr. Rita Maxwell was standing behind her desk as usual as David Blank entered her office. It was best to be standing, smiling, and putting the patient at his or her ease, yet still maintaining a position of authority.

"David, it's good to see you again."

He smiled back. "Same here, Dr. Maxwell."

How amiable and cooperative we are this afternoon. "Why don't you sit down, David, the clock is running."

He grinned wider. "Isn't that the truth, Doctor?"

She sat down on the sofa this time, very informal, as he lowered himself into the recliner he liked, tilting the backrest so he was lying almost horizontally. He watched her from that position from the corner of a narrowed eye, almost like someone feigning sleep.

"We're in the truth business," she said, keeping it conversational and meaningless for now. She was determined to make appreciable progress this session, to peel back another of the layers concealing the real David Blank. David Blank—who wasn't in the phone directory, who didn't appear on any of New York's public records she could access on her computer. *Who are you?*

Again he nudged her off balance. "I'd like to apologize for being evasive," he said, his eyes closed lightly. "I've been avoiding the truth, lying to you."

"I suspected," she said, keeping the irony from her voice.

"This is difficult for me," Blank said without changing expression. His eyes were still closed, as if he were napping and talking at the same time.

"Like a confession?" Dr. Maxwell asked. She wondered if he might be playing her, setting her up for an even bigger lie than the ones he'd told earlier. If that were possible.

"Well, maybe . . . Why would you describe it as that? A confession?"

"To be honest, I interpreted some of what you've told me as a manifestation of guilt."

"What kind of guilt?"

"There is only one kind."

"Ah, that's wonderful, Doctor! You *know*! Guilt is like every color always, a dreadful buzzing gray."

"That's very descriptive. Really. I do want to assure you that confession here will be confidential and liberating. And between us only, I promise you."

"Liberating . . ." He seemed to taste the word as he said it.

"Do you believe that?"

"Oh, yes. It's why I'm here."

Dr. Maxwell liked that answer. She glanced at the tiny recorder on the corner of her desk to make sure it was running. Though it was soundless, its red pinpoint of light glowed reassuringly.

"We might start," Dr. Maxwell said, "with you telling me your real name."

"*Your* real name is Rita."

Deflection. And unabashedly obvious. He wasn't quite in

a mood to relinquish control. "Yes, of course it is." Keeping her tone neutral.

His eyes remained closed as he spoke. There was no sign that the pupils were moving beneath the thin flesh of his eyelids. "If a person did have something he wanted to confess, Rita . . . say, that he *had* to confess, if you know what I mean . . ."

"I know, David." *Keep talking, keep talking.*

"Say, like a serial killer who secretly yearns to be stopped, to be caught; how would a serial killer deal with the sly pressure, the self-destructive danger of his increasing need for confession?"

Whoa! "That's quite a question."

"Do you have quite an answer?"

"I'm afraid I don't. Not yet."

"I do."

Dr. Maxwell found herself glancing at the closed office door. It wasn't often that she'd been frightened during her sessions. And she wasn't ready to admit she was frightened now.

Uneasy, yes . . .

"What is your answer, David?" She felt a chill as she asked. She was playing his game, she knew, finding herself being led. *To where?* "What would such a person do?"

"Obviously, he'd find someone other than the police to confess to."

"To what effect?"

"Why, then the buzzing would stop, the pressure would ease, and he'd be unburdened, liberated, and free to kill and kill and kill."

My God, it made sense! A horrible kind of sense, but sense.

"Anyone he'd confess to would have to notify the police," Dr. Maxwell said. "Even a priest. Even a psychoanalyst. Of course, we're speaking hypothetically," she added hopefully.

Knowing on some level, beneath so many layers of her own, that she'd lost control of what was happening here.

His eyes were open now and he was looking directly at her. His right hand crept beneath his unbuttoned sport coat and emerged holding a long-bladed knife. The blade had obviously been wiped recently, but there was still a smear of what looked like blood on it. Dr. Maxwell's mind darted to her receptionist in the outer office.

Hannah! If I can somehow alert Hannah!

If he hadn't . . .

"Only one of us is speaking hypothetically, Doctor." His voice was calm, and somehow different. This was the real David Blank, whatever his name, *whatever his ancient name,* and he terrified her.

"Hannah?"

"She's in the closet, where no one coming into the office will notice her. The phone's disconnected, but it doesn't matter. She won't be booking any more appointments."

Dr. Maxwell heard herself swallow, a sound like tiny bones breaking beneath flesh. Words froze in her throat. She didn't know what she was trying to say, anyway.

David Blank sat up and swiveled his body on the recliner so he was facing her, holding the knife up and out so she could see and appreciate the length of its gleaming blade.

"We have another twenty minutes, Doctor."

She swallowed again.

He smiled. "All these weeks are about to pay off. You've gotten what you wanted. We've finally made a real breakthrough. I'd like you to hear my confession."

Dr. Maxwell knew that this time none of it would be lies.

Her insatiable need to learn, the driving curiosity that had propelled her to a scholarship to one of the toughest, most prestigious universities on the East Coast, then through a near-fatal bout of meningitis, then through medical school and a grueling internship, and all the way here, to a plush office on Park Avenue, somehow found its way through her horror.

"Why don't we start with your real name?" she managed to croak.

Dying to know.

51

"The part's good and the money's good enough," Jubal said to Claire over his glass of wine at the Café Caracole on West Fifty-seventh.

Claire took a sip of ice water—no alcohol for her while she was pregnant—and nodded agreement. Jubal's "almost sure thing" as a soldier in *Winding Road* had fallen through without explanation, as so often happened in their business; hot could become cold in less than a minute.

Now, undeniably, it made sense for him to accept this role of the helpful and romantic neighbor in *As Thy Love Thyself* at a theater near Chicago. It was just that right now, especially right now, Claire didn't like the idea of being alone.

"Who's going to put on his shoes and run out at midnight to bring me my blueberry muffins?" she asked. During the last few weeks she'd developed a craving for the oversize, shrink-wrapped muffins sold by the deli down the block.

Jubal stared at her, then realized she was joking and laughed, dribbling wine onto his good green tie. He shook his head and dabbed at the wet spot with his napkin, but she knew the tie was probably ruined. Merlot was like grape paint.

"I should have known you were joking," he said, "but women, all of them, seem to lose a measure of logic during pregnancy."

"You're saying we think with our hormones?"

"Pregnant women do. Temporarily. Nothing wrong with that. Mother Nature."

"Mother Nature makes me want you to stay here in New York, even though I know you're right. The part's a real opportunity for you; it suits you."

"I suit it."

"Whatever. Our lives can't be freeze-framed until I deliver, and I'm only into my third month."

"And it doesn't even show."

"No need for bullshit, Jubal. It's beginning to show too much. I know you should accept this offer. Go to Chicago, do the part, and don't worry about me—us. I'm still getting by with the help of wardrobe and oughta be able to fake it until the end of your run."

"Then we can be unemployed together."

"But with more than enough money to get by, and with bright prospects when we feel like finding day care and going back to work." Day care. She couldn't imagine it. Not with her—their baby. But she knew it would come to that someday soon. Other women managed the painful, early parting, the surrender of some of their responsibility for what was so precious to them. She'd be able to handle it when the time came, she was sure. She thought about how that first day must be, the looks, the puckered mouth, the tears, the leaving behind. . . .

Not sure.

"We can both still practice our craft," Jubal said. "We have to."

Claire wasn't positive she still *had* to, hormones having reshuffled her priorities at least for now, but maybe he'd meant they had to continue acting for financial reasons. She smiled. There was always that, even though right now they had quite a pad and it was growing. But there were expenses, medical bills, decorating the baby's room; it all added up. At least they had some insurance to cover medical expenses. Not much, but some.

"Too bad we don't have decorator's insurance," she said.

"Huh?"

She smiled. "Just thinking out loud. Not making much sense. It's a preggy prerogative."

"Point taken." He poured more wine. "This bother you? Me drinking in front of you?"

She shook her head no. "I don't miss it. And it's not forever."

"I'll have to leave for Chicago tomorrow evening. They want to get into rehearsal right away."

"You've only just read the script."

"I can read it again on the plane. There's a red-eye to Chicago. I can read instead of sleep."

"Yeah, then you can be so tired, you'll fuck up during rehearsal."

"Not to worry, I have a contract."

You have phone conversations. "Signed?"

"Well, no, not yet."

"Thinking with your actor's hormones," Claire said.

"Okay, you've topped me—I can take it." He raised his glass. "To the future."

She lifted her water goblet and they clinked glasses. "Our future."

Jubal peered around his raised glass at his wife seated across the table from him. *Actor's hormones. She has no idea how grateful I am for this role.*

He knew Claire had always underestimated his acting abilities. Of course she wasn't alone in that.

They drank to the rest of their lives.

Pearl having sex.

Her tiny bedroom hot and humid with the scent of sex.

She'd personally checked with Dr. Liran and knew it was okay; men with hearts like Quinn's seldom suffered an attack during the sexual act. Better for him than a drink and a cigar, the doctor had said. Pearl sure as hell hoped so.

She'd already been satisfied. Quinn had learned about her fast and knew how to bring out a tenderness in her that even Pearl hadn't suspected she possessed. He could make the uneasiness and loneliness dissipate, at least for a while. With Quinn she was herself. With Quinn she was reborn.

Pearl was no stranger to multiple orgasms, but she doubted it would be possible this time, though she wasn't sure why.

Quinn's weight was heavy on her, even though he was propped on his elbows and knees. The bedsprings were squealing, the headboard banging against the wall. His labored breathing was harsh in her right ear. She adjusted her legs, trying to get more comfortable.

Jesus! What am I doing?

She couldn't help it. Something about the ceiling fixture directly above held her attention. The fixture was old, metal of some sort, with a stamped floral design that had been painted over so many times it was almost indiscernible. It held two lightbulbs, and if their glare needed softening, it was up to the tenant to buy some sort of shades to fit over the bulbs.

Quinn gasped and his body became rigid. She thought he'd climaxed, but he hadn't. He began thrusting into her again. And again. It wasn't that Pearl wasn't still enjoying it on a certain level (what the hell, it was sex), it was just that by now she was out of the mood.

That fixture has to go. Has to be replaced. Maybe by something on a chain that throws more light. Or a paddle fan with a light kit. There's an idea.

My God, I'm like that unfeeling woman in the joke who's trying to figure out during sex what color to paint the ceiling.

Well, maybe not quite that bad.

This isn't like me!

Then she realized why staring at the light fixture so intrigued her. It had sparked something related in her mind. Something about the Night Prowler investigation. It was so strange, how the mind worked. She couldn't quite get a grip on what was nibbling at the edges of her consciousness.

Something on the other side of the wall that the headboard was banging against crashed to the floor. Probably something in the closet that held the painting supplies Pearl seldom used or even looked at.

Decorators!

Yes, decorators!

Additional suspects. Stones unturned.

She lowered her legs. "Quinn!"

Startled, he straightened his arms and reared back, withdrawing from her. "Wha's wrong . . . I hurt you?"

"Decorators, Quinn."

"Huh?" He glanced around as if he'd been warned. His unruly hair was damp and mussed and a bead of perspiration dripped from his forehead onto her pillow. She heard it plop onto the taut linen. He drew in a deep breath and released it slowly, then peered down at her quizzically. "You did say *decorators*?"

She squirmed out from beneath him, which wasn't difficult, the way they were both sweating. "Everyone who might have been given a key to enter the victims' apartments in the times leading up to their deaths—supers, trusted neighbors, tradesmen like plumbers and electricians—have all been questioned by the police."

"Including interior decorators."

"Exactly. When people can afford a professional decorator, they often turn over the apartment to him and trust his judgment on everything."

"Everything?"

"Yes. And they don't want to be home while the work's being done."

"You know this?"

"Sure. Every woman knows this. Who wants to live with sawdust in their hair? And if the owner or tenant wants to give the decorator free rein, he usually gets a key to keep the entire time the job's in progress." Pearl was staring at Quinn, a bit surprised that he seemed dubious. "Something, no?"

"Something, maybe," he said. "The murder apartments had been redecorated within the past few years—like a lot of apartments in Manhattan—and the decorators were given keys by their clients, like you said, but they've been cleared. They all had alibis that checked out."

"But what about the tradesmen *they* hired? We talked to tradesmen hired by the building owners or supers, usually to make repairs. Interior decorators often subcontract out the painting, carpeting, whatever. They want things done right, so they like to use people they usually work with and can trust. *Their* people."

Quinn sat up cross-legged on the bed. "I follow. Who might the *decorators* have given keys to without the clients even knowing about it?"

"Right. So, we might have more suspects. We talk to the decorators again and see if they gave apartment keys to any of the tradesmen they hired. If so, whoever they lent the keys to might have secretly had them duplicated."

"So they could come and go as they pleased from then on," Quinn said, "and learn all sorts of things about the occupants by looking through their desk and dresser drawers."

"And searching their computer hard drives, especially if they figured out how to get online. Most people have their passwords written down someplace handy to the computer, in case they forget. Like they do with safe combinations."

It made sense. Enough sense, anyway. Quinn stood up from the bed and used the heel of his hand to wipe perspiration from his eyes.

"Where you going?" Pearl asked.

"To take a shower. You and I are gonna get dressed and make some phone calls, set up appointments to talk to decorators."

"You're gonna leave me like this? Unfinished and unfulfilled?"

"You were the one thinking about work."

She grinned. "This isn't the NYPD way. This is 'copus interruptus.' "

"Don't worry, we'll get back to it. Wanna take a shower with me?"

"You bet."

She scooted down to the foot of the bed and stood up, wondering if they'd slip and fall and break something in the old claw-footed tub. "What do you think of that ceiling fixture?"

He glanced up. "Looks more like a glob of paint with a couple of dirty bulbs screwed into it."

"So you'd replace it?"

"Yeah, definitely."

"With what?"

"I dunno. Maybe I'd ask someone, or hire a . . ." He gave her a suspicious look, obviously wondering at what point she'd been thinking about light fixtures and decorators during the past half hour.

Pearl was afraid she might have hurt his feelings. Men were so vain when it came to that sort of thing. And she really, truly did *not* want to hurt Quinn.

If she had bruised his ego, she made it up to him under the shower.

52

Claire borrowed Maddy's old Volvo and drove Jubal to LaGuardia for his flight to Chicago.

"Don't think too much about me or the baby," she told him as they walked toward the security area leading to the concourses. "Concentrate on the play."

"That won't be easy." He was holding a black carry-on, which contained his laptop and a copy of the *As Thy Love Thyself* script. He sneaked a peek at his wristwatch, the way people do when they're in a hurry.

"Good luck!" Claire said. *Don't go! Don't leave! Damn hormones!*

He slung the carry-on's thick strap over his shoulder and smiled at her, then kissed her, letting his lips linger. "Be careful driving home. Take the tunnel."

"I always do. You be careful yourself. Love you."

"Me, too."

They kissed again, and then he was gone from her, striding toward the metal detector with the shortest line. He swerved to avoid a couple carrying an infant and trailing wheeled suitcases and a portable stroller laden with wadded blankets and a stuffed animal.

Us in less than a year.

Within a few minutes he was through security. He turned and waved to her, giving her another smile. *Handsome actor. Colleague, lover, husband.* She loved him so fiercely at that moment she was afraid she might break into sobs.

Goddamn hormones!

It's worth it. It's worth it.

The drive back to the apartment alone seemed to take forever. Then she spent another twenty minutes finding a parking space within two blocks of her building. Why Maddy even owned a car in Manhattan was beyond Claire.

To lend to needy friends—like me.

She wished she were thinking more clearly these days.

When she walked into the apartment, she immediately felt better. Balanced on the sofa back, where it would be clearly visible, was a large shrink-wrapped blueberry muffin from the nearby deli, the food that had become her vice during pregnancy. This one was particularly large, perhaps six inches across the top.

Jubal must have bought it earlier and stashed it, then sneaked it onto the sofa just before they left for LaGuardia. Yes, she'd walked out of the apartment first, and he'd followed with his luggage, then keyed the dead bolt.

Or had he stepped out into the hall first?

Claire couldn't remember and soon gave up trying to reconstruct in her mind the sequence of their departure.

It didn't matter. There was the muffin, his gift, his thoughtfulness.

There was his love for her.

The direct flight to Chicago had taken a little less than three hours. The carry-on strap was digging into Jubal's shoulder with every step as he strode toward the point beyond security where people waited to greet incoming passengers. It hadn't been an easy flight. An infant two seats in front of his had begun wailing during takeoff and only stopped occasionally to catch its breath so it could maintain volume. Concentrating on *As Thy Love Thyself* was impossible, so Jubal had put the script back in his carry-on and, despite the din, had dozed on the plane and was still slightly groggy.

He became more alert when he saw a slight, shapely woman leaning casually against a post with her arms crossed. Her posture was one of easy grace, one leg slightly bent at the knee so her pointed toe retained balance, her body elegantly curved. A dancer's line. She was wearing tight blue slacks and an untucked white T-shirt snug over small, pointed breasts. Her blond hair was styled close to her head in a boy cut to emphasize her gamine features.

Dalia Hart.

She spotted Jubal and came alive with a glow. Grinning widely, she pushed away from the post she'd been leaning on and ran to greet him.

He let the carry-on drop to the floor and gathered her close in his arms.

She nuzzled the base of his neck, flicking with her tongue. "Glad to see me?"

"Understatement," he said.

"I know," she said through her smile. "I can feel it."

He kissed her hello as fervently as he'd kissed Claire good-bye only hours ago in New York.

53

Rain had begun to fall, or rather hang in the air, a heavy mist that made umbrellas useless and found its way beneath exposed cuffs and down the backs of collars. At least the heat had broken, Quinn thought as he struggled out of a cab and stepped into a puddle, which made his right sock wet.

A woman wearing rubber boots sloshed through the water and claimed his place in the back of the cab even before he had a chance to shut the door. He barely got out of the way and avoided being splashed as the vehicle rejoined start-and-stop traffic on Park Avenue.

While Pearl and Fedderman were continuing their interviews with interior decorators who'd been employed by Night Prowler victims, Quinn had cabbed here to meet Harley Renz at a psychiatrist's office. Renz had requested the meeting but hadn't told Quinn the reason for it. As he crossed the wide street toward the sedate, prewar building, Quinn thought it was way past time for Renz to find his way to a psychiatrist's office.

The lobby was gold-veined gray marble and soft oak paneling, understated and elegant. It was unattended. Quinn paused on a large rubber mat and stamped water from his shoes, noticing a security camera mounted in a corner and aimed his way. He found a directory near the elevators and quickly located his destination.

The office, on the ninth floor, was at the end of a wide hall. Its door was open about six inches in coy and silent invitation.

He pushed the door open all the way and stepped inside. Something about the subtle, chemical scent of the place alerted him. Then he noticed smudges on various objects, like someone had gone through with a greasy feather duster, from when prints had been lifted. Now he recognized the scent; more obscure prints had been made visible with the Super Glue method.

Crime scene.

Quinn was in a receptionist's outer office and waiting room. There was a desk with a computer on it, a bank of tan file cabinets, softly painted earth-tone walls, restful prints of water lilies. Current magazines were spread out on a coffee table before a long beige sofa, a *Forbes*, a *New Yorker,* an *Architectural Digest.* A Mr. Coffee sat on a small table in a corner, a stack of white Styrofoam cups next to it along with packaged cream and sugar. Mr. Coffee's burner light wasn't glowing, but the glass pot was half filled.

Quinn saw that a closet door on his left was hanging open. A man's worn blue windbreaker on a wire hanger was the only garment. There was an X of masking tape on the floor, no doubt to indicate where a body had been stuffed into the narrow closet. The tape was smeared with blood and curled where it lay over a dark stain on the carpeted floor. Quinn noted that the carpet had absorbed a lot of blood, so when the door was closed, it wouldn't be visible to anyone coming in from the hall. *A killer thinking ahead?*

He went to another half-opened door alongside the reception desk and used the back of a knuckle, so as not to disturb or leave a print, to push it open all the way. Not necessary, since the scene had obviously been gone over by the crime scene unit and the body removed, but habits formed in the presence of death died harder than some homicide victims.

There was Harley Renz, lying on his back on a brown leather sofa, his legs crossed at the ankles, his fingers laced behind his head. He looked over and smiled when Quinn entered the room. "Welcome to the confessional."

"Sorry I missed it. I bet you had some doozies."

"I was too late myself." Renz motioned lazily to where an outline of a human body had been marked out crudely with tape on the carpet near the desk.

"Was that the Dr. Rita Maxwell whose name was on the building directory," Quinn asked, "or was she the one in the closet?"

"This one was Dr. Maxwell." Renz sat up but remained slumped and relaxed on a corner of the comfortable-looking sofa. "The vic in the outer-office closet was her receptionist, one Hannah Best. This Dr. Maxwell"—he pointed to a wall displaying photographs and framed diplomas and certificates—"was some impressive babe."

"I read about the case in the papers," Quinn said. "The doctor and her assistant were stabbed to death. The pattern didn't fit the Night Prowler, so I didn't pay too much attention."

"I don't think it fits, either," Renz said, "but I thought you might wanna take a look at the scene. You never know what might trigger an errant thought, wandered somehow into an infertile brain."

"True enough. Any leads?"

"One. Like I said, there's probably no connection, but sometimes New York can be a small town. Both these women were stabbed only a few times each, as if more to send them on their way without a lot of time, trouble, or passion than for any sadistic enjoyment. Not like what your guy does to them. Still, we got women stabbed to death here. The media's taken note. And a Park Avenue analyst murdered in her office—lots of people will be disturbed by that."

"You mean people who were disturbed to begin with and had motive and opportunity to kill Dr. Maxwell."

"Among others. Just think of all the secrets passed in confidence in this quiet, restful room." Renz grinned. "But we know there's really no such thing as secrets in confidence."

"They exist," Quinn said, "but briefly."

"Like true love."

"I noticed a security camera in the lobby. Did it show anything?"

"You mean like a shot of the killer on his way in or out? No. It had recycled and was on its next loop by the time we knew it was there. Everybody coming or going on the tape was here well after the murders."

"What about the doctor's files?"

"They don't appear to have been disturbed. It seems the killer entered the outer office, killed 'Hard Luck Hannah' the receptionist, and hid her body in the closet. Then he came in here and did the doctor."

"Maybe a patient thought twice after revealing something during analysis and wanted to take it back."

"Always that possibility, with a victim like this."

"It wasn't done on a whim," Quinn said. "The only blood from the receptionist is in the closet. Looks like she was knocked out and stuffed in there before she got knifed."

"That's how I figure it. The killer just wanted her out of the way. Dr. Maxwell was the primary target."

"Have you searched her files?"

"That'd be a touchy matter legally," Renz said. "We're working on a warrant right now."

"Have you searched her files?" Quinn repeated in the same tone.

"Yeah. And found about what you'd expect. But there are some interesting names in there."

"Potentially useful to a shameless climber like you," Quinn said.

"They might prove useful to our side."

He was right. *Our side. Our team.* It made Quinn wince.

"And aren't you just the one to talk about shame?"

Quinn felt his anger rise but pushed it back. "You mentioned you had a lead."

"Sort of a lead. The receptionist kept a patient schedule on a software program in her computer, but she was old-fashioned and distrustful of technology. Like us. So she also kept names and appointment times in a book. One of the names in the book is missing in the computer and file cabinet. A patient named David Blank."

"So, you think Blank did the killings, then deleted his appointment from the computer calendar and removed his file, but he didn't know about the book."

"So I surmise. He was the last appointment the afternoon of the murder. The first appointment the next morning discovered the bodies and called the police. We're pretty sure Blank had previous appointments, because the records show gaps in the doctor's schedule. Several of them. Damned computers. Global search and delete. Handy for felons."

"Bits and bytes have no moral compass."

"If you say so. There's a recorder over there on the desk. Some of the other patients said it was how Dr. Maxwell worked. She listened to her patients and recorded the sessions so she could review them later, then placed the tapes in the files. There's no cassette in the recorder."

"So, David Blank wanted to remove all evidence of his having been a patient."

"Sure looks that way. And turns out he's proving difficult to locate. The few David Blanks we can find have been eliminated as suspects, so all we have is a name. The David Blank in Hannah Best's appointment book didn't and doesn't exist. Only he's real, because he probably murdered these two women."

Quinn walked over and stared down at the taped outline on the floor, trying to imagine a human being lying there. A woman Renz had called a babe, with friends, family, and a medical degree. Looks, brains, she'd had it all, but *had* was the operative word. *Don't get sentimental. Maybe she didn't have a family. But even I have a family. Some remnants of a family. The soon-to-be Franzine family.* "If Blank did the deed after taking pains to create a false identity, he planned to kill the doctor from the beginning of his visits."

"Why would anybody do something like that?" Renz asked, sounding deeply perplexed. "Go to a shrink knowing you were setting up to kill her?"

"I have no idea," Quinn said. "But then, I don't think I need one. Like you said, this doesn't fit the pattern."

"Still, it'd be nice to solve it. Throw some meat to the media wolves and take some heat off you."

And you. "I'll point out one thing. There might have been someone else who deleted and removed files. Somebody more successful than David Blank at covering his tracks."

Renz looked at him with a kind of growing anger. "A killer who might have been a patient we never heard of and never will?"

"It's possible. Somebody who knew about or never made it into Hannah's appointment book. Who wants you looking for David Blank instead of him." Quinn motioned with an arm toward the file cabinets in the office, then toward the reception area on the other side of the wall. "How can we know what else might be missing?"

Renz ran a hand down his face, stretching the flesh beneath his eyes so he looked mournful. "Jesus H. Christ! Leave it to you to make everything complicated."

"It's what you get for leaving it to me, Harley. And almost everything *is* complicated, if you're really trying to get at the truth."

"I'm not interested in the truth, Quinn. I'm interested in evidence. That's all that counts in court."

Quinn thought Renz might have something there.

He thanked Renz for calling him to the scene, then filled him in on what Pearl and Fedderman were doing and left.

He didn't try pointing out that evidence was supposed to lead to truth, no matter how it played in court. There were only so many links in Renz's chains of logic.

Enough to reach where he wanted to go, but no further.

As Quinn closed the door on the bloodied office, he wondered if the law would ever catch up with David Blank.

But then, it wasn't his concern.

54

Successful decorators were a flighty bunch, flitting all over the city as if in a panic, difficult to catch up to. They were late there, in the wrong place here, ahead of schedule there. Apparently, they could arrange anything but time.

Pearl finally located Victory Wallace at a crumbly red-brick building just off Christopher Street in the Village. It was obvious that the building was being refurbished. A tubular slide ran from a second-floor window down to a rusty Dumpster. The front shop window was covered with graffiti-marred plywood featuring BOOK 'EM ALL in large black letters. The first three letters looked somewhat suspicious, and Pearl could interpret the original message. Sometimes she shared the thought.

Two vans and a pickup truck overloaded with debris—rotted lumber, broken wallboard, splintered lathing, an old door—were parked near the entrance. The building's front door was not only open but off its hinges. Pearl wondered if it was the door in the truck.

She heard hammering as she stepped inside. Daylight streamed narrowly in through the few unboarded windows, completely missing areas that were illuminated by flood-lights. A fine dust hung in the air. Plaster dust, Pearl assumed. A burly man in jeans and a sleeveless shirt was on a ladder, using a trowel to spread drywall mud over seams in newly applied wallboard. A skinny, shirtless teenage boy, his upper body covered with tattoos, was sanding dried applications of the putty-colored substance—the cause of so much dust. His dark hair had a film of gray over it, making him look prematurely aged. At the far end of the area, whose interior walls had been removed, a man in baggy overalls was using a circular saw on boards laid over a pair of sawhorses. To Pearl's left, another workman was on a stepladder, wielding a red-handled hammer.

In the middle of all this heavy-duty, purely practical activity stood an improbable figure in tight black leather pants, boots with built-up heels, and a sky blue shirt with puffy sleeves. Pearl wished she had the guy's waist, not to mention his ass.

"Are you Mr. Wallace?" she asked between passes with the power saw.

He turned toward her, quite a handsome man, with a firm chin and dark lashes, and held up his middle and forefinger in a V gesture. "Victory, my sweet. I'm Victory." He looked her up and down without being bashful about it. "And you are Detective Kasner. The one who called."

"Unless there's another Detective Kasner," Pearl said. *Keeeeeeeyow!* went the power saw. *B-bam, b-bam!* went the hammer. "Can we please talk someplace quiet?"

"The walls!" shouted Victory.

If they have ears, they are surely deaf. "What about the walls?"

"What do you think of a subtle flesh color for the walls?"

Pearl glanced around. "I don't know. What kind of place is—" *keeeeeyow!*—"this gonna be?"

"An erotic Internet dessert cafe."

Pearl cupped a hand to her ear. "Exotic desserts?"

"Erotic!"

B-bam, b-bam!

"Ah," said Pearl. She pointed to her right ear and shrugged. "Someplace quiet, okay?"

Victory nodded and led her to a back entrance, then through a door to a small, shaded courtyard with dead flowers surrounding a maple tree. The hammering and sawing were barely audible out here.

"Better," Pearl said. "Now, how do I get a job at an erotic Internet café?"

Victory gave her a dubious look and smiled. He said nothing, still trying to figure out the game. After all, cops, murder, it was all more than unsettling.

"And what *is* an erotic Internet café?" Pearl asked.

"Like any other Internet café, dear, only we subscribe to the most amazing Web sites, and the confections are of different shapes. Dough can be worked into many forms other than bagels and doughnuts, some of them quite suggestive if not titillating."

"And you've been hired to decorate the place?"

"Indeed I have."

Good choice. "Flesh-colored walls seem right, then," Pearl said, "but without a trace of blush."

"Consider your vote cast." Victory waved an arm for emphasis. Pearl saw that his shirt had French cuffs with gold-coin cuff links—probably real gold. There was profit in bullshit. "If this is about poor Marcy Graham and her husband, I already talked to one of your fellow officers. To what do I owe this second tête-à-tête? Am I perchance a suspect?"

"Nope. You're in the clear. So far," she added, trying to wipe the smarmy smile off his face.

The smile didn't waver. "I watch *Law and Order*, dear detective. I know that truth always rises to the top."

"In real life it takes someone like me to push it up there."

"And where might we find real life?"

Pearl laughed. "It'd take a better detective than me to tell you that. But Marcy Graham and her husband found real death just months after you decorated their apartment. It says in the file you were given a key by Marcy."

"Indeed. That isn't unusual. Most of my clients don't mind me letting myself in, and they prefer not to be home during remodeling."

"Did you give the Graham key to any of your subcontractors? The tradesmen who do the physical part of your work."

"A few times. But I always got it back from them before nightfall. I am not unmindful of security. I mean, these days . . ." He waved a hand as if to gesture toward particular days all around them. *These* days.

"Did any of the people you hired have the opportunity to have the key duplicated?"

Victory looked nonplussed, and that was the only word for it. "Oh, my!"

"That a yes?"

"I'm afraid it is. But all the people I use are old acquaintances, each and every one of them totally trustworthy."

"We both know it's impossible to be sure of that."

"True. But this isn't love or war, dear, it's interior decorating." He raised a ringed forefinger. "Strike that. It can be like war sometimes. When the client thinks something doesn't *tie in.* Or when it comes time to pay the cost of art, instead of simply talking about it."

"I'd like a list of all the tradesmen you employ," Pearl said.

"I hate to cause them a problem."

"Do I look like a problem?"

Victory grinned lewdly. "Oh, do you ever!"

"That would be a yes on the list?"

Victory shrugged. "I suppose."

Pearl gave him her pen and notepad.

When he was finished writing, she said, "What are they using for bedroom ceiling fixtures these days?"

"Retro crystal chandeliers, stained-glass Japanese lanterns, brushed aluminum—"

"What about one of those ceiling fans with a light kit?"

"Oh, my God!"

Brushed aluminum, Pearl thought.

As she was leaving, the guy working the power saw glanced over at her and managed a kind of come-hither motion with his tongue. Pearl tried to ignore him but had to admire his dexterity.

Keeeeeeeyow!

Pearl hoped he was cutting off a finger.

Victory watched Pearl through the bright rectangle of the front doorway as she crossed the street to her parked car.

I wish I had her ass.

He liked the lady cop; she had balls. But he certainly didn't want to see her again. It was unnerving, being so close to an actual murder case. A homicide was déclassé, but nothing compared to an arraignment and trial, not to mention prison, not to overlook. . . . Well, it could prove squalid and mortifying. Judges, juries, could be so unpredictable in these times. Victory knew innocent people were convicted of murder with alarming regularity. What was that movie . . . ?

It had gotten four stars—he remembered that. It would come to him.

He went over in his mind the names he'd written on the detective's pad. He needed to be thorough so as not to invite suspicion of some kind, or suggest complicity with a monster.

He'd listed everyone, he was positive. The detective with the delectable derriere had the names of all the tradesmen he'd employed in the past two years.

Satisfied that he could put the entire dreary business out of his mind, Victory returned to contemplating the walls-to-be. It wasn't only the color that concerned him; he had to co-ordinate other elements with the carnal and crust motif. The walls were background; something now needed to be on them to pop and provide contrast. Perhaps clear-laquered, risqué lingerie, framed as art. And surely there were baking utensils that suggested erotic usage.

Yes! But possibly he was approaching this backward. First the lingerie and utensil wall hangings, then the color? There was still time to decide. And he knew someone who might perfectly match color with context to combine sex and food, two of the basic human imperatives.

Victory hadn't for a second considered including Romulus in his list of tradesmen. That was because Romulus wasn't a tradesman. He didn't merely glow in the galaxy of simple craft. Romulus was too complex and brilliant for that. He was unique. A bright star rather than a workaday drudge with a talent for hammer, saw, or paintbrush.

He was hardly a slayer of anything other than poor taste.

Romulus was an artist, like Victory himself, a spiritual brother and not part of the mundane world that so often tried to intrude on their own.

A genuine artist. And in this fucked-up, fucked-over city, what was more precious than that?

The Night Prowler watched Claire leave her apartment building and stride with her incredibly graceful walk on the opposite side of the street. How she could move—her hips, her arms, the kick of her legs—in time with some celestial music he could hear and see in elegant kaleidoscopic wonder. Was she also a dancer? So many Broadway stars could dance, as well as sing and act. Many had begun as chorus line dancers and had become actors. Or was it the other way around? He didn't know, actually, but to him Claire was a dancer.

She was walking with bold purpose.

On her way to meet someone? Someone who should be me?

She turned a corner and the Night Prowler had to jay-walk, jogging across a lane of slowly moving traffic to keep up. An annoyed driver screamed at him that he was an ass-hole. The Night Prowler ignored him instead of killing him and walked swiftly on.

Ah! There she is! In the shadow of the valley of—

Then she walked into the brilliant pale light cast down-ward by a theater marquee. She was going to see a movie? Alone?

But she didn't stop at the glassed-in booth to buy a ticket before entering the lobby.

The Night Prowler slowed and moved sideways to skirt the closed shops.

He watched through glass doors as Claire talked smil-ingly to the young man taking tickets. Finally he grinned back at her, charmed as he would be, and Claire brushed past him and across the carpeted inner lobby.

The Night Prowler pushed the door open and pretended to study movie posters in the outer lobby while actually keeping an eye on Claire. The theater was having a science fiction retrospect, and the poster was for *I Married a Monster from Outer Space*. He was pretty sure he'd seen that one years ago; he remembered the luscious brunette with the bangs, screaming on the poster. *Four stars.*

Claire was at the concession counter, waiting patiently behind a bald man buying popcorn. The Night Prowler moved closer, standing before the poster nearest the main lobby en-trance. It advertised the feature for tonight, *Creature from the Black Lagoon*. The Night Prowler recalled that one, too, and knew it was a classic. Richard Carlson spitting into his scuba mask and swimming around in Florida. Didn't Carlson also star in *I Led 3 Lives*? Of course that one was television. *Three lives? That was nothing!*

After the bald man had sprinkled salt on his popcorn and finally walked away, Claire moved up a step and pointed at something in the display case. The woman behind the counter stooped, straightened, and handed her a large box of candy. The Night Prowler recognized the brand even from this distance—chocolate-covered mints in a green-and-white package. He recalled from an e-mail he'd read on Claire's computer that they were her favorite candy.

So, she was weaning herself away from the muffins, or suddenly they'd become repulsive to her. Women—

Coming this way!

He turned away so she wouldn't see his face, and in the reflection of the *Black Lagoon* poster glass, he watched her walk past, not glancing at him. The creature, some sort of amphibian with a permanent scowl, glowered at him. It knew what he was about.

The Night Prowler waited at least a minute before turning around. Then he went outside and bought a ticket, even though the woman in the booth warned him the movie was well under way.

Inside the theater he went to the concession stand and bought half a dozen boxes of mints before going into the darkened auditorium and finding a seat.

He got comfortable, opened one of the mint boxes, and began eating Claire's favorite candy. He let the chocolate melt on his tongue while he thought about her. On the screen an attractive scuba diver, with long, beautiful legs, was swimming in dark waters. She was obviously afraid even as she stroked deeper, propelled by the screenplay. Danger, death, could suddenly embrace her from any direction in the murky depths. It was much like life outside the movies.

Someone in the audience tittered. The Night Prowler pressed a fingertip against the back of the unoccupied seat in front of him and thought a sharply pointed knife would penetrate the material easily, then cut through the back of anyone seated there and reach the heart. *Bloodred, scarlet blue in the dark.* If he acted out what he was thinking, the person, the titterer, would die immediately and the few other patrons in the theater would assume he was simply asleep, while his killer got up and walked out.

It could be done. It was a thought. People who talked in movies, who rudely intruded in other people's dreams and diversions, deserved death.

The volume of the music rose, and so did the swimmer. Wide-eyed and fearful, she was yanked up, just in time, into the boat, where she was safe.

At least for a while.

Not very realistic, thought the Night Prowler, forgetting about the titterer.

It would have been better in color.

55

The sun was bright and there were no clouds in the morning sky, but thunder roared like a distant lion in the east. Quinn was sitting on one of the concrete and wooden benches just inside the Eighty-sixth Street entrance to the park, looking out at a gentle slope of ground shaded by mature trees. Beyond the slope a few sunbathers were out on towels or webbed aluminum loungers, though it was still early and the day's heat was just beginning to build.

Quinn thought it was a beautiful morning that belied his troubles. He glanced at his watch. Pearl and Fedderman should be along soon.

"So, this is where you meet," said a voice behind him.

Harley Renz walked into view. He was wearing a dark blue suit with a light pinstripe, a blue shirt and patterned red tie fastened with a gold clasp. Somebody had spent a lot of time buffing his shoes to a high gloss. He belonged in the park like Fred Astaire belonged at an Ozark clog dance. Quinn figured there must be a TV interview scheduled for this morning. He could see a shiny black Lincoln at the curb out on Central Park West and thought it was probably Renz's driver waiting for him.

"You might get rained on," Renz said with a smile, as if he didn't think that would be so bad. "Hear that thunder?"

"It's out at sea."

"Where you are," Renz said, still smiling. He lightly hooked a thumb in his belt, so he looked like a catalog clothes model, and glanced around. "Your roach trap apartment's in the Nineties. There's an entrance to the park closer to where you live, so why don't you meet your partners in crime solving there?"

"This is more central to us." Which was true. It was also true there was a playground near the Ninety-first Street entrance, and Quinn didn't want to spend time on a park bench too close to it. The media had enough to work with, as it was.

"I was on my way to Channel One, then the precinct, and I thought, I bet Quinn has something to report. I knew this was where you and your team met sometimes, so I had my driver stop off here so we could chat."

Quinn told him about Pearl's key-reproduction theory.

"And?" Renz asked.

"We're still checking it out. It makes sense."

"Which is your way of saying you don't have diddly shit."

Quinn nodded. "Your way of saying it is better. But we're not done. Pearl and Fedderman have been on it and might have something when they get here."

"On it how?"

"Checking places where apartment door keys might have been duplicated."

"Jesus, Quinn. Do you know how many—"

"It's not as long a shot as you might think. There are certain blanks for particular kinds of locks that are usually on apartment doors."

"Blanks?"

"Plain, unnotched keys that haven't been cut."

"And there are only millions of apartments in Manhattan. If one half of one percent of their occupants had duplicate keys made, it'd mean you only had hundreds of thousands to check out."

"Remember, we're looking for tradesmen who had keys duplicated. That narrows it down."

"To only tens of thousands."

"Harley, you've been spending time trying to trace a silencer that doesn't have an individual serial number."

"And found a guy living on the West Side who threw one out in his trash a few months ago."

"If it's the same silencer."

"It might be."

"So do you have your troops searching landfills?"

"No. Too much of a long shot. And I wouldn't have them going around visiting hundreds of places that duplicate thousands of keys."

"Pearl and Fedderman might come up with something. They'll sense where to go. They have good cop instincts."

Renz looked away, up at what might be the only cloud in the sky, then back at Quinn. "Yeah. Pearl's a hell of a detective. And some parts of Fedderman's brain are still active."

"You assigned them to me."

"Shows what I know. Pearl's a good fuck, would you say?"

Quinn felt the anger rise hot in him, almost lifting him off the bench.

"Cool down," Renz said. "The word is out about you and Pearl, and even you have to admit the relationship isn't very professional."

"It's not professional at all. It's personal."

"Quinn, there is no personal."

Quinn thought he might be right. If you were a cop long enough, groping around in other people's dirty secrets and desires, your mental fingertips grew calluses. You lost a certain respect and sensitivity for privacy. He leaned back on the bench and crossed his arms, looking up at Renz. "You mentioned you were on your way to do some media this morning. About the Night Prowler?"

"Sure. What else is New York media interested in?"

"You said the word was out about Pearl and me. Has it hit print or TV yet?"

"No, but it will. And when it does, they'll hammer both of you hard. It'll be rough, but you'll still have a little time. Maybe. Depending. Possibly. How can anyone say for sure, other than the participants, what happened behind closed doors?"

"Somebody must have said," Quinn pointed out. "How else would the word have gotten around?"

"Nobody in the NYPD had to be told. All anybody had to do was look at Pearl to know she was in love and in heat."

"Dammit, Harley!"

"Okay, I'll show some respect. But you know the news wolves in this town. And they've already fallen in love with Anna Caruso and are leaning toward lynching you. They probably won't feel too kindly toward Pearl, either."

Thunder rolled again, but it sounded farther away.

Renz shot his cuff as he glanced at his gold watch. "I gotta stop wasting time talking with you. After Channel One I got another interview with Kay Kemper. If it isn't one info babe, it's another."

"Careful what you say to Kemper. She likes to rake the muck."

Renz laughed. "You, the muck, telling me to be careful. Telling anybody."

He turned and gave a dismissive wave as he walked toward his waiting car and driver. Quinn had to admit the suit looked great on him. It was the only thing he liked about Harley Renz.

Other than he was better than Vince Egan.

* * *

Ten minutes later, Pearl and Fedderman drove up in the unmarked and parked in the space Renz's Lincoln had occupied. As they approached the bench, Quinn thought Pearl looked businesslike in a gray jacket and dark slacks, a V of white showing where the coat was buttoned. Fedderman limped along as if his feet hurt; compared to Renz's nifty attire, Fed's brown suit hung on him like rags. One of his shirt cuffs protruded from the coat sleeve, unbuttoned and flapping around as he swung his arms. The general effect was that of a portly scarecrow on the move.

"Traffic," said Pearl, who'd been driving. She said it by way of explanation, nothing of apology in her tone. *Could* she apologize? For anything? "Been waiting long?"

"No, and I've had company." Quinn told them about his conversation with Renz.

"Guy's a genuine prick," Pearl said.

"So everyone says." Quinn used the back of his hand to wipe sweat off his forehead. Pearl had to be hot in that blazer, and Fedderman in his shoddy suit. "Was Renz right to be skeptical of our search for the literal key to the case?"

"He was right," Pearl said. "I never knew there were so many places that duplicated keys every day in the areas of the murders. The locksmiths—and only some of them *are*— know the blanks and brands common to apartment keys, but lots of their customers pay cash. Records aren't available, and charge receipts yielded nothing."

"Renz has been right so far," Fedderman said, as if he'd only been half listening to Pearl. Quinn could see now there were crescents of perspiration beneath the arms of his suit coat. Or were those stains from yesterday? "But only so far."

Pearl and Quinn both looked at him.

"Suppose we assume the killer duplicated his own keys. You've seen that some of those machines are portable, Pearl, and using them doesn't take a great deal of skill or training. So let's work this backward."

Pearl didn't know what he meant. She looked quizzically at Quinn.

"He means start with tradesmen who worked in any of the murder apartments, and also have their own portable key cutters."

"That'd narrow it down," Fedderman said.

"Would it ever!" Pearl grinned and kissed him on the cheek.

Fedderman blushed and glanced almost guiltily at Quinn.

56

Jubal rolled off Dalia and sighed, still trying to catch his breath. Dalia liked to go twice sometimes, once on top, then on the bottom. He couldn't imagine Claire even suggesting such a thing—not since she'd become pregnant.

They were in Chicago's venerable and almost shabby Tremontier Hotel, where they were registered under their real names, Dorthea Hartnagle and Arnold Wolfe. It wouldn't do to let the others in the production of *As Thy Love Thyself* know they were longtime lovers. Show business could be a small world, and Jubal was married to an actress.

The room was warm and smelled of sex and the rose fragrance perfume Dalia always wore. Jubal had come to love the combined scent. It almost made him hesitate in lighting a cigarette, but he reached over to the bedside table, carefully avoiding Dalia's overturned champagne glass, and got his pack of Camels and a hotel book of matches. He fired up a cigarette, then leaned his head back on the damp pillow, took a long drag, and exhaled.

"Jesus, that's good!"

Dalia was staring over at him, grinning. "The sex or the cigarette?"

"All of it."

"Your wife know you're back smoking?"

"Somehow that doesn't seem like the logical question."

"I guess it isn't."

"There's a lot Claire doesn't know about me."

"Yeah, I bet you're really misunderstood and abused."

"You know what I mean, how it is."

"Do I ever." Dalia rolled onto her stomach and felt around for the bottle of Dom Pérignon on the floor. She found it, then righted the champagne glass and poured what little was left of the bottle into it. She sat up cross-legged and nude on the bed and experimentally sipped champagne.

"Flat?" Jubal asked.

"Yeah, but so am I now, after the way you've been bouncing on me." Another sip drained the glass and she placed it back on the table. "Does Claire know about your sitcom offer?"

"Not yet." The producer of a pilot film for a proposed new cable sitcom, *West Side Buddies,* about a group of female-obsessed New York pals and neighbors, had called Jubal's agent and said he might be right for the part of the Mets bachelor shortstop, Eric. There were no guarantees, but Jubal's agent said he'd gotten word Jubal had a real shot at the role.

"Then you *are* going back to New York to audition?"

"I don't know yet."

"Don't be an idiot. You want the role, don't you?"

"Sure. There are top people involved. But it's in New York, and you're here."

"And I'll still be here when you get back. Go! Astin can stand in for you for a couple of days. You won't be bailing out on us; everyone will understand." Astin was Astin Jones, Jubal's handsome and calculating young understudy. There

were people in the cast who thought he might be better for
Jubal's part than Jubal. "Hell, everyone will envy you for the
opportunity. If they knew about the offer, they'd be urging
you to go for it."

Especially Astin.

"You afraid somebody's gonna take your place perma-
nently while you're away?"

Jubal knew what she meant but played dumb. "We've
been meeting each other for a long time and nobody's taken
my place."

Dalia let him get away with it and didn't say anything.
She pretended to check the empty champagne bottle to see if
anything more could be coaxed from it.

Jubal drew again on his cigarette, then leaned to the side
and snuffed out the butt in the glass ashtray near the base of
the lamp. The scent of tobacco smoke now dominated the
room.

"Maybe I will go," he said.

Dalia dropped to her side, then scooted over on the mattress, snaked an arm around Jubal's neck, and kissed him on
the mouth.

"I'll show you maybe," she said, smiling down at him.

At the airport Jubal checked in and passed through security faster than expected. Before the flight to Chicago he'd
had to remove his shoes at LaGuardia, but apparently what
might have been exploding wing tips aroused no suspicion
on this end. He went into a gift shop and browsed to kill
time.

He wasn't all that eager to see Claire.

He was going to miss Dalia.

Claire was in another city and he'd mentally pushed her
aside; it was difficult now to readjust to her. He was still in a
Dalia frame of mind.

Jubal knew he'd done a good job of pretending with Claire. Well, not at first. Initially he'd been shocked, and he supposed glad, when she told him she was pregnant. Then came the marriage, and reality began setting in. Marriage, an infant realer by the hour, genuine commitment, a mutual checking account, mutual everything; it was stifling. None of it correlated with Jubal's plans.

At first he told himself people had to make concessions in life, that he should grow up. But he wasn't good at convincing himself. He *wanted*. He *needed*. Very badly. And not what he already had. Even he hadn't realized how selfish he was about his future, his career.

Not that he felt he should apologize for his selfishness. Or feel guilty about it. He and Claire were both in show business, and they knew the kinds of sacrifices that had to be made. It was like a religious cult, acting; esoteric, demanding, unforgiving to those who betrayed it. He'd kept his religion, but Claire was losing hers.

So he'd begun seeing Dalia again. Dalia ran in his blood and had done so long before Claire. Their on-again, off-again romance had survived for almost seven years, mainly because of the sex, which seemed only to get better and more imaginative with time.

During an off period with Dalia, while she was away working on the West Coast, Claire had become a force in Jubal's life. She'd spun a web that enthralled and hypnotized him, occupying all his thoughts.

But lately, not only because of his deteriorating relationship with Claire, but also probably because of his marriage making Dalia forbidden fruit, and only more desirable, Jubal thought more and more about Dalia. Even making love to Claire, he thought about Dalia.

Dalia was the woman he thought of when he saw the ruby necklace in the airport gift shop showcase.

Dalia loved rubies. She had several ruby rings, a ruby

bracelet, and at least one ruby pin that Jubal knew of. He couldn't recall her wearing a ruby necklace.

This one held a single large stone in a silver setting on a unique silver chain. It reminded the already-lonely Jubal painfully of Dalia. He longed to make her a present of it.

The necklace was overpriced, like almost everything else in the shop. Jubal stood staring at it, considering.

Every addiction is expensive. Even Dalia.

He knew if he didn't buy the necklace now, it might not be there when he returned from New York, so he decided to purchase it, then conceal it someplace for a while.

"Can I help you?" a voice asked. The graying, matronly woman behind the counter had been observing him in his reverie. "Help you?" she asked again.

Jubal didn't think she could. Not really. He'd have to figure out a way to help himself.

"That necklace . . ." He pointed. "The ruby one. Would you show it to me?"

Every addiction . . .

57

Hubby was home.

The Night Prowler had left the apartment after observing Claire sleep. He'd known Jubal was gone, and that he wouldn't be away for very long. Chicago wasn't all that far from New York.

But he hadn't expected him tonight. Not at this hour.

Close! This had been close! And I'm not ready for it yet. I don't want it to happen.

It was past three A.M. when the Night Prowler had left Claire. He'd felt secure standing at the foot of her bed, knowing that if he chose to stay, he'd be alone with her until dawn. *As I would be if I chose to wake her.*

Not yet, not yet. . . .

So he'd left. He was surprised when he'd crossed the street and happened to see Jubal striding toward the apartment building.

You're supposed to be somewhere else.

But here he was. Handsome young would-be celebrity, moving confidently and with a preoccupied air about him, almost floating down the street, a parade all by himself.

Nicely cut suit, tie loosened and askew, hair mussed in a carefully arranged manner, as if he suspected there might be cameras about and wanted to convey a candid flattering moment. Always on; that was the rule. Practicing for greater fame and the fortune that must accompany it.

Jubal Day. *Home to Claire!*

Must have taken a late flight. Cheaper, or the only seat available. Jubal was carrying no luggage. *Traveling light. And why not? I've seen your closet; you have a wardrobe here. It's waiting for you. Like Claire.*

Like me.

"Thanks for the mints," Claire said. She'd gotten up early and decided to let Jubal sleep. Then, when she'd gone into the living room after getting the coffee brewer going, she noticed the two green boxes of chocolate mints on the table. Her favorite candy. Jubal must have bought them for her on the way home. It was so thoughtful and loving of him. She wouldn't tell him she'd experienced one of her sudden cravings and consumed an entire box of the mints only last night.

Barefoot and shirtless, he stood staring at her, puzzled. "Mints?"

She grinned. He was an actor, all right. And if he wanted to play it this way, that was fine. She went to him and kissed him, standing close while he held her. "Never mind. Want some coffee?"

"Can't think of anything I want more."

"I should be insulted."

"Don't be. I didn't mean—"

She laughed. "You're still half-asleep. When did you get in?"

"About three."

Claire glanced at a wall clock. "It's not even nine o'clock. Go back to bed, darling, and have your coffee later."

"Can't. Audition at ten. That's why I set the alarm."

"I didn't hear the alarm."

"My watch."

"I didn't even know your watch had an alarm."

Jubal's heart jumped. It was the watch Dalia had given him. He'd forgotten to exchange it with his old one before leaving Chicago.

He went to Claire and kissed her. "*Every* watch these days has an alarm." He walked into the kitchen and she followed.

"Technology," she said. "I can't keep up."

"Coffee," he said. "And you keep up just fine. The way things are, nobody can know everything."

He poured his coffee, careful to stand so the watch wasn't visible, making it all look so natural, knowing in his bones she was buying into it.

How can anyone who isn't an actor cheat on his wife?

The damned photograph was still everywhere, opening old wounds. The Night Prowler had avoided the newspapers and TV for a while, thinking the media mania would subside, or at least go off on a tangent. There was, after all, other news.

But when he'd turned on the TV yesterday, there was a cop in a suit talking to Kay Kemper about the Night Prowler murders, about how the police were getting closer all the time and it wouldn't be long before an arrest was made. And on the street this morning there was the photograph again, staring from one of the twine-tied stacks of tabloid papers aligned before a kiosk.

It was that bastard Quinn's fault. He was behind the photograph, the demeaning, humiliating news releases, the increasing pressure, everything. Quinn. He was like something out of legend that never stopped, that couldn't be stopped. It made the Night Prowler furious that he couldn't help admiring Quinn even as he loathed him.

Quinn!

The Night Prowler bolted from his chair with the force of his impulse.

No, not impulse, *thought! Idea. Strategy.*

He put on his new NYPD cap he'd bought in a Times Square souvenir shop (*irony-dripping blue*), his amber sunglasses, and went outside and down the street to a subway stop. Not the nearest stop; he wasn't that foolish.

The morning rush was almost over, but there were still twenty-five or thirty people waiting for the next train. No one seemed to be paying much attention to him, staring instead into the dark tunnel in anticipation of the train, or at the littered concrete floor, or down into the shadowed trench where the third rail lay and the gray rats roamed. *Fear and the city.* He was thankful for subway etiquette.

After riding the subway to the Fifty-third and Lex station, far enough from his apartment, he found a public phone near the Citigroup Building. He already knew the number. Had it memorized. Because he'd been considering this not only this morning, but for the past several days. Working out what to say, how to say it, how to be taken seriously.

If they didn't put him on hold and forget him.

Two can waltz with the New York media. Two can use them, the rabid, hypocritical creatures who gorge on other people's grief, then vomit it through mindless smiles and call it news. Two can feel the rhythm and do this destructive, deadly dance of ruination, of blackness and red.

Blackness and red, crimson to black . . .

He punched out the phone number, waited, then told a woman on the other end of the connection he had vitally important information for Kay Kemper.

Who was he?

"I'm sorry, I can't reveal that because I fear the consequences. All you have to know is I'm a former New York cop who was high in the department. I have tremendous respect for Kay Kemper. She's the only one I'll trust. I'm afraid to talk to anyone else. She can judge the veracity of my information."

Afraid of nothing!

After only a moment's hesitation, the woman transferred his call.

The world belonged to the bold.

58

Quinn was tired and felt old. Along with Pearl and Fedderman, he'd spent much of the day talking to tradesmen on the decorators' lists who'd done work the past year in the murder apartments and were known to have their own key-making machines.

There weren't that many, but it had taken a while to identify and then find them. First the detectives asked the tradesmen themselves if they had the machines, then asked them about other tradesmen. Checking, cross-checking, not turning up a lie. As it turned out, not that many carpenters, painters, or plumbers also made or duplicated keys.

When they'd finished going down the list, it seemed they'd pursued another ghost of a lead. It wasn't that Pearl's idea was a bad one; it was just that there was no way to be sure one of the tradesmen didn't possess a key-making machine and the skill to use it and had managed to keep the capability a secret. As well he might, if he were the Night Prowler.

They'd had dinner at a place on the West Side called Placebo, and stayed there over coffee until almost seven o'clock, commiserating with each other over how the investigation was going. When they went outside, they found that while the sun was low, the evening seemed just as hot and humid as the day had been.

Rush hour traffic had died down when Pearl and Quinn dropped Fedderman back where he'd left his car on Central Park West near Eighty-seventh, the nearest parking space he'd been able to find. It was only a few blocks away, but the overheated and exhausted Fedderman didn't feel like doing more walking and they didn't blame him. He lurched like one of the undead in a baggy suit toward his car, opened the door, and dropped in behind the steering wheel.

After watching Fedderman drive away, Pearl pulled the unmarked back into traffic and headed for Quinn's apartment.

Pearl said, "Idiot!" as she yanked at the steering wheel to avoid hitting a house-size SUV crossing the intersection.

She'd been the one who jumped the light, but Quinn said nothing. He became aware that his right foot was pressing against the car's floor on the passenger side, as if there were a brake pedal there. He made himself relax—somewhat. Sometimes he thought it would be a miracle if he lived through this investigation.

A cell phone chirped and he blanched at the thought of Pearl driving and talking on the phone simultaneously. Then he realized it was his own phone.

He dug it out of his pocket and answered.

"Quinn?" Harley Renz's voice.

"Yeah. It was my number you called."

"So what's this latest bullshit?"

"I guess I'm gonna have to ask you the same question."

"Kay Kemper."

"You mean your interview with her?"

"I mean the story about you and those other teenage kids."

Other teenage kids? "Tell me what this is about, Harley."

"You don't know? Sure you don't. On her six o'clock news report Kemper reported that a reputable anonymous source informed her you mighta molested other kids besides Anna Caruso. She said others in the NYPD had confirmed there were rumors to that effect at the time of the Caruso rape."

"Others? You mean somebody in the NYPD is dishing out this crap?"

"My impression is her primary source was a former cop, but she didn't come right out and say that."

"Egan. It has to be Egan, or one of his flunkies."

"If Egan didn't dream up the idea, he'll sure take to it, and he'll try using it against us. So, is it true?"

Quinn was glad they weren't having this conversation face-to-face; he might have grabbed Renz by the neck and squeezed. "It's as true as the Anna Caruso story."

That didn't seem to be what Renz wanted to hear. Instead of saying anything immediately, he made a soft wheezing sound, as if breathing through a stopped-up nose. "Well, in a way it doesn't matter."

"It matters a hell of a lot to me."

"Sure it does. What I mean is, the media's already playing you off against Anna Caruso. Now these rumors, true or not, lend more credibility to her story."

"If there really are rumors, whoever's spreading them can't come up with a complainant or a witness, Harley, because these molested girls they're talking about don't exist and never did."

"Jesus, Quinn, Anna Caruso identified you."

Quinn was silent for a long time, barely noticing when Pearl missed a startled pedestrian by inches. "So where's this leave us, Harley?"

"I said when you started that you had a short shelf life, Quinn. It just got shorter."

"I'm telling you—"

But Renz had hung up.

Quinn broke his end of the connection and slid the phone back in his pocket.

"So what was that all about?" Pearl asked, glancing over at him as the car struck a pothole hard enough to cause one of the sun visors to flip down.

He told her.

She didn't ask him if the new accusations were true. He appreciated that.

"The assumption is that the source is a former New York cop," Quinn said.

"Genuine anonymous sources," Pearl said, "usually try staying as anonymous as possible."

Quinn sat and watched her drive. "Meaning?"

"Maybe the source isn't NYPD. The informer might have wanted Kay Kemper to think so because it would lend credibility to his lies."

A white work van cut off Pearl as she slowed to take a corner. She honked the horn and the driver glared at her and raised his middle finger. Pearl sat quietly, as if she hadn't seen.

It was a possibility, Quinn thought. "The most likely source would be the Night Prowler himself."

"Sure. You're getting under his skin. He had to do something to get back at you, so he used Kay Kemper. It all fits. And it's the way assholes like that operate."

"The Night Prowler—"

"I meant Kemper. She probably knows the story's bullshit, but she'll do anything for ratings."

"He must be getting frustrated, to pull something like this."

"That's the idea, isn't it?" Pearl said. "We want him frustrated. We break the fucker so he messes up, and we nail him."

The white van hadn't moved after cutting off Pearl. She

leaned on the horn and the driver, a guy in a dark shirt with a cap set way back on his head, repeated his obscene gesture.

Pearl lowered her window and waved her shield around. "I'm a cop! Move that van now, shit for brains, or I'll arrest you for vehicular stupidity!"

Watching the van driver maneuver his big vehicle out of the way by putting two wheels up on the sidewalk, Quinn thought again that Pearl was some item.

"He has a lotta nerve, that stewhead!" The car shot forward and Quinn noticed his foot was mashing down again on his nonexistent brake pedal.

"Guy's probably tired and on his way home from work," he said.

"Not the van driver, the Night Prowler."

Quinn sat back and closed his eyes. *Pearl . . .*

"I'm staying over with you tonight," she said.

He didn't answer.

"You need me, so it's settled."

She was so right. And she still hadn't asked if the rumors about him were true.

Pearl.

There was still enough daylight to see to shoot. The setting sun had turned the horizon, barely visible beyond a dark row of trees and distant buildings, a vivid burned orange threaded with gray.

The Night Prowler was standing on the slope of an abandoned quarry outside Newark, New Jersey, where many amateur target shooters, not to mention rat hunters, went to sharpen their aim. He was the only one left in the orange-tinted, failing light, but still he sighted in carefully on bent tin cans or beer or wine bottles protruding from the landfill near the base of the quarry.

He stared intently over the sight of his handgun, squeezed the trigger gently, and saw a slight puff of dust as the bullet struck a yard to the side of what looked from this distant like a pound coffee can.

Not good enough!

He had to improve! Had to learn to shoot for distance. And he was lucky enough to have the handgun; he couldn't risk buying or stealing a rifle, as difficult as they were to conceal. And using one would be a problem, anyway. Long guns were, let's face it, noticeable. New York wasn't Wyoming.

It amazed the Night Prowler how swiftly Quinn had struck back. *Tit for tat, this for that, death for that.* He squeezed off another shot. *Closer.* It seemed that Kay Kemper had no sooner mentioned on TV the rumors of more child molestations by Quinn, than Victory called and told the Night Prowler he'd learned of a woman cop—Detective Pearl, no doubt—asking about key reproductions. The hardware store where she'd been making her inquiries was not only in Victory's neighborhood, it was also in the Night Prowler's, and only a few blocks from his apartment.

Drab gray officialdom in my personal territory! Intolerable!

So, the law was concentrating now on who might have had keys to the murder apartments. No problem, so far. But it was only a matter of time before they learned he had a portable machine for setting locks and cutting keys. And he'd done work in all the apartments where the murders occurred.

Only a matter of time. In-fucking-tolerable!

Another shot.

Another miss.

At least the phone call to Kay Kemper had gone as the Night Prowler expected. She'd been interested and tried to pump him for more information about himself. But he'd sold her on the idea that he was a former cop, and he was afraid for his life if it became known he'd turned snitch on the NYPD. He had a pension and a sick wife to consider. Kay Kemper had bought it, *true blue,* probably because she wanted so much to believe him, wanted the story.

And as the Night Prowler had suspected, Quinn's enemies in the NYPD took the opportunity to stick more barbs into him. Yes, they'd heard the rumors, they said anonymously. No fire, but a sky full of smoke. No proof, but then there hadn't been any lock-tight proof in the Anna Caruso case, and everyone in the NYPD knew who'd committed that crime. Everyone in the city.

The Night Prowler smiled, aimed, shot.

Another miss.

Smile became frown.

Is Quinn impossible to kill? Is that what the message is here? Is Quinn being favored by fate?

There! Something!

The Night Prowler had glimpsed movement about twenty feet away, where there was a low mound of what looked like cinders and assorted trash someone had dumped. It had been there awhile. The labels on cans and bottles were faded, and even in the dying light swarms of flies were visible droning around the base of the mound.

But something other than insects had moved. The Night Prowler was sure of it.

He crept closer, holding the gun before him in both hands, like cops on countless TV shows.

And there was the movement again!

A rat?

No, an ordinary squirrel.

The Night Prowler aimed, fired, and the squirrel leaped into the air violently as if electrified, then dropped to the trash pile dead.

Blood makes the difference! Shooting for real. The blood!

He walked over and looked down at the gray and the red that was the squirrel, the glimpse of white that was the purity of bone. Most of the animal's head was missing.

Fate was no longer something to fear. Neither was time. Death was an ally. The Night Prowler's luck had changed.

And Quinn's.

"Bad luck, I'm afraid," said the voice in Jubal Day's ear.

Jubal was in the living room, on his cell phone. He'd just returned from reading for the role in *West Side Buddies* at a small studio on West Forty-fourth Street. He and the producer and Jubal's agent had gone out for drinks afterward. There were two more auditions to be held, they said, two more candidates for the role. If neither of them made the grade, then Jubal looked good for the part. His world was opening before him. His career was about to be launched big time. If only—

"Jubal, did you hear?"

The caller was Don Henson, the director of *As Thy Love Thyself,* in Chicago.

"Yeah, Don, so what's going on?"

"Astin's come down with some kind of bug that's got him flat on his back with a hundred and three temperature. We're lucky the theater's black tonight, but we have to have you back here."

"How soon?"

"Yesterday. Tonight. Early tomorrow morning at the latest. We've made some revisions, and you're going to have to run through them before going on tomorrow evening."

Jubal's mind was bouncing around in his skull. Would it hurt his chances for the TV series if he cut and ran out of New York? Probably not. He'd already read for the part, and it was doubtful they'd want him back for another reading.

Unless one of the other two candidates for the role came through big and made the decision difficult.

"Jubal, you're all we've got, my man. No troops in reserve. You've gotta do this!"

"I will, Don. Don't sweat it. I still have time to catch a flight out tonight."

"You're a prince, Jubal. I owe you a piece of the kingdom."

"Careful, Don, I might claim it one of these days."

"Hey, that's how it works."

"When it works. I'll be at the theater tomorrow morning, I promise."

"Early?"

"Before you get there, Don."

"I doubt it. I don't do much sleeping lately."

"You can sleep well tonight," Jubal said, and hung up.

Now what?

Claire was in the kitchen puttering around, trying to decide if she was hungry. She wasn't going to like Jubal dropping in for a few days, then streaking back to Chicago. Jubal didn't like it himself.

But then there was Dalia.

Jubal realized he had something to do before he told Claire he was packing and leaving within an hour. While she was busy in the kitchen, he went into the bedroom so he could retrieve the necklace he'd bought for Dalia. He'd concealed it well by taping it to the outside of the back of one of the dresser drawers. The drawer would have to be completely removed before the necklace was visible.

He was reaching to remove the drawer when—

"Jubal."

Claire's voice spun him around.

She was standing in the doorway, smiling. "Scare you?"

Almost to death. "No, not at all." He grinned. "I was just about to start packing."

Her smile disappeared. "For what?"

He told her about Henson's phone call.

"What about *West Side Buddies*?"

"I don't think it should make any difference."

Claire looked disappointed, even for some reason afraid.

He tried to lighten the mood. "I don't feel like cabbing back to the airport and jumping on a plane again, but it's nice to be needed."

She came to him, moving more heavily in her pregnancy, and kissed him on the lips. "Now more than ever." When she pulled away, she said, "How soon do you have to leave?"

"Within an hour at most. I'll grab something to eat at the airport." He extended his hands, palms out, a gesture he'd practiced before a mirror: *Nothing I can do about this, and I'd move heaven and earth if I could change it.* "I'm really and deeply sorry about this, hon."

"I know," she said, biting her lower lip but not crying, *not* crying. "I'll help you pack."

Jubal decided Dalia would have to wait for her necklace.

There was no choice, as with so much else in this world. Women. The way they got beneath your skin and into your blood; they ran like a chemical in your veins.

Women were a problem.

"You're telling me," Harley Renz said the next evening on the phone to Quinn, "that you've got nada times nada."

"So far," Quinn admitted. He was sitting in the heat on the bench inside the Eighty-sixth Street entrance to the park, waiting for Pearl and Fedderman. The bench was in the shade, but that didn't help much, hot and muggy as it was today. "We're not a helluva lot closer than we were last week."

"Last week when you were shot at?"

Renz rubbing it in. "That week," Quinn said. He'd been

there awhile and wondered if his rear end might be welded to the hard slats of the bench.

"Listen, Quinn, my sources tell me there's another TV feature on Anna Caruso in the works, this one by Kay Kemper. She's making this her story."

"Anna Caruso's?"

"Kay Kemper's. She cares not at all about Anna except that the kid means ratings. You mighta noticed, local news in this city is a competitive business. The thing is, whenever Anna's sweet young face appears on television, you look more and more like the villain in the piece. Especially with your rugged bad looks. Especially now that the rumor is you're a serial child molester. There are voices telling me to yank you off the streets, Quinn."

"Arrest me?"

"Of course not. Not without proof. But lots of people in the department and at City Hall would like to see you run over by a cab and no longer be a problem. Pressure keeps building, Quinn, on me, on you—"

"And on the Night Prowler. He'd love to see you take me off the case. He's probably the one who planted the child molestation story with Kay Kemper."

"Maybe. But don't bet against Egan."

"Point. Where we going with this, Harley?"

"Nowhere, faster and faster. That's the fucking problem. It's a matter of days, and you're gonna be gone. I've got no choice, Quinn. I talk to you and you keep coming up blank."

"Speaking of blank," Quinn said, "did you ever get a lead on Dr. Maxwell's patient David Blank?"

"Nothing. The guy doesn't exist."

"You've come up blank."

"That's cute, but—"

"You'd think the Night Prowler would have broken under pressure by now, wouldn't you? He's been at it a long time with us on his heels."

"He's one of the toughest," Renz said.

"Suppose he had a way of relieving that pressure. Like seeing a good psychoanalyst. Somebody he could talk to about these killings."

"Confess to, you mean?"

"Maybe even that."

"The analyst is obligated to tell us about criminal activity, especially murder."

"Unless the analyst becomes a victim herself."

Renz didn't answer for a while, his breath hissing into the phone. "David Blank and Dr. Maxwell, huh? It's a stretch, but possible. Sick fucks like that do suffer from a growing need to confess. That's why we got the Miranda law. But even if true, it doesn't help us. If the Night Prowler and David Blank are the same person, his charade worked. We got us a dead analyst who served her purpose, and David Blank is still nowhere to be found."

"It gives us more insight into the Night Prowler. And that's what this is all about, figuring how he thinks."

"It doesn't help us," Renz repeated. *Not as much as you being a serial molester.*

Quinn couldn't deny it. All he could muster was "But it might."

"There's only a few grains of sand left in the hourglass, Quinn. This is something I can't control. Keep that in mind." Renz hung up without saying good-bye.

Quinn sat in the shade with the dead phone and watched the unmarked pull to the curb out on Central Park West. He watched Pearl and Fedderman climb out of the car and make their way toward the park entrance and bench. They looked tired again. Pearl was plodding and Fedderman seemed as if he could barely drag his cheap suit along with him. His pants had worked themselves so low he looked like a prison gang-banger; they puddled around his feet and would have dragged the ground if not for his big clunky shoes. These two did not look like the NYPD's finest.

Unsurprisingly, they reported no progress.

Quinn related the conversation he'd just had with Harley Renz.

"Sounds like we're royally fucked," Fedderman said, mopping his forehead with a handkerchief that looked as if it had been used to change oil.

"I can't think of a better way to put it," Pearl said.

"We're all in a lousy mood," Quinn said. "Let's get outta here. Get into some air-conditioning."

"I gotta get back to the precinct house and pick up my car," Fedderman said. "I'm going out to dinner with the wife. We got reservations."

I'll bet she does about you. "Take the unmarked," Pearl said.

"Thanks. Drop you two at Quinn's place?"

They both nodded, and the three of them trudged glumly toward the car. Nobody spoke because there wasn't anything to say. That was the problem. They were headed toward a wall and they all knew it, and talking about it wouldn't change a thing.

Pearl was driving, Fedderman in front with her, Quinn in the backseat.

The car had just pulled out into traffic and was starting to accelerate when gunfire came at them from the park.

59

There was a muted cracking sound from outside the car, and a louder crack as a small hole appeared low in the passenger-side window. The sounds were so close together it was impossible to know which came first. Fedderman said, "What the fuck?" and held out a bloody hand, then slumped forward.

Pearl figured it out right away but couldn't accelerate out of trouble because of stopped traffic ahead. The car jerked to a halt. Quinn rammed a thumb down and unbuckled his seat belt. "Get down, Pearl!" He slid low behind the front seats.

Another shot sounded off to their right.

Quinn heard Pearl shouting into the radio, loud but not frantic. "Ten-thirteen, shots fired, officer down! Eighty-sixth and Central Park West!"

She repeated the call for help, which would immediately attract every cop within blocks.

"Feds," Quinn said, "you hit bad?"

"His arm, I think," Pearl said.

"Upper arm," Fedderman said. "I got the bleeding stopped. Can't you move the fuckin' car, Pearl?"

"Sure. Other than the motor's dead and we're blocked in." Another shot. "I can't see him. I can't see him, dammit!"

Quinn sat up straighter and saw the top of her head above the level of the dashboard as she peered into the park trying to spot the shooter. "Get down, Pearl!"

"I can't see the motherfucker."

"Down, Pearl. Goddammit, get down!"

Another shot. The rearview mirror suddenly became detached and whizzed and whirled, clattering around the confines of the car like a gigantic insect trying to escape. The passenger-side window turned milky as the deflected bullet snapped over the slumping Fedderman.

Pearl got down.

It had been quiet but for the shooting. Now sirens were yodeling all around them. There were shouts and blaring horns outside. A siren so near and loud it hurt Quinn's ears, and the screech of tires as a vehicle braked hard.

The siren growled and grumbled to silence. Quinn cautiously raised his head and saw a police cruiser directly alongside. He pointed toward the park, and the cop riding shotgun nodded. The two uniforms piled out and the near one took shelter behind the cruiser, while the other jogged bent low toward the stone wall that ran along the edge of the park.

"Stay low and call again for an ambulance," Quinn said to Pearl as he worked the door handle and prepared to slide out of the car.

"Radio's damaged. They know Fedderman's shot and should be sending medical."

"Look after him till they get here."

"Look after yourself, Quinn. Remember your heart."

Quinn knew she was right about an ambulance being on the way, but he wanted to make sure, so he used his cell phone to verify the request. Then he was aware of his heart fluttering like a panicked bird in his chest. But what else would you expect? It was the rush of adrenaline. And there was no pain.

He stayed low, opened the door, and eased out of the car to join the uniform hunkered behind the patrol car. Smashed sunglasses lay flat on the pavement near one of the cops' regulation black shoes. Quinn could see other units that had responded. Sirens were still wailing and an ambulance with lights flashing was picking its way like a broken-field runner through stalled traffic on Central Park West.

Slowly the cop behind the car stood up straight. His partner was still crouching with gun drawn behind the low wall. Beyond him, Quinn could see blue-uniformed figures moving among the trees in the park. The cop next to him, an old-timer with gray tufts of hair sticking out from beneath his cap, looked at Quinn and said, "All the noise we made, the shooter's shagged ass outta here by now."

Quinn nodded, feeling a lot of tension flow out of him. It had been a while since the last shot was fired, and a virtual army of blue was on the hunt in the park.

He walked around the unmarked to see how Fedderman was doing. Behind him, he heard the gray-haired cop say, "Stepped on my fuckin' glasses."

The paramedics were already moving Fedderman out of the car and working him around so he could lie on a stretcher.

Pearl was also out of the car and had come around to Fedderman's side. She touched Quinn's shoulder lightly as if to assure herself he was solid and all right; then he was aware of her moving away.

"It's just my arm," Fedderman kept saying, trying to sit up. One of the paramedics, a guy with biceps the size of thighs, gently forced him back down.

"Call Alice and tell her I'm gonna be okay," Fedderman said, looking up at Quinn.

Quinn nodded. "Soon as you're in the ambulance."

"Get her on the phone now. I can tell her myself."

The oversize paramedic shook his head no.

"Sorry, Feds," Quinn said. "He's bigger'n I am."

"Bigger'n anybody."

"You better cooperate and let them stop that bleeding."

"Yeah, I guess so." Suddenly pale, as if what happened had finally caught up with him, Fedderman settled down flat on the stretcher and remained motionless while they strapped him in and transported him to the ambulance.

There had been a lot of blood, but Quinn didn't think the bullet wound was life threatening.

Still, you never knew for sure until the doctors got to you.

A uniform came over and handed Quinn a slip of paper. "Number for you to call."

Quinn thanked him. He didn't recognize the phone number written on the paper, but he figured the call would be from Renz. He looked over to where Pearl was filling in a couple of plainclothes detectives as to how the shooting occurred. There were people who looked like reporters huddled around them, but, so far, no TV camera crews had arrived. Quinn decided he'd call Renz back and then get out of there before TV did close in and spot him.

It occurred to him that he was the one tracking a killer. The one who'd just been shot at. And he was the one running from the press as if guilty of something.

Quite a world. Upside down.

It wasn't Renz who answered Quinn's call; it was Egan. He'd know about the shooting. When a cop was shot anywhere in the city, it didn't take long for the word to spread.

"Where are you, Quinn?"

"Outside the park on Central Park West. Shooter was inside the park, firing out."

"I thought maybe you were the one that got shot."

Hoped, more like it. "Pearl and I are okay. Fedderman took one in the upper arm."

"You think the Night Prowler was the shooter?"

"Yeah, I think we can be sure of that."

"Does anybody in that fucked-up situation think he can be nailed before he gets out of the park?"

"No, and there's not much chance of it. He was probably out of the park before we went in after him. And even if he stayed in the park, he'd be hard to find. It's gonna be completely dark soon."

"Far as you're concerned, it already is completely dark. You gonna be there awhile?"

"Not much longer. Soon as Pearl and I are done here, we'll drive to the hospital to check on Fedderman. I've gotta call his wife."

"Okay. Stick at the hospital till I see you there. I wanna talk. I want you to listen."

"I'll be there."

"You better."

"And Fedderman's gonna be okay. Thanks for asking."

Quinn cut the connection.

The Night Prowler sat on the subway, which was rattling its way downtown. He tried to look relaxed. It wasn't easy. The risk he'd taken! If he hadn't been alert, even lucky, and made his way out of the park several blocks away on Central Park West, they might have had him. Quinn might have won.

He concentrated on sitting still and looking at the ghostly reflection of his pale face in the opposite dark window. The man in the window, with the darkness sliding past behind him, appeared calm, but tension was running through his body like a spasmodic electrical current. The gun was an unyielding lump beneath his belt at the small of his back, concealed by his untucked shirt. *The gun.*

He'd missed! He was sure of it!

He'd assumed the detective in the car's front passenger seat would be Quinn, but the second he squeezed the trigger and caught a glimpse of the man's profile, he knew it was the other one—Fedderman.

The trailing shots had gone into the stalled car; he was sure of that but couldn't know if any of the bullets found their mark.

He could hope they had, but that was all. Soon as he got back to his apartment, he'd check TV news. Surely, Channel One would have something on the Central Park shooting. And the other local channels might break into regular programming.

This fucking city will jump to attention when I make it jump!

The Night Prowler shook his head, causing a woman seated on the other side of the subway car to glance up at him curiously, then quickly look away.

He struck a casual pose, a bored expression, while his mind worked furiously. *What am I thinking? That's not what this is about, making the city jump. That's not what I'm about.*

He needed, first of all, to find out about Quinn. Maybe Quinn was dead. It was difficult to imagine, but maybe one of the wild shots into the car had struck him in a vital spot. Maybe he was at least wounded.

Stress.

He could *feel* the word even as he thought it. Could feel it insinuating itself throughout mind and body. He knew he had to hold stress at bay so he could function at the high level he demanded. That his mission demanded.

Benzene.

But lately the fumes that had carried him to a placid and

advanced mental state hadn't worked their magic as quickly or as well. The body adapted to everything eventually; the Night Prowler knew that.

But he had to do something to relieve his stress. And soon.

Knowing Quinn was dead would help immensely. Would change the world.

But right now he looked down and saw that his hands were trembling in his lap.

The train lurched and slowed and light crept in at the edges outside the dark windows.

His stop.

Almost home.

Alice Fedderman took the news like a cop's good and faithful wife, stricken with worry but with a calmness about her.

She'd been expecting this for years. Any phone call, long ago and long forgotten, might have brought her the same news. And now here it was.

But not as bad as it might have been. That was the kind of thing you told yourself, that you grabbed hold of and clung to at a time like this.

Her husband was alive.

She was on her way to the hospital and not the morgue.

60

Because of the incompatibility of cell phones and hospitals, Quinn had used a pay phone near the waiting area to call Alice. He'd noticed while talking that his heart rate had picked up again.

He hadn't thought about his heart during the action at the park until Pearl cautioned him. It had slowed its rhythm and seemed normal since he'd arrived at the hospital. But maybe talking to Alice Fedderman was more of a strain than he'd imagined.

May had waited for phone calls like the one to Alice. So would Pearl, but in a different way, because she was a cop herself.

And I'll be waiting.

There was a thought that sobered him.

When he returned to the waiting area, a spacious, carpeted alcove off the main hall, a tall, redheaded doctor, wearing wrinkled green scrubs, was talking to Pearl.

When Quinn joined them, the man identified himself as Doctor Murphy. He had about him a sharp scent that might have been medicinal or simply an agent in soap.

Pearl, sitting slumped in one of the carefully arranged gray chairs, said, "Fedderman's going to be okay."

Quinn had thought that would be the word, but still he was relieved. "His arm . . ."

"The bone was nicked," Dr. Murphy said. A green surgical mask dangled high on his chest like some kind of neckwear he'd loosened. "Most of the damage was done to soft tissue. The bullet appeared to have struck something and was flattened before it hit him, or it might have penetrated the bicep and gone into his side. As it is, his arm will be in a cast for about six weeks. Then, with therapy, he'll be able to recover ninety percent of previous mobility."

"What in the movies they call a flesh wound?" Pearl asked.

The doctor looked at her and raised an eyebrow.

"A car window," Quinn said. "That's what the bullet went through before it hit him."

"He's lucky the window wasn't down. Detective Fedderman is still under anesthetic and will be a while in the recovery room."

"His wife's on the way here."

Doctor Murphy smiled. "She won't mind the news, considering how bad it could have been. I'll instruct the nurses to inform me when she arrives." He nodded to both of them and stalked back to the hall and through wide swinging doors, which hissed open at his approach.

"Egan's on his way here, too," Quinn said.

Pearl snorted. "Tell me it's because he's injured."

"Pissed off is what he sounded like."

"Well, he'll cheer up when he sees me."

"He doesn't have to know you're here."

"Yes, he does."

Quinn sighed. "Listen, Pearl—"

"I'm thirsty." She stood up and strode toward a drinking fountain in the hall near the phone Quinn had used, a woman beyond reason.

Quinn sat down, leaned back, and stretched out his legs, crossing them at the ankles. All things considered, he didn't feel so bad about this evening. The essential news was good: no one had been killed, and Fedderman would be his old self once his arm healed.

Yawning, Quinn reached over to a lamp table and picked up the only magazine, a dog-eared *People*. Jennifer Lopez worked hard to keep in shape. There was scandalous news about a distant Kennedy relative. Sean Penn was acting up again. A new movie was going to star the winner of a cable TV talent hunt show. This he learned just from the cover.

"Getting educated?"

Quinn looked up to see the blocky, muscular form of Captain Vincent Egan. He was surprised to see that Egan was wearing a tuxedo, his face flushed above the tight collar and white tie.

"On your way to the prom?" Quinn asked.

"On my way to a banquet at the Hyatt, as a matter of fact. Where I'm going to see the commissioner, where maybe a lowlife like you might find part-time work next year serving the haut monde."

"There's fish on the menu?"

"Be as much of a smart-ass as you want, Quinn. I won't have to put up with you much longer. I'm gonna recommend at the banquet that you be taken off the Night Prowler case. It's beginning to look bad for the department, setting a serial child molester to catch a serial killer."

Quinn felt himself getting angry and tried to control it. What Egan wanted more than anything was for him to stand up and lose his temper, take a swing at him as Pearl had done. *Pearl.* He caught sight of her down the hall, talking on the pay phone, and hoped she'd have sense enough to stay away until Egan was gone.

"What I came here for," Egan said, "was to see if you had

anything to say that would lead me to believe you were any closer to the Night Prowler."

Covering your ass. "I'd say we were pretty close to each other a few hours ago."

"That's true. When he unfortunately missed who he must've been aiming at. But that's not quite the kind of close I had in mind. Out of fairness, I stopped by to give you one last chance to come up with something positive that suggested progress."

"That'll be your story, anyway."

Egan pulled a cigar from his pocket and fired it up with a lighter. The hell with hospital rules. And New York rules that said you couldn't smoke anyplace other than inside your house or apartment and within five feet of an ashtray and exhaust fan. "That'll be my story," he confirmed, and blew an imperfect smoke ring.

He turned and swaggered away, not an easy thing to do in a tuxedo, and it took all the willpower Quinn had to remain in his chair. He hadn't budged through the entire encounter with Egan.

A nurse said something to Egan, no doubt about the cigar. Egan blew smoke her way and didn't break stride.

He did break stride when he saw Pearl.

Now Quinn stood up. *Don't be stupid, Pearl, please!*

Pearl walked toward Egan, smiling. Quinn had seen that smile. *No, no . . .*

She leaned toward the surprised Egan and whispered something in his ear. Then she walked away, toward Quinn.

Egan stared after her and seemed to puff up with rage. His flushed face glowed like red neon above the pristine whiteness of his formal shirt and tie.

Quinn thought surely Egan was going to come after Pearl. Instead he whirled and trod swiftly down the hall, then stamped around the corner as if trying to crack walnuts with every step.

"What did you say to him?" Quinn asked Pearl.

"That you were my fella and he better get off your ass. That you had a health problem, and if anything happened to you, I'd hold him personally responsible."

"I sincerely doubt that'll help matters," Quinn said, and told her about his conversation with Egan.

Pearl seemed unimpressed.

"It'll help," she said.

Quinn didn't feel like arguing. He wasn't sure he believed Pearl, but whatever she'd whispered made Egan seem almost to explode, and that was all to the good.

Besides, here came an angry, frightened Alice Fedderman, charging down the hall toward them at a run.

61

Unlike Dr. Rita Maxwell, who leaned toward earth tones, Dr. Jeri Janess favored green. Her office was furnished mostly in shades of green. It was a restful color and many psychoanalysts made it the basis of their decor.

The office wasn't as plush as Dr. Maxwell's. It was on Second Avenue near the turnoff to the Queensboro Bridge. An air conditioner, taller than it was wide, hummed smoothly in one of the casement windows, softly overwhelming any sound that might filter into the office from the street nine stories below. Dr. Janess wanted to avoid the stereotypical setting for analysis, so there was no couch. Other than her desk chair, there were only two extremely comfortable leather armchairs, both green leather with brown piping.

Dr. Janess sat now in one of the chairs across from her new patient, Arthur Harris, and continued sizing him up, looking and listening for clues. She was sure she'd heard his name somewhere before. He was well dressed, and in many ways average-looking. *You'd make a great spy, Mr. Harris.* There was his mustache, which was darker than his hair, and she suspected it was false. His wire-rimmed glasses looked like cheap drugstore frames, and if they weren't clear glass, the lenses were incredibly weak.

Jeri Janess was an attractive African American who'd spent her formative years in a rough section of Harlem as one of six children raised by their mother. She'd listened to her father's bullshit on the rare occasions when he visited. Listened to her brothers justify behavior that had gotten two of them shot and another beaten so badly he was in a wheelchair for life. Listened to the lines of her uncle and the neighborhood creeps who tried to get into her pants from the time she was thirteen. And she'd watched her mother taken in by her father. Watched one of her sisters marry at sixteen, then turn to drugs and hang herself in a neighboring vacant apartment. It all made Jeri want to learn why people behaved that way.

And she had learned.

Arthur Harris, my ass.

But it wasn't unusual for new patients to be coy about their identity. At least Harris hadn't told her he was there because "a friend" had a problem. Dr. Janess decided to play along with the lie for a while. Eventually she'd find out everything she needed to know about Arthur Harris, what was bedeviling him and why, and perhaps how she could help him.

"How would you describe this tension and restlessness you mentioned?" she asked.

"It's like something expanding under my skin, squeezing me in at the same time it's pressuring me so I might explode."

"Like a secret that needs to get out?"

He stared at her. "Oh, that's wonderful! Yes, like a secret, buzzing inside me. And if I confessed it, I'd relieve all the pressure. The tension would go away. Only I don't know the secret myself!"

Obviously, you've read Freud. "Perhaps we can find it out

together. When you have more confidence in yourself and in me."

He put on a shy act, lowering his gaze. "Maybe someday I will have that confidence, Dr. Janess."

"You and I both need to work on it, and it will happen."

"I believe you."

I don't believe you. *Not yet.* "Would this problem be about women, Arthur?" she asked with sudden directness. An ambush.

The shyness lifted from his features. "If you're a man, everything's about women. So the answer's yes and no."

"That's how most men feel about women," Dr. Janess said, smiling to let him know she was joking and their appointment time was up.

It wasn't until several hours after Harris had left that she remembered where she might have heard the name. In a college history class years ago, or more recently watching a documentary on television.

She sat at her computer and went online to Google "Arthur Harris" and make sure.

Her memory was correct. Arthur "Bomber" Harris, sometimes referred to as "Butcher" by his countrymen, was the British vice air marshal who'd enthusiastically overseen the RAF's carpet bombing of German cities and the deaths of thousands of civilians during World War II.

Of course it was a common enough name, and it could be coincidental that her new patient had it.

But she doubted it. Considering his behavior and obvious prevarication, she was sure he'd simply recalled the name as she had and borrowed it.

The first piece of the puzzle. Now she was determined to learn more about her Arthur Harris, and about this pressure he described. And she had something to work with. Maybe she'd ask him if he was aware he had a historical name, see how he'd react.

Dr. Janess signed off her Internet service, sat back, and smiled.

Arthur Harris, you and I are going to get to know one another sooner than you think, and better than you think.

Quinn called Harley Renz from his apartment at eight the next morning, using the kitchen phone so he wouldn't wake Pearl. When he'd left her in the cool breeze from the air conditioner, she'd been sleeping soundly, something not to be prodded.

"Has Egan talked to you?" Quinn asked when Renz answered his cell phone.

"No." Renz seemed puzzled. "Was he supposed to?"

Quinn told him about Egan coming to the hospital after Fedderman was shot.

"I haven't heard anything about you being yanked off the case," Renz said. "That's supposed to be up to me. And if Egan mentioned it to the chief or commissioner at the Citizens Award Banquet, I'd know about it by now. Probably would've learned about it before the banquet was over."

"What do you think stirred him up so that he came by the hospital and made that kind of threat?"

"Like all predators, he sensed weakness and saw opportunity. A cop was shot and civilian lives were threatened. It looked like your lack of progress was starting to endanger people. And you know what, it looks that way to me, too."

"But I'm all you've got, Harley, and we both know I'm getting closer. Old cops like us can feel it when a case is coming to a head. The Night Prowler can feel it, too. That's why he shot at the car."

"Shot at you, you mean."

"Probably. Are you warning me to be more careful?"

"I'm remembering what you said about being all I've got."

"I still don't see why Egan would spout off to me at the hospital, then go to the banquet and stay mum." Quinn had decided not to mention to Renz that Pearl whispered something in Egan's ear that almost made him launch like a rocket.

"Obviously, he changed his mind. But he might not keep it changed for long. Here's another piece of information for you, one Egan doesn't have and won't for another two or three hours. I had my contact in ballistics run another quick comparison for me. The bullet that was dug out of Fedderman's arm isn't from the gun that was used to take a shot at you outside the florist shop on First Avenue."

"So Lunt watches cop shows on TV and knows about ballistics tests, so he ditched the First Avenue gun. He's not stupid."

"He's not that."

Quinn watched a small cockroach wander into a patch of morning sunlight on the kitchen floor near the window and stagger toward the wooden molding. It reminded him of Egan. It reminded him of his life the last few years—trying to escape the light.

"You still there, Quinn?"

"Yeah." The roach flattened itself and disappeared in the shadowed space between molding and floor. With the rehabbing and so many vacant apartments in the building, it was impossible to get rid of all the roaches, no matter how much insecticide was sprayed around.

"Quinn?"

"Fedderman's okay, by the way. I tell you because I'm sure you were going to ask."

"No, I wasn't," Renz said. "I already called the hospital this morning and they let me talk to Fedderman. He's gonna be released this afternoon with his arm in a cast. And he wants to keep working the case."

"He shouldn't."

"That's what Alice says."

"What did you tell him?"

"I said, sure he could work the case, no matter what his wife says. Let the two of 'em fight it out."

Quinn started to tell Renz what a jerk-off he was, but he realized Renz had hung up.

Quinn did the same, and looked over and saw Pearl standing in the kitchen doorway. Her eyes were puffy, her hair was a mess, and she was wearing only Quinn's oversize T-shirt that she'd slept in. He thought she looked beautiful in the morning sun that illuminated her half of the kitchen. He forgot about the cockroach and how bad life had seemed a few minutes ago.

"Who were you talking to?" she asked.

"The hospital. Fedderman's being released this afternoon."

"Great! He can go home and sit on his ass and eat chicken soup for a while."

"He's gonna keep working the case, unless Alice wraps him in duct tape to stop him."

"Duct tape. We haven't tried that."

"Pearl, get dressed."

"Like you are?"

Quinn realized he was sitting at the kitchen table in nothing but his Jockey shorts.

"We don't have to meet Fedderman at the bench this morning," Pearl reminded him.

"True. Let's go out and get some breakfast, read the paper."

"I'm not hungry. And we pretty much know what's in the paper."

"Pearl—"

"There's no reason we can't go back to bed for a while. We're undressed for it."

She had him there.

* * *

Claire woke up craving chocolate.

Her unreasonable and overwhelming physical cravings during pregnancy made her uneasy. They were so *unnatural*, so unlike her, that they reminded her of the profundity of what must be happening inside her body and mind. To be so at the mercy of one's nature, one's hormones, was unnerving. If she had to, no matter what, have chocolate on waking in the morning, what other irresistible urges might compel her?

She climbed out of bed, pulled her nightgown off over her head, and examined her nude body in the full-length mirror on the back of the bedroom door. She was still able to disguise her pregnancy with the right clothes, the right costuming in *Hail to the Chef,* but she knew it wouldn't be long before she'd have to remove herself from the cast. She wanted to do it herself, and not force Fred Perry, the director, or Chris Jackson, the playwright, to inform her when it was time.

She decided again that she enjoyed being pregnant, despite the many complications. *Stretch marks—who cares? Morning sickness—so what?* She smiled in the mirror and patted herself on the belly before padding barefoot into the bathroom to shower.

Claire was careful climbing into the high-sided porcelain tub. Lifting one leg high and balancing on the other was becoming noticeably more difficult every day, and a fall could be disastrous for the baby.

She pulled the plastic curtain closed, adjusted the water to warm, and luxuriated in the shower. All her senses seemed more alive these days.

Back in the bedroom, after drying off with a fresh towel, then combing her wet hair, Claire opened the third dresser drawer to find a pair of panties, and her eye fell on a glint of silver.

She pulled the drawer open farther, nudged lingerie aside, and saw what looked like a silver clasp for a chain, maybe to a necklace or bracelet. When she moved a bra at the back of the drawer, there behind it was a beautiful ruby necklace.

Claire was astounded, and after her initial surprise, pleased.

The necklace had to be a gift from Jubal, one he hadn't had time to present to her properly, so he'd hidden it in the drawer for later. Odd, though, that he'd chosen her lingerie drawer. But he knew she was dressing casually these days and seldom wearing a bra, and the necklace had been in the very back of the drawer.

Or maybe he'd intended for her to find it. A surprise. Like some of the other surprise gifts he'd engineered lately.

She glanced at the bedside clock radio. It was almost nine-thirty, eight-thirty in Chicago. Jubal would be awake, not yet at the theater but possibly at breakfast.

Claire was chilly after her shower, so after holding up the necklace to admire it, she slipped on a pair of panties, then her robe and slippers, and went into the kitchen to put on some decaffeinated, doctor-approved coffee. She realized she was still holding the necklace. Her craving for chocolate had suddenly abated. She smiled. Jewelry could have that effect on a woman, even pregnant.

She got the coffee brewing, then put on the necklace and fastened its clasp behind her neck. It felt cool against her flesh. She checked her reflection in the dark, mirrored door of the microwave oven and approved.

When there was about an inch of coffee in the glass pot, she interrupted its flow from the brewer to pour a warm but too-strong quarter of a cup. Then she sat at the table with what she thought of as an espresso and used her cell phone to call Jubal's.

* * *

Jubal was kissing Dalia's left nipple when he heard the opening notes of the *William Tell Overture*.

"What the hell was that?" Dalia asked, pushing his head away.

It took Jubal a few seconds to refocus his mind and give her an answer. "Cell phone."

"I thought it was the fucking Lone Ranger."

Jubal scooted away from her on the mattress, rolled heavily onto his side, and reached for his sport jacket draped over a nearby chair. Locating the phone and digging it out of an inside pocket took more time than he wanted, more overture.

"Yeah?" he said into the phone. Too early for manners, and his sleepy mind couldn't quite shake thoughts of Dalia. Thoughts and possibilities.

"Jubal?"

Jesus! Claire!

"Hi, Claire." Sideways glance at Dalia. "I was just thinking about you while I was getting dressed to go out for breakfast."

"I called about the necklace."

Necklace? No, no! He couldn't think clearly. Had to answer her. And without a meaningful pause. "Necklace?"

She laughed. "Don't sound so guilty. I think you know the one I mean. It's a ruby on a silver chain. Elegant. Perfect."

"You, uh, found a necklace?"

"In my dresser drawer, hidden among my lingerie."

"Hidden?"

"Well, it was way in the back of the drawer."

"I don't know anything about—"

Jubal understood then what must have happened. The necklace had come loose from where he'd taped it to the outside back of the drawer above her lingerie drawer. Dalia's necklace. And as luck would have it, it hadn't dropped to the floor or bottom of the dresser but had snagged on something and fallen into the drawer below. Or maybe she hadn't pushed the drawer the necklace was taped to all the way closed.

Either way, she had the necklace.

He thought about lying, but he was committed now to an earlier lie.

Jubal knew when not to push. If he reversed his field here and took credit for the necklace as a gift to Claire, she might sense something was wrong. He decided his best course was to continue playing dumb.

"I'm tempted to pretend I meant this necklace as a gift," he said, "but I have to be honest with you. The sad truth is I know nothing about it."

Dalia knew he was talking to Claire and was staring at him from her side of the bed. She puckered her lips and sent an air kiss his way.

Damm it, Dalia!

"Jubal?"

"Honestly, Claire. We bought the dresser secondhand. The necklace must have belonged to a previous owner. Or still belongs. It's probably just paste, maybe a kid's necklace, or it wouldn't have been left there."

"I don't think it's paste. It looks pretty good. And I think there's a tiny silver stamp on the clasp."

"Real or not, Claire, it isn't from me. I wish it were."

She was silent.

"You *do* believe me, Claire?"

"Of course I do."

"Show it to me when I get back. If it's high quality, we'll see if we can find out who it belongs to. And if we can't . . . finders keepers."

"Okay, Jubal." A beat. "Any problems with the play?"

"No, I slipped right back into it. Born for the part. Any part."

"No news yet on the sitcom?"

"Nothing yet. I told you, they had two more auditions to consider."

"That's right, you did. Love me?"

"Love you."

"I'll let you get to breakfast."

"What? Oh, yeah. How are you? How's the baby?"

"We're both fine. Both hungry. Like you must be."

Jubal glanced at Dalia and felt a stab of guilt. But only momentarily.

"Love you," he said again to Claire.

She told him she loved him, too, then hung up.

"That was pretty damned convincing," Dalia said. "Maybe too convincing."

Jubal set the cell phone on the chair and lay on his back next to her. "Damn it! Claire found the necklace."

Dalia raised her head and propped her chin on her elbow. "What necklace?"

"One I was going to give you. Since I left on such short notice for my flight out of New York, I couldn't get to where I'd hidden it in the apartment. I was sure it'd be safe where it was for a while, though; then I could remove it and give it to you. But obviously I was wrong."

"Claire suspects you bought this necklace for someone else?"

"No, I played dumb, as if I knew nothing about it, and I think she believed me."

"My guess is she did. I only heard your end of the conversation, but like I told you, you're good." She smiled. "At everything."

"If I wasn't good enough just now, we've got a problem."

Still sprawled on his back, Jubal stared at the smoke alarm above the bed. He was pretty sure Claire had believed him, yet there was something about her voice. And she'd been acting strange lately in ways he ascribed to her preg-

nancy, pretending to find other, smaller gifts and not knowing where they'd come from. It was damned weird. Something
seemed to be going on, and he couldn't quite figure out what
it was.

He felt the mattress shift as Dalia slid over to be near him,
her body hot against his. She kissed him wetly on the neck.
"I know how to solve the problem," she whispered in his ear.

"Oh? How?"

"Buy another necklace."

Claire sat by the phone, holding her coffee cup but not
raising it to her lips.

Something was wrong. She could sense it. Maybe being
pregnant gave you ESP.

She got up, poured a full cup of coffee, and carried it into
the living room so she could sip it while sitting on the sofa
and watching local news.

When she used the remote, it was already set for Channel
One. A slick anchorwoman and a guy in a suit were talking
about that serial killer, the Night Prowler. The suit was a cop,
and he was assuring her that the police had leads they were
following and would soon bring a resolution to the case. By
that, Claire assumed he meant solve it.

Then the woman began asking about gifts the Night Prowler
had apparently left in his victims' apartments, often in the
kitchen. The candy, gourmet foods, yellow roses, jewelry.

Jewelry!

Claire stiffened, spilling coffee onto the rug.

Oh, Christ! She hadn't thought of this. She should pay
more attention to the news.

She found she was standing but didn't recall getting up.

*Wait a minute! Calm down, for God's sake. Think about
the odds on this. You're being stupid. You're being . . . pregnant!*

She went into the kitchen and ran water on a paper towel, then carried it, along with a dry towel, back into the living room. She rubbed the coffee spots on the rug with the wet towel, then patted them with the dry one, standing and using the sole of her slipper to press moisture from the stains.

It was an effort bending over to pick up the towels. Claire carried them into the kitchen, depressed the foot pedal on the plastic wastebasket so the lid would lift, and dropped them in with the trash.

And noticed something green in the wastebasket—an empty chocolate mints box half concealed by crumpled junk mail.

The mints she'd assumed were a gift from Jubal, and that were uneaten when Jubal left town.

The mints whose box she hadn't thrown away.

Claire felt her throat tighten. If not Jubal, *who* had eaten the mints and put the box in the wastebasket?

Jubal might really not have known about the mints. Or about any of the other gifts.

Or the necklace.

He wouldn't have lied to her about something like the necklace. Not Jubal.

The sense of dread she felt was for good reason.

I'm not being an alarmist. I'm not! Pregnant isn't stupid.

She went to the phone and called the police.

62

"We've gotta go with it," Pearl said. "It's the pathetic sum total of what we've got. And maybe Claire Briggs really *is* in danger."

"We all listened to her story," Fedderman said. He was on the outside in their booth in the Lotus Diner because of his arm, which was still in a plastic cast and a sling. The breakfast crowd had thinned in the diner, leaving behind unbused tables and the strong scent of burned sausage and toast, ignored coffee residue cooking in a pot. "I don't know about you two, but my guess is she's got a problem with her husband. He probably bought the necklace for somebody else and she found it."

"Hidden in her drawer?"

"Like the purloined letter."

Pearl and Quinn stared at Fedderman. Pearl said, "The purloined letter wasn't hidden under a bra."

"She's been getting anonymous gifts," Quinn pointed out. "Including food."

"Or so she says." Fedderman inserted a finger beneath his

cast and tried to scratch an itch, then gave up. "The woman's a confessed chocoholic."

"So am I," Pearl said. "If that's why you don't trust her, you don't trust half the human race."

"I don't trust anywhere near half. And Claire's an actress. How can we know if she's telling us straight? A pregnant actress, at that."

Pearl glared at him. "Meaning?"

"Hormones," Fedderman said.

"Hormones what?"

"Just hormones. If you'd ever had a kid, you'd know what I'm talking about."

Pearl wished she could reach his injured arm.

Fedderman sipped his coffee, thinking his hormones explanation had carried the argument. "I say we have the local precinct run some extra patrols past her building. There's millions of single women in New York, and every day hundreds of them place Night Prowler calls, none of which pan out. I don't see why this Claire woman's anything special that needs our personal attention."

"She's a celebrity," Quinn said.

"Not much of one."

"Costarring in a Broadway play."

"Not for much longer, the way she'll put on pounds. And every other woman you pass on the street in New York's an actress. All you gotta do is ask 'em." Fedderman scratched again at the plastic cast. It was obviously driving him nuts. Pearl was glad.

Quinn looked at Pearl, who was calmly buttering her toast. Apparently, both detectives had had their say about Claire Briggs.

"Renz thinks she's enough of a celebrity that we have to cover ourselves just in case she's right," he said.

"What do you think?" Pearl asked.

"I don't think we can ignore her story. She fits the pattern.

And I know, before you tell me, the problem is that lots of women do. And lots of husbands with twisted senses of humor in this city are giving their wives anonymous gifts just to throw a scare into them as a joke."

"Some joke," Pearl said. "Really fucks *us* up."

"We'll look over the Briggs apartment, give Claire some instructions, then put a nighttime stakeout on her building starting tonight. We'll work in shifts so we can all get at least some sleep."

"We'll be doing nothing but waiting for Egan to drop the hammer on us," Fedderman said.

Quinn thought he might be right, but he didn't see that they had any choice. And in truth, he didn't so much mind concentrating their efforts on Claire Briggs. Something was going to break soon; he knew it in his mind and his gut. Almost thirty years as a cop told him something was going to break. And Claire Briggs might be the reason. Maybe Fedderman was right about her being an actress and able to take them in, but Quinn was sure one thing about Claire wasn't an act. She was genuinely terrified.

So, they'd establish their stakeout and wait and wait. And maybe Quinn's gut would be right again.

And if it wasn't . . .

Quinn didn't have much time to agonize over the possibility.

Pearl fell asleep holding a Styrofoam cup half filled with cold coffee. She was behind the steering wheel of the parked unmarked down the block from Claire Briggs's apartment building. The car's windows were down and the damp, close night had permeated the interior and left a film of condensation over glass and metal. That and the bitter aftertaste of too much coffee had put Pearl in a lousy mood.

She awoke with a start and a curse as she realized the cup

had tilted and coffee spilled onto her thigh. The sudden action caused her to drop the now-empty cup to the floor between her feet.

Stakeouts. She'd always disliked them. She licked her lips. They felt gummy. She was glad she couldn't smell her own breath. *Stakeouts.*

The Briggs apartment was a high corner unit, and Pearl had a fix on its windows. Claire had left the street-side blinds open as instructed. If a light came on in the kitchen or anywhere else, even a faint one, Pearl should be able to see it. Late as it was, the windows in all but four of the other apartments were dark. Pearl glanced at her watch—three-seventeen.

She felt some relief; she'd dozed off only about ten minutes ago.

Not that anything figured to happen. Claire Briggs's story was only slightly more credible than those of so many other callers who'd contacted the police lately. It was odd how a killer like this affected a certain kind of woman. Loneliness probably made some of them pick up the phone and tell someone on the other end of the line anything that would create interest, draw attention. Loneliness was such a powerful driver of single women.

It's as if we—

Pearl sat up straighter as she saw one of the building's street doors open and a man emerge. He paused and looked around, then adjusted his cap, pulling it low as if a wind might blow it off, though the night was calm.

She watched the darkly dressed man walk along the deserted sidewalk, in the opposite direction from where she was parked. Probably, she told herself, he was a tenant. Or a late-night poker player. An insomniac out for a stroll. A guy who worked odd hours, though that didn't seem likely.

Yet here *she* was working odd hours.

It wouldn't hurt to talk to him, listen to his story. She

wasn't here just to sit in the muggy night without moving, like a human mushroom.

Anyway, there was something about the way the man was walking, with a deliberate casualness, his shoulders slightly hunched, now and then glancing off to one side or the other.

Pearl realized she was feeling more and more that the man was acting as if he might have something to hide, slinking along in his dark pants and shirt and wearing what looked like a blue or black baseball cap pulled so low on his forehead.

Slinking?

Yeah, slinking.

When he was almost to the corner, she started the engine.

But when she pressed her foot down on the accelerator, something was wrong. There was back pressure. The car lurched forward and the right front tire dug into the curb, causing the steering wheel to come alive and jerk from her grip violently enough to bend back her thumb.

The engine died.

Pearl contorted her body to reach down low. Her fingers closed on the Styrofoam coffee cup that had dropped to the floor and gotten wedged beneath the accelerator pedal.

Disgusted, she flung the empty cup aside and got the car started again. The front wheel jumped the curb, then bounced back into the gutter, and she pulled out into the street.

But by the time she'd driven to the intersection, the dark man was nowhere in sight.

She worked her aching thumb back and forth a few times to make sure it would be okay, then stepped down hard on the accelerator and did a fast turn around the block.

Still no sign of the man.

Pearl slowed the car and used her cell phone to call and wake Claire.

She hoped.

63

Pearl knew there was a phone on the nightstand beside Claire's bed. Unless she had the ringer turned off, it had to be jangling almost in her ear.

It rang four times before it was picked up.

"Claire?" Pearl asked.

"Who is this?" The voice on the other end of the connection was small and afraid.

"Detective Kasner. I don't think there's anything to be alarmed about, but I'm coming up to talk to you."

"Is everything okay?"

"It is. I'll explain when I get there. When I knock, check through the peephole and I'll show you my badge. Check everyone who knocks, just like we told you."

"This sounds creepy. You sure something's not going on?"

"Yes. I'll be there in five minutes."

After breaking the connection, Pearl called Quinn on his cell phone.

Their conversation lasted as long as it took Pearl to park in front of Claire's building.

Using the key Claire had supplied so they wouldn't have to be buzzed in, Pearl entered the building. She crossed the deserted lobby and pressed the elevator button. The elevator was at lobby level and the door opened within seconds. The man who'd left the building must have ridden it down.

Pearl took the elevator to the twenty-ninth floor. It took longer than she would have liked. She walked fast down the hall to Claire's apartment and knocked three times.

The light in the peephole dimmed almost immediately and Pearl held up her shield.

Locks snicked, a chain rattled, and the door opened.

Claire had on a blue robe and slippers. Her eyes were puffy and her hair mussed, but she looked wide awake as she stepped aside so Pearl could enter. She also looked scared.

Pearl assessed her. *Pretty, even rousted out of bed at three in the morning, but not* that *pretty. Maybe I could have been a Broadway star.*

"What's going on, Detective Kasner?"

"Call me Pearl. And probably nothing's going on. I saw a man dressed in dark clothing leave the building a little while ago, and he acted a little furtive. When I tried to catch up with him in the car, he was nowhere in sight. I wanted to check to make sure you were all right."

"Nothing woke me up until your phone call. And the chain was still on when you knocked."

"There are lots of ways to refasten a chain lock on the way out. If you don't mind losing a wire hanger, I could show you."

Claire's pretty face turned pale as she realized the significance of what Pearl was saying. "You mean you think he might have been in here while I was asleep?"

"That's how we think he operates."

"Yeah. It was a dumb question. I read the papers and watch the news. Here's another dumb question: do you think he had time to come back into the building after you drove away?"

Pearl knew what she meant: *might he be in the apartment now?* "Not such a dumb question, Claire. I don't think it was possible, but we can have a look to put your mind at ease." Pearl got her gun from her belt holster, though she was sure it was unnecessary. Sometimes you had to act for show instead of go. Claire was a taxpayer and no fool; if they did find somebody in here, she'd want her protectors able to react and save her from injury or death. "Can I do a walk-through?"

Claire shivered. "Can I stay close?"

Couple of yeses. Pearl smiled. She moved to the side to make sure there wasn't enough angle for anyone to be crouching concealed behind the far sofa arm; then she walked to the closet by the hall door and opened it.

Nothing but a few coats and bare plastic hangers. And on the single shelf a couple of shoe boxes and a collapsible umbrella.

Pearl continued clearing the apartment, room by room. She went down the short hall to the kitchen, feeling Claire close behind. She groped around the corner and flipped the light switch.

No Night Prowler.

Using faint illumination from the previous rooms, she checked the bathroom, then went into the bedroom, which was brightly lit. Claire watched while Pearl investigated the closets, the small bathroom off the bedroom, even under the bed.

Pearl straightened up and smiled. "We're alone. Unless there's another room."

"The baby's room," Claire said. "Baby-to-be."

Bolder now, she led Pearl down the hall to a closed door. She rotated the knob and pushed the door open, then backed away so Pearl could enter first.

There was enough light from the hall for Pearl to see pretty well, but she threw the wall switch, anyway.

Unoccupied.

Great room! Pearl noticed the stars that had been glittering on the ceiling were no longer visible in the brighter light. There was a section of white picket fence on one wall with painted flowers behind it. A white crib. A padded love seat lined with stuffed animals. The room was ready for baby.

"The stars come out when the light's turned off?" Pearl asked.

"Every time. Just like outside." Claire was relaxing now. Whatever threat this night had brought seemed past. "My husband Jubal thinks she—or he—might grow up to be an astronomer."

"Let me take a look in the closet and we'll be clear," Pearl said.

There was a knock on the apartment door, and Claire jumped. "Damn! I didn't know I was so nervous."

"Healthy to be nervous," Pearl assured her. "That should be my boss."

"Detective Quinn?"

"Yeah."

"He looks kinda tough, but he seems very nice."

"Yeah. Wait a minute while I check the closet and we'll go let him in."

Pearl walked to the closet door and pulled it open.

Empty. Not even hangers.

"We need to know the sex before we buy baby clothes," Claire explained.

"Can't you find that out ahead of time?"

"We'd rather be surprised."

Another knock on the door.

Pearl holstered her 9mm and led the way to let Quinn in.

Rumpled and tired-looking, he said hello to Claire, smiling to put her at ease. Then he turned to Pearl.

"Any sign of him having been inside?"

"None. We just did a walk-through."

He only nodded to indicate he'd heard as he looked about, then began idly moving deeper into the apartment.

"Everything's no doubt fine," he assured Claire as she and Pearl followed him. He drifted down the hall to the kitchen, the bath . . . tracing Pearl and Claire's earlier route, glancing about in case he might notice something they hadn't. Of course he wouldn't come right out and tell Pearl that, for fear she'd get ticked off and start acting like . . . Pearl. "Your husband left town last night?"

"Yes. He took the red-eye to Chicago. An emergency. Well, an emergency if you're an actor. The understudy who took his place in a play got sick and Jubal had to fill in for him." Claire realized how ironic that sounded and shook her head with a grin.

"I get you," Quinn assured her. "The show must go on," he added unnecessarily, drawing a look from Pearl. Anything to soothe poor Claire.

"Would you like some coffee, now that we're all awake?" she asked.

Pearl was surprised when he said he would.

When Claire had bustled off to the kitchen to put coffee on, he said to Pearl, "The Night Prowler might not have known hubby wasn't home. He might have come in here ready to kill if he had to, as usual, then noticed Claire was alone in bed."

"You think that would've stopped him? Being one victim short?"

"He's always killed in pairs before. It seems to be the happy couple that sets him off."

"So he might come back when he figures hubby's returned."

Quinn smiled. "You're ahead of me, Pearl."

Keep it in mind.

He moved away from her, into the child's room.

"Marvelous," he said, glancing around.

"When you turn out the lights, there are stars on the ceiling."

"Really?" But he didn't try it to see. "If I'd had a room like this as a child, I might have grown up to be president."

"Probably happier, whatever you turned out to be."

Claire was back and had heard them. "Look," she said, and flipped the toggle switch back and forth to demonstrate the stars set in the ceiling.

"Ah, that's something rare. You'll be raising a future astronomer—"

Quinn stopped talking when he heard Claire gasp and saw how pale she was. Pale, but her eyes were dark with terror.

"Claire?"

She was pointing at the love seat with its lineup of stuffed animals. "There! That stuffed bear! It wasn't there! The brown-and-white bear!"

"You're sure?" Pearl asked, unable to help thinking Claire was sounding a little like Dr. Seuss.

"Positive. I bought all the stuffed animals myself. Four of them. There are five now." She moved closer to the love seat, so it was obvious she was pointing at a small brown-and-white bear with a toothy smile. It was wedged between a stuffed dog and a fuzzy alligator and was wearing a pinstripe baseball uniform and a Yankees cap. "It wasn't there before!"

"We believe you," Quinn told her. He absently clutched her shoulder and squeezed gently to reassure her.

Then he went to the bear and picked it up, wondering if the paw he couldn't see, because of the way the bear was angled between the stuffed animals flanking it, would be wearing a fielder's glove or catcher's mitt.

It was wearing neither.

It was clutching a single yellow rose.

64

The Night Prowler rode the elevator up to his apartment, touching a fingertip to the hard steel surface of the knife taped to his chest beneath his shirt. He stood motionless but feeling the motion as he rocketed through the dark core of the building.

He'd been ready for the unexpected, expected the unexpected. But Claire had been sleeping in the big bed alone.

Where was her husband?

Away somewhere, probably in some other city, some other world. He was an actor, so maybe he had to reshoot a scene in a movie or TV commercial, or had to attend a story conference. A business trip. But he'd return—*Me! Home, dear!*—to where the journey began and where it would end.

No one could plan for everything, so tonight had been simply another night.

It wasn't yet time to act if Claire slept alone. She and her husband would understand that; being actors, they would surely know the entire cast had to be in place before the curtain was raised, *lowered,* and the lights came up, *died.* It was all necessary for effect, for illusion layered over illusion until it became reality.

So, for a long time, he'd simply stood silently in their bedroom, a dark angel at the foot of the bed, and watched Claire sleep. Watched and listened to her breathe. Then he'd gone into the smaller bedroom, the room of the child that might have been, and lay on his back on the carpet and stared at the stars.

He left the gifts, the stuffed bear for the child-to-have-been. *Irony, the cuddly, smiling beast that rips with razor claws.* And he'd fixed to its paw, with a piece of cellophane tape from the desk, the single yellow rose for Claire.

He looked in on her before leaving, to make sure her sleep hadn't been disturbed. How safe and beautiful she looked, the paleness of her flesh where her leg extended from beneath the white sheet, as if she were seeking in sleep a foothold in the waking world. The slow pink rhythm of her breathing was hypnotic. . . .

The elevator stopped its ascent. The door slid open. The Night Prowler didn't move.

Finally he pressed the down button.

He couldn't go home yet, not to needs unfulfilled and gray terrors that wouldn't remain dead. Not to the buzzing he knew would begin and would become louder and louder.

He couldn't and wouldn't.

As on so many nights lately, he'd roam the colorless, early-hour streets, where there were few to see him. Sometimes he'd wear his sweatpants and jogging shoes so he wouldn't arouse suspicion as he ran faster and faster and farther until the needs and terrors were left behind, at least for a while. Some of the terrors had faces only glimpsed. Quinn's broad, powerful face. Quinn, the god of the law; Quinn, the chess master, *red and black.*

Quinn the hated and feared. *One can't exist without the other.*

Hate, fear, frustration, *needs*. A recipe that boiled in the brain.

Quinn knew that and was counting on a mistake, an opening, a checkmate, and a death.

Soon the husband half of the acting team would return to wife and apartment, his final destination. *Home, dear!*

And soon enough, when the cast was reassembled, the Night Prowler would return to his stage and play the role he was born to and borne to. Destiny from the womb. There was a birth order worldwide, not only within families.

Chess has nothing to do with fate.

He wasn't wearing jogging shoes tonight, but he would run.

Anna ran in the building's basement on the industrial-model treadmill her overweight neighbor Mr. Jansen had offered. It helped him to run off stress, he'd told her, so maybe it would do the same for her.

And it did help. This wasn't the kind of neighborhood where people jogged along city streets for their health. For their health they went most places in pairs and avoided certain street corners. For their health they stayed indoors most nights and kept their drapes closed and their shades down and minded their own business.

Mr. Jansen called his treadmill "Mr. Torture." Joking, of course. He was diabetic and his doctor said he had to get his weight down, so it wasn't as if he had much choice. It was the kind of treadmill that had a digital display showing how far you'd gone and how many calories you'd burned. And you could put a headband on with a wire that plugged into the display so you could observe your pulse rate in red digital numbers. Anna's heart rate was well over a hundred. More than it should have been, according to the table stuck on the treadmill's control board.

She was winded. Her legs ached and her sides hurt with every breath, but she continued to run. She felt oddly detached from her discomfort, her legs and arms pumping mechanically. Physical exhaustion could do only so much to alleviate stress. It was the mental friction that set thoughts on fire and burned away the soul, and that you could never really outrun. But you could try, so the treadmill growled along while Anna's jogging shoes beat out their weary, relentless rhythm on its unforgiving rubber belt.

While she ran nowhere she thought about Quinn.

She thought about her gun.

Finally she pressed the off button and the treadmill slowed and then stopped. She leaned forward with both elbows resting on the steel handrails, her head bowed, and tried to catch her breath.

This was, she realized, quite literally getting her nowhere.

She thought about her gun.

65

Jubal and Dalia showered together to cool down and relax, but wound up having sex again in the tiled shower stall of their Chicago hotel room.

When finally they were soaped, satiated, rinsed, and dried, they decided there was another atavistic desire to appease— hunger. Jubal phoned down to room service for a late supper of club sandwiches and French fries, a beer for him, an iced tea for Dalia, who was worried about her weight.

By the time they were dressed, the food had arrived. The bellhop set everything up on the table by the window that looked out over downtown, and Jubal tipped him and ignored the way he glanced sideways at Dalia, who had a kind of glow about her.

Since there wasn't much to see out the window at night unless they switched off the room lights, and they didn't particularly want anyone to see in, Dalia closed the drapes before they sat down to eat.

"Claire called my cell phone number again a few minutes before you got here," Jubal said, and took a huge bite of his sandwich. Plenty of mayonnaise. Good!

Dalia looked a bit surprised. It wasn't like him to bring up the subject of his wife during meals. She simply stared at him, slowly stirring her tea, until he was finished chewing and could continue.

"She's got things stirred up in New York. Called the cops. For some reason she thinks the Night Prowler's after her."

Dalia looked blank for a moment. "The serial killer who's got every woman in New York scared shitless?" It was a rhetorical question. "Why would she think that?"

"A few objects she can't explain—probably because she doesn't remember—have turned up around the apartment. This Night Prowler jerk leaves his intended victims anonymous gifts before he kills them, like he's courting them or something."

"Can you explain the gifts?"

"Not other than Claire's hormones are running wild with the pregnancy. Her mind's fucked up."

Dalia, who'd never been pregnant, mulled that over and came to no conclusion.

"She does say when she called the cops, she found an extra teddy bear in the room she's got decorated for the baby. Said she bought four and now there's five, and the new bear was holding a yellow rose."

"Is that significant?"

"According to the news, the Night Prowler likes to leave his victims-to-be yellow roses."

Dalia delicately placed a few fries on her sandwich plate, then pushed the rest of them away, where they wouldn't tempt. She sipped her iced tea and sat back. "Sounds creepy."

"Sure. She's probably imagining it. That's all I can think of."

"And she wants you to come home so she'll feel safe?"

"No, she told me I should stay here and do my work. She said the cops'll be looking out for her."

Dalia gave him a level, questioning look. "You worried about her?"

"Sure. I don't want some crazy killer to carve her up."

"I mean *really* worried?"

Loaded question. Jubal wished now he hadn't mentioned Claire's phone call. Women were . . . women. *Careful here.* . . . "Not really worried," he said, "because I don't think anything's really going to happen to her."

"How can you be so sure?"

"I know Claire. And I know Claire pregnant. She could let her imagination get the best of her and one thing would lead to another. Right now, it's how she is."

It wasn't how she was, not really, and Jubal knew it. It was probably the ruby necklace that had started Claire's mind whirring. She might not have entirely believed his lie, and he didn't like the cops involved. He knew how to handle her. She needed reassurance. He should bolster his story, maybe surprise her, and soon, with a matching ring or bracelet.

His explanation was good enough for Dalia. She opened her mouth wide, cocking her head sideways in a way that reminded Jubal of a shark about to close on its prey, and attacked her club sandwich.

Jubal thought there was something wonderfully carnal about her.

The next night that the stakeout was in place, Quinn ran it from the vestibule of an apartment building across the street that had a clear view of the entrance to Claire Briggs's building. They were going on the assumption the Night Prowler hadn't noticed Pearl starting to follow him last night in the unmarked car. Or if he had seen the car, as far as he knew, it had been innocently parked down the street, or was accelerating after turning a corner.

Fedderman was inside the building across the street, Claire's building, positioned in a storage room with its door propped open a crack so he had a view of the lobby. He had a hard wooden chair to sit on, which would help keep him awake, and a thermos full of strong coffee. He'd been on a lot of stakeouts during his years as a cop, and he knew how to maintain a kind of not-quite-asleep awareness that allowed him to survey an area for hours effectively without moving and without missing anything. He thought when he retired, he might find a job as a human security camera.

Pearl was parked in the unmarked half a block down, near where she'd been last night, using binoculars to help her keep an eye on Claire's apartment windows. It was warmer than last night, without much of a breeze, and she was uncomfortable even with the windows down. She knew she couldn't start the engine and switch on the air conditioner; noise and exhaust fumes might give her away. She, too, had a thermos full of coffee, and also her portable plastic potty. She'd considered telling Fedderman about the device, then figured it wouldn't be worth the grief.

A couple of undercover cops were nearby, one in a closed dry cleaners a few doors down the street, another dressed as a homeless person in a doorway. In Claire's living room, reading by one of those lights you clip on a book, was a tough, reliable cop named Ryan Campbell. Quinn knew him from the old days, when Campbell had once taken two bullets in the arm and still hauled down a stickup artist who'd just shot a bartender. Campbell had held the man in the iron vise of his uninjured arm until help arrived.

Claire had shown herself several times at her apartment windows so it would be evident she was home. Home and vulnerable. She was being brave about this. Or acting brave.

Quinn checked with his two-way to make sure everyone was in position; then he settled down and smoked a cigar, making sure its glowing ember was shielded from sight by his cupped hand.

Stakeout mode. One of the things about police work he hadn't missed. Wait, wait, wait . . . and almost always nothing happened until the next night, or the next, or the next.

Then suddenly everything might happen.

66

Sometimes Quinn sat, and sometimes he stood so he wouldn't fall asleep.

But even standing and leaning against the wall in the black vestibule, he was in danger of dozing off.

He looked away for an instant, changing position to rest his weight on his other leg, and didn't notice the darkly dressed figure that appeared from deep shadow beneath a neighboring awning and entered Claire's apartment building.

Pearl had seen the man, almost rubbing her eyes to convince herself she was awake and hadn't imagined him. He'd suddenly appeared out of darkness, strolling casually but quickly, and entered the building as if for the thousandth time, as if he belonged there. *Cops can move like that after a lot of years on the job, as if they belong wherever they happen to be at the moment.* Pearl knew she hadn't yet reached that point and wondered if she'd be a cop long enough to achieve such natural invisibility.

She used her two-way to contact Quinn.

He came awake all the way and alerted everyone: "Somebody in the building. Might be our guy."

Who else, at two forty-five in the morning?

"Got him," Fedderman said softly from his vantage point in the storage room. "He's crossing the lobby."

He watched as the man pressed the up button and stood seemingly relaxed, absently rolling something minute between the thumb and middle finger of his right hand, waiting for the elevator to arrive.

It must have been on a low floor, because it didn't take long to reach lobby level.

Fedderman was patient and waited until the elevator door had slid closed behind the man before making any more noise.

Fedderman, louder: "He just stepped into the elevator."

Quinn made sure everyone else knew what was happening, then left the shelter of the dark vestibule and crossed the street.

Half a block down, Pearl climbed out of the unmarked and moved toward him at a fast walk. This part made her nervous. The Night Prowler would be out of the elevator soon, might even glance out one of the windows at the ends of the halls and check the streets below. Pearl definitely didn't belong in the neighborhood, a lone woman cutting across the street diagonally to save time.

Don't fuck up now.

Quinn was already in the building. She picked up her pace.

Campbell, likewise, knew what might be coming and was ready for it.

He left the lights out in the apartment, and in the dimness moved quietly down the hall and into Claire's bedroom. He didn't want to wake her, have her hysterical before anything happened. Most of all, he didn't want her harmed. He'd make damned sure she wasn't harmed!

But he wanted this asshole to actually enter her room and make it official, wanted him nailed in the courtroom the way Campbell was about to hammer him here in the bedroom.

He took up position in a corner, close to the wall the door was on. When the sick fuck entered—*if he enters—if he even comes to this apartment*—Campbell would be like God Himself meting out rough justice.

When the elevator had risen several floors, Fedderman pressed the button to bring the other elevator down to the lobby from where it was high in the building.

The elevators were the old, slow kind, and the one containing the Night Prowler suspect was still rising when Quinn and Pearl entered the building. Quinn looked tired but alert. Pearl looked so eager she reminded Fedderman of a wirehaired terrier he'd owned long ago. *Better not tell her that.*

Quinn looked at the glowing elevator button, then glanced up at the floor indicator light. The rising elevator was only a few floors below Claire's.

"He had a building key," Fedderman said. "Didn't even hesitate opening the inner lobby door and coming in."

"Maybe one of the tenants," Pearl suggested, not believing it.

"We'll have a better idea in a few seconds," Quinn said.

The indicator light stopped at twenty-nine. Claire's floor.

"Jesus!" Pearl said.

Quinn glanced toward the street door, which he'd left propped open. "The uniforms are on the way."

"So's the other elevator," Fedderman said, staring up at the falling indicator light, "but it's slower than a damned diving bell."

* * *

In the bedroom's quiet darkness Campbell heard only Claire's even breathing.

Then he stood straighter. He'd heard what had to be the front door's dead bolt snick, then the door open and the faint click of the latch. His mouth was dry cotton and his drumming heart was the loudest sound in the room. He worked his fingers in and out of fists and smiled thinly, not surprised to realize he still enjoyed this. It was what he was about.

Claire moaned in her sleep, then rolled onto her side.

Not now! Don't wake up now!

She wasn't breathing as deeply and evenly, perhaps rising toward wakefulness. Campbell was getting worried. But didn't something always go wrong?

It was a well-built apartment and the floors didn't squeak. He couldn't be sure of the location of whoever had entered. He stood staring fixedly at the bedroom door, which he'd left open about six inches.

C'mon in, asshole. Come right on in.

And the intruder did come in. Quickly and quietly. He seemed almost to float across the room, then stood motionless at the foot of the bed.

Campbell held his breath and watched. *Fuckin' creepy.*

The Night Prowler stared down at Claire in the dim, buzzing silence. Almost as if he were offering a prayer.

For someone about to die.

Then he turned toward Campbell.

67

The figure at the foot of Claire's bed was on Campbell in a second. The veteran cop had no time to react. He felt a burning sensation in his left arm. One he'd felt before.

Knife!

He knew he was cut.

Instinctively he grabbed the knife arm of his assailant and bent it back. Not easily. He was shocked by the man's physical strength. Campbell head-butted him, gave the arm an extra twist, and the knife dropped to the floor.

Something slammed into the side of Campbell's face. The Night Prowler's fist. *Other goddamn arm!* He moved in close and the two men began to grapple. Campbell knew he must be losing blood, but the wound couldn't be serious or he'd feel a greater loss of strength in the arm that was cut. Still, this asshole was powerful. The Night Prowler wrenched his arm free from Campbell's grasp, gave the veteran cop a bear hug that lifted him off the floor, then flung him halfway across the dark bedroom. The nightstand toppled and the lamp on it went flying.

The Night Prowler was struggling toward the door now,

with Campbell hanging on and trying to trip him up, drag him down. A small, pale hand clutched Campbell's opponent's throat, surprising Campbell. *Claire! Awake and in the fray! Jesus! No!*

Campbell felt the Night Prowler's weight shift and saw the man's open hand slam into the side of Claire's head. She fell back into dimness and he heard her body hit hard against a wall. Campbell didn't think she was badly hurt, but in the corner of his vision he saw her slide to the floor, stunned.

Then he felt something behind his left knee, pressure on his left shoulder, and he was on the floor himself with a jolt. *Pain! Base of the spine.*

The Night Prowler was loose and darting toward the living room, the door to the hall, and escape.

Never, dammit!

Campbell scrambled halfway to his feet and launched himself after the fleeing dark figure. He managed to grasp an ankle and hold on as he was dragged across the floor. Frantically he tightened his grip, until his fingers ached as if they might break or his nails might bleed.

They were in the living room, where it was darker than the bedroom. Campbell reached up with his free hand, clutched the fleeing suspect's belt, and hauled himself to his feet. For his effort, he was punched in the stomach, grabbed beneath the arm, and spun around. *Strong! I'm getting old or this is one powerful guy.*

As they clung to each other and fought to control the fight, they turned in a clockwise circle. Furniture bumped and scraped the wall. A lamp crashed to the floor. Neither man spoke, but they were breathing hard and grunting in their battle to gain the upper hand. It was almost as if they were locked in a mad dance, but the direction was steadily toward the door.

Campbell was losing, and he knew it.

* * *

In the hall, Quinn, Pearl, and Fedderman heard the struggle. They ran toward the apartment door, and Fedderman was about to put a shoulder to it when Pearl reached out and turned the knob.

The door opened to the living room and the two powerful figures grappling in the dark.

Quinn went in first, feeling the others close behind. He heard the door bounce off the wall and slam shut again behind them, cutting off even the dim light from the hall.

No time for that now!

He led the charge.

Campbell's breath whooshed out of him as something drove hard into his left side. He was forced back and away, losing his grip on the Night Prowler and collapsing to the floor. He was in a three-point stance, his knees and one palm rooted to the carpet.

He knew what was happening. Help had arrived and made the wrong guess as to which of the struggling shadows was the Night Prowler.

Not me, damn you! Not me!

But Campbell could only scream the words internally. He was still trying to inhale before his heart gave out, when someone grabbed his injured arm. Somehow a yelp of pain made its way out of his gaping mouth.

Apparently, it was enough. The arm was released and a voice in the dark said, "Campbell?"

Campbell finally gasped and drew in wonderful oxygen.

Still unable to speak, he blocked out his pain and managed to get to his feet. Around him in the dark he could hear a lot of movement, but not as if there was a struggle. *Lucky fucker's gonna make it outta here!*

Campbell had lost. A sense of hopelessness and defeat rushed through him so forcefully that he felt like weeping.

The lights came on.

Pearl, groping over rough plaster, had found a smooth plastic wall switch and flipped it up.

In the almost blinding brightness, everyone stared wide-eyed.

Standing with his hand on the knob of the door to the hall, staring back at them, was Jubal Day.

Campbell tried to take a step toward Jubal but couldn't get his body to respond to his will. *You didn't make it out, you bastard. I beat you!*

Jubal, as surprised by the sudden brightness as Campbell, was also motionless.

With everyone momentarily paralyzed, this was a game that could be won by whoever moved first.

68

Fedderman was closest to Jubal, which was why he might have been the first of the good guys to move. He took a long step and reached out for Jubal but was met with a stiff left jab. Pearl was there. She slipped another left and got inside Jubal's arms so he didn't have leverage to punch hard. He immediately backed away and raised both arms in surrender.

She spun him around and shoved so he was pressed with his chest and the right side of his face against the wall. He didn't resist as she worked his hands behind him and cuffed his wrists.

"You can't do this!" he said in a shocked voice as he felt the handcuffs dig into his flesh. He turned around unsteadily and stared at everyone.

"Can and are." Pearl pulled her shield and held it up where he could see it.

The door opened and the two uniforms from downstairs, who'd been on the last elevator ride, came in with guns drawn.

"We got him," Pearl said, waving at them to lower their

weapons. "We nailed the bastard before he could get out the door!"

"Jubal?"

Everyone turned to look at Claire standing in the living-room doorway. She was sagging against a wall, staring uncomprehendingly at her husband. "You're in Chicago. . . ."

"He's here," Quinn said. "And he's under arrest for murder."

"Don't listen to this bullshit! Call me a lawyer, Claire!"

"Jubal . . . ?"

"A lawyer!"

Fedderman read him his rights, then grabbed his left arm above the elbow. Pearl had the other arm.

"I notice you didn't ask if your wife was hurt," Pearl said to Jubal.

He glared at her in a way that made her glad he was cuffed.

Quinn looked over at Campbell. His left arm was bleeding, but he otherwise seemed all right. The knife wound didn't look too serious.

"Knife's in the bedroom," Campbell said.

Quinn sent Fedderman in to bag it. Fedderman seemed awfully reluctant to release his grip on Jubal, as if nobody in his right mind finally captured something so elusive, then didn't hold tight to it.

"Looks like this is what we want," Fedderman said when he returned holding up the plastic evidence pouch containing the knife. He displayed it like a prize. "Thin blade about ten inches long, sharp edge and point."

"It's goddamn sharp, all right," Campbell said.

"You want an ambulance?" Quinn asked, making sure but knowing the answer.

"Fuck a bunch of ambulances," Campbell said.

Tough old bastard. We need more like you. Quinn glanced

at one of the uniforms, the younger of the two, black, with a calm look about him, eyes never still.

"We'll drive him to the hospital in the cruiser," the cop said. He looked at Campbell and grinned. "You'll need some stitches, Sarge, if you're not too scared."

Quinn expected Campbell to explode.

Instead, he said, "This little prick's kinda my protégé."

The cop nodded. "I'll see the old fart's taken care of."

"And I'll see you spend the rest of your career chasing Times Square sketch artists," Campbell growled.

They threatened each other all the way down the hall to the elevator.

Claire was staring at her husband, still trying to grasp the metamorphosis. This man who looked exactly like her husband was one of the most brutal and dangerous killers in the city's history. "Jubal? Can you explain? Will you tell me what's going on? Please?"

"Are *you* hurt?"

"No, I'm okay."

"I shouldn't talk without a lawyer, Claire. You know that. I'm sorry. Just get me a lawyer."

"We don't even *have* a lawyer."

Quinn knew Jubal was being smart, but he didn't say so. "Do you want someone to stay here with you?" Quinn asked Claire.

"No. Really, I'm all right."

"Take the suspect down to the elevator and wait for me," Quinn said to Pearl and Fedderman.

Each of them gripped Jubal by an arm, and Fedderman used his free hand to bunch the back of Jubal's collar. They marched him toward the door he'd been so anxious to exit.

They could have been more gentle.

69

When Quinn was alone with Claire, he went to her and rested a hand lightly on her shoulder. He'd expected her to be trembling, but she was steady. *Strong inside, even if she looks frail as a bird.*

"Can I go with him?" she asked.

"You can, but there's no point to it at this hour. He'll go through the booking procedure; then he'll be moved to a holdover cell. You get referrals in the morning and contact an attorney. In the meantime I'll see he gets a public defender to protect his rights. I promise you that."

He could see her thinking about it, trying to sort out her allegiances. *Should I take the word of the arresting officer? Who saved my life. Or should I stand by my husband? Who tried to kill me.*

It took her longer than it should have to make up her mind.

"Thank you," she said.

"Do you think you might need medical attention?" Quinn asked. "I mean, for your pregnancy."

"No. I'd be able to tell if I were hurt that way."

"Someone will call you tomorrow morning. We'll send a car for you."

She nodded.

"Sure you're gonna be okay?"

"Okay as anyone can be, lost in all the questions."

"We'll sort things out and have the answers for you. Meantime, try to worry as little as possible."

"Easy to say."

"Yeah, I know. Like so many things."

"I didn't expect *this*!" she said, then bit her lower lip and stared up at the ceiling. She didn't look as if she were going to cry, though.

Quinn glanced down at her pregnancy, which was beginning to show, and thought of what she faced alone. *God help her.*

"It'll all be okay after a while," he lied, and patted her gently on the shoulder. He felt suddenly cheap, conning her along, even though he was trying to help. "Better, anyway."

He could find nothing else to say to this woman whose husband had been about to murder her, so he turned away.

After Quinn left, Claire went to the door and locked it, then trudged back into the bedroom.

Jubal! How could this be happening?

She'd never felt this way, as if she were alone at the edge of a cold hell. As if there were some dark inadequacy in her. As if this were all because of something *she'd* done.

Was it . . . was it something I did?

Or didn't do?

She sat stunned on the edge of the bed and tried not to sob.

Was it?

She wanted to scream.

She wanted to throw herself on the bed like a child and beat the mattress with her fists until she was exhausted.

Her misery was a weight that would never lift. She felt beyond crying, but tears that were someone else's tracked down her cheeks.

She wanted to die.

The baby!

She didn't want to die.

She wanted chocolate.

In the dark closet near the door, the Night Prowler waited.

70

They were all gone. The Night Prowler was reasonably sure of that.

Better to make absolutely sure.

So Romulus, whose real name was Tom Wilde, stood in stifling heat and darkness, smelling the white acrid scent of mothballs, waiting for his breathing to even out, listening for movement or voices outside the closet.

He'd entered the apartment just before the husband, Jubal, and had been surprised in Claire's bedroom by the big cop, the tough one. He'd gotten the cop with his knife, which was a damned good thing because it took at least some of the fight out of the determined bastard.

The cop had clung to him all the way down the hall and into the living room. In the mad struggle in the dark and the confusion after the other cops arrived, Wilde was shoved against the coat closet door and felt the knob jab him in the hip. He turned in the blackness and found refuge in the closet, just before the lights came on to show at the bottom of the door as a thin yellow line.

Certain he'd be discovered, he was about to make a hopeless, desperate break for freedom, when he heard the cops turn their attention to someone else.

It took Wilde a few seconds to realize what had happened—Hubby had flown home unexpectedly and surprised everyone.

And been surprised.

They must have caught Jubal at the door when the lights came on and assumed he was *leaving* instead of *entering* the apartment.

The Night Prowler almost fainted with gratitude.

He's me! Tonight he's me!

Wilde could have cheered when he heard Jubal insist on a lawyer before trying to explain himself to the police. A homicide charge was nothing to mess with unless you had counsel.

Damned right! Wilde had known that ever since Hiram, Missouri.

Since the night of the Sand murders.

He'd suspected Luther was still seeing Cara and followed him to the Sand house, waited for him to emerge, then realized he must be sleeping there. Years before, Wilde had lost his teaching job because of a secret affair with one of his art students, Cara Smith, who'd later married Milford Sand. The embers of that affair had never died, and they became flame again—at least in Tom Wilde.

He went to the Sand house late one sleepless night to talk Luther into leaving, for the boy's own good, and had seen lights and heard shouting coming from the kitchen. When he investigated the source of the commotion, he found opportunity as well as pain.

In his rage it had seemed so simple, the desperate logic that had moved countless men before him: if Cara couldn't be his, she'd belong to no one.

The scene in the kitchen, the brilliant colors, remained vivid in Wilde's memory; the blood, the interrupted meal that he could *taste,* the interrupted lives. . . . How suddenly everything could change, could stop.

When Luther regained consciousness and was still in shock, it hadn't been difficult to convince the intoxicated and naive young man that he'd committed the murders. And, of course, his good friend and mentor, Tom Wilde, would help him to escape, would send him downstream to safety in his boat.

And that part of it was God's truth; Wilde did want Luther to get clear and free.

But Luther must have recalled what had really happened in the Sand kitchen, and in a fury tried to kill Wilde but botched the attempt. It was Wilde who took the boat out from the bank. A mile downriver, Luther's weighted body sank to the bottom and was never found.

Wilde had taken the advice he'd given Luther: lose yourself in a large city and become another you. Be a different man living a different life.

It hadn't been easy, this creation of another self. It didn't happen overnight, but it happened. Wilde had found in himself a resourcefulness and talent he'd only faintly known existed.

But over the years Wilde-Romulus came to realize that the past was always there, as if it were upstream and around the bend in a winding river, invisible but there, always there, while time flowed on. *Cara! . . . Claire! . . .*

Now, hiding in the dark closet, Wilde thought enough time had passed. Besides, the police might soon realize their mistake and return.

Timing . . . so important.

He was sure he'd heard the faint shuffling of feet, probably Claire walking back to the bedroom. Since then, no sound from the other side of the closet door. She was alone.

Thought she was alone.

The buzzing . . .

He swallowed, steadying himself for what was to come, maintaining control.

Soon.

The police would have taken the knife, but there were others in the kitchen. Lots of them.

Very soon.

Night. Black. Red.

The elevator arrived at the end of the hall on the twenty-ninth floor.

When the door opened, Pearl and Fedderman guided the handcuffed Jubal inside, and the three of them stood huddled as far to the rear as they could move.

Quinn stood facing away from them and pressed the button for the lobby. In the reflection of the polished steel control panel, he watched his two detectives and Jubal Day. Quinn seemed relaxed, but he was tensed and ready to help if Jubal panicked or for some other reason got rambunctious. That happened sometimes. The suspect, facing a hopeless future, suddenly decided to lash out at his fate, his past, his sickness, at anyone close enough to reach. The demon in him trying one last time to escape.

The door slid closed, and the elevator began to drop.

71

Now!

The Night Prowler soundlessly rotated the knob and opened the closet door about six inches.

The living room was still dark, but there was a light on somewhere in the back of the apartment, the bedroom.

For several seconds he stood without moving, listening, listening. . . .

Then he stepped from the closet and silently made his way toward the kitchen.

Claire would be in the bedroom, still trying to figure everything out, nursing her grief and pain, too much of it to allow sleep.

She'd be awake and alone.

That was best, that she be awake. *If it's going to be just the two of us.*

In the kitchen he tried to decide between a boning knife—perhaps too flexible and fragile—and a serrated bread knife with sharp twin points.

And, of course, the sturdy, all-purpose chef's knife. *Hail to the Chef!*

Did he want her to come here, to the kitchen, or should he go to her?

Where will you die, Claire?

He decided on the bedroom. Enough had gone wrong tonight already, so why take chances?

It would be quick. He'd be careful not to make any noise on his way to the bedroom, then when he entered she'd be astounded and paralyzed with terror. Her throat would be solid. She'd be unable to breathe for a moment, much less cry out.

Then it would be too late.

No one spoke as the elevator descended. Quinn resisted the temptation to stare upward, as people did out of habit in elevators, instead keeping his gaze fixed on Jubal's reflection in the shiny control panel.

Suddenly he saw an arm extended alongside him.

Pearl pressed the emergency stop button, and the elevator slowed, lurched, and was still.

Fedderman said, "What the hell, Pearl?"

Quinn turned and looked at her. "Why?"

She jerked a thumb toward Jubal. "He's just been in a fight for his life with a tough cop and made a run for freedom."

"And?" Fedderman said.

"He isn't breathing hard."

Quinn stared at Jubal.

It was true. Jubal's complexion was pasty and he was obviously distressed, frightened, but his chest wasn't heaving and his pale lips were pressed together. His breathing was even. *After going several rounds with Campbell?* And he wasn't marked up from his struggle with Campbell and then with Campbell's reinforcements.

He isn't the Night Prowler!

Which meant . . .

"Good Christ!" Fedderman said.

All three of them had figured it out and were reaching for the *29* button. It was Pearl who pressed it, with Quinn's finger mashing down on her thumb.

The elevator began its slow ascent back toward Claire's floor.

72

"Cara?"

Claire gasped and looked up from where she sat slumped on the edge of the bed, her elbows on her knees.

In that instant the Night Prowler hesitated.

So beautiful in her sadness, in her secret knowledge. Not now, not yet. . . .

She sat up straight. It took her a few seconds to recognize the man standing in her bedroom doorway. *The decorator.* "Romulus . . ." Then she said automatically, "Not Cara. It's Claire."

He smiled as if embarrassed. "Yes. Claire."

"What on earth are you—" And she noticed the knife in his hand, pressed flat against his thigh. From the kitchen. Her own knife.

Her right hand rose to touch her lower lip. "My God! You're—"

"Don't scream, Cara."

Cara again?

She couldn't move or look away from him. Her breath

wouldn't come. Her heart went wild and seemed about to explode.

He sighed and moved toward her.

Not Cara! I'm not Cara!

When finally the elevator door slid open, the three detectives left a baffled Jubal Day standing alone in handcuffs and ran down the hall toward the apartment door.

"Hey!" Jubal called after them.

They didn't turn around; their hurried feet made a desperate shuffling sound on the hall carpet.

"Hey! What is this? What's going on?"

They ignored him.

The door glided shut and the elevator began to descend before Jubal could stop it.

Claire found the strength to move and scooted back across the mattress, staring at the knife, then up into Romulus' eyes. They were such a beautiful blue, so sad and serious. And intent. Terrifying in their certainty.

He's ahead of me. He knows what we're going to share and he's going to make it happen. There's no changing his mind.

She decided to pick up a pillow and throw it at him, thinking that in the few seconds he was blinded when it struck his face, she'd make a run to get around him and reach the door. The element of surprise. It wasn't much of a chance, but it was everything.

It was as if he'd read her thoughts.

He simply sidestepped the pillow and began moving around the bed toward her, his expression unchanged.

Smiling, he gave her the angle to the door now, and she

knew he wanted her to run for safety so he could intercept her, so she would come to him. He was waiting for her nerve to break. Giving her a slight chance. Knowing she'd take it as he got closer, because what else could she do?

What else could she do?

"Fast and hard," Quinn said, thinking the noise might help, might stop or at least delay what was surely about to happen.

If it hadn't happened already.

Fedderman, huffing like a winded bull, knew what he meant and lowered his shoulder as they neared the apartment door.

Pearl already had her gun drawn.

Claire had taken her first running step, and the Night Prowler his, when the sudden crash of the apartment door flying open made them both freeze.

There was no thought of fighting them this time. Instinct and logic were the same. The Night Prowler bolted toward the window. If he could smash through the glass, reach the fire escape!

Claire knew what he was doing and picked up the other pillow on the bed and hurled it at him as she had the first, with all her might.

This time it struck him in the face and he paused, brushing it aside.

The cost of his hesitation was only a second or two, but it was the ultimate price.

Quinn was through the bedroom door first, Pearl and Fedderman almost running up his back.

The Night Prowler lifted his right arm and at first Claire

thought he was raising his hands, giving himself up. But his hand held the knife, his arm drawn back as if he were about to throw it at her.

Giving them no choice!

She knew somehow he wasn't going to throw the knife. She didn't even bother trying to get out of the way.

The bedroom roared with the thunder of gunfire and the Night Prowler dropped the knife and staggered backward, hugging himself as if cold. He stared at Claire for a long moment.

As if I betrayed him.

Rolling his eyes in what might have been sudden panic, he dropped to a sitting position, then keeled over and lay curled on his side as if preparing to take a nap.

His cheek was pressed against the carpet and he knew he was dying. His final horizon was only inches away.

The last thing he saw was the vivid scarlet of his blood clashing with the blue carpet fibers.

It was wrong, all wrong!

73

"His name's Romulus," Claire said, standing numbly and staring down at the corpse in her bedroom. "He decorated the baby's room. Painted it."

Quinn didn't have to bend down and examine the dead man on the floor to know he wasn't Luther Lunt.

"He called me Cara."

Quinn stared at her. "Cara?"

"Never before. But when he first came into the bedroom. And just before you got here. Is he—"

"Dead?"

"No. I know he's dead."

"He's the Night Prowler," Quinn said.

"And Jubal? Where's Jubal?"

Quinn glanced at Fedderman. "Take her to her husband, and get the cuffs off him."

When Fedderman and Claire were gone, Quinn and Pearl looked at each other.

They'd read a few things wrong. They both realized now that the victims who scratched at the freshly painted door and wall were trying not only to leave dying messages but to direct attention to the paint itself, and to the painter. Mary Navarre's inverted V, or caret, that Quinn thought might be the first two strokes of an M or A scrawled in blood on the wall, was actually the first, vertical stroke of an R; death had come just as the second, horizontal stroke was about to begin, and her lifeless hand dropped almost straight down.

And they hadn't delved deeply or soon enough into suspects who might have duplicated keys to the murder apartments. The decorators obviously regarded their specialists, people like Romulus, as unlike the other tradesmen they employed, and above suspicion because they were fellow artists.

"We should have figured it out," Pearl said.

"Maybe," Quinn said. "Unless the name Romulus is on this guy's birth certificate, we're going to find out who he really is, and what might have made him do what he did."

"And who Cara is."

"Was," Quinn corrected, recalling the information in Nester Brothers' crinkled brown envelope.

Pearl had gone over to the window near the body and was looking down at the street. "Everybody's gathering down there. More cruisers, unmarkeds, media wolves. And I think I see Renz. There's somebody down there that might even be Egan. Can't be sure, though. One asshole looks pretty much like another from this height."

Quinn grinned at her, loving her just then the way maybe Jubal Day loved Claire. A couple of actors, not acting.

"Bring 'em on," he said.

74

Two days later, Quinn learned what Pearl had whispered in Egan's ear that day at the hospital, what had infuriated Egan so and made him back away from his threat.

Using the hard drive Pearl had given her, Michelle had matched the incriminating e-mails and Web site visits on Quinn's NYPD computer with days, and even times, when police records showed Quinn was somewhere else.

Someone had learned Quinn's password—easy enough to do with a glance over Quinn's shoulder when he was signing on—and had used Quinn's computer.

Of course Michelle was implicated in stealing the computer's hard drive, and the actual crime had been committed by Pearl. But if Egan wanted to charge either of them, they could take him down with them. They could take him down even further than they'd fall.

Egan had no bargaining chips and knew it. The only way he could prevent the hard-drive information from being made public was if he revealed who'd really raped Anna Caruso, which would clear Quinn. Mercer, the actual rapist, had duplicated the scar on Quinn's forearm and made sure

Anna saw it. And he'd stolen a button from Quinn's shirt in Quinn's locker and left it at the scene of the rape. Mercer would try to implicate Egan. But without the hard drive, there was no solid evidence that Egan was involved.

The purpose of the rape was to get rid of Quinn and stop an internal affairs investigation into a narcotics kickback scheme involving Egan, Mercer, and half a dozen other cops.

That investigation would become active again, and the chips would fall wherever.

What Egan would have to do even before that happened, if he wasn't fired, was resign from the NYPD with his skin intact but not his reputation.

He was, in short, where Quinn used to be.

Well, maybe in a worse place.

Anna Caruso made a public apology to Quinn, who was reinstated in the NYPD. There were photographs in all the papers of them hugging each other while NYPD brass smilingly looked on.

Only the day before, Anna had thrown away in a storm sewer her father's gun she'd used to shoot at Quinn on First Avenue. The night he'd chased her on foot and almost caught her before his heart acted up.

Anna decided life was a series of near misses, and sometimes hits, and the thing to do was to forget about them and live on.

And play music.

Dr. Jeri Janess was gratified to be making progress with her new patient. He'd come to her and confessed what was plaguing him: his drug addiction and increasing desire to enter into sadistic relationships with willing participants. As was inevitable, the victimization of his subjects was working its internal destruction in him. He sought now to escape his compulsion, and had come to Dr. Janess for help. So much confidence was he placing in the doctor that he'd finally offered up his real name: Lars Svenson.

After Svenson had left her office, the doctor leaned back in her desk chair and couldn't resist a satisfied smile. She switched on her recorder to make a brief oral summation, as she always did immediately following an appointment. She recited the patient's name and the date, then heard the hope in her voice as she said, "We're getting somewhere. . . ."

May Quinn married Elliott Franzine in a small, private ceremony in a seaside chapel on the California coast. Quinn didn't know whether he should send a wedding gift. Pearl told him only if it might explode.

They settled on a silver serving platter. Quinn received a polite thank-you note, and a month later a note from Lauri complaining that "Elliott" was seriously dorky and way too strict.

Quinn decided May's new marriage was going better than he'd expected.

Quinn and Pearl worked smoothly in the NYPD for a while, then they broke the rules again and moved in with each other.

The Village apartment they rented needed painting, but instead of hiring someone they decided to do the work themselves.

Jubal Day didn't get the *West Side Buddies* sitcom role. And after *As Thy Love Thyself*'s run in Chicago, the roles he landed came further and further apart.

"It'll get better," Claire would assure him. "Something always comes along. Some perfect part, or one that doesn't seem perfect but turns out to be. You know how this business is."

Jubal did know, and knowing didn't help.

His days grew longer, and so did his black moods and frustrations.

On nights when the baby let them sleep, and the only sound was the high breeze down the avenue playing at the windows, he would lie in bed desperately missing Dalia, finding his life more and more intolerable. With misery came sleeplessness and contemplation.

It was odd the way people thought, the way destiny directed their minds and lives. They assumed they had free will, but sometimes they didn't. They were simply rushed along by fate, making up their minds the only way they could, helpless even though they sensed what was happening.

That was how Jubal felt, moved by dark powers he couldn't understand, much less escape. If this was true evil, it was irresistible, and indistinguishable from fairness, from what he deserved. It masqueraded as hope. That was why it would win in the end.

He couldn't help thinking back on what happened the night he returned to New York unexpectedly to smooth over the necklace situation with Claire. When he opened his apartment door, it was as if he found yet another door. Whether he opened that door was now his choice. It was a choice he was terrified to make, though he knew that on a certain level he'd already made it. In something like this, there were really no surprises.

So, here he lay beside Claire, wondering if the baby he didn't want would again begin to bawl, missing Dalia, missing the life he'd envisioned for himself. Trapped like so many poor fools. Resigned like most of them. Thinking the forbidden thoughts.

Suppose there'd been no necklace, and no Jubal Day or Arnold Wolfe on the passenger list of the late-night flight from Chicago. Suppose he'd flown to New York under an assumed name, using identification he could buy at half a dozen places in Times Square or the Village. Suppose he'd arranged for an alibi in Chicago with Dalia. She'd swear to anything for him, for the two of them to be together. Suppose he'd been in his apartment for what the police had first assumed.

Suppose . . .

One intolerable gray morning, when Claire unfolded the stroller and left the apartment to take the brat for a walk in the park before it started to rain, Jubal phoned Dalia.

The moment she heard his voice, she realized she'd been expecting his call, and knew what he was going to suggest.

Don't miss John Lutz's next spine-tingling thriller
starring homicide detective Frank Quinn . . .

IN FOR THE KILL

Coming from Pinnacle in November 2007!